Praise for Chris Campanioni

"Award-winning author Chris Campanioni may, for better or worse, be the voice of our generation in which the internet is our stomping ground and making eye contact with our friends and family is a rare treat. . ." —*Your Impossible Voice*

"A hashtag, abbreviated quality . . . both deeply intimate and thrilling." —*Metal Magazine*

"He is Frank O'Hara traveling the hyper-connected contemporary landscape via iPhone—spawning, recording, discarding speculative versions of himself. . . He carries his Situationism between cities, between countries, between periods in his life without rest or regard for boundaries. Campanioni isn't playing at being clever; he is erasing himself to locate the sublime." —*The Brooklyn Rail*

"Campanioni's writing is playful, unflinching…a much-needed reminder of our endless potential for duality, in a world that too often suggests only polarity is possible." —*Harvard Review*

"Bolaño meets DeLillo meets Borges . . ." —*Red Fez*

CHRIS CAMPANIONI is a first-generation Cuban- and Polish-American who lives and writes in Brooklyn. His "Billboards" poem responding to Latino stereotypes and mutable—and often muted—identity in the fashion world was awarded an Academy of American Poets Prize and his novel *Going Down* was selected as Best First Book at the 2014 International Latino Book Awards. He edits PANK, At Large, and Tupelo Quarterly, and teaches Latino literature and creative writing at Pace University and Baruch College.

DRIFT

CHRIS CAMPANIONI

KING SHOT PRESS
PDX / ATH

King Shot Press
P.O. Box 80601
Portland, OR 97280
www.kingshotpress.com

First Trade Paperback Edition
© 2017 by Chris Campanioni
Cover design © 2018 Matthew Revert
www.matthewrevert.com
Typesetting & additional design by Michael Kazepis

Grateful acknowledgement is made to the editors and readers of
the following publications, in which some of these stories originally
appeared: "Shooting the Breeze," SunStruck Magazine (Fall 2015);
"Time and Time Again," Hypertext Magazine (November 2016);
"Nobody," La Pluma y La Tinta's New Voices (2014) and Duende
(Exodus, Spring 2017); "Life (or something similar)," Williams Writing
Prize (2007); "Excerpt from SCREEN, May 26, 2008," theNewerYork's
The Electronic Encyclopedia of Experimental Literature (July 2014);
"Criminal Tendencies," Quiddity International Literary Journal
(Volume 8.1); "Wonderland" Williams Writing Prize (2007); Parts of "A
Good Story" appear as "Ocupar" in Lime Hawk Literary Arts Collective
(Issue 2, July 2014); "Just One Line," Sliver of Stone (Issue 11); "Study
Abroad," Red Fez (Issue 80); "A Slice of Lifé," Carbon Culture Review
(Fall 2016, Issue 3); Parts of "The Fleeting Moments Between Here and
There," including the chapter, Remain in Light, first appeared in Across
the Margin (January 2015) as part of the "Coda to the Twenty-First
Century"

ISBN 978-1-7321240-0-4
Printed in the United States of America and worldwide.

For L,
Who makes life move, and time stand still

I believe that we are entering another time, a time that has not yet revealed its form and about which we can say nothing except that it will be neither linear time nor cyclical time.

OCTAVIO PAZ

here's that rhythm again
here's my shoulder blade
here's the sound I made
here's the picture I saved
here I am

TALKING HEADS

Death is nothing

SPRING

Deep and Violent and

You can always tell you're in California by the colors.

You could wake up in the middle of a dream and know exactly where you are—the state, I mean—by the colors above your head. Gray, orange, red, royal blue. And tonight it's purple. A deep, violent swath of purple streaking across the sky. The color purple and the hot night air and the howl of a coyote—I think—and the murmur of water hitting rocks—pitter-patter—the rush and stream from a waterfall.

We'd gone hiking all afternoon, curving upward and around Yosemite and taking photographs of particular trees, particular rocks, particular poses at particular moments, all of it to be relived at a particular time. A particular degree of posterity.

"You ever see a sky like that?" George Rizzoli asks. "You ever see a sky that color before? You don't see a sky like that back East."

I bend down, pick up a rock, hold the smooth curve in my hand, feel it between my fingers, squeeze tight.

"You don't see a sky like that anywhere else," he continues. His voice is hoarse in the evening. His voice cracks and creaks with his bones and he wipes his nose with the back of his palm and I notice the rolled-up newspaper in his back pocket, half of a headline still legible. George Rizzoli always keeps a newspaper in his back pocket, and I wonder if he's got his Reporter notepad wedged in there now too. I wonder if he's got a pen for writing but I stop wondering because I hear a scream.

Another coyote howls (I think). Or it's the same coyote and another howl. The water continues slipping past each groove of earth. Every rock. Pitter-patter. Rush and stream.

"You know what I mean?" he says, as I turn around, look at him with his head held high, hands on hips, staring at the stars. "Anywhere, anywhere . . . where else can you see a sky like this?"

I look up too, and it's purple. Deep and violent and beautiful, and I nod my head.

"Nowhere else," I say.

I say: "But I've never really been anywhere yet."

Shooting the Breeze

"It's really not so bad, you know, once you get past the taste."

And here I pause, because I know what you're thinking. You're thinking the same gutter-gathering thoughts that all of us sometime think when we are subjected to a title, like, say—but I won't even say it—only to add that it was never at all about oral sex, at least not consciously.

We are in the desert, talking about eating dog biscuits between camera flashes and sunrise—once again—the sun is about to rise, but not yet. It's a long story but I'll fill in the most salient details.

March 17
The crew rented three black vans—nearly identical, except for the license plates, of course—with power locks and tinted windows, and a built-in GPS in case we ever get lost in the desert.

We drive everywhere here. We drive in circles.

The houses and the trees—and the streets—the long, wide air-brushed streets look like scenes from *Chinatown*, from *Mulholland Drive*, from a movie I'd had, once, in my head, the kind of movie you sometimes only dream about—the kind that replays every three or four months— the kind you try to explain to a friend or lover by simply saying: "I've dreamed this before."

It looks like that.

Dust clouds, manicured lawns, a chemical sky.

I imagine all the pornography that has been filmed in these homes, these palatial all-white sculptures of 1950s concrete.

March 18

"I want to capture everything."

This is what Jared Garrett keeps saying, shouting, demanding. But that issue keeps coming up. The budget. The issue of the budget. Jared calls up Mega to call up *Voidyeur*, to call up their art directors, to implore the finance team for *more money*.

They deliberate. A day passes. There is talk of a hunger strike when the call comes in: as long as they can capture my abs in the morning light, as long as those abs are slicked with enough moisture—natural or otherwise—then the editorial is golden. "The abs—" my abs, which cost nothing, I remind them, "—the abs are absolutely essential to the editorial."

But the money comes anyway. Money for makeup, money for strobe lights, money for more reflectors, and lassos, and moisture, and caravans wrapped in burlap; money for the dog treats which they use to tip the housemaids at the hotel. "Says it tastes like filet mignon," Ronnie, one of the lighting assistants, says. "Says it right here." (He points to the bright yellow package: the dog, a black Lab, smiling wide-eyed and apparently sated.)

"Would you eat it?" I ask. "Would you eat the dog biscuits?"

"If I was a housemaid," Ronnie says, laughing like a hyena, jiggling his rotund torso, looking at the brown bone like it's a fossil he's found at the Museum of Natural History, clutching it between his thumb and middle finger, squinting and still wiggling. "If you paid me."

Every morning we drive to the same spot. El Mirage. We park in the same lot; we walk the same distance and then I take off my sneakers. I take off my clothes.

"I want to capture everything," Jared says, and he says this even as we get the news that the eight-page spread is now a four-page supplement. Curses ring out, several objects are thrown. Not even the biscuits are spared. The money keeps coming.

March 19

They've rented out the whole kingdom. That means seven rooms at the Desert Princess, bed and breakfast, with complimentary newspaper service (*The Beacon*) thrown in.

There are two TVs in each room that are never turned off; there is one room filled completely with camera equipment. Camera equipment and dog biscuits. Articles of clothing are strewn everywhere, forming an archipelago from A1 to C1, and the Jacuzzi and swimming pool that separate the three apartments.

Breakfast is served in a quaint kitchen adjacent to the lobby, so I routinely see the faces of rejected guests when they are casually informed by Jeff and Tom, the couple who own the property, *the whole hotel has actually been rented out this week*.

Jeff and Tom are always smiling and asking if we'd like more coffee; if we'd like more cream for the coffee. The gold-wrapped rectangles of butter house yellow bricks, rows and rows of yellow bricks in a ceramic casket.

There are many moments afforded to things like *self-reflection* in a place like Palm Springs. But just as often, my cell phone rings.

Dave Goldstein—again.

He was having a moment of self-doubt—he had been having the moment for a while now—a prolonged bout of hysteria in which he asked himself (and then me) whether or not it was right—if it was morally sound—to refuse the role of Artiste Savant. And why does everyone care so much about the fact of his being a Genius? It isn't the first time he's asked the question.

It is becoming impossible to live up to the expectations bequeathed unto me.

I would like to respond. I think about responding. I start to form a response.

Bequeath? Really?

March 20 (morning)

Jared Garrett wants to know what my story is. You know, like what I do when I'm not modeling. "Example: I am a surgeon," he says. "Jared Garrett isn't even my real name. Jared Garrett is my *brand*. The kind of art I'm creating. The medium of my message. (He pauses here.) My true voice . . . but at my *other* job, I operate on people's *mouths*. 'Open up.' (I don't think he can shut his.) 'Bite down hard.' Et cetera, et cetera. Lots of gagging and spitting. (Laughter like an infant's whimper.) Imagine that. So what about you? . . . Everybody does something else; wishes they did something else. You really need to reinvent yourself these days, you know? Master multiple fields. Like Ronnie—you know he's a deejay right? And Marissa (makeup)—well, she does *a lot* of makeup. Roger is a singer. Rhythm and blues, right, Rodge? And we are all finding ourselves."

Unless we are losing ourselves, I think. But I don't say it. I don't say anything.

March 20 (afternoon)

"So what *is* your story?"

They always want to know. They always want to hear you tell.

Pieces of something that would never (not ever) be what they were expecting you to say, pieces of something you yourself hardly knew you'd say (now or ever), as if anything ever came out just the way it was supposed to—supposing any of it could ever be told.

"You mean, the one I'm writing?"

And the whole effect would be like speaking Russian without having any knowledge of the language. The whole effect would be nothing but big signboards blaring *vacancy*.

"Or the one I'm living?"

Or maybe what would follow would be epiphany, unbearable resonance of anti-thought, which is to say *feeling*, lingering deep in the marrow below the skin and suffocated almost immediately by canned laughter and tired phrases, preset selections played at random. You've read that chapter before. A feeling like a door slammed in your face, and yet . . . and yet, a long hall, another door at the end . . . a walk that resumes.

I have the vague sense the same thing that had happened to me is happening to other people, everywhere.

"What's the difference?"

March 20 (evening)

Jared Garrett (why didn't he pick a better name?) talks the whole way from El Mirage to the Desert Princess, turning his head from the front passenger seat, smoothing out his thin eyebrows with his slim fingers and saying things like, "It's not easy to explain the difference between 'fun' and 'pleasure' since they are quite similar . . ."

We pass the Champion Institute of Cosmetology. We pass two golf courses. We pass a gymnasium with the name "Golden Age" etched across a neon-lit sign with the first "G" and the "en" completely dark.

"I have been trying to figure out the difference between things that are 'fun' and things that are 'pleasurable,'" Roger returns. "For instance (we pass the Desert Princess, but the van hurtles on), lying around all afternoon reading mags and drinking coffee while wrapped in a warm blanket is one of my most delicious of pleasures, but I wouldn't call it *fun*. When I think of all the things I like to do (performing on stage comes to mind), I don't think of these things as 'fun,' particularly. They are richly satisfying, enjoyable and engrossing, but there is often a lot of resistance going in. They require discipline, you know?"

"Example: I told you already—right?—I'm actually a surgeon," Jared Garrett interrupts, craning his neck, smiling wistfully. "Back home—back in New York—that's what I do. And when I go to Cornell Medical to analyze X-rays, maybe to rehearse a few different techniques, I feel completely powerful. But it's often mentally frustrating when I can't get it *perfect*. So I think the way I would distinguish fun from pleasure is that fun is novel. Fun takes you out of your routine."

"For me," Roger picks up the thread again, "fun is when I'm practicing a number twenty-thousand times and I'm performing it not thinking about making a mistake but simply enjoying it because I've mastered every move, there's nothing to worry about but to simply have fun . . ."

The day grows darker, and more clear. I stare out the window of the van as it races on: the long, wide streets, the purple sky, the tumbleweed, the stucco homes, the homes that look like palaces, gated entrances, driveways that spiral forward like a wave . . . and think about lines to a poem I

will probably ~~never~~ write[i].

---

[i] ***Shot On Location***
On the way to El Mirage we passed
the windmill farms, each fan turning almost
indiscernibly. I felt the wind come in
from canyons, a montage of
scorched earth, rust and fungus
clouds, rolling hills, *The Sun Never Sets*
On the Mighty, arid, shrill heat
of a California morning
rising higher when I stepped outside:
vista of a million Jeep commercials
in the drive-in of my mind.
There's Only One.

Cut to white noise on the screen.
Cut to a man in the waiting room
accosting the maid who only came to clean
up the mess. Desert Princess.
67967 Vista Chino, Cathedral City. Cut
to some passerby's careless spit, the ice-scorched sand,
my saliva and sweat, the director's demands,
hands on hips, altering after every other
"How the West Was One"
—interruptions—
(my head in one place,
my body in quite another) . . .

the Ferris wheel I rode all night,
one night in childhood, back flat to feel
the world move. And then I stopped too,
halfway there, halfway not,
paralyzed at the apex of the loop,
frozen in a half frown to hover,
helpless, above the ground where

we come around,
we come around.
we come around.

"'Pleasure' is sublime," someone says. "It speaks to a state of mind."

"It's all about entertainment, people." Another voice. Another mouth. "Fun happens when one switches off the brain."

I see another palm tree pass, leaves swaying like a stream of rushing water in my eyes. Jared Garrett turns to me. "Do you do that? Do you like to sometimes turn it off?"

"I can't," I say, still looking out the window. "I can't sometimes even think one thought at a time. Thoughts overlap other thoughts, interrupt and bleed across, cancel each other out, sometimes combine or curtail thought completely . . . like the sentence and its goal of moving across the page in a single direction (always down, I think), moving swiftly and sometimes without punctuation, and how it all comes crashing the minute you pause to consider a thing like posterity."

I wait for a response but they're already talking about pleasure again; pleasure and fun.

"Doing doing doing, I find myself all the time insistent on *doing* things—for no other reason except to do them."

(We turn at the traffic circle, going down a long stretch

Palm Springs was a dream
I'd run along: long, wide streets, wide-
eyed awake and still longing
in the moments before sunrise.
Manicured lawns, espaliers, trestle-table patios, palm trees,
1950s swimming pools and the despair
of a million zigzagging fantasies
dissipating the moment they arrived
at El Mirador, or Araby Cove.

All of us and everything are born
in desperation and hope, and the swarm
of sightseeing captured in a magazine
for posterity, or for pleasure,
or for proof of something more.

of asphalt, sand, neon lights, as it gets darker. The purple sky.) Language is a valley. Words rise and fall, too, I think. We make and remake them.

They make and remake us.

March 21

> You're invited to: Dave Goldstein—A Retrospective
> Celebrate the smash hit—four years later. On October 6, be prepared to be shocked all over again. Featuring a round-table discussion by Mr. Goldstein and several special guests and industry experts, including leading academics in film theory and cinematography. RSVP until March 31 by including your first and last name, and a donation (suggested) in the box below.

I click out and turn inward, thinking about replying, about saying I'm out, I'm out of town, I'm stuck in Palm Springs if you can believe it, I'm still shooting, I'm still not sleeping if you can believe it, I can't make it, thank you, I'm honored but—*I don't do anything.*

March 22

Idyllwild was the greatest thing I'd never seen.

The village is located in the mountains above Palm Springs—about fifty miles from downtown on Highway 74. But the one thing the crew doesn't have is patience.

"An hour and a half? In an hour and a half, we could *create* Idyllwild on a computer screen."

So that's what Jared Garrett did. And it was great—the greatest—thing I'd never seen. Tall pines, sweet-smelling cedars, legendary rocks. I'm reading from a tourist brochure (we picked one up, too, in the Desert Princess lobby), and it sounds about right, because the image they've created on the massive iMac—the new backdrop for Page 1 (eventually, they'll stick my body somewhere among those pines)—makes tears form, just a little, in my eyes.

March 23

"Ours is a generation with empty ambitions, unfulfilling experiences. Ours is a generation of delayed growth, stilted maturation, Emerging Adulthood; we are in permanent limbo."

Ronnie is riffing on what he calls "the plight of our generation." He's taking online courses at the University of Phoenix—I know, because he had an exam during a coffee break yesterday afternoon—and he's been riffing since we've met.

"That's exactly what I was saying the other day," Jared Garrett slides into the van, slides over to me. "Our generation is in constant need of re-invention. Like—what do you want to do now? *Who* do you want to *be*?"

Jared is going bald and the hair he does have is a wispy dark gray but still, he says "our generation" and when he asks his questions, I know that he doesn't expect—that he doesn't even want—a response, and maybe that's what he's doing, after all: re-inventing himself. Jared Garrett. After all.

"Can we please—can we just talk for a moment, can we linger on the question that's just been killing me lately."

"Which is?" Roger perks up, twists his baseball cap sideways, rubs his pointed chin. We pass Marilyn Monroe (twenty-six feet tall) on the corner of Palm Canyon Drive and Tahquitz Canyon. *Forever Marilyn* is inscribed on the sculpture. Seward Johnson. Marilyn's white dress forever fluttering in the still air of a desert afternoon; a frieze-frame from *The Seven Year Itch*.

"Beauty and attraction. Same or different?" Jared answers. "And if so: how do we define *beauty*?"

March 25

"It looked better in pictures."

We passed the windmill farms and I tried to watch each fan turning almost imperceptibly. We drove too fast.

Then we stopped, reversed, parked in a grotto nearby.

"It looked better in pictures," Marissa repeats, dabbing my forehead with some kind of powder. Fairy dust.

"Well—that's exactly the *point*," Jared Garrett intones audibly, slapping his right thigh with his left hand and laughing too loud. "Hence the whole Edelweiss Village situation."

"Idyllwild," I correct, craning my head above Marissa's gaze, trying to see the windmills, trying to see the motion of each fan. "Not Edelweiss."

"Every morning you greet me . . . small and white, clean and bright . . . You look happy to meet me . . ."

We take some shots. I try for stoic, solitary; maybe I try for bored.

I remember the graffiti slapped across the Desert Princess's patio fence:

ALL HORRORS ARE DULLED BY ROUTINE

I think about the repetition of a push-up; I think about the moment I stepped into J&P Talent's dilapidated offices. I think about the news and it terrifies me.

March 25/26/27/28 . . .

"I want to capture everything."

"I thought we captured this already?" I ask. We've been shooting in El Mirage—this exact spot—for the last nine mornings.

"We did. We have. But the lighting . . . I didn't like the . . . It didn't feel as if . . . You weren't exactly . . ."

Ronnie says Jared Garrett's inability to complete his thoughts stems from our culture's overabundance of communication; our too many ways to communicate.

Ronnie (he also works as a deejay, in Vegas) says the dog biscuits really do taste like filet mignon, and I wonder how music can be Ronnie's forte, music, mixing music, when all he finds on the radio is Miley Cyrus and Lana Del Rey.

"Should I try AM? Should I try talk radio?"

Dog biscuits. Filet mignon. We've come full circle, I think.

Someone's phone rings and more curses ring out. A coyote howls in the distance. The sky is beginning to turn purple again. That deep, violent purple that maybe characterizes every evening in Palm Springs. The order for the foggers we will never use has been delayed.

We'll be here for another week, at least. Probably we'll never leave.

"Do you think I can capture the silence?" Jared asks, and I know—I already know—nothing in Palm Springs requires an answer. The hours rise; time slips past.

Now we are standing, huddled around the van, waiting for the sun to rise. It's a fleeting moment, you know. We have only eight or nine minutes each morning. Sometimes only seven.

Jared keeps talking while the sand burns my feet—the sand is so cold in El Mirage at 4:35 that it burns; my feet are on fire. I wish I had my sneakers on. I wish I had on all my clothes.

"Or—is silence more about the sculptural values of *sound?*" Jared continues. "The flexible medium of the future and the nascent breath of something like . . . a sentence?"

Nothing. Not even the breeze. Not even the rustle of limbs, in and out of a torn pair of blue jeans.

24

"Could I capture it? Could I even articulate it?"

For the first time all week—all week-and-a-half—I laugh. The feeling could best be described as a smile, or the mystery of a smile—or right before a smile—the melancholy expressed by the tilt of a body stretching toward the sun.

We are still shooting the breeze.

Time and Time Again

TIME

We take the Subte two stops on the blue line and ascend on foot through San Telmo, the cobblestone streets. The moon reflects our footsteps on each brick. It is beautiful in the way only a picture can be. Beautiful in the way life is when viewed from afar, illumined, sometimes even framed.

This is not a photograph.

I am here and she is here, and we are *here*, walking, hand-in-hand through La Manzana de las Luces. Train whistles in the distance. Her hand inside mine. She pulls me closer and I surrender: we move along, one body floating through the night.

This morning was *A Walk in the Park*, but I could hardly concentrate. I was thinking about her. She who is so close to me. I was thinking about Isabella. She turns her head, as if she can hear my thoughts, as if she can hear me speaking her name in silence. She pulls me further and we descend.

"We have to go down," she says, laughing, her voice slipping through me. "Everything is connected by a series of tunnels."

"Everything, but everything," she continues, breathless, "is connected."

In English, her voice sounds staccato. Stopping and starting, italicized at the most unexpected moments. English with an English accent. A sense of urgency.

I am panting alongside as we pause, breathless, still trying to breathe inside each other's mouths. The air is damp, wonderful, moist, heavy with the smell of rain, a passing storm or a storm that's passed, but the sea is calm tonight. The sea is calm to-night. The sea is calm to-night . . .

I search for the first verse. The second line. When I am nervous, I recite poetry in my head. Arnold, Eliot, Cummings, Marvell, Rilke. Sometimes even Ovid. All of the favorites. But I am too nervous, too nervous to recall anything but this moment, trying to capture it before it passes, too.

I have been here for three days. Dining on bife de chorizo and morcilla in between a billboard for Bolivia and a Deberser look-book—or maybe the other way around— Dave Goldstein following me for all of it. Except Dave Goldstein isn't here now. And what a pity. For him, not for me. I'd rather remember Isabella from memory. I'd rather forget everything else.

What else is left?

Next week I will be doing the same thing, but in a different place. The same thing. We move past Plaza Dorrego. A dozen vacant café tables and signs pointing nowhere. The party has been packed up, gone until next week. I know because I've seen pictures. Metal trinkets, leather belts, necklaces: antiquities. Remainders of the day. I feel the sweat on her palms, the heat of her skin. The earth moving under our feet.

And what would Ana say to me now, if she were here? What would my mother say if she were still alive?

"A mist all the scams and backstabbing, and all of those false promises, and no one to trust, and so many horror stories . . . a mist all of it, you have gotten on so well. And I am so proud . . ."

And maybe I would realize that what she was saying was everything was a mist; everything and all of it, a thin film of reality, cupped and suctioned like a contact lens in each eye, and it had become impossible for me to see beyond the haze. And yet I had to try. And yet I was trying now.

I try to picture it again.

All I remembered from this morning was Isabella, her enormous eyes, her slender nose and pointed chin and round lips. Isabella who was not in the park, who was not in Belgrano at all. But she was there all the same, a projection in my mind, there as I stood silent, filmed or not filmed—I never know when the camera is rolling, I only know there is more than one, and if one isn't on, another one is—there as I wondered what had happened to my life, wondered where all of it went. Except I know, at least, that answer.

All of life is misunderstanding, miscommunication. Contact cut just when the moment becomes possible. A look in the street, a handshake, sometimes even a hug. All the familiar signals, everything reduced to formalities. Like walking on eggshells. We turn away from ourselves. We turn inward. It's as easy as putting on a pair of slippers. Going to the movies, going to the bar, holding hands, holding hands but never touching, a nod of the head, a hello, gestures of salutation or farewell, graceful contacts . . . contacts? Message-as-massage, well-wrought conversation . . . an *excuse me* or *pardon* or *no problem* (what ever was the problem?) or *sorry, do you have* . . . (always apologizing but for what, I never knew) *please, don't mention it* . . . a high-five at a Mets game, a day at the races, a shrug, a wave, a seat given or taken on the F train, an outstretched hand on the cool pole. We shut up just when we should say something, just when words could have some use. As easy as putting on a pair of slippers. Two lips moving. An outstretched hand . . .

You came to me. Touched me. Entered me. I saw with your own eyes.

This passage is addressed to me, but it is written for you.

Will you find it someday, months or years later? Will you find it, read it? Will you know me? Can anyone?

We slip into Iglesia Nuestra Señora de Belén and I lose myself in a maze of pews, concave domes and grooves, nooks, cupolas, everything painted white except for the stained-glass windows, an opaque reflection. It might suggest a strobe light throbbing at untimed intervals.

I often have these fainting spells. In bars, hotel lobbies, concert halls. In the passenger seat of a cruising taxi, doing fifty, maybe sixty, hands and head out the half-held sliding translucence. Flickering black spots weave in and out of focus like cue marks in an old film. Imperfections of reality. My soul contracts until my body crumples to the floor. I never remember anything else. Is it jet lag? Is it euphoria? Is it my body, every fiber and neuron, and each cell exasperated; is my body giving up?

Either I suck in life too fast, or too much, or too often. Or life sucks me dry. A hiccup in the vacuum of eternity. I am choking.

Every time I come back, I'm a little bit less.

Every time I come back, pieces of me get chipped away. What is left?

A child's room: four walls devastated by time. Scotch-taped boxes. An empty valise. Things I will never remember, or never sift through, or never see. Things that have been lost for good. For good or bad, but for good.

My petrified smile.

Isabella finds me ten minutes later—maybe fifteen—neither of us wear a watch.

"What were you doing," she asks, "staring at the window?"

"Checking myself out," I say.

We laugh. Or rather, she does. We exit through the side doors left ajar, aged wood creaking, air rushing in as we rush out.

I don't tell her what she doesn't know, what she could never guess. I don't tell her I am just checking my self out. Making sure I am still here.

TIME AGAIN

They watched him from a park bench. From the center of Barrancas de Belgrano, the breeze coming in from the Río de la Plata—or an automated fan. From the sun streaking through at seventy-six degrees, the angle of the moment passing. From a reclining position, legs shifting, lips wet, cigarettes dangling from the corners of their mouths like lollipops. Sucking sounds. Smoke blowing through the trees: pines and Jacarandas, and an enormous Ombu at the center. Cars shrinking to a halt on the corner of Arribeños. Laughter. Film rolling. They watched. Time and time again.

He came closer, emerging from the dog run, and they collectively sighed. It was all very audible amid the noise of afternoon. A boom mic hanging from every branch.

"Is he giving them *dégagé*?"

"Is he giving them *onda*?"

And when they said, "them," they meant, "us."

They weren't sure what he was giving, but they were taking it. They took it in three-quarters and in profile, in close-crop and in tracking shot, and from their personal mobiles too, streaming a sequence of indefinitely proceeding images that could eventually, in days or weeks—or maybe hours—form a coherent narrative.

We hear the breeze pick up from the bay, audible whistles and the shrill sound of brakes as you come into view: a look of inconsolable sadness STOP enter camera left, with a stronger gait, the sun enveloping your eyes as you enter across and STOP descend through the dog walk on foot, bending and leaning here and there, perhaps petting a pooch if time allows but always moving STOP hands in pocket, craning neck, in search of something but still smiling

STOP

A narrative copied and cut, transmitted via telegram. Piece-mail.

Actually, he emerged through the shade of a pine and paused mid-stride at the wrought-iron gazebo, as if uncertain, suddenly reluctant to proceed, oval eyes enlarged unnaturally, according to the law of divine proportion[ii].

He was smiling.

Standing—"con la lengua en la mejilla," someone uttered—legs taut, as if he were ready to spring into action, sprint through the curving pathway that led to the river. As if he were ready to escape. A forearm came into view, veiny and robust in the plummeting perspective.

"Now *that's* a *figure* of speech, darling."

Voices. Passersby. An audience. The hush of silence. *La Glorieta at noon.*

But he did nothing, but nothing. He stood there, smiled, one hand in his jeans pocket, the other running through his wavy hair, blond strands flowing in and out of his eyes; in and out and in and out of focus, standing expertly and absently, like a mannequin. A bust at the Barrancas de Belgrano scaled to size, a statue of limitations. And a few yards away, the Statue of Liberty in miniature.

The Director entered along that nine-foot replica, camera right, under the unwavering torch, shaking his head, pursing his lips, running his hand over his head (he was bald), muttering stage directions, spitting into the wind, asking Chris Selden if he could be *more natural. And lose the shirt completely. Please*—

[ii] Also called: *the golden ratio.*

Give me something masculine . . . Details which said more about the Director than they did about the subject.

"Is this the breathing version?"

"Is this the real thing?"

He could feel the words crawling all around him and under him and past his unblinking eyes like ants.

A voice-over drowned out the rest[iii].

The agents, the publicists, the journalists. Squawking in the background, hawking their wares: each part partitioned to meet the current need, and then redistributed. *Taking a cue from Satan, their greatest strategy was to make the world believe Chris Selden didn't exist.*

•

He knew Ana was in the box. And not in the box. He knew Ana was everywhere, as evidenced by his thoughts; he couldn't stop thinking about her.

For a while he looked at her; then he no longer knew where to look. And this gesture or lack of gesture repeated, until he could no longer decide whether to keep his eyes open or to hold them closed; he could no longer decide because he couldn't tell what the difference was, and anyway, it made no difference. Open, closed. It could be neither because it was both.

The way when Ana was still alive, when she was still dying, she had become a child too. Everything, but everything, he thought. Everything repeats. And he thought of her now, like he thinks of everything.

[iii] *He was unable to create that true sense of identity and livelihood that must go hand in hand in order not merely to exist, but to survive. That love every artist feels for his work was absent, because the artist himself could not identify with his creation, which was himself. He hadn't yet realized that he would have to destroy the portrait and begin again.*

•

Humility is a trait that can only come from its root word, or origin: Humiliation. And such is the case in this book and the one following, and especially, in the one that came before. Chris often felt that he was traversing a world that had as its soundtrack "A Dancing Shell" by Wild Nothing—only one song, played without pause until it began again—walking along the streets while the verse *"I sold myself for a shot at the moon . . . I sold myself so I could be a big star . . . And I'll be your monkey, every night, if it makes you love me, watch me now. Watch me, watch me . . . "* rang through his ears.

He'd do everything they'd ask him to. Within reason, but reason was another word that has its origins elsewhere. Underneath it all, the power of comprehending, the rational ground or motive, the exercise of the mind . . . all of these definitions can best be explained by *a treatment that affords satisfaction.*

Walking along the streets with his camera eye and his mask in place, with the secret knowledge that he was not who he was to the world, or rather, that he was more than what the role called for, more, even, than what comprised the whole play; this was a satisfaction in itself.

It was the greatest one.

•

The lesson, if there was a lesson, if there were lessons embedded in events, seemed to be accounting. That he should have gone into accounting, or finance, like his father, and the father before him. That he should have been a banker. That he should have bowed down to the dollar bills the way anyone else had, anyone or everyone; the way they worshipped the paper; the way they feared it too; like anything worth worshipping, it was fear, not love, which kept its parishioners devout.

Still, he preferred not to think of this story as a fable, and liked less to consider the prerequisite of a moral. Unless, he conceded, it amounted to pleasure.

·

A few extras pushed a piano across the dirt. Violin, double bass, a bandoneón. Tango sounds. A cloud appeared, expanded across the sky.

The lighting changed.

They watched it all unfold, simultaneously seeing and shooting, and dreaming, too, dreaming until they couldn't stand it any longer, couldn't stand, couldn't sit. Their hands fumbled for an opening between buttons, ran down their navels, found their way to their crotches, clasping their inner thighs until they cupped their groins, rubbing vigorously through their jeans, unzipped in fleeting moments, fingertips reaching back toward each vent, opening up and unfolding, feeling the heat, and the flow, and especially, the longing. Beating around the bush.

They took turns until the scene faded out.

UNA VEZ MÁS

"Repita eso, por favor."

I start. Stop. Sputter out more Spanish mixed with English. I only want to order another Malbec. Malbec from Mendoza. I try pointing to a photo of a llama hanging from the wall behind the bar, a llama that looks like the one on the cylinder's seal, smiling with its big buck teeth, inflated further to reach around the bottle, but I mispronounce that, too. Yame? Lama? All I get is raised eyebrows and curled lips.

My parents never taught me Spanish when I was a child. Instead they each spoke English with indelible accents. I got fucked. I can't speak Spanish right, I can't speak English right. My parents' accents ruined any chance I had of speaking properly.

So instead I just speak.

Outside, the earth changes color, from royal blue to purple. Three clouds in their slow procession across time. The moribund sun.

When I finally receive my glass of wine, it's white, from Mendoza. A Torrontés. I smile and take a sip anyway, turning my attention to my notebook.

What is left?

I had been writing. Writing and re-writing. I try to write *Going Down* again, this time in nine pages. It takes me eight minutes. I make a note to play it during intermission.

Why always this desire to repeat?

My thoughts drift to last night. To yesterday morning. They drift until I am thinking about my past life. I rewind.

There were no Cubans in Oradell. Hardly any Latinos at all. My popularity in high school depended on it. I was a novelty. The blond-haired Cuban who turned brown in summer. I had the feeling friends invited me over just to show me off.

Look! And he speaks English!

But please, Mom—can we keep him? At least till dinner?

I often wondered why my parents moved there in the first place; was it, after all, a performance? Were we masquerading as *The Whites*—the new Genet being staged in Bergen County?—and if we were, I never got the script.

I picked up comedy instead. I played *Class Clown*. For a while, I forgot I was any different from anyone else.

For a while.

I think of numbers. Situations. The arrangement of events that form a life. It has been three years and ten months. That's 1,155 days since I walked into J&P Talent, into its dilapidated office: the lobby and everything else. I never walked back out.

I have traveled the world.

I'd like to think I learned things, soaked them up like a sponge—an old nickname at OPS—discovered something about *life*. If I learned anything, it is that I don't know a damn thing. I am here to be taught.

Everything is passing. And everything passes me by.

I caress a shiny, copper lighter: two figures locked in a thrilling tango stare-off. A parting gift from Isabella. Something to remember her by.

A memory.

I'll caress it again, and again. Finger it. Watch the flame flicker. Maybe I'll remember her each time. And maybe each time it will be different.

"Drone On" by Physical Therapy begins to blare on the bar's speakers.

"What do you see when you see me?"

Glasses clink. People I've never seen before sing along.

"You're alive, you're alive . . . You're alive now . . . I see you again . . ."

The beautiful thing about death is that it keeps repeating, and in repeating, it multiplies and disseminates, it folds in and erupts, and isn't it true that it's not the living who are at our mercy but the dead, the dead who exist in us and who exist *for us*, in so many more ways than when they were alive.

It's my last night in Buenos Aires, I murmur, sipping slowly, tasting the saccharine at the back of my throat. And I am alone. I look around. Maybe I look like a mannequin. So used to people looking that if they stopped, if they shut their eyes, if they didn't look, I'd feel as if I was not there. As if I am not here.

I glance at a watch that isn't there and wonder when Dave will arrive; one final ride, cruising along the Río de la Plata until the first light of dawn, and for a second, everyone and everything freezes mid-frame, lips open, eyes half-shut, and everything is silent except for the drizzle, the pitter-patter of rain against windowpanes—a sound effect played on a loop—and then the second comes to an end. Another one begins.

I see you again

Repeated indefinitely.

I like music so much because it is liminal. Temporal. Three minutes. Four? Sudden illumination, I think. And with a countdown. I like music so much I let it bleed across the pages, too. I look at the camera. I look right at you.

"I know you want, I know you want. I know you want, I know . . ."

"I am listening to the same song you are," I say.

I have a habit of breaking the fourth wall, and now the whole structure collapses. Outside, the pale light illumines each brick. A puddle reflects the shimmering sky
and then dissolves.

Dave appears outside, motions to me, dangles a set of keys. I leave four pesos on the counter.

"How do I look?" I ask as I slide in, recline the seat.

The convertible turns. The panorama of Puerto Madero opens up, unfolds, surrounds me.

"Same as ever," Dave says.

"Same as ever?"

He nods, shifts the stick into sixth-gear. I want to ask where he learned to drive like that. I want to ask, from which movie. Instead I ask him how I look. A third time. Staring at my darting reflection at fifty, maybe sixty miles per hour. And repeating, repeating . . .

Fast-forward through warehouses and high-rises, the hum of the engine. Ripping wind. Boats at anchor in a freeze-frame: *River of Silver*. The way I like to always name a moment. Something like torque shoots through me. The dimensions expand until they explode.

"Same as ever."

But I only realize later.

He means it as a compliment.

Nobody

My name is Nadié and I am nineteen years old but my agency tells clients I'm sixteen—that I, in fact, just turned sixteen—so it is as if I'm sixteen every day because people keep smiling and wishing me a "happy birthday" whenever they meet me.

Everything in this country, it seems, gets lost in translation. When I arrived, people called me Natalie, Nadia, Nadine, Nena. The agents at Fusion had so much trouble pronouncing my name that they stopped saying it altogether and now they call me something else entirely. It costs less to print comp cards without accent marks— something about special codes for symbols—so now I'm Nadie, which, where I come from, means Nobody.

I walk in through the sunlit morning.

The wall-length windows bathe the wooden floor in shadows and I see half a dozen people slipping in between racks of clothes; a steamer; a long, black, conference table; an ornate mattress; a row of mirrors. I am slipping too, moving like a ballerina because I used to be a dancer and the most that came from it is my body—Fusion calls it elastic, lithe, supple, but sometimes I feel like I am barely-there.

No one has congratulated me on reaching sixteen so I say hello, drop my saddlebag and ask where the restroom is. I see two stylists standing hips out and turning a man's head like it is on a swivel, deciding on the hair's part, I think, or maybe the amount of glue to apply. I had seen him before—was it on television, or a bus stop? Or maybe a magazine?—but we had never met in person. In New York City, it seems natural that everyone eventually sees everyone else—whether or not we ever meet.

The man smiles, moving his eyes higher, looking right at me through the mirror's gaze. He is tan, a darker shade than me, with hair that is between brown and blond and eyes that are either brown or green—I can't tell. It is not the distance but the way the light frames each iris, as if they altered every time he blinked. I did not want to stare and now I was, wide-eyed and curious. I have always been curious. I think that's what made me move to New York City in the first place.

When I return from the restroom, nothing has changed, except there are more people slipping between everything, moving quickly and with small cardboard cups in their hands; the scent of roasted coffee and toasted croissants rising in the studio. I run my fingers under my halter top and around my navel, hearing my body talk. It speaks some more and a tall, wiry man I recognize from the casting welcomes me. Art Director.

"Clothes make the man," he says, pointing to a black tent. Two assistants are unfolding and unzipping it, and taking turns hopping inside.

"Or woman," I add, managing a smile. Lips barely parted.

"Of course," he says, sucking in his cheeks and then sighing. He points back to the tent. "Dressing room."

He is holding a clipboard and I see the schedule: chance meeting on Broadway, a sequence shot—pedestrians moving, smiles and laughs from a café, suggestive looks under the awning—a romp in the bedroom. Lunch at noon. He walks me over to hair and makeup and as I brush past the other bodies, I look at him—the other model—

and he is still smiling or smiling again or always smiling. He has thick, dark-red-almost-purple lips.

I sit down next to him and he turns his face to me and I notice he is reading a script. *One Life to Live* is scrawled across the manila envelope unfastened on the counter. He tells me his name and I tell him mine, my real name. The stylist standing over us moves his head in place, pressing both of his hands to his temples, then continues snipping away, the small scissors so close it almost feels like it is my hair that is falling on my shoulders to my feet.

"Ever done this before?" he asks, pointing to the lingerie arranged on the rack across from us. Sheer, lace, nylon. Another stylist dabs his neck with cotton. *A romp in the bedroom.*

"Of course," I laugh. "Just not in photos."

I hear the sound of film rolling before I see the men crouching behind us and around us, both of them balancing big, black video cameras on their shoulders. I remember the papers I filled out at Fusion the day they booked me for *Harper's Bazaar*. There will be a second camera crew at the shoot. A reality TV pilot. Nothing to rehearse. No nude shots, of course. Statutes and definitions. Clothes, noun: a covering for the person. Implied terms and conditions. Sign here, and here. *Bravo.*

"'One crew filming another crew filming Chris . . .'" Chris recites, turning to me again. "I wrote about this situation. Now I'm living it again."

I nod my head as one of the cameramen rises and juts sideways.

"A tracking shot," Chris says, nodding his head toward a lens. "Living it again," he repeats, whistling. I turn to him.

"We all are."

•

When we break for lunch Chris is already sitting on one of the leather couches in the lobby with his legs crossed, staring at a pamphlet.

"I study menus like they're letters from Rilke," he says, not looking up.

"I don't know what Rilke is—" I reply, pointing to the flimsy purple paper folded in his hands. *Hill Country BBQ* is etched across the front. "But it must be very interesting."

He nods and shifts his body so I can join him on the couch. He starts talking about food—breakfast, lunch, dinner, and of course, dessert. And then we get on the subject of chicken and he tells me he read a news report that said that men always go for the breast and women for the thighs, the tender parts, the dark meat (does he notice I am staring at his legs?) and I say I am beginning to get hungry. "Ravenous," he returns.

When I turn back to him, he is looking at something else—writing fast, moving his hand fervently across the pages of a small, spiral-bound notebook.

"What are you doing over there?" I ask, but his gaze remains glued on his notebook. "Are you writing a letter to Rilke?" I try, smiling, and finally, he turns his eyes to mine and laughs.

"I'm a writer," he says.

"A writer?" I repeat. He nods mechanically, like he is used to the question, or at least the question mark. "I thought you were an actor," I say. "An actor who writes, or a—"

"Writers make the best actors," he says. I inch closer. Maybe I think I am about to receive some important advice, something they don't teach you in the crowded conference room at Fusion. "Writers make the best actors," he repeats. "Because they write their own stage directions, and scene descriptions, and—" he says, and now he inches closer, almost blowing breath in my ear. "If the studio is smart, their own dialogue, too." He pauses and I wonder if this is my cue or if the gap is intended: a space he can hold, or behold. "And even if they aren't speaking it (he points to his eyes), they're thinking it."

I don't know what to say so I tell him I am going to order the thighs. The wiry man with the clipboard appears above us and starts speaking, talking about out times and flesh thongs and syndication rights and potential residuals but that's really as much as I get because I am thinking about the reason why I am here. Besides the last shot—striped sequin satin gown from Alexander Wang—I am just a prop and this shoot is Chris Selden's. Or rather, it belongs to neither of us; it belongs to *Harper's Bazaar*; it belongs to their Night on the Town feature and the promotional video they are shooting alongside it, the reality TV pitch, and the best models, Fusion always told me, are the ones that can sink into the feature, the frame, the clothes, the image. The best models sink into the photograph.

•

They are pulling my leg or at least pushing it into place when Chris smiles that same smile and puts his lips close to mine and whispers in my ear: todo está bien, tranquilízate, and I can see we are from the same place, or somewhere nearby, except he speaks without an accent and I am rolling my Rs and mixing my Ys and Js and feeling foolish and at the same time petrified, rigid and stiff, and I think I probably look more like a mannequin than a model but I wish I was a ghost, a nobody, utterly invisible, because the first thing that shows up in photographs are human emotions like *fear*.

Chris takes my hand and presses it closer to his chest. I wonder what he is thinking, and if I could read the book he is writing—I mean the narrative in his head—if I could read his mind, I would read it in italics and parentheses:

(It is the naked truth but it isn't real and what it is is aural intercourse because I am only listening. Listening for the sound of stage directions and camera flashes and my own distorted voice, too, on each command: speaking louder and kissing harder and touching more touching and doing everything with the volume turned up because the boom mic and the camera and even its micro-macro zoom lens can't catch subtleties, slight expressions and gestures, or whispers, and especially the sensations of being here at this moment and this place, with this girl, Nadié was it?) She wrapped her legs around him naturally, like they were meant to be there, springing from his ankles and calves and the back of his thighs like the roots of a tree, like tree branches, and they held the look— the feeling, the before-the-kiss-and-after-the-realization- that-lips-are-imminent—and more shouts interrupted the moment, *this* moment, and then they relaxed, both of them, all of them, in the back and on the bed, unclasping their limbs and breathing because the camera was out of batteries *(or how it feels for her, and what it is she must be feeling now, or tomorrow looking back on it, or what she'll be feeling remembering it alongside the sight of whatever it is they'll print or release on video, streaming across months, years, eternity . . .)* and after a few tense moments—the socket! the charger? where is it?—they faced each other again, this time in-profile, one pillow dangling from his outstretched palm, the others perched under the shimmering sky—

•

"You have this tendency," Chris says, spinning the swivel chair around to face me. "You sneak up on people like a suggestion."

"A suggestion?"

"A whisper," he continues. "A tendril of air."

I don't laugh. I want to ask him if this is how he always talks or if he's reciting lines for Rilke. Instead, I ask him what he's doing. A stream of images radiates from the enormous iMac monitor. Images from an hour ago, two hours ago, the whole morning, and Chris is scrolling through the day.

"Fascinating how many we take," I say. The photographs are bridging, blurring, moving faster, moving more like the pilot of the present (is there a fishpole hanging to my left?) than the frames of the past.

"This is nothing," Chris returns, spinning the chair around again to face the computer, clicking, moving, scrolling. "When Randall Mesdon shot me for Levi's Go Forth six years ago, a lot of people were still using film."

"Film?" I ask. I point to the cameramen that were— even now—hovering around us, hovering through us. "For video?"

Chris shakes his head. "Ever been in a dark room?"

"Never," I say, smiling, briefly showing my teeth. "Not unless you count the bar on Ludlow."

"I saw how Go Forth developed," Chris says. "How it took shape."

Chris starts talking about enlargers and safelights and chemicals and water. "And voilà!" he slaps his palms together. He is still scrolling, or trying to, but the arrow on the toolbar won't move. The monitor had frozen on a black cloud where my face should have been. Overexposure, I murmur. Chris spins back around to face me.

"A star is burned."

•

I am standing erect, as upright as possible, when they begin measuring the distance from my waist to my toes and drape the sequin satin over my neck. I look at Chris and he is smiling again; he always seems to be smiling, or half-smiling, or at least smiling with his eyes. But it is his eyes. Green or brown or maybe neither. Those deep, melancholic eyes give him away.

I have never seen anyone so confident and so sure of himself, and at the same time, so desperate. It's as if there's a sandglass sifting in his head and he seems to think the top bulb is always on the verge of emptying. Maybe I am seeming too much, or seeing too much. I have a natural curiosity. That's why I came here in the first place. To find things out.

"Your body is a perfect match for this fabric," a woman says, holding a plastic clip in between her lips. "To be honest," she pauses to fasten a zipper and removes the clip, letting it fall to the floor, "we don't even need to pin you."

Another voice: "You slip right in." Coming from behind me.

"He's right," the Art Director says. He is still holding his clipboard, except now he is smiling. They all are. "That's why you're here."

Tell me again? I want to ask, but my lips remain shut. More hands move over and around me, flattening out the satin waves that ebb every time I breathe.

"Wrinkles . . ." someone mutters.

"There's hardly any," another answers.

"You are a canvas, honey," the woman that dropped the clips purrs.

"You don't wear the clothes," the Art Director says. He lets his clipboard fall to the floor to situate my shoulders. "The clothes wear you."

"Perfect fit," a voice hums.

The photographer is nearly flat on his stomach, legs spread on the wooden floor, camera tilted, shooting skyward. It creates structure, he is saying. *Body.*

I take a look at the wall-length windows, and now it is the moon creating the shadows.

"Nadie—you're a gorgeous backdrop!"

"Absolutely textbook!"

"Turn your head more—"

"Look away, don't look here—"

"Now *that's* a pretty picture—wouldn't you say?"

"Nadie—"

I walk in through the pale light.

"That's why you're here—"

To find things out.

"Nadie—"

I am Nobody.

The Americas

I catch a bus from Galeão International to Copacabana and ten minutes in, I'm already sweating like a hooker in church. Rio de Janeiro is *hot* and I might be the hottest one here. I take a peek at my reflection in the window (I've got an aisle seat, so I crane my neck to accomplish this), in the sunglasses of the silent passenger sitting next to me, and finally, in my own BlackBerry, the black screen held up to my face, turned off for a few perilous seconds.

Besides the driver, the whole lot looks like members of the Newark bowling team.

Before I die of asphyxiation or heat stroke, or just plain boredom (*reading* material? I don't have to tell *you* that no one reads anymore . . . and my phone is still turned off, totally and completely: no juice), passing the same road or a road that looks just the same, miles and miles of road, palm trees, crumbled walls and buildings, a piece-of-shit-set if you ask me, I make it to the city, or what I take to be the city, but at least it's a pretty picture—I mean a Kodak moment—and there's a lake encircling everything (I could probably see my reflection here, too, if I were walking outside), and a massive statue of Jesus Christ (I'm still sweating, but this time more like a nun in Amsterdam), and bodies by the bucket-load, sweat-glazed and smiling, with more fake muscles and buckets—I mean tits, bodacious ta-tas—and bom-boms, too, and God knows what else, more fake body *parts* than real ones. Welcome to the plastic surgery capital of the world and damn, I can't wait to take a big bite out of it.

I've always taken whatever I can get and only asked for more in return. And that takes a special skill-set, I think. I think that takes a special kind of person. Maybe I think about Oliver Twist because I played the little twerp in an Illustrated Classics picture book, three hours of shooting and a lifetime ago, but I'm special; I really am. I'm a carnivore, baby. I want to take a big bite out of everyone and everything. And I start with *Fabulouso*.

Mega sent me here for a few under-5s and probably to check up on Chris Selden, but hell if I'm going to let him have all the fun. When I arrive on set, he's already looking at me with those wistful eyes, those sad, tragic, enormous anime eyes, and of course, reading. He's poring over some New York rag in between takes and I want to tell him, hey buddy, we ain't in the Big Apple anymore. I want to tell him so much more, of course, but instead of talking, I observe the scene. It takes patience.

IS COLOR REALLY IN FASHION
THIS SEASON—OR ANY?

I see the headline and make out a few other words but really, it's no news; it's never any news. And Selden is only an exception to the rule.

I want to tell him: You want to know why there are so few Latino models? Because the model is white. The model, the measure, the ruler. The world.

I want to tell him: People want the white life, the white picture, and the less color, the better.

I want to tell him: That's the writing on the wall, or at least the picture on the wallpaper.

Get into it.

But I don't say a damn thing but blow him an air kiss and try to graze his ass with my index finger (I fail) and tell him that Mega has sent me to Rio for all of the above reasons, and move over brother, because it's my time to shine. In this story, I'm the main character.

I haven't gotten any work in Manhattan in three months, and the last time I saw myself on print was an advertisement for Munchos, right above the small-print caution about anal leakage.

"Do you ever see me at night?" he asks. "And does it please you at all, with my head on your wall?"

Selden is always saying weird shit like that, talking in song lyrics or just nonsense, asking questions never meant to be answered, so I shrug it off; I shrug it off and slide right into the scene, the scene on set but off camera, I mean; I slide right in and get comfortable and start playing my role before it's even time to start rolling.

I don't even know my character's name.

I say: "I like your image, baby." I whistle; I pat my forehead, the damp, cool, skin. I say: "I like your poise, your pose. I like the way you are *appearing*."

I say all of this to Selden but he's not listening. Neither am I.

I'll never know what Alice saw in him unless that was just it, what she *saw*, what she saw with her eyes and nothing else. Chris Selden's face. Those fucking eyes. Like a glitch or a discrepancy, his face came unsewn, rifted and stretched out, before it finally came back into view.

"So how do you like Rio?" he asks, turning to me. Standing up now, too.

"I like it just fine," I say. "I feel like I'm in another world. I feel like I'm out-of-this-world. I feel like—"

"It's the Americas," he interrupts. "We are the same people, from the same mother; the same mother but a different point of departure. Why do you try to make every single person into some *other*?"

And I want to stop him right there because I don't look a thing like anyone on this island, least of all Selden. I want to tell him, Hey, my parents are from *Europe*—but he keeps on talking—like I said, questions never meant to be answered.

"Only difference is which direction we're headed."

"Well, amigo," I say, sidling up again, introducing myself to the makeup artist, too, "can you point me in the direction of the nearest drug distribution center?"

I wink at him and he just laughs.

"Come on," I moan, "this island probably has more drugs than all of the Northeast corridor."

"We're not on an island, Bailey."

We're not on an island? Is that a password? Is that the key? I whisper in his ear, hands cupped to mouth, but he gets the idea, and he tells me to meet him later that evening at his hotel. Says he knows somebody, says he's dating the guy's sister, and I want to tell him, bad idea, babes, but we move on to New York City, at least in words, we move on and we start talking about Alice, inevitably (and it's clear he *hasn't* moved on), and Dave's new film (while Dave inches closer, and the film is rolling, of course), but Chris is so interested in *Fabulouso*, so meticulous about his lines (all five of them, I think), I don't believe he even notices, but I swear—

Sometimes I catch his gaze, and he looks at me with a death stare, a look that says, You disgust me; a look that says, I'm going to kill you someday.

And I want to tell him, you'd never do a thing like that, honey. You think too much before you do anything.

Did You Get All That?

We watched Lifetime. We watched the Game Show Network. We watched MTV all afternoon, and I remember my favorite song: "She Drives Me Crazy." Quick cuts to close-ups of a television for a head, synchronized hopscotch, hands on hips, limbs slipping, jumping and squatting, in black and white and color, in wide-screen and split in two, halfway and in three-quarters, blurred in the back or bleeding into the foreground, fast-forward and rewound, played back in slow-mo.

We were playing hooky. It was fall. It was winter. No—it was spring. Or else it was summer and we weren't playing hooky at all.

"Everything you say is lies
But to me there's no surprise"
A television for a head.

I was just a boy, I remember that. Eleven, or twelve. Fascinated by music, but more than that, the music video, the way the image and the music played together, streaming in continual frames of revision to reveal other things—things I couldn't understand but only feel, which is to say emotions or sensibilities, faint rhythms tapping from my brain to my fingers and toes, and every sensation heightened with each passing

"She drives me crazy!"

Like no one else, or nothing else, the video did it to me, the music with the image flickering alongside and in between and inside out made me restless; *"I can't get any"* and still I tried, searching for the words that were not words and would never be but—

"I can't help myself"

I never could. So it's often better just to stop altogether, turn off or turn in or tune in and sink toward the image, the one on screen or the one I'm projecting because the things I do don't seem real.

Sometimes.

But they are, or they were to me: the superstitious rites of a child, at eleven or twelve, reading *Batman* and *The Flash* tucked inside of the Torah. Etmol, hayom, mahar, akhshav. *Stop. Rewind.* ". . . streaming in continual frames of revision to reveal other things . . ." And the way I walked outside, skipping over the cracks, stomping and swinging and passing the tenuous time when there was no MTV or no Fine Young Cannibals or no mammals at all, whether human or animals; when there was nothing but imagination and memory, in a waiting room or at temple, or on the school bus or in a crowded cafeteria: always in my own solitude, and especially in the company of others. Good as Gold. *Stop. Rewind.* "Like no one else or nothing else . . ." I imagined the scenes I saw on screen and transposed them onto life—and then there was music, and then there was the moving image, and then there was life, but this time more melodic and more manifold and more momentous to me.

We watched everything, the chorus and refrain collapsing into an eternity of three minutes and thirty-five seconds, sliding forward until silence, or until another video blared on, creating the illusion and destroying it at the same time.

Like the moment I first wore headphones under my yarmulke. An iPod, portable disc player, Walkman, any of these things; the privacy of it, the shock, the way it colored my surroundings as if they were set-pieces—but I don't exactly remember that, the first time, not at all, or not like this.

But why do I remember that day among all the others?

And why right now? *Stop. Rewind.* ". . . a television for a head . . ." *Fast-forward.* "It was fall. It was winter. No—it was spring. Or else it was summer and. . ." Those headphones changed everything. I could carry the soundtrack wherever I went. I could alter the score over and over again . . . one minute, an unrequited romance, the next, a spy thriller . . . over and over again.

When I met Chris Selden I knew he was just like me, except from the opposite angle. He believed he was always in a music video, and I thought I was the one filming it. We were a perfect match, a timeless story, too good to be true, or at least too good for Hollywood—and of course it was, because we're in Cannes now.

A moment before my own film debuts internationally— "Good as *Gold!*" they've been saying, slapping my back and shaking my hand and shouting half my surname three more times—and all I can think about is this memory from childhood, this fleeting moment of eleven or twelve in some basement, on some couch, with a girl named Carol or Joanne or Carol Anne, and worse, I can only tell you about it on *film.* Everything recorded or pre-recorded or misreported (ask Selden about that) for some other time, and who will ever watch this one, who will ever listen to *these* words? *Stop. Rewind.* ". . . creating the illusion and destroying it at the same time."

Stop.

(off camera, *sotto voce*) Am I not allowed to ask questions? . . . But I've already asked a few . . . Okay, let's do it over then. Just keep recording. Did you get all that?

We watched Lifetime. We watched the Game Show Network. We watched MTV all afternoon, and I remember my favorite song: "She Drives Me Crazy." Quick cuts to close-ups of a television for a head, synchronized hopscotch, hands on hips, limbs slipping, jumping and squatting, in black and white and color, in wide-screen and split in two, halfway and in three-quarters, blurred in the back or bleeding into the foreground, fast-forward and rewound, played back in

Life (or something similar)

THEY CALL THAT SKIING

They call that skiing.

"Dummy," Johnny Baker barked and cracked his neck to the side with confidence, flipping off the TV and turning his attention to something new.

"I know, I was just kidding around," Dave started. "I *know* how to ski."

Dave had just made a joke about the Winter X Games, asking why the people on screen pump their wrists up and down as if they were milking two cows at the same time. It fell flat. Everything I say, Dave murmured, falls flat.

Johnny was already discussing plans for the night. He thought it was a good idea to throw a party. "Let's throw a couple of kegs into the mix and make it a good time."

Anything that involved booze and bitches was a good time to Johnny. The guy has been swimming in both since we met, Dave thought, but he never gets tired of it. In fact, Dave could recall only one time in which his housemate put any limits on his restless libido. It was last February, when Johnny had given up sober sex for Lent.

"Alright," Dave said, after a long pause. "Only if we can get Sarah to come."

Sarah, Sarah, Sarah—the object of affection—countless sperm had been murdered in her name, by her image, since Dave met her, wide-eyed and sweating, hands jammed in his pockets outside Linderman Library. She had gone out for a smoke and he was just looking for some fresh air.

Johnny grinned and got up from the couch, walking

toward the kitchen to begin placing calls. Dave sat and stared at the chipped wood floor of their parlor, both hands on his forehead, complaining about waiting to talk to Sarah before doing anything drastic, citing a reluctance to sully his record before he even got a chance to apply to law school.

"She's a lock," Johnny said, his hair hanging effortlessly in all directions, and Dave almost became nauseated at his friend's good luck, or maybe his lack of any. "I'll invite her myself."

Dave's eyes lit up. He tried his best to remain calm as he walked—two steps at a time—up the stairs to his bedroom on the second floor. He began by making a list of possible outfits he should consider, different lines to say and approaches he could take, once he spotted Sarah. He clicked open the Internet and scoured the boundaries of Facebook until he came upon her screen name.

Dave had always had a thing for blonds, so when he began to take an interest in Sarah—slender, C cups, auburn hair, cheerleader—he knew it was something special. But Dave's thing for blonds wasn't at all reciprocal. No girls, in fact, had slept in the second-floor bedroom at 618 Pierce Street since Dave moved in with Johnny last year, excluding the one time Johnny left his girlfriend with Dave to attend to while she was hooking up with the toilet and *he* was on the howl with some transfer student from Colombia—the country, not the school.

Dave often wondered why Johnny had all the luck: a great tan, a sinewy build—years of lacrosse—cool, blue eyes, a nice smile . . . and why God couldn't bear to share any of that Manhattan Upper East Side charisma with him; he who was considered, by most measures, a townie born and raised fifteen minutes across the way in Allentown; a hell of a fun time if you got no idea of fun.

He wasn't unattractive and he jogged every other day, but Dave seemed resigned to his role as the quiet kid in the back of the class whom no one ever quite knew. And he was satisfied for a time with the secret knowledge of his mental superiority, until even that phase of intellectual egotism wore off and all he had left was the label of insecure nerd.

He imagined breaking out someday, just morphing into somebody he'd have liked to meet. Life, or something similar. He'd have a fast car and nice clothes, aviator sunglasses maybe, and a bomber jacket with a sheepskin collar. Maybe Sarah and he would walk across Fifth Avenue and Broadway until they got to Greenwich Village and there they would sit and talk about life over a croissant and a cappuccino while something jazzy echoed in the distance, the sun warming their skin . . . he had never been to New York City but frequently envisioned what it would be like to move among the herds of people huddled around Times Square, feeling au courant at the center of the universe.

Later that night, Dave took off his glasses and examined himself in the mirror. His nose was long and narrow and occasional freckles spotted his pale cheeks and under his small, dark eyes. His receding black hair was stuck up in various directions in a fashion that looked more authentically bed head than the reproduction of sleekness Johnny's hair wax was supposed to suggest. He grimaced at the reflection and carefully put on his contacts, which he reserved for special opportunities, such as the one who would present herself tonight.

He remained optimistic. This was life—but only a preview. Only the coming attractions. This was life, but . . .

Life would change, soon, just as soon as he graduated, moved away, got a job . . . life would open up—*he* would open up, say hello—soon, life would be quite different. It had to. It would. It *will*, he thought.

How could anyone get on if they didn't believe in that?

"Cheer up, kid," Johnny said, smiling his game-show smile and slapping Dave on the back, on his way out of the bathroom after grabbing the tube of wax near the sink. "Everybody's gotta get laid sooner or later," he called behind his back and Dave laughed, briefly believing it.

When the moment came, Dave wasn't the sparkling image of James Bond, or even Johnny Baker; there was no slow-mo time-stop assurance of sophistication that would make Sarah lock eyes with him and instantly fall into his arms, perhaps while something romantic ("Enjoy the Silence"? "Strangelove"? Master and Servant"?) played.

There were only two Ping-Pong balls and one open table, a pyramid of half-filled eight-ounce plastic cups and warm Natty Light shimmering in the translucence. Sarah wasn't lucid at all. She was carrying a half-empty handle of Banker's Club vodka in one hand, her beautiful face splotched with makeup and sweat, those soft blue eyes nearly rolled back inside the crevice of her skull. Dave was transfixed.

"Sure," she stammered, nearly falling in his arms, "I'll play with you." Dave fidgeted with his fingers, inching them toward his eyes until he remembered he wasn't wearing glasses. He regrouped and extended one hand, stammering his name. She shook it and smiled.

"Okay *Dan*, you ready to play with some little white *balls?*" Sarah hollered at her own joke. Dave smiled, seeking out Johnny in the corner of the room—Johnny talking to his girlfriend over a beer—as if to solicit his approval, signify the accomplishment—*Look, my love has arrived*. Johnny pointed back with his beer and reverted his attention to his girlfriend's breasts, the tops of which were busting out of her violet Donna Karan dress. Johnny was wearing a fire truck red muscle-fit polo from Abercrombie & Fitch and washed-out Mavi jeans with tan flip-flops. Dave felt resplendent in tight beige Dockers and an olive Seville Row flannel button-down, collar secure, sleeves firm. He wore auburn boat shoes he hoped would give him another connection to Sarah, something else to talk about before they made love. Johnny would correct him tomorrow.

Dave looked back at Sarah, who was looking at Chris Selden, who was looking at another girl—a freshman? a prospective? a townie?—who was looking back at him.

Dave touched his pointed ears; the sides of his thin hair. He could feel the heat filling up his cheeks, shooting through his arms and legs. The beer, he thought. The beer and the flames of love . . .

While Dave and Sarah sipped quickly from cans and lofted Ping-Pong balls into cups, the music radiating from Johnny's iPod grew louder on the speakers. This time it was "Castles in the Sky" by Ian Van Dahl, and Dave started pumping his fist to the thumping bass, his confidence soaring along with his blood alcohol level; he thought about taking off his shirt and swinging it between his legs, of throwing Sarah forcefully onto the antique parlor couch—cushions ripped and stained—and making love to her right then and there, eye candy for all the partygoers at 618 Pierce Street.

Then the flames tapered and he simply held Sarah's hand, flimsily at first and then firmly, with conviction and determination, squinting his eyes just enough to see clearly and fixing his jaw tight; some semblance of manly bravado he'd noticed countless times in the collection of Paul Newman movies he had back home. Introspection, self-assurance, maybe a touch of chivalry?

Sarah was, after all, he reasoned, a good, innocent girl. The kind you'd like to marry. The kind you could take home to your parents, and he wondered, taking another greedy gulp of beer, what his parents would say when he brought *her* home, what they might talk about at the dinner table as his mother and father exchanged knowing looks, communicating their acknowledgement that their son was having intercourse with a beautiful woman. Dave wondered if Sarah had had many lovers, or if he would be her first.

She smiled at him, as if his thoughts were transmitting from his cerebral cortex to hers, and the saliva forming on the edges of her chapped lips radiated something to Dave which looked like bliss. It is finally starting to happen, he thought. My life is turning around . . .

He began planning first dates and anniversaries—a trip to the park for a picnic, a night of bowling, a holiday cruising along the Delaware River in Sarah's family yacht . . . weeks would trail weeks as he sectioned off whole months from the calendar and allotted each to quality time with Sarah. It was The End of the World Party, but to Dave, it seemed like everything was only just beginning.

When he suggested they move to the second floor, Dave stopped on the third step of the staircase, halting mid-stride as if the sight of the party, the parlor, the reclining plastic table and the eight-ounce cups, the brass chandelier and all of the people swerving underneath were much better from there. Just the right angle, Dave thought, just the right lighting—there's real presence here. But when he looked back, Sarah was gone.

The music got progressively louder and more people poured into the small house on 618 Pierce Street: herds of acne-faced freshmen and salacious sophomores, the over-twenty-one crowd just coming back from Leon's or MacGrady's, looking for a little more of whatever it was they were hoping for in the first place when their descent into the night began.

Fifteen minutes later, as Dave sat idly in the backseat of a cop car, wondering how to explain the whole ordeal to his parents—the specific details to leave out, what exactly to alter—Sarah was in the second-floor closet, giving a hand job to two JV hockey players.

They call that skiing.

CHAMELEONS

There are over seven and a half billion people in the world, and none of them will ever know each other. Not really.

This was Chris's cynical viewpoint, probably ever since he saw *The Rules of Attraction* and realized he had more in common with the film's vacuous characters than would be favorable to admit. But he got over it quick, and even as he prescribed to the self-loathing philosophy of "romance is dead," so did he also tend to reproduce it, going with one girl after another, a different face for each week or whim.

He was living out scenes from a movie; his ideas about romance had become his reality, but at least he was cognizant of the anomaly between the two, the idea and the reality, firmly believing that who you were to the world was not who you were inside, and everyone and everything was some kind of chameleon, flip-flopping identities like they were jeans. Being one's self required being invisible and alone, he thought, and Chris couldn't think of anything worse, except not being himself all the time.

So when he found himself at a party at 618 Pierce Street—Johnny Baker's place; the two hated each other but free beer was free beer, and pussy? Well, that was always free—he played the role of passionate Lit major, one which wasn't too difficult to perform, having just ended a relationship with the girl he thought he might marry. Jules left him for her Brazilian yoga instructor a month before, breaking up in an e-mail, and all Chris could think about was why she couldn't have sent a singing telegram instead.

At least that's what he'd been telling people.

Chris liked girls like they were songs from his mixtapes, intensely preoccupied with a few at a time for a week in a seemingly endless loop before discarding each into the recesses of his library for something new, something forever more exciting. Then, they were just auto-tunes, just a fleeting guitar riff or buoyant chorus that occasionally popped into his head when he least expected it. How could a person become a feeling and a feeling become a memory and a memory become an afterthought? How could a person disappear?

The difference between understanding and harmony is that understanding is only a word, and harmony is music.

The difference between understanding and harmony is . . .

He slowed down, paused, rewound.

"What I mean is, what else is there anyway? What else is there when it comes down to it except for those five minutes of heaven—"

"Seven—"

"Or seven—" Chris resumed, swallowing another swirl of Natural Ice and furrowing his brow, which was not part of the performance. "Seven minutes of heaven with the lights turned off." He coughed, resisting the urge to spit out the beer. "If you're lucky."

There was something he wanted to say; something he wanted to tell Dave. A word or words. He wanted to tell him he was miserable; he wanted to tell him he was lost. He wanted to tell him he could not live without her, because she had taught him new ways to live. But he said nothing, but nothing. Instead, he had one of his spasms of comic relief.

Relief from what? Every revelation in life cut short by insecurity. The same way he would sooner tell a stranger on the bus an intimate confession, the same way he couldn't tell Ana, his best friend, his mother, anything. The same way that everyone's greatest conversations are the ones they have with themselves. The poignancy, the honesty. The right-word-at-the-right-moment kind of truth. And anyway—he told himself, everything that was ever said was spoiled by saying it.

Yes, the difference between understanding and harmony was music. Chris was thinking that at the same time he was talking to Dave Goldstein over a game of flip-cup, standing over a plastic fold-up table, swarming the party with his eyes (Who's the new girl? Who's *she*? The small button nose, the blue eyes, the brown bangs . . .) concentrating hard and furrowing his brow to appear somehow more thoughtful, more contemplative, maybe more sensitive. Furrowing his brow. Bobbing his head from time to time to the beat of "Take On Me" by A-Ha, which was blaring from his headphones. It was The End of the World Party; the music characteristically sucked.

Dave was someone he knew, someone he liked. Someone he had even spent two hours of silence with at the movies—a handful of times—someone who'd taught him how to cook couscous. Someone who'd shown him the exact way a stage should be set, the proper lighting, the best angle. Intro to Cinematography. I can talk to him—really say something. Can't I?

"If you really want contact," Dave observed, seven fingers still raised, eyes still locked on the brunette on the other side of table, framing her with his camera eye, "sometimes it's best to shout."

Chris smiled and removed one headphone from his ear, patting Dave on the back.

"What were you saying?"

COCKTAIL HOUR

There were moments in Johnny's life that constituted total happiness and tranquility—his darting reflection in the dark windows outside Neville Hall, hearing his name being called on the PA system at lacrosse games, nailing a random freshman on his girlfriend's birthday, for instance.

But this was not one of them. This was disappointing, nearly depressing. This was Johnny at the gym, half an hour in and a good pump flowing through his veins, interrupted by the realization that his housemate Dave Goldstein was certainly not any cooler than he was when he first met him a year ago, which is exactly when he asked the shy secretary of the Hillel Society to move in with him at the three-story house on 618 Pierce Street. It had been a spontaneous decision; they had only just run into each other moments earlier at 48 Hours Video, but he was in desperate need of another mate to pay the rent, and although popular among a variety of people on campus, nobody liked Johnny well enough to actually *live* with him. In the back of his mind, Johnny knew this too.

But the real truth was that Johnny loved the idea of living with someone whom he considered so socially inferior. He thrived on it. It revitalized him in ways even admiring himself in the mirror after a fake tan and a lukewarm shower (not especially hot—steam slackened the muscles) couldn't achieve. Dave's complete lack of social skills only boosted Johnny's confidence further and soon, his immense ego had ballooned to Herculean proportions.

Dave, too, was delighted. He savored the idea of being seen with Johnny, even as Johnny carefully distanced himself from Dave in most social settings, simply arriving with his housemate and dropping him off at the keg, in search of more exciting action.

His protégé, Johnny knew too well, was aloof and insecure around all women. He tried to imagine what a simple conversation between Dave and his mother would be like, but couldn't find the words. So in exchange for paying the utilities every month and taking care of his laundry, Dave became the subject of Johnny's version of *Extreme Makeover*. Johnny believed he had embarked on a mission of unabated altruism; he was firm in his mind-set to shape Dave into a more sociable, likable human being. He would model Dave after himself, of course, telling him how to act, what to wear, how to present himself at public gatherings, which fraternities to mingle with and the houses to avoid. He might even get the kid laid in the first month, he thought, back then. But it was all wishful thinking. And this latest discovery sent Johnny's ego tumbling down, at least until his next set of triceps extensions.

"Yeah, tell him he should get out more," Jenny said, sweating in her navy blue spandex shorts, her long brown hair tied in a bun, blue eyes a little red from running. "I'm starting to get worried about him."

Jenny was one of Dave's few female friends, an acquaintance he met, of course, through Johnny, who used to sleep with her on Wednesdays. "Worried?" Johnny grinned, cracking his neck to the side with confidence—a habit he formed years ago when he couldn't think of anything significant to say and had to fill the space with *some*thing—and wiping the sweat from his lip.

"Yeah, last Saturday for instance," she returned. "He spent it at the circus." "The *circus?*"

Johnny now posed the question to Dave, back in their parlor, as they sat on the couch watching television. "Where the hell was the *circus*?"

"Hey, it was free," Dave protested. "And I got the ticket from a friend. It was in old town, on Main Street," he said, raising one weak hand in rebuttal, "and it was actually really cool, like a criticism of the circuses of old."

Dave was constantly finding ways to support the unconventional, or avenues for facilitating his affinity for overturning the popular, which made it even stranger that he would relish the moments being seen in public with somebody like Johnny. In another life, Dave always told himself, he'd be a freedom fighter, some sort of gung-ho ass-kicking anti-establishment liberator. But in this one, he was shackled to his inept, enfeebled frame, and the role of unkempt Cinema Studies student, handcuffed to emotions of self-loathing and reserve. Although even that was changing by the minute, with every passing day he spent with Johnny, as the confident lacrosse star taught him new ways to lose his individuality and replace it with something more easily consumed by the general public. Clearly, something else had been lost in translation.

"So," Johnny said, shaking off the realization, "did you meet any hot girls?"

"No," Dave replied, quieter. "Only children and seniors."

"Seniors?" Johnny scowled. "*Old* people?" He shook his head and trudged upstairs. Dave was getting sloppy, Johnny reasoned. He was only playing the role assigned to him at birth, not the one he should have been reciting in front of the mirror every night before bed. The kid is a lost cause, Johnny muttered, and turned his mind to other things.

What better way to shake off the boredom than to throw a party? But the notion dissipated before it touched his lips with the realization that convincing Dave to play host would be akin to getting him a date, and that, he knew too well, was nearly impossible.

Johnny walked back downstairs and sat on the couch, budging only to reach for the remote, flipping through the channels till he got to ESPN. The Winter X Games? Johnny sneered. I'd rather watch professional bowling.

"Hey, what are we watching?" Dave asked, grinning and slapping a knee. "'Agriculture Anonymous'? Looks like a couple of farmers milking cows."

Johnny shook his head and shot back an insult—regretting it almost instantly. Persuasion is, he understood under his breath, a pill swallowed slow and gentle.

And so he started step by step, inching toward the kitchen only to turn his face back toward Dave and nod twice: a Biblical offering. The End of the World Party. Dave agreed enthusiastically, nodding back after a bout of silence in which Johnny prayed for positive results—with the added exception that Sarah come. Sarah was a sultry sophomore cheerleader, auburn-haired and unethically-thin with fake tits and an airbrushed smile. She lived on a diet of cocaine and pretzels, and lived in a galaxy far far away from people like Dave Goldstein.

Johnny knew she wouldn't come, not if Dave asked her, so he quickly added that he'd call her himself, a detail which energized his housemate even more (Johnny knew it would), and the plan was set in motion. Johnny walked back toward the kitchen and started making phone calls while Dave hustled up the stairs. Five minutes later, Johnny received a tap on the shoulder and turned around on the couch to see Dave again, mentioning a computer problem and asking for his housemate's help. Johnny was confused; he didn't use the computer for very much at all besides chatting and pornography, but as he walked into Dave's room—immaculately maintained with Depeche Mode posters and black lights adorning the walls—the topic came into view. Dave pointed to his laptop and began to rub his palms together.

"So we need to devise some carefully-worded IMs, something clever and casual," Dave said, "but keep in mind—sarcasm doesn't translate well on screen."

Johnny shook his head. Dave wanted to drop a few lines to Sarah before the evening's entertainments commenced. But Johnny quickly suggested that no talk was good talk. "You know, make her sweat it out a little." So Dave did, satisfied in his knowledge that he was finally playing the game. The only one that mattered.

As the time for festivities drew near, Johnny made sure *he* had his A-game apparent. He waxed his hair with Göt2b Ultra Glued Invincible Grit then waited eleven minutes for the follicles to congeal (the back of the bottle suggested ten). Afterward, he put his hands to his head lightly, being careful to fix only what needed fixing and not to disrupt any aura of spontaneity he'd managed to achieve with the bed head replication. Satisfied, he finished the procedure with a few spritzes of hair spray, remembering that the forecast had called for a slight breeze this evening.

He put on his favorite Mavi jeans, fabric as soft as butter, and felt the denim slide in between his legs like liquid. He was going to get laid tonight, that was a given. Marcy, his adorable girlfriend of six months, was obviously a guest of honor, but even better was the invitation sent to her hot eighteen-year-old sister, May, whom Johnny likened to an innocent version of Marcy herself—though (and here was the departure that made Johnny's heart flutter) unspoiled, untouched, removed of baggage, or only a syllable. She was visiting from high school, come to Bethlehem to see what all the rage of the number-three party school was about.

The occasion started well enough. Neighbors showed up, followed by a couple of doe-eyed Jewish girls from a sorority nearby—already dripping with cheap vodka and perfume—but after eleven o'clock, when the music started thumping (Johnny's favorite Sag Harbor mix, a staple during his perennial surfing adventures in the Hamptons) the party really got rolling.

It seemed like everyone knew about the event way in advance and they were simply waiting it out to make Johnny sweat. But Johnny had done his part well, working the phone lines like a telemarketer, except the only thing he was selling was excitement, some kind of antidote to boredom, some better way to pass the time.

And it passed quickly.

By midnight, the first floor was packed, and girls and guys were complaining about getting their asses slapped on their way to the bathroom. Fraternal life ruled stronger outside of the fraternities. There were the popped collars, the sweater vests, the pink corduroys and North Face jackets, a dozen chants and yells and hoots to fill an arena.

Johnny glanced at Dave and smiled in between sips of warm Natty Ice. The kid isn't doing so bad after all, he murmured, but he guessed that Sarah was talking to him more out of pity than anything else. Dave wasn't dressed for any kind of success and Johnny grimaced at the image of a balding thirty-something celibate bookworm accountant Dave conveyed in his tight pale Dockers and Seville Row flannel tucked in at the waist. He had totally misinterpreted Johnny's suggestion of looking *smart*. He would correct him tomorrow.

Dave smiled slowly and hesitated to move in closer to his Beirut partner. Sarah was so drunk she was practically being held up by Dave. He probably feels more like a ladies man than ever before, Johnny thought. *His* arm was around Marcy's and in between glances at her perky tits popping out of her violet dress, all eyes were on May; May the beautiful, May the coveted, who, at this very moment, was in deep conversation with some senior from Jersey whom

Johnny regarded as a complete douchebag, as if anyone from the state could be considered the least bit significant.

Chris split his time at the track, the humanities center, and avant-garde art galleries—probably postmodern circuses, too—and when he wasn't in the public gaze, there were rumors circulating around campus that he wrote poetry. He's a Russian Doll, Johnny had heard people say around campus. A Russian Doll? he thought now. But isn't Chris Polish? . . . Or is it Cuban? Except isn't his last name—

It was precisely this allure that made Johnny dislike Chris so much. Whattafag, Johnny thought, and smirked at all six feet of him, dirty blond hair and hazel eyes and hairy, thick eyebrows and a long, solid—the kid was definitely too into himself to be interested in May but there he was, romancing her like a snake charmer on the crowded intersection of a faraway tourist trap. Johnny wondered what they must be talking about, what Chris must have said to draw her attention away from the party and locked solely on him.

Probably something poetic, the fucking queer.

Probably he's writing this down too, Johnny sneered. Probably he's using *this* for the scene of a story. It was no secret that Johnny was jealous. Jealousy was fine, jealousy was good. Jealousy spurred him to action. But he'd forget all about it as soon as he was alone with Marcy, who at this very moment was rubbing Johnny's crotch with her knees, standing erect, brushed up against him from the front. It takes talent and the girl had plenty.

And then the shit hit the fan. Somebody—Johnny would later blame Dave—thought it would be a good idea to let in a forty-something dressed in suspenders and a red flannel shirt (C'mon, what is this, *Kutztown?*), who turned out to be an undercover cop. It was "Ride of the Valkyries," *Apocalypse Now*, helicopters in motion, and citations were being thrown around like machine-gun fire from a bunker nest hidden away in a smog of intoxicated bewilderment.

Escape routes became predictable. Everyone went for the back exit, busting right through the wooden door, knocking the weak frame off the hinges in a stampede of Sperry flip-flops and UGGs. Johnny watched Marcy get arrested (she was only one year older than May) then bolted outside into the cool April night. He felt like a fugitive on the lam, like Henry Fleming in *The Red Badge of Courage* (though this particular literary connection was filled in by the narrator, not Johnny himself, since he had not read many books since the sixth grade), and he would say, years later, at every cocktail hour he went to, at every bar he sat at, that you haven't really lived until you've run away from your own house.

HUMANITIES

Cell phone, text message, middle of class, blinking at you sporadically like old Christmas lights. This is how it happens. Places and dates, how a plan gets made.

Sarah looked at her inbox and sighed. Johnny Baker.

End of the World Party tonight at mine. Come thru.

The kid was sketchy as all hell; Sarah had known him since she was a freshman, and she didn't have enough fingers to count the number of her friends he had slept with. In her opinion, the kid was a walking STD, some curiosity to medical science, but that didn't discourage her too much (that's what condoms are for), just enough to make him sweat it out till the end of class—Humanities—to text him back.

Everyone was sweating; everyone would always be sweating.

Sarah could picture him sitting by his phone, his phone on his lap in case it vibrated, waiting for her reply, checking every other minute in case he had suddenly gone deaf in the heat of the moment.

She was the kind of woman who relished being in complete control over the opposite sex; she enjoyed making them squirm like goldfish in a tank full of piranhas. The only thing she felt truly hesitant about was Johnny's ultra-creepy roommate, Dave. Oddest couple in school, Sarah thought, so she figured Dave had to be dealing coke or something just as expensive to make the relationship worthwhile. She wondered if she could score some tonight. The secretary of the Hillel Society and the captain of the lacrosse team don't just get together one day and decide to live with each other. Sarah wondered how the question got posed; did Dave beg, or did Johnny suggest it? She bet it went down in the beer-soaked lino of some party, Johnny too drunk to realize what the hell he had just done until he woke up in the morning to a few unwieldy knocks on the front door, staring face to face with Dave Goldstein and two suitcases full of whatever it was he decided was important enough to pack.

Sarah started early, sipping on vodka cranberries around eight, taking fifteen-minute breaks every half an hour to blow lines on her roommate's computer desk. At around ten, she wandered up on the Hill, getting lost in the maze of faces tightly packed in the corridors of some nameless frat house. To Sarah, they were mostly all the same. It was a hotel party and she took her turns around each room, getting shuttled to the front of the line almost immediately; she was queen of this broke-down palace and everyone else were just subjects, she thought, worker bees ready at a moment's glance to do her bidding.

She didn't want to get roofied, at least she didn't *ask* for that cocktail. Before she blacked out completely, she backed out of the party, stumbled down the snaking campus, and by sheer providence—in behalf of Dave Goldstein—made it to Pierce Street.

The next morning, she woke up in somebody else's closet, her makeup caked dry across her face, left nostril peeling, blood stains above her lips, BCBG leggings torn slightly at the crotch, next to two freshman boys she had never seen before.

What sweethearts, she thought. They must have taken care of me last night while I was sick.

She noted the vomit on the carpeted floor beside them—all three bodies tangled in a pile so that respective limbs were unidentifiable—and texted Johnny Baker, apologizing for never making it to his party.

Excerpt from SCREEN, *May 26, 2008*

Dave Goldstein's disarming debut "—" is a raw fact, gathering into itself and reflecting its own gaze.

Mr. Goldstein directs it with the poise of a seasoned auteur, segueing between the imagination and the real, and most dramatically, the collision of the two. Chris Selden is an actor, but he doesn't act; he transforms into a gesture, a symbol, a mode of expression. Mr. Selden becomes a mirror, too, and one that reflects back to the audience all of its private desires and subterranean yearning. He sparkles and explodes from scene to scene—scenes, which, are not scenes at all but rather points on a map; the whole world is a vast film set, Mr. Goldstein seems to be saying, and the division between the reality and the movie is so slight that even the participants are sometimes confused. Dennis Romero, a New York City caterer reprising his own role, is one such example. Mr. Romero is brilliant, touching, funny and brutal in his portrayal of himself; one would think he was more real than reality; truer than life. Alice Waters is a walking zombie, moving with the speed of an old Kodak disposable, blinking her eyes toward the audience like a shutter when she speaks. What is she communicating? We can hardly guess, but it's not our job to impose meaning on a human life; a human life that is represented in the em-dash enveloping the blank title screen. Mr. Goldstein's map is not fixed, it sprouts like a tree, the assemblages of which reach exhilarating heights, shattering the linear unity of the word—shattering, even, the conception of language. We see this moment from outside as from within.

Mr. Goldstein produces the unconscious with a statement about authenticity, the compulsion of curation, the desire to document everything in and around us. And likewise, "—" has no beginning or end; it is always in the middle. The film moves in a kind of suspended motion; an excursion through a spectral landscape with a shape-filled foreground and negative outlines. Mr. Goldstein keeps the audience jumping with cuts; shifting camera angles, juxtaposing images, implying connections, tracing lines in the snow. I have watched the film on nine occasions, and each time, the experience is not unlike walking into the cinema in the middle of the film; one cannot tell whether it is a preview, or the real thing, halfway in, or at the climax, and it hardly matters. Mr. Goldstein offers us something and withholds it. What is offered is not narrative, plot, a look behind the red carpet, glamour, or even Chris Selden, but proof that he exists. And it is *our* landscape, too, proof that we were there, proof that we bore witness to it all; every breath as a breath breathing into each other.

Mr. Goldstein drapes the audience in his myth; he lets it flow over all of us, and we cling to it like a blanket. We stare; and he returns our gaze by winking.

The movie, exhilarating in its wild complexity, constantly transits between documentary and fiction, actors and characters, black-and-white and color, 16mm and 35, past and present. That there is more than one way to perceive and inhabit reality is the most basic of the film's many truths.

The experience is not unlike waking, except "—" is a new dream, a dream with all the texture of life and memories that causes telescoping, interruptions, a breaking down of images—too many images. We dream that we awake. Even now, as I write this, as you read this . . . even now, I am unsure whether I am awake. The film excavates whole lifetimes—whole histories—within an image—histories of the media itself, a fountain of LIFE that is many times more interesting than Aronofsky's tepid version in 2006. Everything the camera gives us is interesting. Not for long; just for now, but *now*, Mr. Goldstein seems to be saying, *now* is all that actually matters.

"—" is fundamentally about experience and sensation; a striving for identity through the harmony of form and content, style and substance. Mr. Goldstein glorifies the camera, to show how it can perform better than the eye, to show how it can discern tiny differences, and to show that these differences add up to an unbroken alteration of reality. "—" flatters us with suggestions, hints, moments of awareness; "—" beckons us closer and whispers in our ear: You have something in common with celebrity. You are just as important—more important—than the celebrity. Because you are rare, discerning, a connoisseur of culture. You—the film says—are a spectator. No one can be greater; nothing else matters.

Accordingly, the film is shockproof despite scenes of sordid sex and creation, a surface with slips that eventually slips away, shifting into its duplicate; a perversion of itself. When the mask is torn off only to reveal another mask, what is one more illusion? Everything is false, except the audience's conviction that matches the director's: The film is true. This is complete negation, a perpetual fall, a charged vacuum; a recall of the beautiful mushroom clouds at the end of *Strangelove*, except varnished in HD.

"—" is a system of signals that signals itself.

Mr. Goldstein seems to say, in the end, rather simply, that it is *you* who made this. You who is we. The audience's gaze. All of us. Therefore, "—" is the truth. Pass it on.

In a Portrait

Calvin had just finished saying something stupid, something like "clothes without bodies." Something about the most beautiful image being a pair of jeans draped on a desk chair. Something about something.

"Get into it."

And I cringed and sipped and shuffled my feet, clad in what? I don't even remember . . . tapping them under the table as I always do when I'm nervous, anxious, bored. But now I was thinking, too, about the suffocation of surveillance, the vulnerability of a figure unwittingly being watched, the absence of an unattended cummerbund. Oh, God. The *helplessness*. The difference between a person in a portrait and an unposed figure. And then, I thought about him. He had a name. Of course he had a name.

"Get into it," Calvin repeated. Everyone was squinting, squinting and withered and spectral, oozing airlessness, breathing out the same air-condition they were taking in, sucking long and hard on their flutes. They were like vampires, the whole table, except for Dave, who was barely breathing. (You must always keep looking, Dave thought, without for a second relaxing the intensity of the gaze or the mood that is beginning to swell in the body, outside the body; you must hold the scene, the moment, the relatively boisterous silence, and let nothing in.) Then someone laughed, then someone hiccupped, and finally, I heard a scream.

Someone recognizes me. Someone recognizes me, I murmur, and turn my head as slow as I can make the capitis muscles go.

And look—now you are coming my way.

I Am Reading My Own Lines

In my dream, I am at ABC waiting to tape my scene and revising a hardcopy draft of *Going Down*, the part of the novel where Chris Selden is also at ABC. 320 West 66th Street. They call my name on the PA system and I scamper up one flight of stairs to the studio floor. I tape my lines, all the while thinking that I left my manuscript in the dressing room. A week passes. I am at ABC again, waiting to tape my scene, which is the same scene except now I'm the cabana boy (last week I was Juan in the Buenos Días Café) and I thought of the T-shirt again, *Same Shit, Different Island* except the island is the same now, too. When I look at my script, I am reading my own lines; I mean, my own lines that I wrote in *Going Down* for Chris Selden at ABC. Like everything on TV, rehearsed once in somebody else's life and once in ours. As I turn the page, read further, keep turning, now faster, I realize that ABC has found my manuscript and is using all the dialogue and scenes for the soap opera that I am acting in outside the novel. How would they ticket that in a coming attraction? *The horror of being stuck in your own soap opera* except the more I start to feel it around my lips, I think that could describe anyone, anywhere, because that is the human experience: your own soap opera. I fictionalized the real story, then the fiction became a new reality. The process of reimagination went one step further, turning and shifting even when I stopped.

I wake with a start.

Over and Out

María, ¿qué tal? Bien, gracias. Bueno, bueno . . . pues, Robert is good, Robert is working like a maniac—ya tu sabes cómo él se pone—you know how he is. Casi nunca en la casa. Ah, y hombrecito—¡Dios mío!—how quiet he can get some times once he shuts his mouth. Nothing but nothing. No—I wish he would talk to me now. He won't be able to talk with me forever. One day he will realize it and then it won't matter; it will be too late to talk, too late for anything. But he should talk to me. I'm his mother. You know, the one person in the world who he can trust, who he can always talk to and who will always love him. I will always love him. And I can see he's scared, or desperate; I don't know what? Is René like that? Was Ángel? Well, Ángel is still a boy, too. I still think of him as a boy. They're all boys! C'mon María—he's a good kid. You raised them the best they could. Drugs? I don't think Chris touches anything like that; he barely drinks chocolate milk after eight in the evening. Well, I don't know what it is but he is certainly quiet these days, so that's that. Espero que todo esté bien y solo son mis nervios que están hablando. I see him in photos more than I get a chance to see *him*. Life is an optical course, isn't it? Vallas y aros. Well, you should come over and bring the boys. No, really, come over and outside by the pool; we just opened it this week. Well, it *is* must-see television, María. No, let me tell you what—give it a try tonight and I guarantee you'll be hooked. That's my guilty pleasure. What's my *pleasure*? Oh goodness, I don't know! I mean, I like cooking, you know, dancing, who doesn't—I like taking care of my boys . . . let's not get philosophical. Ay pero you should hear some of the things that come out of Chris's mouth cuando llega por sermonear. Thank goodness *I* never went to college—I would outsmart myself! Sí, claro, claro. Ah, the new neighbors show up yesterday morning y la mujer fue vestida como prostituta . . . she comes prancing through my living room pointing at photos and asking me if *the kid is mine*—do you believe that?—looking at me and pointing at Chris's face and I want to kick her out before I can offer her some café and galleticas pero tú sabes que no lo apreciara. Una mujer así se metiera en la boca y tragara sin masticar, como perra. She was wearing a skirt and heels—¡descarada! Like skin on bologna!—Oh, speaking of which—what was that? There is so much static on your end, María. Oh no, unless it is coming from mine . . . Well, I got a George Foreman grill—no, the new one, the one on sale at Sears—didn't René tell you? . . . but anyway, it doesn't have to last forever . . . no you're right, that's exactly it. Nothing has to last forever.

The Cuban way of life is to talk a lot, to eat a lot, to joke a lot, to laugh a lot, to do everything a lot, and especially with the mouth. Music has always been a part of me, music, music, in every room of the house, and most of all, the rumes in my head; my ruminations. Music, music . . .

Criminal Tendencies

You're walking down the street thinking about the Mona Lisa, not thinking about the expression really, not the woman in the portrait, certainly not da Vinci, thinking about *Mona* and feeling both syllables on your tongue while Bradford Cox croons out the lyrics on your earphones and you almost sing along, walking to the M train no less, heading south on Montague when you hear the name around the block, someone calling *Hey Monica*, someone screaming out her name.

She's brunette, brown-skinned and lip-glossed and smiling a half-smile and showing teeth, actual teeth that look like fence boards they're so white. And if she's Monica, Monica's beautiful.

She clambers down the stairs not looking behind her, not pausing at each step, not taking two at a time but nearly sliding down the whole set. You think about the man—you didn't see him but you heard his voice; the note of anger, fervor, sadness . . . you wonder who she was running from, what she is running to.

And when the train arrives, Monica slides over to you, to the pole you're gripping, looking around, trying to see if she's been followed, except it's only you who's watching, and when your eyes meet, it isn't fear or ire, or even exasperation you see, but the look of someone who's just fallen in love. Love, lust, longing—it's almost all the same. What matters is the falling.

These things happen.

"Oh God—thank you so much."

"Don't mention it," you say. You say: "My pleasure" as you hoist her up and hand her her purse too: a black leather saddlebag. She fell (what—did you think I was being metaphorical?) and now you put her back together again, except this time you're sitting, as the train doors rattle open and people disperse, more people clamber in. *The next stop is—*

"So where are you headed this morning?"

You seldom ever talk during moments like this; you seldom ever allow words to creep in and occupy the space, and you manage to surprise yourself. (Imagine that.) Her hands are folded on her lap and you notice the green scrubs, the white sneakers, the pencil holding up her hair—and still, she's beautiful.

A nurse? you think.

"I'm going up to 68th," she says, and you see her brush her hands over her lap—a nervous gesture? A gesture of boredom? An unequivocal act of—"I'm a nurse practitioner," she explains. And then, after a pause, another stop, a loud voice scratching on the PA system: "Well, I'm studying to become one. I volunteer most mornings."

You ask her her name and you tell her yours and there's that look again, like falling, except this time her legs are crossed and you start to imagine things.

This is what makes you you, you think. This is what makes you a liar.

And you've always been good at it—or at least it's always come naturally. The imagining, the reimagining. And you start to think about everything else, you start to put it all in place as her hands fall away and find your own, as your fingers touch, slower, more carefully, but they touch, finally, yes and it feels cool and warm all over and at the same time; you've been waiting for this. You piece together her life— this Monica, this nurse practitioner volunteer—and what in the world was she running from this morning, who was the man calling her name, pleading her to acknowledge his presence, or at least his salutation? *Hey Monica!* Unless it was a warning, a precaution, a signal of distress, and you think: Shit—there's a storm coming, isn't there? But the thought recedes almost immediately because who has time to think about the weather at a time like this?

This is how it always begins. A passing thought, a fleeting melody, the title of an e-mail on your cell phone's screen, a storefront's awning—coincidences, really; "reality favors symmetries and slight anachronisms[iv]," isn't that right?—a name, a face, two pairs of eyes meet. And you think how beautiful she really is—another stop, another voice on the PA—you think she's so beautiful, it's almost criminal, but you don't say it, you don't say anything, you certainly don't say *it's criminal.*

Tendencies like this are your forte, your modus operandi. She's so beautiful but even her—even her face, her sierra skin, her dark eyes gleaming in the half-light of the M train . . . even that simper, that Mona Lisa smile . . . even that is disappearing in the distance, disappearing in the face of the Mona Lisa on this page.

You meet a girl and instead of getting to know her you'd rather remember her from memory. Instead of sharing your life, you'd rather write hers. You'd rather write people in as characters—and why? You hardly ever ask anymore, because you know the answer. You hardly ever ask because you know how bad it sounds. How utterly appalling.

The real person will never be as real to you as the fiction you've created.

[iv] Jorge Luis Borges, "El Sur."

Foot Prince

Francis Carter elevated his heel and flexed an ankle as another flash occurred.

"By the way you moved your right foot I knew you were a god[v]."

Francis looked up and laughed. A painful, guttural sound. I can't even laugh anymore, Francis murmured. I can't even pretend to laugh.

"Left. Now, with the left," the man behind the camera instructed. He stood above Francis on a stool, pointing to an assistant with his free hand, signaling her to adjust the lamp's brightness.

Francis was a foot model. "The Foot Prince," actually— the nickname J&P Talent had given him last summer. Shoes, socks, slippers, fungus treatments. He even did high heels. All the major companies booked him.

Royalty, he thought, as he slid his other foot toward the mark, indicated with an enormous black "X" taped to the tiled floor. He imagined the masking tape over his lips, spread tight and pressed in. Life had become that way, a series of speechless acts.

"Can you arch your ankle a bit more? A little higher, a little . . ."

Francis obliged, letting the words wash over him. And what *exactly* had his life become? A seesaw of excess and absence, the living and the living death, a new party every

---

[v] Severo Sarduy, Cobra.

night—Grey Goose and Cuvée, and lots and lots of cocaine, and he was either swimming in it or cleaning it up.

But mostly cleaning it up.

And spending his afternoons in small, strobe-lit studios like this one. Moving his body into place.

Did I come to this city to be a waiter? he thought, as another flash emitted, three at a time, the sound like gunshots and each bullet left its mark on the monitor: the primary shot replicated and draped in blue, and black, and red, and whatever other colors were being produced for the Havaianas Urban Style double footbed flip-flop—and so fast, he could hardly tell which was the original and which was the copy.

No, I came here to be an architect. Fucking magna cum laude graduate student. The most educated architect in the city. No—

He corrected himself. The most educated foot model in the city. There used to be hope. There used to be possibilities, he murmured.

He could hardly tell which. The original? he repeated. The copy?

"Loving it, Francis," the man said, not lifting his eyes from the camera. "Absolutely *gorgeous* form. (click-click-click) Loving—"

There was a time I knew I could do anything I wanted, and all that I wanted was to design buildings for people, homes for families. Re-conceptualize the way people saw their *structure*. Every day brought with it the unmistakable imprint of an unexplored idea. *Imprint?* Francis turned his face down and let loose an ad-lib laugh. I used to feel this way, he whispered. Now what do I feel?

He saw the reflection of his stretched calf in the mirror, the sole of his foot sinking into the seamless paper as if it were another body, in and out.

Is this something that gets inevitably lost as we get older

102

and experience disappointment after disappointment?—and one day there is just one disappointment too many and you never again feel like life's waiting around the corner, but that it very likely got on a bus and is happening elsewhere, without you, to someone else? Where did the bus go? Where, he thought, am I? In and out—he swung his other leg back, a calf stretching toward the beauty lamp, the black umbrella which looked, Francis thought, more like a mushroom cloud.

This was the aftermath.

Last night, he was at Cedar Lounge, booked by MAC Cosmetics. It wasn't foot modeling, but it wasn't bad as far as day rates go. Five hundred dollars to dress up as a giant kitten—Dear Daniel, Hello Kitty's best friend, from South Africa—and pose for photos. Pose for photos, but never talk. The number one rule. "Kittens can't speak," the event coordinator had told him, as soon as he'd arrived, and five minutes later, Francis was wearing black leather pants and hardly anything else, an enormous helmet with a pink bow on one ear situated on his neck, digging into his flesh. "Dear Daniel doesn't know *English*." And she laughed, patting his bare shoulders, almost snorting as people backstage zoomed by at the speed of light (until his sense of sight adjusted, Francis could only hear them inside his helmet), patting his shoulders and laughing, laughing like this was all obvious, all so very on-the-face apparent. *Duh*.

So he stood in place, like a statue, breathing heavy, almost breathless, because there were only a dozen tiny holes around the kitten's whiskers in which to breathe, barely moving to wave and crack his knuckles, and sometimes give a thumbs-up or clap his hands to the beat of the music blasting in the event space—everything was muted but the music, which actually seemed intensified by his face's lack of space—and at one point he saw a very beautiful girl—a woman, he corrected himself—a truly attractive, amazing-looking knockout woman with big lips and enormous blue eyes, at least that's how he'd like to remember her. And when she asked what his name was, when she asked what he looked like under the hefty kitten helmet which, by the minute, was more discomforting—his neck strangled and sore and twisted and tight—all Francis could say, silently, that is, all Francis could *think* was:

This is really happening.

And it was, it *had* happened, all of it. It was still happening, he thought now, as another flash erupted, and this time it sounded like lightning, like a storm approaching, an enormous black mushroom cloud pointed straight at him.

"Are you suffocating?"

He looked over at the window, the only one in the small studio, and saw rain falling. Pitter-patter—*flash*. What would his parents say, if they knew what he was doing here, right now, in New York City? What would they think of their only son? *The Foot Prince.* Royalty, he repeated.

Except his parents were dead. His mother, first. And when she was dying, his father's way of denial was to continue buying things for her. A fur coat, and a gown, and cashmere sweaters, and silk curtains, and a pearl necklace, and another juicer. Where were they now?

And could he ever find a way out of this hell? Turn around, head home, pack up the duffel bag and suitcase, and his sketchbooks, stuff them all inside the backpack he carried everywhere, and forget it all happened.

Could he retrace his steps?

Wonderland

The closet doors creak open slow and startling. It is the summer for remembering lies and forgetting about how life really is, the summer of Bennys and the Seaside boardwalk, the morning surf and sand castles disappearing in the afternoon haze of someone's careless feet, the fluorescent lights and cat-calls, the shots of sex on the beach and tank tops and tube tops and miniskirts and lip gloss and fast cars, submarine yellow and candy apple red speeding left right, zipping inside and out of the breeze where man's dreams go to die.

"Gimme a beeh."

Sammy slaps down his palm on the counter, traveling to far away thoughts and getting lost in the journey.

"Ain't it three o'clock?"

And Sammy glances at a watch that isn't there and shrugs, "Corona. With a lime, thank yah," rubbing his scraggly chin like he caught a glimpse of what he was trying to think about before his first sip.

He shakes his head loose like some screws might fall out and his whole body shakes, ripped jeans not for the style and half a blue tank top shredded at the bottom so his hairy gut peeks out.

Outside, mobs of young people, tan and beautiful and some a beach-bum red strut and pout, *"Kid's a fucking Benny."* "What's a *Benny*?" *"You know, Bayonne, Elizabeth . . . an' everything else. Don't belong."* "Oh." And four jokesters zip by in matching blue Speedos while guys scream *"Fags!"*

and girls coo and whisper and jiggle with excitement or surprise and Sammy goes, "What you lookin' at?"

"Last one was free. Gotta pay some time, man."

And the two argue and Sammy offers his left sneaker, a raggedy white Adidas with no laces, and the bartender, tanned and confident with short, spiky gelled black hair (who doesn't?) and a porcine nose, he says, "Maybe ten years ago."

Outside, the boardwalk is still brimming. It's a buzz, a chatter, and everyone's smiling confident and cool, picking out a group or two to say hello and make plans with for later. Cracker Jack, Yakety Yak, Bamboo?

"Nah, tonight's high-class, we're going to Temptations."

So it's settled.

•

He loved the beach, the sand; especially, he loved the water. In that shimmering sky, he could get lost. He could lose himself and let the surf rock him until the sun fell into the sea and exploded into evening. Fade out to purple dusk. A pretty picture. Remembering, remembering—a cadence of thought and texture. So many breaths of air. The wind on his face. It had been that way since he was a child. He loved the way the water felt; the smell, the rhythm, and it was as much an act of art as sex, and poetry, and the countless stories he would write on the bus, on the train, between classes; morning, noon, night. Love-making. Always in love with making. Submerged and surrendered. It was a way to perceive reality, it was a way to transcend it.

•

Oh my gawd.

Kacy sits on her stool on the deck of her parent's beach house and admires her friend in the new bikini.

The new bikini.

"Oh my gawd, *oh my gawd!*" she's saying in between big New Jersey chews of gum, stopping periodically to blow a bubble until one blows up on her face.

"You think tonight's the night?" Gigi shouts, not expecting an answer. She asks again anyway, her dirty blond hair flapping in the wind coming in with the waves close enough to feel in the breeze.

Kacy nods and both women are giddy with excitement, jumping up and down in each other's arms, Kacy with her Bebe gray sweatpants on, lips across the ass, black bikini top to whet the imagination until a pack of guys (Kacy sees at least two) speed by in a green Mazda Miata, top down, screaming cat-calls.

"Shut up, you fuckin' guidos!" Gigi screams, and the pack shrugs it off and speeds on.

"Ya think they liked me?"

But Kacy isn't listening, she's wondering which guy to sleep with out of the four she'd met earlier. The whole group of them probably have something, but what's a girl to do? Chlamydia can't be *that* bad these days . . . like a one in eight chance; besides they have medications for those scabs . . . you know, kind you see in those funny commercials . . . nah . . . I'll be fine, and Johnny's gone for least two more weeks, and he—

"Hey, dumbo!" Gigi does everything but slap her friend across the face. "I says, ya think they liked me?"

Hey, dumbo.

"Huh? Oh. Yeah, sure, G. Tonight's the night."

Gigi's eye-shadowed lids are brimming and she begins to sway to the Black Eyed Peas blaring in the kitchen inside, her tits popping out of her small bikini top and her ass a gleaming glaze of oil and sweat.

"Dolce & Gabbana,
Fendi and then Donna
Karan, they be sharing
all their money, got me wearing
fly gear but I ain't asking"

"Hey G, did I mention the folks aren't comin' home this weekend?"

•

Fucking rock stars.

The wild boys scream and shout and take turns lunging headfirst into the huge waves and come out flapping their arms like they're wings and people are in awe. These fucking jokesters and their Speedos—"I was kinda nervous about wearing the Speedo until I saw my abs in the reflection of some girl's sunglasses"—and back and forth, the one with the wavy blond hair and dark eyes oozing with confidence and bravado.

And the four jokesters in the Speedos come running up Q Street and straight onto the sand, bypassing the lady selling beach tickets in her green lawn chair but even *she* doesn't give a shit for long as long as she gets to see some eye candy on her ho-hum day. They hop past the guardrail on the boardwalk and slide gracefully on the sand, throwing bits of rocks and shells everywhere as they sprint from side to side, disturbing the middle-aged couples with the umbrellas and the moms sleeping on their backs, eyes closed but secretly smiling.

"Wooooh*ooooooooo*!!!"

Gimmeabreak.

The bandits are renowned throughout the state for their daring and audacity; they go from Seaside to Belmar to

Wildwood and countless clubs in the tri-state area, invading DNA's Underwear Night in Astoria, rubbing up against chicks while the girls sneak grabs at their crotches, such a summer sensation that KTU starts talking about them the morning after—2006's Jersey Shore Sex Bombs. This is before the college diploma, and the job, and maybe the wife and two kids (if you're lucky) and the rest of the stuff that makes growing old a nuisance rather than a novelty; the celebration of youth rolling on for now in one frenetic orgasm.

"Hey, fuck those guys!" and footballs and volleyballs and curses ring out (it was inevitable), some hitting the group of four, others ignored and dropped to the sand. "Must be kinda cold in there, eh?" Ha-ha-ha, and the laughs ring out but the Speedo Bandits could care less. Well, most of 'em.

"That's what your fuckin' mom said!" Mark yells and George mentions something about the whole world being jealous and the group collectively agrees and calms down. Well, most of 'em. "We're like fuckin' rock stars, man!" Mark hollers. And girls in droves come up, young, teenaged, high schoolers and college freshmen, nervous, fluttering, "Heyyy . . . can we *please* take a picture with you guys?" biting nails and giggling; Eric makes a comment about a school trip, "Just our luck!"

Mark complains that one of the broads is blocking his abs—"What, you came for the view didn't you?" he's saying between deep breaths ("Blow out your air, it makes your abs look tighter") and Chris is just trying not to laugh, the whole ordeal so fucking ridiculous while George and Eric strike goofy poses on each end.

"Wow, thanks guys," one girl is saying, her tits not fully grown to shape but her ass is tight enough and she's got nice long legs, toned and brimming, Mark's thinking, he's whispering, whimpering, it's been way too long, "It's been six months since I touched a cooch," so maybe the sixteen-year-old will have to do.

"Say, what are you doing later?"

And Sally gurgles some more laughter out of her shy lips while Mark whispers something in George's ear, George the fucking short peerless Greek, bronzed and waxed like some museum showcase; George just laughs and calls Mark a sicko.

The four run off after Mark nabs the girl's number (Mark just glad someone brought a cell on their scenic jaunt) and they continue on their merry way, prancing up and down the beach: "Stop thinking about it Mark, you gotta stop thinking about it—" "—Fucking *six months*, man! I might turn gay soon . . ." toward the lighthouse until they find a big, craggy rock higher than the rest and Eric thinks it's a good idea to climb it while someone takes pictures and then switches.

"I'm not climbing that thing," George shouts, eyebrows raised until Eric hops on and sucks in his stomach real tight and puffs out his chest in a fighter hen's grin and even Eric, George agrees, the least toned of the group looks good enough for a picture so sure, why not?

"Alright alright, four poses each. Then we switch."

"What?" Chris whines, rubbing oil on his pecs ("Who the hell brought this?" *Who knows!*"), greased up and smiling.

"Only four?"

•

"What da fuck you lookin' at?"

"What you mean what I'm lookin' at? I'm just lookin'."

"Tony, ya starin' right at me. Quit before I stick you in a jar of mayo." Mike is picking chicken kebab out of his teeth with his fingers. "What are you, a fag?"

"Sure thing. You said it." Tony whispers a curse under his breath then pauses, "What we talkin' 'bout anyways?"

Tony and Mike talk it over some more on the boardwalk between Italian ice and snow cones and cotton candy and shops advertising everything from fried chicken to fried Oreos and signs promising Lemonade Waffles and other things you wouldn't expect but really, it's just a lack of punctuation.

"You want to hit up a bona fide *gymnasium* or are we just gonna do some push-ups an' shit before tonight?"

Mike looks at his watch and shakes his head, "Nah we're early still. Let's cruise around in the grill for a while. See if we catch some broads to throw a few fucks in for latah."

"I hear that," and the two laugh and envision their night, which would not be a night if it didn't end in some broad's bed sheets. Mike slaps on his Varsity high school football jacket from five years ago, the one with the big QB on the shoulder and captain's badge and squints his eyes deep into the distance, looking at nothing in particular, his arms looking like two cannons in his tight black guinea tee. Tony, he's been Mike's sidekick since he was four; guy follows him everywhere he goes, his puppy-dog face more like a pit bull's with a couple lazy eyes and if it hadn't been for the hooker Mike got for him on his twenty-first, he probably wouldn't know what *a few fucks in a few broads* even meant. He's shy and awkward but he's a nice guy. And that stuff's important too, Mike would always say. That way, chicks get to choose. They want badass cool bro, they go with me . . .

"How ya doin' how ya doin' *ham sand-weech*?" Tony's carried away and confident, poking his head out the window and hollering at two Grade A choices of meat on a porch. "I'd like to show you my Premio Italian sausage someday!" He's laughing spit he's so silly. "Maybe tonight?"

and one of the girls (the one in the skimpy thong) curses him off but they're long past by now.

"Hey, I think someone's getting laid tonight!" Mike howls, punching his buddy in the chest with one solid fist.

•

In between all the cursing, the crashing of words and foot stomps and pint glasses shuffling back and forth, you might not even notice the tears in old Sammy's eyes.

"Why in hell do ya treat me like this?"

"What?"

"*This*!" Sammy throws up one arm in disgust. "Do you even know my goddamn name?" And the tears keep streaming down his tin-foil cheeks, rough and patchy like sandpaper from too much sun.

"Yeah. Sammy. Good ol' Sammy, okay? You been coming here for years," Jake returns. At this point, he's thinking, I could care less about the three bucks and more about getting this fuckin' liability out of shop before the rush comes—the throngs of hot, young bodies looking for happy hour.

"Samuel *Jenkins*! That's my stinkin' name, and if you was old enough to know, I use to be mayor of this *stinkin'* town!"

"Whatever."

Jake gets a rag out and starts to wipe the bar clean. "What? So it's free now?"

"No," Jake shoots back, not even bothering to sigh, "it's cause yer a fuckin' *bum*.

"Now scram."

Samuel Jenkins is long gone now. Like a bullet to his brain, he sinks to the floor, crushing himself limp, curled into a ball, head under the stool.

"Get the fuck up, you loony."

Sammy tries to keep his eyes closed but the tears ruin it. An itch on the eyelid. Whattafaker.

"C'mon, stop screwing around and get your ass up."

Sammy slowly rises, his gut bouncing up and down like a man on the moon minus the fanfare. "Well, least you can do is spare the old Mayor a few singles for a hot meal."

But Jake stopped listening an hour ago. Sammy wipes up his tears and sniffles a good-bye while a crowd starts to stare.

"Just ten years ago, just ten years . . . '96 ain't just yesterday. . ." he mumbles, walking in whatever direction the wind carries him.

"Think he's telling the truth?" Jake asks, turning to the owner, hands on each hip. "Nah, guy's a nutjob. Always has been. Thank God ya got 'im outta here before the stampede."

"You're telling me. God knows I need the tips," Jake returns, looking back at the owner, grinning. "Weekly allowance ain't doin' it for me anymore pops."

•

Robert was a money-maker. But he didn't just make it; he loved it. The design, the artistry. He loved the symbol, too. The figure eight, the curve of the S—like *Selden*—the dash down the middle, bisecting the haves from the have-nots with a single stroke.

Did he know that the sign originated from Hermes, from his caduceus, his staff from which snakes dangle in a sinuous twist? Venomous, they could kill you if you looked them in the eyes.

The snakes and the money.

No, he doesn't know that, Chris murmured. Another wave crashed at his feet and the foam brushed against him, brushed past him. He heard the hollering of the other bandits up ahead, getting softer. He hardly knows my birthday.

·

Don't take it so personal is all.

—Personal? How else I'm supposed to take it?

—However the hell you want, but you can't keep coming in here, you can't keep harassing the customers.

—I'm a person, ain't I?

—. . .

—Ain't I?

·

"Now are we wearing red, or green?"

Kacy moves from one corner of the room to the next, inspecting every inch of the outfit on her body compared to the one lying on the floor at her feet. The outfit, these strips of cloth ain't much of an outfit, but that's the point.

"Ugh . . ." she lets out a groan and begins to rip off her clothes, draping a floral dress over her head before hesitating again. "Hey. I asked you a question, hun: red or green?"

"G, what is this, fuckin' Christmas? No wonder you're still a virgin."

Oh shit. Kacy's thinking, Oh shit, did I just say that? And Gigi starts to say something but crumbles, ruining the face she'd just put on.

"Hey, G, I didn't mean that, I . . ." Kacy rushes to her friend and hugs her. "I'd rather be a virgin than a whore anyways," she lies. But it works; Gigi wipes away tears and examines her dirty blond hair in the mirror, gelled and curled then blown dry and hair sprayed.

"Anyone can be hot, Kacy," she says, looking at herself in the mirror, her eyes unblinking. A track of teardrops fading on her cheeks. "But if you really want to *be* somebody, you have to be what doesn't meet the eye." She pauses, turns around, sticks out her tongue. Kacy laughs. The two women hug and for a moment, Gigi catches herself in the mirror again. "That," she adds, still staring, "is the fashion of the season."

"What is?"

"Okay, I'm good," Gigi declares, forgetting the question or just ignoring it, sliding, instead, into a short white skirt and a blue tube top. Kacy's wearing dark blue jeans and a black halter top that matches the thong jutting out at her hips. Kacy walks away for a second and returns with two plastic cups and a bottle of Georgi.

"Ready when you are."

Five minutes later, they're four shots deep and ready to roll. Purses click, cell phones shuffle, and then there's the last-minute check; Kacy does the front door while Gigi is stuck using the shoddy bathroom mirror and after a few fusses and laughter (girls got the giggle fits), they're off.

"Temptations won't know what hit 'em!"

•

The sun has nearly set and the water grows colder, and dark. The throngs of people on the beach have packed up and left by now, trudging their coolers and umbrellas and beach towels away with them but leaving their garbage—the soda cans and plastic bottles and thin napkins the only evidence that anyone was even there at all. The only four left at this hour are the Speedo Bandits, hollering and hooting, so immersed in themselves they don't even realize what time it is—or where the world has gone.

"All I'm saying is, we're pretty much any girl's fantasy," Eric remarks, not even breaking a smile, snaking a path through the sand, "look at it this way, we got something for everyone, the short jacked kid (he points to George), the medium ripped dude (Mark blushes)—that looks like he's five . . . (Mark screams something inaudible) the fuckin' A&F model over here (Chris grins) and . . ."

"You, Eric, the guy who looks like my sister with shorter hair," Mark retorts and everyone but Eric laughs.

"Not funny dude."

"So," Mark interrupts, bouncy as ever, "like I was saying before, this eight-some should happen. And if—"

"*If,*" George interrupts.

"Yeah, *if* it happens," Mark resumes, "these girls are going to go fucking crazy. Oh man, think about what's gonna be going through their minds . . ."

"Think about what?" Chris says, kicking sand around his toes, his thoughts turning, again, to his father. Producing, producing. The excess of returns. Maybe we aren't so different . . . "You ever think about what a waste of time all this is? You know, working the weights every day, sculpting our bodies to *perfection* . . . up-down, up-down . . . grilled chicken and boiled tofu and fucking rice cakes—all so we can have the same wrinkly-lookin' corpses as everyone else, Mark's sister wouldn't fuck if she had to."

Mark's eyes begin to water and he runs at Chris, shoving him toward the waves.

"You bastard! You stop that!" Mark is wailing, dizzy and spitting until George gets close and whispers, "He didn't mean it," while staring at Chris from out the corner of one eye, mouthing, "You're scaring him dude," and Eric just laughs, scratching his nuts and smiling, "Okay, first off— I'd fucking *do* Mark's sister, secondly . . ."

"No, no, what if he's *right* though?" Mark asks, maybe not expecting an answer. "What if there's nothing else either. If there's nothing at the end of it . . ." he throws up his arms and pouts, frustrated like this is the first time he's ever contemplated mortality, the first time he's ever given it a color or a shape. Fucking rice cake. "You can't lift, can't run, can't *eat* . . ."

"Fuck," Eric points out.

"Trim your pubes," George says, expecting a laugh from Mark but getting silence.

"Shut up, man," Mark finally returns. "This shit is serious."

He sighs and the waves moan in return; for a split second, Mark considers getting lost in the murky darkness but it's too cold to play games.

"The rest of our lives are gonna suck."

•

And it was like looking for a door in the dark, for a way through.

The warm breath in his ears, the blue-green body unfurled until the world was flat again. Until he could hold it in his hand.

•

Out on the boardwalk at night, it's like visiting a cemetery. Out on the boardwalk at night, you better have a few beers in your hand or at least a friend in one arm because it doesn't get much lonelier than this.

Where *this* is, is nearing ten o'clock. Where this is, is long past wading time, long past the fun and the sun and the laughter, a long stretch of darkness hovering over a splintered concourse of solitude. Of course, even solitude has its occasional visitors.

Sammy stumbles from one bench to the next, hovering between vacant ice cream parlors and arcades, lights out, noises mute, skeletons by evening. He is sputtering, muttering fierce shouts and indignant whispers, tripping over his bare feet he almost fumbles into two passersby who just look at him sadly, the old sack of bones, before shoving on, hurried; everyone always pressing on.

"Guy hasn't gotten any tail in ten years!" the one in front shouts. Partner to his right, taller and goofy, smiles and nods, "Nah, I'd say fifteen!"

They hurry off in their laughter, not bothering to glance behind them but all they would have seen is Sammy's bloodshot eyes, fierce and forlorn and lit by the moon. He is hungry for something that alcohol can't satisfy anymore. He is craving flesh.

"See, things could be worse," one kid in the distance is saying over his shoulder, walking to the parking lot, stopped on the way by the big sagging lump of skin to the right as it came into their vision and how can you not stop to stare, if only for a moment?

"You could look like that," he says, pointing to the old man, comforting his friend, his friend just shaking his head. Two others behind them laugh, clap their hands, and whistle. Old Sammy just curses under his breath, old Sammy's just a scavenger now.

•

To love with someone else's mind, in that moment. Outside of that moment. That's why he loved reading. That's why he loved writing. To feel their life slowly sliding into him, to share his own.

•

The signs are all there: the flashing neon lights, the tight-shirt bouncers, the energy, the excitement, the drugs—mostly E and cocaine, if you can pay that bill—the thumping bass of whatever trance anthem is reverberating across Seaside right now, the DJ's sound system at Temptations so loud it could probably shatter a few windows if this was a cartoon.

A few liberal arts-types in tight button-downs and girl's jeans (NYU fags?) are having a roundtable discussion on the merits of Internet dating, one saying, "When girls have a profile photo that's taken at a Myspace angle and they're posing duckface, you just know they're ugly in person . . ." the others all agreeing, talking to no one in particular and everyone, "We know your tricks, stop trying to be cute because it will never happen. You are a fraud, a phony, but most of all, a shame to our country . . ." and the table erupts in laughter as another pitcher is emptied and refilled.

Tony and Mike are hugging the bar, ordering a round of shots for two broads they just picked up while nursing their Budweisers and saying things like they're big-time college athletes, or else they're the two youngest members of Fortune 500, or simply with the mob.

"Sex on the beach alright with you two?" Mike shouts over the thumping bass. The chicks are sorority sisters who stumbled into the wrong joint (hell, the wrong *state*) and decided to stay for whatever reason and they make a face but tilt their heads back and drink it down anyway when it comes.

"To Seaside!" Mike shouts.

"To dancing!" the two girls squeal, tipsy as hell.

"To big Mike!" Tony proclaims, and locks eyes with Mike, giving him a nod of the head and a look; I'm not sure what kind.

The four move from the bar and onto the dance floor, Mike grinding up on the blond while Tony the lumbering oaf does a two-step next to her red-haired friend. Eventually, he gives this up for a fist pump and thinks it might be infectious enough to pass around, but Mike's hard at work on the blond—literally—and seeing her friend out of the loop, he makes the signal for a time-out, motioning to

Tony to head to the bathroom while the girls stay put.

"What the fuck ya doin' out there, man?" Mike's shouting at Tony in the cramped bathroom and simultaneously putting a few delicate fingers to his hair but Tony's tipsy and staring at the snake coiling up in Mike's jeans; he's still got a semi from dancing and Tony has the wrong idea; his eyes open wide and his nerves tingle, his mouth goes dry from the anticipation—he's been waiting for this moment to happen in God knows how long and in the middle of whatever the hell Mike was telling him to do (or trying to), Tony shoves his best friend against the stall and starts sucking on his lips, striving to squeeze his tongue through the crease of Mike's mouth. "What the . . ." Mike mutters, but he can't form the words.

The shock wears off when someone knocks on the door ("You alright in there?") and Tony yells back, "We're *fine*," and Mike just winds up and slams him to the ground, the whole room shaking, the mirror maybe marked with one more long crack down its center, pushing Tony's face to the tiled floor until he can taste the lino.

"No, we ain't fine at all. Oh, no sir . . ." He returns, letting go of Tony's neck and dusting off his hands with a paper towel. "Ya lucky I don't kill you," Mike spits. "*Fag*."

He slams the door in Tony's face, Tony left holding his egg-shaped head, bloodied and shaken.

Meanwhile, fifteen feet in the opposite direction . . .

"Jesus Christ, what's takin' so long, I gotta *pee*!" Kacy bangs on the unisex toilet door again and this time some greased-up guido ("Have we met?"), muscled and hair-spiked, rushes out, not even giving her a gaze.

"Asshole."

Five minutes ago, she was enjoying some conversation with Gigi and two baseball players and after that, some yuppies who were real keepers but then the seal finally broke (inevitable, it had been long enough) and she had to rush off to the toilet all the time worrying about whether or not G would do well enough in her absence to keep them at bay until she returned—Then we can get down to business, Kacy's thinking while she squats down, levitating her ass above the stool (takes practice) not noticing the groans emanating outside the stall, or too much in a hurry to care.

Gigi, alone and talkative and innocent, playing with her hair and nodding at all the right times, Gigi's doing fine. Then she gets a text message from her ex-boyfriend telling her to call, telling her *I miss you* and she implodes.

"Oh, hold on a sec, I just haveta call someone real quick, okey-dokey . . ." she announces, uncrossing her legs and getting up to leave. Outside, she begins frantically dialing Steve's number, Steve, her first and last boyfriend, what nice hair he's got and oh, I should have just gotten it over with when I had the chance . . .

"Hello?" she gets an answer on the fourth ring, except it's not Steve, it's some girl.

Some girl.

"Yeah, is Steve there? Steve, yeah, he just called me. Yeah . . . well, *texted* . . . so *can I speak* with him?"

"He's . . ." the voice on the phone giggles, "kinda busy right now," and Gigi doesn't even bother with the string of curses she had been thinking up since the bitch picked up the phone, she just hangs up.

Outside, the waves keep crashing hard against the sand and Gigi turns her head and starts to walk back toward Temptations to ride the shit out of whoever looks at her next but a warm hand touches her shoulder and she turns, hoping for her knight in shining armor—

"Howdy, miss."

—but getting some old bum instead.

"Listen, I got no cash mister. I'm sorry . . ." she shrugs

him off and turns away but he opens his mouth again: "No, no, I ain't a bum! Hear me out, I'm . . ." he starts, stumbles, keeps going, "I'm looking for a dog. It's my granddaughter's little puppy and it just scooted on over here. Under the boardwalk, see."

He points to the boardwalk and ducks under to get a better view.

"Can't you just help me for a quick second? I'd appreciate it . . ."

Gigi takes one look at his clothes, tattered and repulsive, his gut flopping in the wind and sighs, "Okay, but I can't help ya for too long. Got plans."

"Don't we all?"

The man vibrates a smile and motions her over to him.

"Where is this dog again?" and the old man points to the same spot as before, saying, "His name is Sammy. Like me," extending his crusty hand. "My name's Sammy, too."

Gigi rolls her eyes and continues following Sammy until they can't go any farther. Farther or further, and she can't see a thing. He bends down and calls out the dog's name and tries again while Gigi waits impatiently, standing behind and finally she bends down too to see what the hell's going on, which is when Sammy (the man, not the dog) turns his head and flops his body onto hers, overpowering her to the ground. She squeals and Sammy puts one sandpaper hand over her mouth and with the other, pushes up her tube top and begins sucking on her tits, nipples taut and enormous in the moonlight.

Gigi keeps protesting but to no avail and he runs his hand up against her white skirt, sand flowing in between her thighs, unzipping his dingy old Levi's and forcing himself inside her while the waves continue to break on shore, a few feet from Gigi's head. After only a couple thrusts she's crying and dry but Sammy, he doesn't stop he just thrusts harder, muttering to himself about her being as tight as a virgin, flopping up and down like a fish until he teeters, on the verge of exhaustion, his face beet red and sweating and now he's having a coughing fit too, expelling phlegm all over Gigi and Gigi's crying, bleeding, dirty and sweaty and *terrified* for her life, understanding nothing now but pain and fear, and the distant inward dread that it was somehow always going to go like this, face down, helpless. A phantom pet unseen beneath a stretch of splintered wood, another man who only takes and takes and takes, another man, not another take, a tango in the sand with some prick named Sammy. The man, not the dog.

•

Good morning sunshine, just not yet. The sun has crept back while the world was partying and dancing and dreaming and for at least a couple hours, the boardwalk becomes one long, desolate freeway; the cheer and laughter and megaphones and cheap scams and hustling vendors momentarily disappeared. One kid, shaggy-haired and four-eyed, sits alone on a bench, staring out to the waves, that vast expanse of water that can make even the happy-go-lucky just a little lonely.

Never again will he have the prom, or the after-party, or this here, right now, so he better soak it up while he can—even if nothing went the way he had planned, the way he had always dreamed it would go since, oh, about sixth grade.

The waves dig deep into the sand, bringing rocks and shells and misplaced sandals back with them.

A couple guys at The Sea Shell start setting up chairs and tables for their Father's Day special, an outdoor barbecue with free first rounds for all the dads, Jake doing all the hard work while Lucas, his father, looks on.

"Gonna be another scorcher today Jakey," the owner is

saying, already placing a palm to the perspiration on his forehead.

"Yeah, you're telling me," Jake blurts out automatically, lifting another table in place and setting each chair straight, until a thought pops into his head and he's jumpy and excited. "Say, you know that bum we always get? Sammy?"

Lucas nods his head, unsmiling.

"Yeah, well I looked up Samuel Jenkins last night and turns out the old kook *was* the fuckin' mayor. Back in '95 or something. Had his picture and everything. Same red cheeks and the lopsided smile. Hasn't changed much probably, besides the suit and tie, ya know . . ."

"I don't fucking believe it," Lucas yells back.

"I ain't kidding ya, pops! He's really a stand-up guy, you know? Web site called him a 'community leader' and stuff. I kinda feel bad the way we was treating him the other day." Jake pauses, frowns, looks at his sneakers. "Lost his wife and daughter a couple years ago, you know, that's probably why he's such a dump . . ."

Lucas shakes his head. "Yeah, a real mess he is. Bad things sometime happen to good people . . ." he sighs and wrinkles his brow, his consolation being that he's still got his son and wife in *his* life, but if something ever happened . . . "We should pour him a drink today. He'll be here; he always pops in around three."

"Maybe I'll get him some new clothes, too," Jake returns. "You know, head over to Salvo or something. That's what I'll do.

"You know, ol' Sammy ain't a bad guy after all. Nah," Jake convinces himself, shaking his head emphatically, "not once you get to *know* him!"

Father and son laugh, patting each other on the back and waiting, waiting, waiting for the throngs of people to settle down on the beach and roam the boardwalk, young people, old people, class trips and proms, crowds of people relishing in their youth and exuberance, others recapturing it in the June sun. But for now, it's just the wait, the hangover, the slow drifting low after last night's high in wonderland.

Jake checks his watch.

"We're still early. Awhile till the stampede."

"Good," Lucas grins and puts his arm around his son.

Look at the waves long enough and sooner or later, it's no longer a hundred different ebbs and flows, it's just one big, crashing blur. It's life.

"Enough time for a beeh."

INNERMISSION

*Now wait, now watch, now pass
the time, & wonder how long
this will last, or wonder
where they pick the songs
that play now, from secret
unseen stereos*

"Look at that brunette. My God! What a pair of pinkies on her. Flawless fingers. I'd like to have her give me an injection of the good stuff. Don't you ever have fantasies about nurses? About latex gloves? Gait belts—*shit*. Needles? How about—"

"Sure," Chris murmured. But inwardly he couldn't recall if any of the images he might have ever shared with the man sitting across from him were from an actual dream or from a romance novel shoot. An actual dream or—"How long do you think I have to stay here for?" he asked, as the brunette came into view. Enter stage left. Navy skirt and a blue shirt. Latex gloves. A pair of scissors. A gait belt hanging from one pocket. The whole fantasy come to fruition, he thought. Was Arthur Gerald licking his lips? He looked over at Arthur, Arthur sitting and scratching his flabby cheeks, scratching the folds of flesh as if he had a bite, a tick, a rash; as if he were trying to blot himself out of the picture.

"A little Edison's medicine? They'll fix you up in no time," Arthur said, his fingers moving rapidly from one side of his face to the other, one side of his face—lit up as with a nimbus—to the other. A funeral parlor glow. And Chris looked at the clock, the big black letters, the small second hand slipping past almost imperceptibly . . .

Arthur continued to scratch, peering at the nurse from his bug eyes, uncrossing and crossing his legs, fidgeting in his plastic seat, the nimbus growing brighter. He yawned.

Hiccupped. Coughed. Pulled out a newspaper and began fanning himself as the wooden beams roped idly overhead. Chris shivered. The Velcro straps across his torso felt like manacles. When can I go home? he thought. When can I leave this place? A voice on the PA system sputtered and Arthur Gerald spoke again, nodding his head.

"No time at all."

The Fact Is

From an early age I had a fascination with facts and figures. I played the part of *Journalist* with a touch of bravado and a suggestion of doom, like all good love stories destined to end badly.

The fact is the person I wanted to be was cut for a used car advertisement on A-2. The fact is SPACE IS LIMITED. The fact is the truth of anything always brings me to a moment of disappointment. The fact is a series of snapshots on a refrigerator door, magnetized and magnified for the visually impaired:

Sepia slightly blurred and worn at the edges, two faces dissolved in dusk of a South Florida summer. I remember the warm breeze, wind in ears, the taste and smell of humid grass and plants whose names I didn't know: Gumbo Limbo? Paradise? Heavy darkness, the new moon called Neoma, your small fingers clasping mine, leather sandals on gravel, dirt kicking at our feet, the thoughts we left behind like footsteps . . . "Do you want to come?" We watched a polo game the day before, the sport of kings, misremembered mornings, harnesses and white wooden balls shimmering today as a reflection in my coffee cup:

"Those horses are beautiful."

"Beautiful, right?"

"And so fearless!"

"A product of their training. They train them with blindfolds and tie them to a tree. Then they take turns throwing mallets at them. For hours," she added. "Hours."

Fearless, you say? Earless? Senses dulled, receptors excised completely . . . for hours? Ours? All I remember about summer in Wellington is the polo ponies. Everything else is a photograph.

Now the city moves like a map you are drawing, words lying on the street picked up and put into pictures, daydreams, a whole new way of being in the world as though art on the level of utopia is life itself.

Is the fact of memory that its function is to forget the living things that live in them?

And when the love is good you can really feel it; I mean the spasms of the other body inside yours until you can't tell the difference, bodies clicking; muscles contract and relax in a warm breath. Whose spasm? Whose breath? That tingling isn't the tingle of the color TV . . . for a moment, just a moment. I am you. If the love is good.

(The camera negative was affected by advanced vinegar syndrome—in particular where the duplicate negatives of archival footage were edited into the film—causing a consistent halo on the image . . .)

Into and out of a phone conversation between two boys, talk of modeling and Manhattan, "Do you want to come?" and the question finally hangs there like a wad of chewing gum on the bottom of a classroom desk. I traded in a summer hobby for a season in Brazil. I traded in time for money. A box of cardboard. A magazine cover. An underwear campaign. I traded in the *Journalist* for something more undercover. Telegraphing horoscopes and adverts outlined in red ink from spilled blood.

If you must please
fall on your knees

"So, what the hell is this thing about anyway?"
Characters changing into each other's clothes so fast I get

confused each time I blink. The whole world is a vast film set in which the props are continually shifting, four extras reprising the roles of twenty-four characters and people I've never seen before playing my most beloved ones.

Things no longer run on lithium, only time. The roving camera is a mirror in which the lens's gaze belongs to the audience or else a recurring memory, propped on stilts and a rotating series of images displayed from an old Bell & Howell Cassette Projector in which stutters may result in earthquakes. A vast film set that doubles as Buster's Pub and Cinema in East Hartford, Connecticut; everything you could ever want rolling on camera in one bag of bricks on Main Street.

Are you in the film? Is he? Am I? And Do you want to come? repeated as a lap-dissolve narration through memories and pictures of things I remember doing in a different life, when I was a boy who never would be now . . . I lost him . . . when my life could have gone either way or split into sections, patterns and fragments . . . I lost him . . . Is this what I thought it would be? Is this the person I turned out to be? I lost him. So let's rewind.

(Most of reel 3 was irreversibly crystallized and half of reel 4 was badly compromised by decay . . .)

Take a camera, or better, a camcorder. Press play. "What's it like to be on TV?" What a funny way to say it. But I am in TV, inside the flat black rectangle, and the screen projects me in tiny, fragmented particles, each pixel amounting to something like Me. On location? In a studio? The hovering attendants, the serious-looking men and women holding binders in one hand and three-ounce bottles of Evian in another, the sound of film recording against a dubstep, new wave soundtrack, faces clamoring, computers blinking as a new frame pops up on screen and another replaces it, the rack of garments: underwear, jeans jackets, jock straps, a fire hydrant—a fire hydrant?—sweater vests, turtlenecks, an indigo wrist watch, *turn left* and of course the flashing. *A little less.* No, I don't miss modeling. I don't miss a thing. Scrawling hasty notes, letters pressed up against one another, lines bleeding across the page, frantic, trying to recall the details, sensations of being, everything to project myself as best I can back in time no—I don't miss a thing.

Coming attractions before word games, rearranged names, weight of bodies, expectations; desire for a payoff or to get what we paid for; the movie is the one that is always on. The instant of the present and the past of that instant, everything except the sensations of being, or the disconnect of seeing yourself on film. The moment of unrecognition between the eyes outside and the eyes on set is unsettling—I saw myself grainy, black spots crackling in the foreground of film unspooled in the dark, broadcast in Panavision as a talking picture. Talking the talk.

Take a look in: They had me in various positions, full-length, three-quarters, profile, *the good side*, back arched, legs spread out on the table like a deck of tarot cards— what's your destiny? And is this mine?

You're better than the real thing, Joél with cold thin eyes licking his lips in a lizard grin flipping through a book of photographs. The real thing? Yes, he said, whatever that is *you're it.* No one's ever seen that before and just to make sure it won't happen again, the sign says NO PHOTOGRAPHY ALLOWED—a woman in satin chooses what's *in*, agents squawking behind closed doors, hawking their wares or working the telephone lines like a telemarketer (like Johnny Baker), feeding off the audience, the spectators, feeding off *us*, like a car salesman trading in old dreams for slightly newer ones, or vice versa. Or just vice. Or just voices. Calling, calling . . .

On the street everyone is mesmerized by shoes. The thoughts I leave behind like footsteps. Pitter-patter. Intellect.

I remember warm mornings, the sound of the mower, crackling grass and cicadas stuck to trees, Malta dribbling down my father's chin, the smell of rust and paint and gasoline, and ropa vieja boiling from the kitchen inside and my mother's voice calling ¡Tribilin!—a different time, a different script when what I loved remained in my pre-fading body in coordinates, constellations and right now as you read this is the point where the past touches the future, sitting or standing at a café or on the subway, train doors rattling; breathe deeper and let the recycled air in.

(. . . resulting in a harsh and raspy sound, with noticeable image spread distortion.)

I believed then that I was different, my soul sheathed in its own skin—but I gave them both up a while ago—my body, my soul—plodding toward eternity. Corpses smiling in a magazine.

The fact is a five-page spread in *Supplementaire* called "How the West Was One" and I'm still unsure if the spelling was intentional, all of it Shot On Location, cactus and tumbleweeds drifting in the dirt like a desolate tango show. Traded in my dreams again and again.

Readjust the lens to find emptiness, which is only thirty-three frames per second, a vast expanse of images, the darkness of the cinema, the places my mind goes when I stop to think, an isthmus for hermetic memories lost in the time it takes for perceiving anything. And time's passing.

And as the credits finally rolled on a black backdrop that seemed to scroll into eternity, the only thought that sprang to mind was if I couldn't act all of it out again. In a different room, in a different place. Time and space transported.

And this time it would look different.

I remember turbid waves, the salt wind, blood in sand, my torn skin, suffocating on words until I couldn't breathe; buried half-dead in Brazil until I wrote my way out. Again. Again, again.

I was that boy, after the Rewind. Before daylight and after the black of night has waltzed away is the loneliest place on earth and Do you want to come? between film stutters and reel replacements and my mind in one place my body in quite another. And the big black box broadcasting back our dreams. Killing them softly. Who cares about the serialization, who cares about the show, who cares about the sound? Turn the volume up higher or place it on mute. What matters is the tingle of the color TV. That's posterity. Killing us softly. And one wants to leave something behind. One always wants to leave something behind, something with a life of its own. A project for memory, a project of remembering. To realize myself in my own words.

(Now I must speak about Bailey, the gunshots, the murder, so as to be complete, so as to have told the whole story.) I wrote a trilogy out of order and then rearranged it. The fact is everything can be reworked, remastered, reiterated. Retranslated. Dug up years or moments later like Rossetti's long deceased wife, a rose for Emily, bouquet of flowers a thousand vibrant dandelions exploding in your face.

¡Qué descubrimiento!

Drift: a technique of rapid passage through varied ambiance. A forgotten account with accumulated interest. Effect of any passage. *Drift.* And to give new experiences out of old experiences is the same thing as speaking a new language that has always already been inside the lips. Retranslate and you remember hope of a new feeling strange flesh the mouth and lips dim room pants rip quick and silent coming another scene in the shallow end, "You will now descend," silence and secrecy, chlorine and garden weeds the drift of time a child's room pieces from Monopoly the dark city dying sun three-level sugar maple-split with all the windows open to simulate some sort of movement that the actual home lacked. Fade out to darkness, a black sky, stars dissolved in dust: the season is over; the set has been abandoned.

And when the love is really good I feel your tingle in me as my own rushing waterfall waves exploding eyes rolled back, lapping it up like a Labrador's tongue on a shore of flesh.

> The best kind of love
> is becoming
> the other
> for an instant

Look at me please. Not at the photo but in the eyes. Turn right. A little to the right. Now more. Stage directions and I never wanted to be that, I was only waiting to see what I would be, at the same moment arranged in clothes for every season of the year, sleeves tight, jeans unrolled to my knees *a little less* thinking all the while: And what about my soul?

(Scratches, dirt, and dust on the emulsion caused heavy crackles and clicks during reproduction. Sound restoration was able to significantly reduce these issues.) A Work of Art snap-snap-snap—again, I hear the shutter of the camera, my own shudder . . . Destined to never again be who I am. And what counts is the eyes. To look into eyes that came to me and seized my soul, to look into any eyes . . . how I wanted to know them, to know all of them, only to discover that there is nothing inside—but still worse, much worse, to discover that I am alone, cut off, disconnected, *click*, the line is dead; do you notice you don't get a dial tone when you are hung up on anymore? Just an imperceptible click and silence. Abandoned—and yet, I feel abandoned.

We all live alone. And that is worse than death, that is death in life, that is the living death. That is life. Till deaf do us part.

They were smiling without any semblance of warmth; all of them arranged in a row, bovine, eyes glazed and lips blunted as if immune to any real contact. Talking without speaking, imagine that. But no need to imagine everyone walking around with their receptors excised. Receivers cut. The line goes dead. The line. Long and straight and even. Same as it ever was. Dead. It's like a long line of cars and I'm the only one on the road; the fact is they were like polo ponies. A product of their training. Fearless! And so afraid to live. The sport of kings and all I remember about summer in Wellington is the polo ponies. Everything is a photograph. The fact is I am like the protozoa destroyed by the products of my own disintegration. *Snap-snap-snap*— again, I hear the shutter of the camera, my own shudder.

What are the facts? Lay them out on a table in a row and shoot them off with an imaginary pistol like a lonesome gunslinger. Arrange them in sequence or as constellations, the way life runs in circles and complex diagonals, zigzags exploding in a dust cloud of memories. People live on in other people's memories. I read that looking at old photographs is another form of time travel. My mother's childhood is also her child's. I read that and so did you.

Everything arranged on the coffee table from birth to death.

Question: What would a life look like if moments and events were re-ordered and arranged by the time in which they took place instead of by each proceeding year? Answer:

From an early age I had a fascination with facts and figures. Is the fact or isn't it who, why, what, where, and how? Lay them out on the table, arrange them in a row and fire them off, one by one; a shooting gallery in the movie in your mind. Blow it all to smithereens. The words, the images, the set, the projectionist sitting quiet in the dark room and his big black projector. The soothsayers and smooth-talkers and shit-eaters. Come mierdas. Send home Jason the MC and all the ushers at Buster's Pub and Cinema, and demolish the joint. Burning Down the House real nice choice of a soundtrack SATURDAY NIGHT AT THE MOVIES no more. The fact is on the page in front of you. Open-ended, contradictory, manifold.

And all *this* is is a mass of moving flesh (see how it stretches when I give a little tug). All this is is nothing, nothing, because, dear reader, fifty-years-later-dear-reader, dear reader from the future of the present (look up and wink), I am dead. I am already putrefying.

The fact is a palimpsest. Everything reappears eventually. Memories and pictures of things I remember doing in a different life, when I was a boy who never would be now . . . I lost him . . . when my life could have gone either way or split into sections, patterns and fragments . . . I lost him . . . is this what I thought it would be? Is this the person I turned out to be? I lost him. For my image reflecting back at me. I believed then that I was different, my soul sheathed in its own skin—but I gave them both up a while ago— my body, my soul—plodding toward eternity. Corpses smiling in a magazine. Destroyed by the products of my own disintegration. *Drift.*

Can you see it where the movement of pixels, patterns of gradient textures turns into me? Can you see it? repeated under a blindfold the way they're trained muted to all sensation. Earless. Can you hear it as an echo incantation locomotive slowly building steam by its own repeating? The fact is a return ticket. El billete de ida y vuelta. And as the credits finally rolled on a black backdrop that seemed to scroll into eternity, the only thought that sprang to mind was I lost him. I died. The fact is on the page in front of you.

So let's rewind.

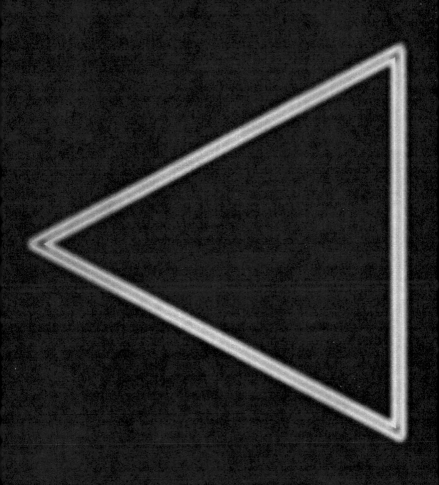

FALL

Dream Pop

We were at Café Orlin.

We were always at Café Orlin. Unless we were sprawled out, sitting comfortably, nestled inside 24P 81 Irving Place. Looking at life below.

There was the matter of who was asleep; of who was awake. It was always like this—would always be like this. And most of the time, it was all a matter of pretending. But you never knew who was pretending what—asleep or awake?—that's how good the act is. When you get the right performers.

"Did you see Mickey Rourke? Did you *see* him give me that look?"

We were at Café Orlin.

Alice kept talking, pointing down the street now, pointing down St. Mark's, peering her head from the patio to get a better view, maybe, and I noticed everybody at the table was looking at something else. Except me, who was looking at Alice, deciding if this was good enough to write down.

But I try to enter the present instead. What does a delay look like? Picture this:

"It wasn't Mickey . . ." Bailey cuts in, looking up from his phone and sighing. Asterisks for eyes, vacant as a waiting room. *Give me languid*, I think I hear Dave whisper, as the recording light turns red. *Give me exasperated.*

"Yes it *was*."

"No. It. Wasn't."

I decide to cut in and mention that there are a dozen Mickey Rourke-lookalikes in this city, two dozen more in the world—at least (I pause here)—and we keep mistaking him for someone else, or vice versa, at the clubs: Greenhouse, Juliet, 1Oak, so what does it matter if *he* just walked by, in the flesh; what does it really matter if he is doing brunch on St. Mark's, or if it's his double?

"It's all the same," I say.

"Well, I've never seen *anyone* who resembles me," Bailey starts, flipping over the menu, sighing again. Audibly. Bailey Lazar would take a job as a human rug if he knew he'd get a few looks. Bailey Lazar, I think, would take the Shake Weight commercial, the clap ad, the cover of *Effluvia Weekly*, the background player on *The Walking Dead* . . . (I shake my head); Bailey Lazar would film his own murder if he knew enough people were watching. "I'm irreplaceable."

I glance at Dave and he's grinning behind the camera. He hardly ever grins.

"A rare breed," I mouth, and turn the subject to who's playing Santos Party House tonight, the secret show.

"Purity Ring?" Alice asks, forgetting momentarily about Mickey, about the look he may have just given her. I nod. She's wearing her favorite shirt. Or maybe it's my favorite shirt. *I'm in love with cities I've never been to & people I've never met.* And I knew very clearly and very closely how anyone could fall in love with anyone else, with people and places they had never met, let alone would never know. Never, not really or not at all. Like all branding devices, any repeated photograph or moving image elicits expectation in the one looking, even and especially if the subject can't look back. This is what we call desire. This is what we call the repetition of *waiting for it*. (I nod again.)

"Aren't they, like, nü-gaze?"

"Dream pop," Bailey cuts in.

"Glo-fi," Dave corrects.

"No, no, no," I laugh, massaging Alice's scalp, feeling the blond locks run between my fingers like silk. "Now it's called *chill wave*."

"How'd you know?" Alice asks. "How'd you know who's playing Santos Party House?"

"You told me," I say, moving my hand from her head to my lap, shaking my head, almost, even, laughing. "Fifteen minutes ago."

"You are *truly* the best listener, baby," Joél cuts in, Joél who, until now, had been mute, relatively soundless, who had, until this moment, been silent, except for a few titters, a few "babys," a few more "we need to chat, we need to really catch up, honey, we need to sit it down and *talk*" and you can always tell when someone is pretending to be on the phone. "Did I ever tell you that?" he asks, slapping the thin rectangle down, turning his head up.

"I have tinnitus, Joél," I say. I say: "I don't have a choice. I hear everything."

A whistle like static, the click of teeth, tongues smacking lips, swallow of saliva, gargled mutters, a pooch panting down the block—

"Everything?" he asks, and I only nod. I nod and murmur, except this time to myself: Even the things I don't want to hear.

And they all just look at me, laughing loud and long as the thin waitress circles the table and someone—Mickey?—walks past, and I think they think I'm joking.

The Anniversary

ME

The morning Clarence decided to break up with Monica, he also decided he couldn't bear to see her again.

Instead, he saw electric scooters and leather messenger bags, lilacs in bloom and oak trees shading bare navels, brick-paved walkways and tall, black lampposts encircling the vast green expanse of a campus quad.

The sunlight slid down the trimmed grass and inched closer to Clarence's seat on the wooden bench and he welcomed it, embracing each ray in his arms, which were clad in an off-gray cardigan he had recently purchased. The sunlight warmed his skin but produced a glare. He squinted his eyes, trying to make the image clearer.

He had been in grad school for all of one semester, but it was enough to convince Clarence that people like him and people like her could not possibly be a full-fledged *couple*, the kind that hosted wine and cheese parties in their manicured apartments overlooking Central Park, overlooking *any* park; the kind of couple that completed each other's expressions, that completed each other's gestures and mannerisms, that completed each other's Facebook statuses . . . their most poignant connection resided in the exchange of bodily fluids they dispensed three, or four—sometimes even five—times a day.

He was an athlete through his early twenties, and his body retained the memory of 400-meter races and suicides on the soccer pitch. She was five-foot seven, lithe, even elastic, from her weekly routine of yoga and Pilates. She had a penchant for wearing ponytails and little else whenever they were behind closed doors. Sometimes the doors were ajar.

And to think that everything had been going so smoothly. He had even briefly compared their relationship to his own parents', whose love seemed only to grow with every passing year.

Clarence glanced at the calendar on his phone and his mind reeled as he stared at the date. He had moved through the morning with a feeling of uncanny unrecognition. He thought about psychoanalysis and wondered how to pronounce Schadenfreude[vi] properly. He had a feeling that there was something he had to do, an inkling that today was somehow significant, but he couldn't pinpoint it. Perhaps it was his soul signaling the breakup.

Clarence considered this while watching the girls sunbathing in the center of the quad, their bodies small and tight and untainted by any semblance of a freshman 15—were they prospectives?—the herd of lumpy TAs jogging circles around the oval, panting in their sweatpants and windbreakers, the plangent proclamations of a debate club discussion in the distance, students of all shapes and sizes exasperating: "The Republicans are filibustering *just* to filibust . . ."

This was his life now. He was en route to his Master's— maybe even his Ph.D. And she was . . . well, what was she?

She was Filipina, with skin a few shades darker than his olive complexion. When she was angry with him she spoke in Tagalog. Or maybe it was when she was happy with him. He could only make out the parts that sounded like Spanish, because he had earned check marks in español, sometimes even check pluses, back when success was measured symbolically: Sí, tienes razón, muchacho.

[vi] Clarence probably means *Unheimliche*.

He paused for a second to consider this latest inquiry. A bright green disc nearly hit him in the face but Clarence sidestepped it as he did most of the obstacles in his life, with calm, discerning penetration.

"Hey nice reflexes, Clarence!"

The compliment came accompanied with a thumbs-up and a grin.

"I used to be an athlete," Clarence responded and shrugged his shoulders, throwing the Frisbee back to the mass of cotton sweaters and cargo shorts and backward hats. Clarence couldn't place any of the faces with actual names, but he was certain he must have met each of them at some point during the semester, at a campus lecture or perhaps at a student social.

Clarence looked past the activity on the quad, squinting his eyes and furrowing his brow, crossing and uncrossing his legs, looking through the bodies and perspiration, wondering what each passerby thought about the man sitting on the bench. He liked to surround himself with crowds of people. He liked to be alone with his thoughts.

Clarence fell back on his meditation as the breeze picked up and church bells began to ring in the distance, mingling with shards of gossip and laughter.

Monica talked often about fake laughs, shoplifting, and dirty underwear in dressing rooms, so maybe she worked in retail. But really, unfortunate incidents like those could happen anywhere.

They talked a lot, but mostly about everyday things, real-life things like where to eat on a Thursday night in the East Village when they couldn't get a table at The Fat Radish and whose turn it was to go to the farmer's market in Union Square for groceries, what to season the beets with before they placed them in the oven—cumin or cilantro, or both?—the physical things that seemed boring after reading Derrida, and Lacan, and Walter Benjamin's manifesto on aura in the age of mechanical reproduction.

But really, they had just been producing a lot of orgasms for the past five months, Clarence considered, stroking his smooth chin. At least he hoped she wasn't *reproducing* anything.

Monica watched the same rotating assemblage of movies every week and Clarence couldn't watch anything twice. What he wanted more than anything was to be interested. Or maybe it was to be interesting. He couldn't tell which.

In truth, he had to admit, they shared a number of magical mornings, afternoons, and evenings together. There were moments—moments that expanded into hours—in which all he did was stare into her eyes while they clasped each other's legs and arms, hands, necks . . . one breathing body heaving on a damp bed in a dimly-lit room. Her eyes became one eye as everything collapsed into a single gaze.

They had done all those things. He had met her parents and she had met his. They had invited each other into their separate lives, into their distinct orbits, shared confidences, let their guards down, and emerged not as individuals but as lovers, as best friends, as electrons orbiting a glowing nucleus; their love growing still stronger as the current of the seasons amplified into fall.

But like a SportsCenter rendering of the Not Top 10 Plays of the Week, the worst bits of their affair kept replaying in his mind.

She read *People* magazine with the concentration of an astrophysicist.

She DVRed every episode of *The Bachelor* and hosted screening parties with her girlfriends.

She listened to the radio, specifically z100.

She could be happy doing anything.

And the real fierceness of desire, the real heat of a passion long continued and withering up the soul of a man is the craving for identity with the woman whom he loves. He desires to see with the same eyes, to touch with the same sense of touch, to hear with the same ears, to lose himself, to be enveloped, supported . . .

Did Ford Madox Ford write that? Clarence shook his head and marveled at the sincerity of Ford's desire, how real it felt to him. Surely, if anyone knew anything about true, undying love, it was Ford Madox Ford.

This is what he would tell her.

He thought of all his options. He wrote them down, and then crossed out each one. Face-to-face interaction was out of the question, but he added that too, as if to remind him of the pain he might endure. Phone call? No, her voice alone was enough to disappoint him. E-mail? Too impersonal, too cold, too recycled.

He fingered the container of floss in his pocket and shuddered. He felt hindered, encumbered, *blocked*.

Finally, he decided. He wanted something she could experience immediately, something that would do their five-month relationship justice, something that would maybe elicit an equally natural and spontaneous reaction.

"Dear Monica," he began, wincing at the formality of it before continuing. The words began to appear faster than he could think them.

"I said I love you. I envisioned our future together: happy, passionate; partners to share the world."

Clarence grimaced. Semicolons seemed unnatural here but he continued anyway, hardly looking up now, entirely focused.

"You excited me as no other person had done before. You were the person I wanted to discover the world with. I plotted timeshares and charted out family vacations. I vacationed in varying degrees of delusion. (*Make the point. Now's when she needs to find out. Just make the point . . .*) I do not love you. I know I said I did and I thought I did

(*Don't say anything more . . . if you say too much it will never be enough and next thing you know she's reading between the lines; next thing you know she's dumping* you) but I do not love you. (*What vigor! What clarity!*) I love the suggestion of you, the you that was indicated to me but never realized (*This is getting good, oh Clarence, this is getting* literary) or else the you that I made myself, a confabulation of ascribed attributes. It is like observing something that doesn't actually exist. I want to see it so bad, so I say it is there. (*Now we need something gray, we need a bit of darkness, a bit of . . .*) You do not think about eschatology or identity, you are not skeptical or even inquisitive. You take everything as fact, and let everything wash over you. Nothing haunts you but the prospect of a pimple on the edge of your nose before an evening in the Meatpacking District. (*If we don't finish this now, it will never get sent at all. And no stock phrases . . . no weak-kneed good-byes, no easy ways out*) You are nothing like the way I had imagined, the way I had hoped, the way your wavy black hair and electric eyes came to me and seized my soul that first night, how I wanted to *know* them, to know all of you, only to discover that there is nothing inside."

It was a long text message.

He had been reading *Moby-Dick* and wondered if he should mention something about pasteboard masks too but figured it would only make her scratch her head a few times and shrug, or something worse, since this was precisely the same reaction he had upon reading Melville. He didn't want to think about all the possible reactions she *might* have; he wanted to produce a very specific effect, so instead he closed with a simple, "Au revoir—good-bye, my love."

Satisfied, Clarence silenced his phone and enjoyed his last few moments of introspection before class.

Her response came an hour later, in the form of an uncomfortable vibration in the side pocket of his skinny black Levi's, perched uncharacteristically close to his crotch. He was astonished at the message's tone. Passion, optimism, excitement, more than anything else, tenacity in the face of a devastating situation. It was just what he was hoping for, minus all the emoticons.

Clarence I luv u sooo much. ☺ We should talk about this in person. Let's do dins tonite. Sorella at 8?

"Damaged and devoted," Clarence murmured, shaking his head in disbelief. "What a plot twist."

He thought about Monica in a new light as Professor Kimble's lecture on Thoreau's fascination with defecation floated through him like UV rays and out the open window. Monica had become his Blanche DuBois. Her stock was experiencing an exponential uptick.

With each passing seminar, Clarence felt his mind expanding. Or maybe it was his head.

He couldn't tell which.

NANCY

Nancy thought about him as if he were a blazing spirit, as if he were an alluring mystery, the enigmatic stranger in the Nora Roberts books she loved to read, just like in the Nora Roberts book she was reading now. He was like the brilliant flash that flickered before a light bulb burned out completely. She had to change hers soon.

Nancy felt her breasts instinctively as her nipples stiffened and her forehead grew damp. Outside, a lawnmower roared and sprinklers pirouetted in intermittent taps. She slipped her bright red apron off and stretched out on her tiptoes, slamming the window shut. She wanted to be alone with her thoughts.

He treated her body with earnest interest, like it was a glimpse into some other world, like it was one worth exploring. She felt like a young girl in his arms. She felt much younger than her fifty-four years.

"Ooh, ooh, ooh
My-my-my-my-my-my
You've got to feel the power
Yeah, yeah"

Her husband's warbling voice interrupted her thoughts and almost made her drop her stirring spoon. Why was he home so early? And what the hell was he humming?

"Feel what, Walt?" she asked, perturbed at the thought of yet another trifling ache or pain that he had diagnosed as muscular dystrophy or osteoporosis on WebMD. Her hands remained at her side as Walter came into the kitchen.

"Bermuda!" Walter explained, spit flying.

"Bermuda?" Nancy looked at her husband with wonder. Was this a mid-life crisis? She observed his snap-buckle suspenders, his gray slacks, his olive corduroy blazer she had been meaning to throw out for the last decade, and decided he was certainly still the same person she had been married to for twenty-nine years.

Walter combed his hair the same way he did when he was young. She knew this because he kept old photographs everywhere. *Walter at the Bergen County Meet of Champions, Walter hoisting the state football trophy above his head, Walter shaking hands with Governor William T. Cahill.* Now Walter was a haggard salesman, but none of the framed photographs around the house corroborated the trajectory.

Walter ran one limp hand through his hair. Oily and cowlicked and slicked to the side. It was the only thing that remained unchanged in twenty-nine years.

Through the course of their marriage, Nancy had flitted between surrendering to daydreams and depression, moving with the elegant wastefulness of the kind of day drunk that's a true privilege of the idle class. She didn't know how to occupy her time. Of course, that was before she met Scott. He was twenty years younger than Walter, but more evident than their age difference was the difference in dexterity the men displayed—or didn't—in the course of making love to her.

Scott was gentle, careful, slow and easy and utterly soothing in his deep breaths and faint kisses and tender thrusts. And Walter, from what she could recall in the recesses of her mind, was plodding, clumsy, too rough and too fast, and he treated her body like it was a piece of meat. Probably brisket, she thought. Nancy looked at her husband and a frown began to form on her mouth as he continued to talk. She turned her head. She wasn't listening. She wondered if Walter had forgotten how to make love completely. She wondered if Walter even remembered what she looked like naked. She remembered the last time she'd seen Walter naked—a few fleeting seconds before he hopped into bed and collapsed under the covers—but it was enough to make her frown deepen. Walter had grown lax throughout the years. His body that had been molded through a persistent routine of track meets and football games was now swollen and flaccid and when he tossed in bed, as he often did, the bed frames shifted and shook and she trembled too.

Thinking about men made Nancy think about their son. She wondered how he could be so good with people, how he moved through life with unflappable cool and imperceptible sophistication, re-inventing himself, adapting for any circumstance life threw at him. In four years since graduating from college, he had become a poet, a personal trainer, a print model, a tennis instructor, a keyboardist in a pop band—self-trained, she shook her head in astonishment—a waiter, and a bartender/cabana boy on one of her favorite CBS soap operas.

She beamed widest at this last acknowledgment and looked past Walter at the Panasonic flat-screen plasma television nestled securely at the center of the den airing *The Young and the Restless*. The television was always on.

He knew how to treat his girlfriend and they were sparkling and vibrant and utterly beautiful together when they visited her and Walter over Thanksgiving. It was almost embarrassing. Where had he learned these gifts?

Nancy envisioned her son's life as he bounced from borough to borough, traversing the city like a nimble courier, moving through Union Square and Madison Park and perched high above the hurry on the High Line as he strode to his graduate classes. She had watched some footage about the High Line on *The Today Show* when the park first opened last summer. Everything looked so scenic and accessible. What she wanted more than anything was to move through the open spaces too.

Nancy poured her thoughts into the brisket stew she had been listlessly stirring on the stove. Canned potatoes were roasting in the oven. Walter could be happy with anything but this simple meal was his favorite.

"It's sunny! It's romantic! It's perfect!" Walter repeated, and his words cut through her thoughts like a cleaver. She seemed to finally grasp everything that was coming out of his thick, smacking lips.

They were going on a second honeymoon. Back to Bermuda.

If Nancy could speak—really speak—she would have told him that she simply wasn't responsible. She would have said, "I'm not responsible for the image that stands beside you. The one you created." Created and preserved, Nancy thought, looking at Walter's face, staring at the cowlick.

Maybe she would have thrown in a bit about the lack of desire, too.

Walter moved in closer for a hug but Nancy was frozen in her spot beside the stove. He smiled wide but all she could see was his troubled gums, the gingivitis glaring at her.

Nancy wondered if Walter suspected anything about her affair with his orthodontist.

•

"Do you want an upgrade?"

Nancy slowly opened her eyes, rapidly blinking into the small, circular bulbs of LED perched above her head, trying to make sense of non-linear images and associations, still believing she was sleeping. Walter gently pinched her arm and any remnants of the dream vanished.

"Honey, do we want a special meal?"

Nancy squinted and the sketch of the woman in the navy blue skirt and white button-down standing above her became clearer. She looked imposing from where Nancy was slumped in her seat and her wide-eyed smile seemed menacing.

"Honey?"

Nancy thought the experience of traveling was going to be liberating. Open space, palm trees, sea breeze.

"The special meal—"

But the long lines of people huddled around blinking computer terminals, the parade of suitcases and duffel bags, and the recurrent security checkpoints reminded her more of the snaking conveyor belt of baggage claim, pausing and stuttering before eventually moving. She was only traveling in circles.

"—do we want it?"

And now Walter's dull voice was blaring in her ears, making the claustrophobia even worse. Walter had escaped early from work and Nancy's escapist fantasies had been cut short as they took separate taxis to meet at JFK at the appointed hour. Walter was never late, and when she had emerged from the black Lincoln Town Car, he was already standing out front, extending his arm to grab her indigo suitcase, the wind howling through the terminal.

Nancy swallowed hard. It was almost time for takeoff. Nancy's ears would pop soon; the air pocket inside the middle ear would expand and stretch the eardrum to its threshold. But her body felt like it was about to implode now. She glanced over at Walter and finally answered him with a nod.

Walter immediately flashed his credit card to the flight attendant and tried to match her beaming smile as he thanked her. Nancy watched him place the MasterCard back in his leather wallet and thought about all the things that money couldn't buy.

"Well, here's to Bermuda, babe," Walter said, and put his palm on Nancy's lap.

She felt a sudden panic shoot through her. It took her a moment to realize she was shivering. Walter quickly took the blanket out of its plastic bag and carefully covered Nancy, bits of navy blue fabric sticking to his fingers.

Nancy wasn't used to spending so much time alone with Walter. In New Jersey, they had rooms to walk through, restaurants with long, narrow tables, friends. Here they had nothing but an armrest that Walter was, even now, overtaking with his forearm.

Nancy sighed and closed her eyes, imagining what it would be like to spend three days with her husband. Three uninterrupted days.

She thought about Scott. About his youth, his vigor, his charisma in the dentist office. All of the female attendants—young, too, and caked with too much makeup and lip gloss—furnished him with the same type of menacing air-stewardess smiles.

Nancy turned her head and was met with Walter's stare.

He is piercing a hole through me, she murmured. And now he can see my soul.

Thoughts rushed through Nancy's mind. Did he know? But how? And how long? She strained her mouth into a smile. Finally, Walter's lips parted.

"So how was your day?"

She paused. Nancy wasn't shivering anymore. She was smiling, the image of Scott dissipating as the engine roared and the plane ascended, shaking the polyester seats and plastic tray tables as the cabin pressure dropped. Nancy raised the rattling armrest positioned between her and her husband.

Scott never asked her anything about her day.

WALTER

The idea came to Walter like a Luther Vandross song.

Actually, it was a very specific Luther Vandross song: "Power of Love," which had been playing on the radio—Walter liked V101.7—during his commute home, which had produced such uncharacteristic passion in him.

Even Walter had admitted as much.

"Gosh," he gasped, turning the corner of Pyle Street before he pulled to a stop in the blacktop circular driveway that heralded the Byrne's sugar maple split-level home. "I really feel it."

"Feel what, Walt?" Nancy asked. Her voice was tremulous. Perhaps she felt it too, Walter considered, hanging up his olive corduroy blazer as he hurried into the parlor. He had worn the sports coat on their first date; was it merely chance that he was wearing it today, during this unexpected epiphany?

"The power . . ." he began, unsure of how to proceed until he recalled Luther's resonant voice emanating from the Subaru's speakers. "The power of love."

This was something new. Usually Walter was too tired from the long day at his miniature desk, inside his miniature cubicle, to produce anything besides a prolonged yawn in between a chorus of sighs. He had been eyeing a promotion from his customer sales position since he began working for Panasonic. That was thirty years ago.

"What's that?" Nancy asked over her shoulder as she stirred the pot on the stove. She was preparing Walter's favorite: beef bourguignon and golden crisp potato cubes, the kind flecked with bits of crunchy onions and garlic, features which always left Walter fascinated.

"Well, honey, it's like . . ." Walter paused again, squashing the image of sautéed vegetables out of his mind. He was used to talking with people on the phone, at his desk, the dangling black cord wrapped around his fingers, the voice across the other line coming through a million miles of unseen airwaves. "How do you feel about Bermuda."

Walter was not asking.

"Bermuda?" Nancy asked. Walter caught her as she spun around, nearly dropping her big black plastic stirring spoon. He was delighted at her reaction. He had really floored her this time. Walter smiled wide at this achievement, a practiced grin he had mastered through so many tradeshows and company meetings, the same spark of charisma he had passed down to their son, to whom he had imparted almost all of his gifts, and all of his finances. He ran one unwavering hand through his meticulously combed hair—parted, always, off to the side with a flourish of mousse—his momentum rising further, and continued.

"Bermuda!" he exclaimed. "It's sunny, it's romantic, it's . . . perfect."

It *was* perfect. Walter and Nancy had celebrated their honeymoon in the tiny Caribbean island, navigating the Bermuda triangle to find true love, and thirty years later, they would return to celebrate their anniversary, reignite their passion, remember why they had fallen in love in the first place.

It was settled.

Nancy remained speechless but a slight crease twisted on her lips; the hints of a smile that would appear fully formed the minute they touched down at Wade International. He marveled at how perfect her teeth were. Those frequent dentist bills were paying off.

She turned her back to him and returned to the meal she had been preparing.

Devoted to the last drop, Walter thought, and he sighed deeply. I really am the luckiest man in the world.

This he said aloud.

The next afternoon, in between conference calls and a splurging customer lunch at Red Lobster (it was Friday), Walter booked the flight on Priceline. Overwhelmed with excitement, he took the rest of the day off, scurrying out of the office while a crowd of coworkers looked on in confusion. Panasonic was in the midst of preparing for its spring trade show.

Walter wasn't fooling around. He did all the research, Googling everything from "best beaches in Bermuda" to "how to find a woman's g-spot"—Walter considered himself an excellent lover, although he hadn't had many opportunities to practice intimacy with his wife in the past few months. He felt listless, even dull, in suburban New Jersey but the exotic sea breeze of a tropical paradise would change all that.

Two weeks before their trip, Walter had the itinerary all planned. He had long ago acquired a fascination for technique, the exact way to do something properly. It took careful preparation. His extensive career at Panasonic had trained him to be efficient and analytical. He assembled his strategy with PowerPoint-like triangular bullets and laid it out on the coffee table. He had to remove his high school photographs first and this took longer than expected.

They would start at Historic St. George, traversing the Unfinished Church in the morning, holding hands through the same Town Hall and Old Rectory the original settlers used. In the late afternoon, they'd rest their weary bodies on the beautiful sands of Horseshoe Bay. At evening, they'd dine on the sand, snuggled into the rocks with waves lapping nearby at Coconuts Trattoria. They would slip each other spoonfuls of broiled conch and beer-battered shrimp under the glow of tiki torches with their toes in the sand. This is how The Reefs Hotel & Club described it on its Web site. He had booked their two-day stay before he had even finished reading the sentence.

After another day of sun and salt water at Tobacco Bay, they'd take in the zephyr at the Royal Naval Dockyard, window-shopping at the numerous art galleries, quaint (though overpriced) shops and waterfront pubs. They'd eat mussel pie and sweet Wahoo for dinner, and he'd profess how much he loves her, how much he's always loved her, and then they'd lay together in their reclining queen-sized bed, solaced amid layers of comforters and blankets and the two or three cylindrical cushions shaped in columns hotels like The Reefs were certain to have. They'd leave the next morning, refreshed and romanced, and arrive at JFK, just in time to celebrate their thirtieth anniversary with a Hudson River ferry ride back to Jersey City.

When they arrived at Wade International, upon Walter's suggestion, which he had gleaned from a travel guide conveniently placed inside their economy-class seatbacks, Nancy ate rancid Bermuda fish chowder from an airport vendor and was confined to their hotel room indefinitely.

MONICA

"Oh. Em. Gee."

"OH-EM-GEE!"

Samantha repeated her response, a deafening squeal inside an otherwise tranquil Starbucks on Park Avenue and 29th Street.

Monica ignored the curious faces, some astonished, some annoyed, all of them utterly confused, and smiled broadly at her friend across the oval table.

"I know," Monica said, playing with her ponytail with one hand and reaching for her iPhone with the other.

"He is so effing *romantic*," Samantha interrupted, pointing at the text message gleaming on Monica's cell as evidence.

"Well, what's up with the past tense, Sam?" Monica asked.

"Clarence is clearly about to propose to you," Samantha replied.

"But what's—" Monica's persistent curiosity halted mid-question. "Are you kidding me?" Monica blushed and unconsciously stretched her delicate fingers out on the table, eyeing her freshly-painted fingernails: pink with white tips. "It's only been five months," she said, not looking up.

Monica considered the brief relationship from her seat on the chicory-lacquered high stool. She could see the crowds of people ambling past Park Avenue, all of them in a hurry, except for one woman clasping the hands of two children, the three of them taking careful steps together.

The children were pale and freckle-faced, brother and sister probably, and both were adorned in the same gray and blue ensemble. Monica wondered if this would be her life in a year, two years, and perhaps another girl would be watching her strolling through Park Avenue, her hands tightly clasped around her own children.

She took another look out the window and caught the woman's gaze as she turned toward the Starbucks.

Dark skin. Flat nose. Wide, kind, brown eyes. Filipina. Like her.

She wondered if Clarence was raised by a nanny, too. She knew that he was lost, even now, amid a constellation of roles that he had willingly played his whole life, layers of insecurities and uncertainties; an innate need to behold or be held. She wanted to hold his hand. He was like a child, she considered, looking back out the window at their fascinated eyes, their confused and curious and fascinated eyes.

He was a child.

"Honey," Samantha interrupted. "I don't know any boy who talks like that in a text." She waved her hand around like she was directing traffic.

Samantha's Italian was coming out, Monica observed, but her thoughts went back to Clarence, and she averted her eyes from her friend's bronzed face and bleach-blond hair so she could visualize a clearer picture of him in her mind.

"He doesn't like chocolate, or champagne," Samantha continued, mumbling from the sides of her vivid, lip-sticked mouth. "And well, what else is there? He must be totally in love with you."

She sucked down the rest of her Frappuccino, chewing on the green plastic straw as her eyes wandered over to the affable barista in front of their table.

"You're getting a ring tonight," Samantha declared. "And me—what am I doing?"

Monica knew that Samantha was hoping to take her place striding down the chapel aisle; it didn't matter with whom. Monica looked sympathetically at her friend; Samantha was still looking at the man in the forest-green apron smiling from across his domain behind the counter.

"Another first date," Samantha groaned, checking the time on her cell phone. "Match.com. I'm about to light *myself* up. And there's nothing in my purse of purses to make me look less *normal* . . . a skirt? Please, somewhere . . ."

"But five months, really Sam?" Monica asked, lost in her thoughts, not wanting a response. "Clarence gets bored with the music on his iPod after five days."

Monica looked down at the phone. She had already read it thirteen times between now and 3:36, which, as the timestamp indicated, was when she initially received Clarence's text. Though each time she read it, her heart skipped another beat. And to think only one hour had passed since it first hit her screen, announcing itself with the panache of the new Lady Gaga single, "LoveGame," which Samantha had carefully chosen as her friend's ringtone. Monica had been meaning to change it and she briefly cringed at the memory of *"I want to take a ride on your disco stick"* heralding such a romantic communication.

Dear Monica, I said I love you. I envisioned our future together: happy, passionate; partners to share the world. You excited me as no other person had done before. You were the person I wanted to discover the world with. I plotted timeshares and charted out family vacations.

And then it ended. She bristled at the thought of him deliberately teasing her with such an abrupt finish. Not even a smiley face or a bracket and a number 3 in the shape of a heart to cap things off.

She tried to imagine him speaking the words but couldn't. Clarence was usually so guarded, so reluctant to open up. She could see it in the way his eyes wavered if she looked into them for a moment too long, how his customary wide smile concealed an indiscernible, barely-there sadness, how he often lost himself in mid-speech, his thoughts forever restless and resistant, as if he were always in another place in his mind, somewhere quite different from where he was sitting or standing, or laying down—even when they were making love. But she felt confident he would repeat every word tonight. He would reveal his inner self, his undying pledge, his hopes and dreams and desires. And she would surrender herself to him completely. This was what she wanted.

"What does he do again? Bartend? Model?"

"No, that was," Monica paused, thinking about all of Clarence's empty-handed castings at ABC. "Like a year ago."

"Oh, okay." Samantha allowed her response to trail off.

"What—are you jealous?"

"So what *does* he do?"

"He's a student, Sam. English literature," Monica said, slightly annoyed. "I've told you all this before. Do you even listen to me?"

"Hmm . . ." Samantha pursed her lips. "I heard the only reason people get their Master's in English is to attend gallery openings and impress other people . . ." Samantha paused, her eyes meeting the Tazo tea bags lined up against the counter, each displaying a different maxim. "With their knowledge."

"You're jealous, I get it," Monica said. "Clarence is different. He has other interests. He's above fads. God, he still owns a BlackBerry."

"Those things still work?"

Monica looked back at the text.

"Of course they do."

"Oh—I don't want to be *alone*, Monica," Samantha shuddered, and Monica nearly did too. Monica gazed at Samantha's slightly swollen, orange-tinted face and the wrinkles under her hairline seemed to grow more conspicuous. A sense of dread washed over Monica too; it was the loneliness that came with growing old, and sometimes even growing up.

"So what are you wearing?" Samantha asked.

Monica was startled. She began to respond but she hadn't even considered the question. Amid all the turbulence and the excitement and now, the caffeine of a double skinny sugar-free hazelnut venti latte, she had not even considered her wardrobe for tonight.

She glanced at the iPhone once more, the clock at the center of the screen scowling at her. It was already almost five.

She looked down at her blue elastic shorts, letters spelling J U I C Y spread across her backside, and frowned as she felt the sticky remnants of her afternoon workout lingering on her G-Star zip-up hooded sweatshirt. It was supposed to snow tonight; the first snowfall of the year.

"I haven't got a clue."

Her thoughts floated from the swarming café to the relative intimacy of Sorella and she began to broadcast the scene in her mind. Monica loved strolling through the unmarked entrance, passing the narrow wine-washed balsa-wood bar to reach the sprawling, candle-lit, glass-ceilinged annex; she never tired of the surprise. It was exactly how she pictured the inside of a hidden Roman trattoria. Eating at Sorella felt like sharing a secret.

•

When Monica finally arrived, Clarence was already seated, peering over the petite menu meticulously, even though he knew she knew his order by heart. Clarence savored his spontaneous do-anything-all-the-time persona, but Monica recognized he was privately a man of ritual. And tonight the ritual was tajarin with lamb ragu, black pepper ricotta, pistachios and mint; and an order of Brussels sprouts flecked with bacon and rosemary aioli to start. She mouthed the words to herself and as she walked toward the small table sectioned off in the corner, she smiled.

Clarence looked up as she came closer and he rose quickly, embracing her with a hug. She held his fitted button-down firmly, feeling his taut back and shoulders through the thin cotton. Everything about Clarence was tight, and yet he seemed so relaxed tonight. So utterly free.

ME & MONICA

"How long have you been waiting, honey?"

Clarence sat down and took another sip of his purple-red cocktail and grinned.

"Just got here basically," he said, turning a sideways glance at his watch.

He had been sitting at Sorella for the past fifteen minutes. He always arrived early. There was a certain joy in the manner of preparation. Clarence relished the fleeting moments before any event; how time froze, allowing him to observe the world as it were being played out, like a spectator in his own motion picture. He had immediately changed from his off-gray cardigan to a dark green button-down in the dimly-lit, private bathroom, and re-emerged into the scene.

Now he scanned Monica from his post on the pastoral wooden chair.

Sorella's webmaster had described it as such. They had been very specific with their description, Clarence remembered. It was *pastoral*. Not rustic. He thought about shepherds and rolling hills and persuasion tactics.

Monica was wearing a cotton floral summer blouse and black leggings and Clarence imagined what her ass looked like, beautiful and round and constrained, momentarily, in spandex. He had read somewhere that men's fascination with asses was a result of their general protuberance: it reminded men of pregnancy, of reproduction; of everything they could not have themselves.

That feeling of yearning reminded him of the evening's objective and Clarence looked at Monica admiringly. She had shown up after all. And here she was, ready to deliver her breathless proclamation, her unrelenting refusal to leave, her demonstration of *pasión*.

What would it be tonight? Clarence's thoughts wandered, they drifted and receded. They danced with anxiety and fervor. What would it be? The tajarin? The garganelli nero? The *gnudi*? (He mostly liked pronouncing the name.) No amount of preparation could make this moment any calmer, any easier. Any less terrifying.

You have to choose, Clarence murmured silently. You have to choose all the time.

They sat in silence for nine minutes, and after the spirited waitress tottered by to take their orders—Clarence ordering the tajarin with lamb ragu, black pepper ricotta, pistachios and mint; and an order of Brussels sprouts flecked with bacon and rosemary aioli to start—nine more minutes of silence. Finally, Monica spoke. Clarence spoke too. Each of them asking the same question:

"Is there anything you wanted to tell me?"

The couple laughed, grinning sheepishly. They responded by taking another prolonged sip from their highballs, eyeing each other from across the table. Clarence inched closer and smelled strawberry and cedar and whatever else was contained in Monica's perfume. He suddenly fretted that he had forgotten to re-apply his AXE spray deodorant during his extensive commute from class, thrown between other sweating bodies on the 4, hurtling toward the evening like a slingshot from a tea kettle.

He had scoured the Internet on his BlackBerry the moment the train emerged aboveground, looking at photographs of food to calm himself.

Monica pressed her delicate fingers into Clarence's outstretched palm, squeezing hard, forcing him to look at her.

Before Clarence could answer Monica's question, or Monica could answer his, Clarence rose from the table. He jammed his hands into his pockets, fumbling inside the tight, distressed denim. Monica's lips quavered.

This is it, she thought, staring at the rectangular bulge in his jeans pocket. Samantha was right! And her skin burned with anxiety. Her forehead was damp with perspiration. Her hands were clammy, too, and she could see her slender fingers, pink with white-tipped nails shaking on the white linen napkin on her lap; she was too panicked to look up.

"I forgot," Clarence blurted out, "I need to call my parents real quick." He swerved, finally pulling out his right hand from his pocket, grasping his BlackBerry. It fell to the floor and he gracelessly bent down, fumbling with most of the keys before seizing it.

Monica's anticipation deflated. She compressed her lips, murmuring invectives in Tagalog, and looked down at her half-empty bowl of rosemary cauliflower mash. The dish was pretty and picturesque and too-lovely-to-eat when it had arrived but now it just looked ordinary, and even dull.

Clarence produced another wide-eyed smile and strode out of the room, turning his head briefly behind him as the moon peeked out from the glass-ceilinged annex above Monica's head. It illuminated the room from another angle.

"Today is their anniversary."

Monica's iPhone buzzed and she idly glanced at the blinking text until she saw the sender.

"Clarence?"

She clicked on the screen and scrolled down, staring at the same message she had been reciting throughout the afternoon, except this time it arrived unabridged.

•

When Clarence returned, Monica was sucking down a fresh guava margarita and making an origami with her linen napkin. The bill was situated at the center of the table, partly obscured by a pile of dollars.

"No service?" she asked from the corners of her lips.

"No," Clarence shook his head, frowning. "They must be in a dead zone."

"Do you think your message got through?"

"I hope so," Clarence shrugged, still standing, indicating his BlackBerry. "You never can tell with these things."

Monica laughed too loudly.

"Well there's nothing like *face-to-face* conversation—is there?"

Clarence nodded slowly. It took him a moment to realize that Monica was staring at him, unblinking, and he felt as if she could see *inside*. Her eyes were deep and probing and electric, the way he had imagined them on their first night together. He could go swimming in those eyes, he thought. He could drown himself in them. He made a mental note to remember that line for an eventual poem.

Clarence sat down and moved closer to clasp her hands. Her delicate fingers were trembling under his and Clarence looked up to catch her gaze once more.

He thought she looked different tonight, at this instant, and he wanted to take a photo of her, freeze the moment in a crux of time to be held and savored. He had been waiting a lifetime for this.

"I do not know which to prefer," Clarence said softly, running one hand through his hair. "The beauty of inflections, or the beauty of innuendoes." "What?" Monica asked, shaking her head. "What beauty is that? What the hell are you . . ."

"I mean," Clarence cleared his throat. "The blackbird—"

"Clarence—" Monica interrupted, looking down briefly. She pulled her hands away from him. "Have a good night."

Monica was gone.

Clarence shook his head, frowning, utterly perplexed. He looked from the unoccupied chair to his cell phone and his legs began to shake uncomfortably, uncontrollably, as young, well-dressed people bustled in and out of the dining room; the verve and spirit of evening just beginning to pick up on Allen Street.

Clarence gazed out the window, watching the rivulets of snow, each silent pearl. It was starting to stick.

"Sir, are you okay? Sir?"

Clarence was speechless as he stood above the scene. A busboy nudged his way past, clearing away everything, readying the table for another couple: handsome, holding hands. A swirl of faces and questions matched his own pressing thoughts but for the first time that he could remember, Clarence was no longer thinking about himself.

A Good Story

I liked to do it on the typewriter. To feel the letters, to really feel them press and depress, and press again—and to hear it all happen, too, because they don't make keyboards like that anymore. Because, sometimes, silence can be stifling.

A room, four walls, a song to lose myself. To lose myself. A song.

I liked to watch things happen; I liked the view. I liked to peer out the window from time to time, and see the dark blue sky, the sun bleeding into night, the purple crescendo of waves rising and receding.

Oradell did not always look like itself, but the setting is secondary in this story.

It is really about desire.

When I turned twenty-eight, I was living in my parents' home in New Jersey. I had lived in North Bergen, Bethlehem, Buckingham, London, San Francisco, Hoboken, Jersey City, Miami, Brooklyn, Rio de Janeiro, and, for a brief time, Buenos Aires. And now I lived with my parents, sleeping in the bedroom of my childhood. When I'd graduated from Fordham's Master's program in English literature one month later, I was looking for jobs, putting my résumé and all my credentials—listing them one-by-one in bullet points—transcribing my life onto two pages, single-spaced and double-sided. Looking for a position.

Realizing that perhaps nothing would ever be good enough. Realizing that perhaps I never wanted it in the first place: the conventions and markers that make life countable, measurable—a life taken slow, and regularly, like vitamins. The things in life that give life meaning, or else squeeze all the meaning out.

And now I am looking.

This is the price I paid for never wanting to grow up, or at least never wanting to grow up *like everyone else*—or else, like everyone else I knew or had come to know in twenty-eight years of living. My perception of everyone else. Riding the escalator of life, until the escalator stopped moving.

Ocupar. What a verb. To take, fill, hold, take up, take over, engage, employ. Occupy. Occupations. To be occupied. To occupy one's self.

I used to envision my life as a beautiful landscape: the half-sheathed sun, the red-bricked house, the garden, the grove, the green grass, the lush trees and leaves and peaks. The stray dogs and cats and kites. The sky. And everything remains there, as if it were a still life, as if it were half-finished, or worse—maybe already done. As if everything would be filled in some other time. Or not at all. Or never.

Unless I could paint it all myself.

Newsrooms, runways, showrooms, television studios in New York City and Los Angeles, and the stop-and-go traveling schedule that accompanies it; broke for six months until the residual check arrives, or a phone call places you in Hong Kong or Rio or the Czech Republic, as phone calls often do, to occupy your vacancy. The more I tried to focus on my writing, to distance myself from the fashion industry, the more successful of a model I became. It was as if everyone knew I was writing about them, and they kept booking me so that I had more to write about.

I have always chosen pleasure over practicality, and my pleasure is words. I think that's why I never could have continued to work as a journalist. My role as Reporter never stood a chance.

Instead, I live to write, and write as I live. If something sounded like it'd make a good story, I'd do it—within limits, of course. I never hurt anybody; I never took drugs. I've always thought the only effect of any drug was to make you lose yourself, and the only time I ever wanted to lose myself was when I was writing, or when I was becoming you. In some act of creation.

No experience is ever truly lost.

When I quit the *Star-Ledger* in the final days of 2009, I didn't write anything for three years. I would have to get further away; I would have to get so much closer to myself to let everything drop, like a trapdoor in the floor, like a public hanging, uncovered and bare. I would have to turn inward, absent myself, withdraw, disappear.

I continued to rove through life. I saw myself as an apparition, a flicker, drifting between a montage of cheaply-edited cuts while "Slime Crown" by Elite Gymnastics played on repeat:

> *"This isn't what I thought it would be*
> *Okay (Okay)*
> *The person who I turned out to be*
> *I hate (I hate)*
> *When any other person would leave*
> *I'll stay*
> *I'll wait*
> *And that will bring you closer to me*
> *One day*
> *One day"*

Or maybe that's only what was playing on my headphones.

I had lost it; I had lost myself, too. And yet I felt somehow different, like a thin sheet separated me from everybody I knew. A feeling of peculiarity particular to all writers, to anyone who imagines people, judges them, gazes and reshapes them, makes them more real by turning them into fiction. Always looking.

Myself outside of myself, in front of myself. Me.

The only thing that kept me going was the acknowledgement that I had to get better—better as a person, better as a writer—so that I could write the story. So that I could save myself. One day.

The story—whatever this is—is salvation. I often think I live only so I can try and write it. And all of life is memory and sensation; all of life is rich, vivid, beautiful, ugly, ugly but still beautiful, like a particular song played at a particular moment, and all the accompanying sensations and memories that spring forth, and each time you hear it, there's one more.

I didn't get flown from Buenos Aires to Cannes for a few pretty pictures.

Appointment, Noon

"I'm underground. Yes, I'm going to lose you. You're gone, gone."

Miranda slid into the crowded car as the train doors closed and the woman in black overalls and a white collared shirt looked at her cell phone and muttered, fumbling with the keys, shaking her head.

"Dead zone."

Miranda thought the woman was looking at her.

No, she murmured, there are probably two dozen people huddled in the rear of the train. She was just another body.

The doors opened, the crowd dispersed, and Miranda thought about what she was doing here; Miranda thought about where she was going. Someone whistled and the train hurtled forward. She looked at the black expanse through the window's dim glass. Everyone, she thought, seems to be going in the same direction.

•

Is it really today?"

Miranda was staring at the bright magnetic calendar fastened neatly to her refrigerator door. Her eyes met the circled date and they stayed there as her mind wandered.

"And so it is," she continued, flipping from October to September and back again. "And so it is."

It was Monday, the day of her appointment. There was nothing else planned. There was nothing else to do.

APPOINTMENT, NOON

The underlining made the words sound ominous. Miranda winced. Why had she used such a thick Sharpie?

She had awoken early, at seven o'clock, and had gradually prepared breakfast. She had burnt the eggs and charred the poblano and now she sat, gathering up the crusty remains into a mass of specks at the center of the plate. Ashes.

She glanced at her watch, and then at the digital numbers radiating from the microwave, and then at the tall oak wall clock, its pendulum swinging at the center of the parlor. Time seemed to drift carelessly into the recesses of the day as the sunlight poured through the half-open blinds in the tidy one-bedroom apartment on Valentine Avenue.

Miranda fidgeted with her cell phone, clicked on the television, and promptly pushed mute on the remote control. Within half an hour, she was underground.

Miranda navigated through the beatboxers and the banjo set, the sea of stone-faced men and women in dark suits and skirts, hurried and anxious, the murmurs of a psalm to her right, the soothing melody of Chopin to her left. She felt as if she were on a conveyor belt, being pushed and shoved toward the platform. Relieved of her freedom to move, to act, she withdrew, distracted and at the same time occupied, remembering those final moments . . .

When she finally arrived, she paused at the black plastic trash bin adjacent to the tracks. She unzipped her purse, rummaging through for old receipts and gum wrappers, captivated with the desire to throw away everything.

Miranda gave up her search as the sound of steel on steel resonated in the dark passage and the car shuddered to a halt. She exhaled as the mechanical voice on the PA system vibrated and the doors slid open.

If you see something, say something . . .

Miranda hesitated briefly, one red flip-flop on the yellow-painted caution step, the other in the car. Briefcases and backpacks brushed her narrow shoulders. Finally, she slid past the bodies. Her frame was still supple and she imagined the static friction of molecules passing molecules, everyone and everything barely untouched.

". . . going to lose you. You're gone, gone."

Now her flip-flops squeaked as she took an empty seat and crossed her legs.

Miranda knew the route by heart, an inevitable system of passages and tracks. She began on the D, switching at Union Square to the L, which she would ride four stops through Brooklyn to Lorimer, getting off and walking sixteen-and-a-half meters—HopStop confirmed the exact measurements—to the G train, where she would wait an indeterminate time—no technological innovation could account for this interval—for the G, getting off at Greenpoint Avenue and arriving intact, more or less, at the doctor's office.

Miranda pictured the modest red-brick building on the corner of Franklin Street, the row of potted ferns heralding the entrance, the ageless Pac-Man arcade game installed outside the receptionist's office and a smile formed on her lips. It reminded her of childhood.

There were plenty of clinics with plenty of doctors in the Bronx and Manhattan, and Miranda was certain that more than a handful of them were very good at their jobs, but she had been going to Kazimierz Grybowski's office since she was seven years old. He was a family friend. He was the only person Miranda could even think to see. The only person that she would allow to see her.

Miranda let her eyes drift from her murky reflection in the window to the series of advertisements plastered to each side of the car.

INJURED? CALL 1-800-I-AM-HURT
DISCOVERY THE MYSTERY OF THE PSYCHIC
THE MOON & STARS CAN BE YOURS
IMPOTENCE GOT YOU DOWN?
DON'T LET IT RUIN YOUR SEX LIFE
DR. ZIZMOR IS A WORLD-RENOWNED
EXPERT
IN SKIN REVITALIZATION
& SCAR REMOVAL THERAPY
I THOUGHT LIFE WOULD BE THE WAY IT
WAS BEFORE ABORTION CHANGES YOU

Miranda averted her eyes and they briefly met two young men sitting directly across from her.

"Hey yo, honey!" the shorter one bellowed. He snickered like a hyena. Miranda had only ever seen one in *The Lion King,* over and over again when she was younger, but he looked like the villain with his beady eyes and bushy eyebrows and fangs jutting outward. Both men were wearing white tank tops and camo cargo shorts and hay-colored construction boots. She saw everything she didn't want to see. Again, again—her mind wandering again toward those final moments. She couldn't help it. Forced down and trapped. Choking on words. She closed her eyes hard and reopened them moments later; the two men were still sitting, inches apart, rubbing their palms together and smiling.

She could see herself in their own expressions.

Miranda swallowed hard and rubbed the back of her neck. She smelled the strawberry and lavender and grinded her teeth. Why had she even bothered with perfume today?

"You got anywhere to be?" the short man spewed, interrupting her thoughts. Miranda nodded her head and quickly picked out a fold of newspaper on the ground to stare at.

"You got a boyfriend?"

"No," Miranda slowly replied, but she regretted it the moment the word left her lips.

Why don't you just tell them your address too? Why don't you just invite them in the door? Why don't you just . . . but her mind stopped there.

"You in a rush or something?" he prodded. Miranda knew the man would never stop.

His taller friend joined in, rubbing his stubbly chin and extending his right arm: "You want to maybe get something going at 145th? I got a nice place."

"I got a Starbucks bathroom," the smaller one added, punching his friend in the stomach playfully.

Miranda looked back at them but their eyes were set below her torso, in line with the opening of her blue floral skirt. She uncrossed her trembling legs and stood up to switch cars at the next stop.

•

When Miranda finally arrived at Lorimer, she plodded through the narrow corridor, rising and then descending. Down the stairwell, she took one step at a time and when she reached the platform, she glanced at her watch.

11:30

There was still time to leave, head uptown, return home. She shook her head and ran her hand through her hair. Auburn. She wondered where she had gotten auburn hair. Her mother was a blond. Her father had always been bald, at least since she was born, and in old pictures his hair looked nearly black. What did I inherit? Miranda thought. What will I pass on?

She recalled Kaz's voice on the other line; his distress and shock moving through miles of unseen cellular bars, traversing boroughs, but still perfectly audible to Miranda. She explained everything and soon he understood.

"Don't worry, Miranda," he had said, his accent thick and foreign and entirely familiar to her. "Don't you worry, Miranda. Let me see you on Monday. Do you have work on Monday?"

She was silent.

"I can help you."

She nodded continually throughout the conversation, imagining his kind face, his pleasant blue eyes, as if he were standing there beside her.

She thought about his offer again, his words echoing deep inside her soul.

"I can help you."

She welcomed help; for the last several years, she had had no mentors in her life. And she, like her parents before her, were without papers. She welcomed help, even as she understood, somewhere, in a place where only she had access, the advantages of existing *without papers* in a culture that continued to accumulate them. Papers, forms, documents, data. Trash. What could or could not be discarded.

"I can help you," Kaz said once again. The blue eyes, the broad smile.

The memory dissipated as a crowd of teenagers clambered down the stairwell behind her, moving loud and speaking loud; the smell of fried onions and charred meat rising behind them. Everybody was moving fast, and everybody was talking fast, and the sounds became magnified, and the looks, too. Each gaze seemed to look through her. Another body.

This is the world, she thought, and let her fingers drift down her abdomen. The world had happened to her. But to be invisible, she thought. But to seek refuge in some fundamental lack.

The whistle of the train interrupted her thoughts and it trembled to a stop far away from Miranda. The G train, she murmured, always stops short.

She stared blankly as the doors opened, the sound of clicking and faint breaths and the barely-there Queens air conflating with Brooklyn air and the smell of fried onions again in the distance now, moving further away.

"Why you moving so slow, lady? Come on, you're going to miss it."

Miranda caught the gaze of the subway conductor, his black face and blue hat and brown MTA sweater and his burly torso stretching to reach as far outside of the unlatched aperture as he could endure. "Come on!"

Miranda's eyes widened and she scampered to the door, her flip-flops clacking loudly on the pavement. This is it, she knew. I am going to miss it.

Before the doors clamped shut, she decided to leave her flip-flops completely. Miranda dived, her purse swinging wildly behind her narrow shoulders, her flowing auburn hair whipping in all directions, obscuring her dark green eyes.

She landed with a thud, ricocheting off the solid steel pole in front of the entrance. Her legs and arms unfurled, her face still on the sticky, caked linoleum. She heard whispers and faint words; stunned silence. She looked up to see a few passengers rushing to meet her. One man, elderly and frail and long-legged, reached her first, helping Miranda to her feet and holding the small of her back as the train continued to sway. Miranda clasped his thick wool sweater and he turned his eyes to meet her.

"God, are you okay?"

Was he asking God, or her?

The man in the wool sweater repeated the question, his voice stopping and starting in staccatos of concern.

No, Miranda thought, remaining silent. She looked around wildly, scanning the faces encircling her like a carousel, her head still spinning. Everyone seemed to be staring. She tasted the bile rising at her throat.

"Please, sit down, dear," the old man said, guiding her to the seat he had been occupying.

Miranda was crying. She saw the tears on her toenails before she felt them. She looked down at her bare feet and her searching hands found her stomach. She continued to cry as the train stopped at Nassau Avenue, then Greenpoint Avenue. She didn't get off.

When the train arrived at Court Square, the elderly man, still holding her hand, motioned for her to depart. She shook her head. The tears slid down her flushed face.

"This is the last stop, dear," he said, pointing to the doors as more bodies swarmed in and a few slipped out. Everyone going in the same direction. She nodded but remained in her seat. She had the urge to place her fingers on his head; to brush his wispy gray strands back into place. Where did it come from or why? Strands, she thought, like yarn or thread. She pictured the unraveling. She had all this time been nodding.

"Don't you have anywhere to be?"

His watch indicated noon. She moved her eyes from his wrist to his face. His eyes reminded her of her mother; of her father, too; of childhood; a fairy tale; a hope and wish; a child. Her hands hadn't left her stomach, would never leave her stomach.

Miranda shook her head, whimpering, the tears still forming like so many possibilities.

"Not anymore."

Step By Step

The pleasure of seeing the morning sun spiral out through the starless Sky-set from the windshield of a cruising chariot on the Gee Double YOU is like nothing else, and even better with a soundtrack.

The first thing I do when I get inside the Volvo (the Volvo!) is look through the CDs. Talking Heads, New Order, Joy Division, Depeche Mode, Cut Copy, Elite Gymnastics, Pictureplane, more Talking Heads. The usual suspects. Where's Ana's stuff? I turn right and get on 17. Chris listens to this new wave, no wave, nudist colony music.

Y entonces, I'm not saying it's got to be Daddy Yankee and Wisin y Yandel; I'm not saying Buena Vista Social Club or bust, but shit, get in touch with your *roots*, man. Volver a sus raíces. That's the thing with him, and I know this, I know because mamita has told me. Ana (I can smell her Agua de Colonia all over this wagon) never taught Chris Spanish because she wanted him to *adapt*. That's straight from mami's mouth. What an ugly word, *adapt*. Adapt, make a better life. Make a better life in English.

A Certain Ratio. Purity Ring, Matthew Dear, Washed Out, Architecture in Helsinki (who comes up with these names?). Another A Certain Ratio. Sure, why not? Mathematics. I take a chance. I'm all about taking chances these days. I quit my day job just last week.

"As night turns to day, I dream some more . . ."

What's the quickest way to Grand Central? I murmur. I usually take the bus into the city. "Planes, Trains and Automobiles," my phone responds, "is a 1987 American comedy film written, produced and directed by John Hughes."

I get in my left, then continue for another two miles. This—this is a real sweet surprise. Picking up Selden at Grand Central. All the way from

L o n g Island. Montauk. A&F shoot. Fucking A&F. The kid has all the luck. All the luck and all the looks but none—none of the street smarts. That's priceless; that's the thing you can't put a price tag on. Anyway, driving is my pleasure. No, not driving. Cruising. Letting the road dip under me, letting the car and the road disappear, and me, too, until we three become one, or nothing at all—just a sound, a whir, a whoosh, the blast of wind or the force from an approaching Hostess truck on the upper level (twenty-minute delay) . . . that's Zen. . . the bow, arrow, archer. . . the apple, too.

"The film stars Steve Martin as Neal Page," my phone announces, "a high-strung marketing executive, who meets Del Griffith, played by John Candy, an eternally optimistic, overly talkative, and clumsy shower curtain ring salesman who seems to live in a world governed by a different set of rules."

"Empty words, nothing to give . . ."

And now I'm singing along. God, if Chris caught me like this. But of course they're empty. Words don't weigh a goddamn thing. Chris keeps looking for words to save him; looking for words to help solve his relationship issues, his expectations, his desires, his *ennui* (I have the Dictionary. com app), all the mud in the world labeled under the general word *problem* . . . but maybe he's looking in the wrong places. Maybe he should be thinking about the absence of words. Maybe the silence will save him. Maybe it'll save me too. But damn (*turns up radio*), this is good.

"*. . . Why is it hurting, I feel the pain . . .*"

Yea, I've got a few problems. I've got a *spending* habit, comprende? New Jordans, old ones, Beats by Dre, PlayStation 3, Nintendo DS, ice, dope rope . . . I'm talking major bling, dinner at McCormick & Schmick's (shortie's gonna love that)—I want all of it, I want it *pronto*. Yeah, I'm a consumer. So what? Who isn't?

"Would you like to purchase Planes, Trains and Automobiles?" my phone asks. "I found five Best Buys near your location."

I love money; I want to bathe in that green oasis. Bills, bills, I want to dive right into the money bin like the opening scene of *Ducktails* (I'm selling seasons 1 and 2, if you're interested). *Money*. But that's just the problem. The money, I don't have any. Or let's be realistic, I don't have much—but I don't look for handouts, either. That's where Chris comes in, in a strange way. Because this shit just isn't cutting it anymore. Selling Spanish-language *Step by Step*, refurbished CD players, Tamagotchis in unopened boxes. It ain't doing it, and there's no ways mami is gonna work another year in that Marriott hell hole, no way she should have to.

Dollar bills, dolor bills . . . shit, yeah, it gives me a headache to wrap my head around it. To wrap my head around the money problem. I'm broke. That's why I'm playing chauffeur, after all. But Selden, Selden . . . that's where he comes in. In that strange way of his. In that little unwitting-tip way of his. Ladyfriend's doing Armani, man. *Armani*. It's Georgey's largest show in years. Three hundred garments in a day, easy. Next Wednesday. And now I know where I can find the whole line, one day early, at the biggest discount: Free. "*. . . The door shuts slowly, the image returns . . .*"

You see, North Jersey has the most shopping malls per square mile in the world. In a radius of 25 miles, there are seven major shopping centers, not including the sprawling outlets in Secaucus or the strip malls bridging Paramus to River Edge to Ridgewood. It's a long, uninterrupted chain of consumerism. It just makes sense. Supply and demand. Market forces. *Mathematics* . . . You know, my boy Johnny—call him Jay Cee—over on Clinton Place? Now that brother knows how to make a buck, a real honest buck. Gots himself an office over there, in *Man*hattan . . . gots himself a view of the clouds, too, I bet. Global Sales Analyst. Fuck, he sounds like a goddamn superhero. Me? I couldn't even do the Sears thing, not anymore. I'm not cut out for the suits. I'm not cut out for *culture*. So I drive, I drive, I keep on driving around but this could be my big brake, ¿tú sabes?

"*. . . I see the picture inside . . .*"

While waiting to merge into Midtown, I Wikipedia *A Certain Ratio* on my black-market BlackBerry and find out why they have such soul in them. A black drummer. Of course a *black drummer*. Anyway, these guys are good; real good. I figure I'll tell Chris about how good they are, how they've changed my outlook, my whole perception on life during this ride today, ~~and maybe we can go catch them at MSG, or wherever~~ (on Wikipedia, it also says they stopped playing—right about the time I was celebrating birthday number five).

Are you alone?

I check my phone at the stoplight on 72nd and still no answer. Just my own message staring back at me. Unblinking like a character in an anime. That's another thing about Chris, he doesn't much like texts, voicemails; hell, the kid doesn't even really like talking on the *phone*.

But I really wish he would, because it's gonna be hell moving around all these DVDs, all these video games, all these watches and sunglasses and leather jackets. The bricks of oregano. The pharmaceuticals. Crackpot Prozac, Viagra, Cialis, Seraphim. The *Hustlers* from 1986. (Yeah, I'm in a little bit of everything.) Vintage, baby. And chances are, the freak—Dan? Dave?—is following him, and with that big, hulking camera too[vii]. Shit—no room for any of it (*opens window*). No room at all.

"*. . . Nothing's changed, nothing to give . . .*"

Still no answer and I'm rolling down 42nd like I own the block. Slow and strolling. I look to the left, I look to the right; all I see is money. As green as Bryant Park. Money in the faces and money in the fat, and money in between each breast pocket of every suit striding to and fro, head up, with conviction. Street theater. Chris can act; I mean, the kid ain't bad. But these guys are the real actors. Chris couldn't touch them. They've got the style, they've got the pose, they've got that money sensibility down, man. Like it's in their skin, like it's underneath them. Like they're running on it. Running to it and for it, and yeah, they're running on it. But why should they have it all? The money is so near I can touch it, even if my fingers are only pressed up against the glass. Maybe it's time I put my whole fist through.

"The soundtrack album was released in 1987," my phone declares, "but has since gone out of print."

I go home and lie down and then it all starts again. I need action, you dig?

"Would you like to view the trailer?"

[vii] If you're reading this right now, if you're coming to this late, if you're just joining us—a note on form: Everything in the world can be separated into AD and BC. Before Chris, and After Dave. (Everything that exists AD exists to be filmed, to be set to music, to be produced and eventually, premiered.) *We flip the switch and make a wish to record ourselves recording ourselves.*

I need to make something *happen*.

Just One Line

Can I tell you something, just one line? I mean, one *more* line. Because, you know, the last one wasn't very good (I'll admit that much), and because, well, I think you're so much more beautiful than all the bad pick-up lines in the world, and even the good ones.

A smile? I see a smile, okay, great. We're on. Wait till we get in the club. Wait till . . .

The waiting was the problem. Johnny Baker had been waiting for over an hour, and it seemed as if he had only moved five feet forward. In actuality, it was only five inches. He was standing outside The Boom Box; he had been standing outside The Boom Box since eleven-fifteen and it was now nearing twelve-thirty. And fortunately, at least The Boom Box had big speakers (with a name like that . . .), so at least Johnny could bump and grind, or at least two-step his way to another (always the next one) pretty face he saw on line, and at least they could talk about what? Life's tragedies, the weather, the common experience of *waiting*, or maybe a story from college? Maybe a story about The End of the World Party, the one that crashed hard. The one in which the cops came and he ran for his life, or at least for his clean record; running away from his own apartment.

Before he could utter a word, or even a line, the girl turned to her friend. Turned away from him.

It's Thursday night, for chrissake! Johnny murmured. Thursday night and look at this fucking wait. My goodness.

Good God. And work is going to bite me in the ass tomorrow. It always does. Work. Fuck.

And here he trailed off, afraid of what might slide onto his sealed lips next, afraid to even think it.

But he was net happy, wasn't he? *Net happy.* That was the phrase he used to describe his current life situation, the last time he had seen his psychiatrist. The last time he had requested a temporary leave from his medication. Prozac and Zoloft, and sometimes Cymbalta. I'm net happy! he repeated, this time aloud, running his hand through his hair, the gel sprinkling snowflakes on pavement. I'm net happy! Making wads of cash, living in Turtle Bay (Turtle Bay!), wearing the best clothes (he looked down at the new Yamamotos adorning his feet and smiled, for the first time that evening), and ~~meeting the hottest chicks.~~

But that's why they call it *net* happy, Johnny said, silently, still talking to himself, lively and charming, as talkative as ever, moving from a moment in his psychiatrist's office to the memory at Lehigh (to be well-liked was all that mattered then), to his office on the twenty-fourth floor of the Bank of America building on Park Avenue (a view of the clouds), to the penthouse he was checking out on Rivington and Clinton (the scene, *New York Magazine* says, is moving downtown)—he was traveling, alright, just not with his feet.

The music grew louder—Rihanna segued into Beyoncé—and Johnny continued to tap his sparkling Y3s on the pavement, looking for someone—anyone—he knew or wanted to know or that he could know for a moment and soak up for the rest of his life. Because that was what life was for Johnny, a memory he could relive at the worst of times and sometimes even during the good ones. And each time would be better, and more meaningful, and more pleasing.

He heard laughter, he heard shouts, he heard the clinking of glasses and the clanking of high heels. He wanted to be inside, *on the other side*, and if he could just move, if he could just slip past the doors, inside the walls that separated him from everyone else, everything would be so much better . . .

He moved a step forward and inched his way into a conversation about Lady Gaga or Katie Osbourne (Gaga, definitely Gaga), the whole time carrying on the conversation in his head that would sound aloud like this:

"There's nothing in the world worse than waiting on line. I rate them in order from best to worst, with AIDS at the top, then terminal cancer—getting my dick chopped off Lorena Bobbitt-style and full-scale paralysis are on the same level for obvious reasons—working at the North Pole the day before Christmas, then random acts of violence that no one would ever willingly subject themselves to but must be included for their potential likelihood to occur at some point (the world's a fucked up place), like circumcision with a butter knife after puberty, or masturbating with sandpaper, followed by world hunger and poverty (lumping them together adds to their standing), and of course, waiting on line to round things out."

While Johnny was talking to himself, he blurted out tidbits of information—"'Alejandro' was on my workout playlist for three weeks straight"—a spattering of nods of the head and faint murmurs to keep it going, anything to stay in the moment and out of it completely.

Why did he succumb to this? Why this seesaw, this tug-of-war with bonding, empathy, companionship? He wanted it, didn't he? Why did he prevent it at the very moment it presented itself? Why was he so immune to emotional contact? Why did he engage in self-sabotage? What was he afraid of?

There were far too many questions swirling in Johnny's head and he stopped listening to everything—himself, the girls—two blonds with hoop earrings and floral skirts—the music blasting from The Boom Box, the telephone ringing off the hook from a nearby payphone (what the fuck is a *pay*phone?), the cat-calls, the questions ("Are you at Joe McNeil's table?"), the tire shrieks, the car honks, every taxi halting to a stop outside the club, everything, and instead only stared, looking from one face to the other until they became a great big box of flesh, one Siamese blond-blur, and he was looking serious, and humble, and studious, looking with great intensity and at nothing at all.

And then the girl—one of them, or both—the girls said in unison: "So what do you do for work?"

Johnny laughed, grinned, ran another hand through his rigid wave of hair and paused to breathe, like he was delivering the State of the Union.

"I'm an investment banker," he said, and for a second he almost handed them his business card. For a second, he didn't feel so excluded, so anguished, so condemned. For a second. "Bank of America."

He thought about the business card: the font (Andale Mono), the name JOHNNY BAKER etched in all-caps across the center, and below that, in smaller type: Regional Equity Analyst

But then he thought about the near-disaster of the afternoon. (He stepped a foot forward.) An e-mail from a subsidiary in China had nearly turned calamitous when he forget to include the necessary data regarding a recent merger and acquisition, or inquisition, which is what he often called it at company cocktail events, sometimes standing with a female coworker, sometimes on the outskirts of a crowd, and always with the same grin, and instead submitted a stream of self-photos he had taken in the locker room the week before, after a particularly good pump (chest and tris). The file names were nearly identical. Did he sabotage himself again? Or was he simply unlucky, an existential hero in his own postmodern tragedy?

He moved forward another step and now he could at least see the thick glass doors, the squat, black man standing in front. At least he could make out the list he was holding in his hand. At least he could imagine his name on there, too (is my name even on the list?). At least he could picture what it was like inside the club: dark, strobe-lit, bodies moving between other bodies, a table full of young, beautiful women, vodka cranberries and screwdrivers in each hand, bass thumping, the crowd clamoring, everyone sweating and slipping deeper into the night . . .

Had he been talking out loud this whole time? The girls turned away from him. Again. He looked behind him, he looked to the side, he looked straight ahead. It was all just one line.

"Attachments are killing me."

Study Abroad

In this part of the story, Francis is playing marbles.

Red, white, and dark green. He's sitting on a wooden bench in the Piazza del Duomo playing marbles, sketching them from sight for the first time, underneath the towering dome. Red, white, and dark green glinting in the sun protruding over the cathedral. Red, white, and dark green etched in pencil in a scrapbook he brought from Buffalo.

Everything else, he left behind.

The Cathedral of Santa Maria del—but to name an object, to name anything . . . is to suppress three-quarters (sometimes all of it; sometimes the whole thing) of life's pleasure, which comes from guessing, little by little . . . which comes from nibbling at the gift—like the way he is nibbling now, even now, on the edge of the bench—which comes from the enigma that must always exist in life—the life, at least the one Francis had made for himself, here in Italy, here in Florence, here in 2005 for three months and seven days—for it to remain exciting in a world of numbers, formulas, cauterized calculations. A world of measurements.

And he is guessing: Julie, Amanda, Mary . . .

She passes again, under the dome, in the midday sun. Always at the same time (Francis checks his watch), always with the same gait: a frisky skip with an air of something practiced.

Mother of God.

He could look at her for hours. Hours that became days, days that became weeks (three months and seven days made thirteen) . . . and sometimes he could (would) look at her, and forget he was even looking at her, forget he was even sketching the Cathedral of Santa Maria del Fiore from sight.

For the first time.

•

Francis had a ritual. Walking through the aisles, peering at the faces. Nuns were good; nuns were the best. There were no nuns. At least there were children—a dozen or so, and almost all under ten years old—and one or two small dogs. As far as he could see.

Walking through the aisles, peering at the faces . . .

The air felt cool and stale as always, except this was only his third time on a plane. Cool and stale and the smell of coffee on carpet and the sound of seatbelts clinking. A stewardess with rosy cheeks and too-red lips smiled above him and began tapping shut the overhead bins. Peering at . . .

"Please direct your attention to the video monitor as we perform our safety procedures and follow . . ."

. . . the faces.

He didn't want his plane to fall from the sky; he didn't want to disappear. Up here, up in the air, alone and lonely, he tried to feel all the love he was afraid to feel on the ground.

•

Born and raised, and born again.

He had to get out, leave Buffalo, study abroad. He had to leave his life there too.

Francis allows a thought to pass before his eyes even as the girl skips by, even as her dark blond hair ripples in the Arno breeze, even as her eyes dart for a moment to meet—no . . .

"You gotta score tonight, Francis, you gotta rail one of these sisters tonight. Plow one of them asses like it's snowing on Christmas. You hear?"

"You hear?"

"You here?"

Francis was here and he wasn't. Francis was just nodding his head. Nodding his head and smiling in the company of strangers he called brothers, as they laughed and belched, as they kept tally with their sport, the kind of game in which scoring was the only thing that mattered.

"She's gonna get the BC tonight."

"What? You never heard of the BC?"

"The BC, baby."

"The beautiful cock."

"And she's gonna wish she had two."

"And she's gonna wish—"

Francis had spent a lifetime just nodding his head, clutching a beer he never quite finished, smiling on the outside. Wishing.

"What, Franny? Are you a faggot now? Are you a queer? Are you a fucking *pussy*?"

Coercion, aggression. Masculinity through violence, especially useful at parties. Masculinity which depended upon every man's capacity to conquer women, fulfill them, wipe them away like leaves on a rake. These roles were learned in childhood, Francis thought, just not his. These roles . . .

These people, they know nothing, he thinks now, as the girl stops skipping, stands in front of the bench where he's still sitting, smiles. Nothing, nothing. These people know nothing about life and me—at least I know *that*. And it's getting worse, all the time, worse, much worse. All the time. Worse instead of better. Much worse.

He looks up, blinks twice, smiles back. She was gone.

And Florence provided the backdrop for his beautiful escape. Rising over the city, winding through the hills, he could move; he could breathe. Along the banks of the river, under the stitches of the past, he felt as if he were present for the first time.

Francis had been studying architecture at the University of Buffalo; now he studied a stranger: the swell of each breast and the curve of her hip when one foot touched ground and the other soared behind her in an S. The shape of her face in profile, long and slender and lovely . . . the way her thick brown eyebrows almost met during certain expressions, a silhouette of shadows flickering across her cheek when she walked under the dome, just before noon, soft as breath. He would trace a line down the center of her forehead, nose, lips pressed together in his scrapbook, shading the tensions of her torso as her blouse ruffled in the breeze.

She was gone.

•

And he was sad for no reason, or no reason he knew of or could guess. Just being there, alone in the plaza filled with people, walking with his headphones on again, walking along the curved sidewalks, which weren't even sidewalks, again.

All he could think about was his memory of himself, who he was or what he had been doing for the last several years, walking along with the street-corner wind and the sad smell of time (his scrapbook almost filled) . . .

What have I been doing? (Walking with his headphones on again.)

The everyday repetition of the same phrases, the same faces, the same smiles at the same intersections of each conversation (which, although sometimes different, all ended with the same graceful good-bye). Tacit answers as soft as sand, a faint nod. He had an obscure panic of entering into an angle of a room that was not already shaded by the comfort of custom.

He was sketching again, but this time his eyes were closed.

•

"It would be interesting to find out what goes on in the moment when someone looks at you and draws all sorts of conclusions."

"One moment? But there are so many . . ."

"Per favore," she tilts her head back, laughs. "Tell me something, then, so that I don't have to make a false picture."

"At school," he says, clearing his throat, "my thing was sketching."

"Sketching?"

"Yes," he nods, bites his lip, messes around with his hair, scratches the lobe of his ear.

Francis and the girl—he never asked her name; she never gave it—are at a café on the other side of the Arno, a panorama of the city spread at their feet. The moon is out, the stars are out . . . her décolletage glistens in the dim light when he pushes her seat back in.

"I could sketch anyone, anywhere."

"Fond of looking?" she laughs, pointing at Francis's scrapbook, inching forward, uncrossing her legs and pressing her knees together. "Or is this not a sightseeing trip?"

He averts her gaze and slips into silence, looking at her, looking at her and him and the round table and the stilted chairs they're sitting on through the mirror behind the bar he's looking into.

"At school, everyone needed a thing. That's just the way it was. The way it is," Francis says, another thought passing through his mind. He removes it the moment he turns his face back to meet hers. "Maybe it goes for everything. Maybe it goes for life, too, because without my drawings, I'm nothing."

"I think you are funny; I think you Americans are all— aren't you even going to ask me my name?"

"What can you be," Francis interrupts, looking back at both of them in the mirror, "if you don't have anything to call your own?"

"But why do you have to *own* anything?"

"We always make objects of each other," Francis returns. "Don't we? I mean not you and me, specifically, but we do. All of us. It's . . ." he pauses and looks directly at her. She is biting her lip and her forehead is furrowed. She seems out of breath or hardly breathing or breathless. He knows there is a difference. "Unavoidable, isn't it? Something we can't rid ourselves of."

"What's that? And aren't you even going to—"

"Our desire to occupy space. Our desire to . . ." Francis frowns, letting his gaze linger again on the tattered scrapbook. "I don't know. Hold on to each and every piece of it. Like we might die if we didn't."

"You think people can just disappear like that?"

"You think people can't?"

•

Before Francis fastens his seatbelt, he reaches over to slide the window shut.

The Waiting Room

Let me just say from the outset, I'm an impatient man.

"And I bore easily," I added, as I dotted the last *i* in my name[viii] and glanced back at the receptionist. She was a young girl with shoulder-length curly brown hair and hoop earrings. She is wearing too much makeup, I thought, as she pointed past me, indicating the stacks of magazines in a pile on the coffee table at the center of the waiting room. Each couch was empty.

"Make yourself at home."

•

The sun was fierce, the land seemed to glisten and drip with steam. Here and there grayish-whitish specks showed up clustered inside the white surf, with a flag flying above them perhaps. Settlements some centuries old, and still no bigger than pinheads on the untouched expanse of their background. We pounded along, stopped, landed soldiers; went on, landed soldiers; went on . . .

Jackson paused for a moment to turn the page that was fluttering in the wind.

"Went on . . ."

"Went on?" one passenger asked. Her face was like an alligator's: reptile grin and scaly tan skin and a snout, and

---

[viii] Sometime I forget who is meant to speak and when. Sometimes I forget if it's really Chris Selden, or me.

eyes shrouded in big, oval sunglasses. She was leaning back on her cushioned seat aboard the ferry, clicking her heels impatiently.

"Went on, landed custom-house clerks to levy toll in what looked like a God-forsaken wilderness, with a tin shed and a flagpole lost in it."

Jackson paused to wipe the sweat forming on his forehead, brushing his parted, oiled hair to the side, and pointed to the brick buildings and factories dotting the African coast with his green-lined parasol, instructing the passengers to follow along with their tour maps as they went

DEEPER INTO CONRAD'S
HEART OF DARKNESS

as the brochure indicated.

"We passed various places—trading places—with names like Gran' Bassam, Little Popo; names that seemed to belong . . ."

Jackson kept talking, hardly hearing anything—least of all what he was saying; only the gentle lapping of the Congo River: the River Congo by-way-of-Red Hook—as the woman with the sunburn and big sunglasses followed the stops along her map with one distended index finger, the tip painted white.

Inner Station, Central Station, Play Station— where passengers could pick up their children before disembarking—if he was lucky he'd make it back to port by six o'clock. The chick who plays Kurtz's mistress, Jackson was thinking, is a total babe; the kind of woman I could really do a number on, the kind of

". . . warm, thick, heavy, sluggish . . ."

woman I could take to dinner, spend a whole evening

". . . cut off for ever from everything you had known once—somewhere—far away—"

with, the kind of woman who is

". . . monstrous and free. It was unearthly. And the men were—No, they were not inhuman. Well, you know, that was . . ."

worth every dollar.

Or at least equal to the amount he had spent on the latest 76-inch LG plasma. But at least that was on sale.

Jackson was so deep in thought that eventually, even the calm lapping of the river became inaudible; even the splash of water became inaudible. Eventually. The gurgled shriek. The flop of limbs. Someone screamed. Inaudible. When he looked up from his pamphlet, the lady with the alligator snout was gone. Eventually.

"The horror!"

Something unutterable.

And then a faint murmur, a dim buzz, an almost indiscernible hum. A vibration. Something unutterable.

LOL what's up? You still at the dentist?

•

"I'm burning up!"

"You're not convinced that that is enough?"

"Doc—"

"Yes, Tyler?"

"I'm on fire."

"Yes," Doctor Ydobon held up a vanity mirror in front of Tyler—Tyler hot and damp and coughing ash, smoke rising from the cuffs of his jeans—and nodded his head. "That you are my boy."

Ydobon turned the dial on the Victrola on the counter and Madonna's voice came in louder through the static and scratching. He thrust a thermometer in Tyler's lips—Tyler's lips, those pencil-thin lines of red ain't much for lips, but—

"That you are."

"I'm burning up, burning up for your love."

"For your loveeeee," Ydobon interrupted the music, his loud croon spiraling down the hallway as nurses and administrative attendants poked their heads in. He waved to each passerby with white latex gloves, dabbing at Tyler's face now and then with some more mothballs soaked in a milky solvent, the needle still spinning wildly on the phonograph.

"Doctor—what'd you administer to the patient now?"

"Administer?" Ydobon asked, twirling a reflex hammer around his wrist like a pistol.

Minister? the echo followed.

"Administer?" Ydobon asked, twirling a reflex hammer around his wrist like a pistol.

Minister? the echo followed.

"Administer?" Ydobon asked, twirling a reflex hammer around his wrist like a pistol.

Minister? the echo followed[ix].

Tyler spit out the thermometer as his mouth evacuated his face, each gum making a fleshy slap as they hit the floor, the needle still spinning. Ydobon threw a stethoscope over his head and began to crawl on the tiled linoleum.

"Do you want to see me down on my knees?" Ydobon asked, before Madonna had a chance to.

"I'm on fire."

The words came from Tyler's eyes, since he could no longer speak, and Doctor Ydobon nodded, cocking his

---

[ix] It's so damn hard to concentrate with the same song playing on a loop, and the receptionist's cackle, and the rattle of cars passing by, somewhere outside . . .

head to take in Tyler—Tyler's straw blond hair blazing red, his green eyes a charcoaled ash. "Of course you are."

Without a body, without a voice.

"They call that smiling with your eyes. Old modeling trick," Ydobon added, pirouetting on his tiptoes, lips parted halfway like remembering a story he read as a child. "Or was it smoldering?"

"Do you want to see me down on my knees . . ."

"I'm burning up!" Tyler's eyes screamed again, both palms pressed to his flushed cheeks, the smell of flesh dissolving like month-old pastrami in the microwave . . . "For chrissake—" his eyeballs bulged. "I'm on fire!"

The fire alarm's shrieks tore through the small examining room as water cascaded from above and Doctor Ydobon flicked his nametag around and threw his spindly arms up toward the ceiling in ecstasy.

"Doctor—what'd you administer to the patient now?"

"Administer?"

Minister?

A twirl. Whirl of metal splitting air. Reflex hammer like a pistol. Tilted. The vanity mirror. Nametag gleaming back into view.

Minister?

NOBODY

•

"What was his name?"

"That guy?"

"Yeah, your ex—the model."

"Oh," Alice hesitated. Everyone at the crowded booth was speaking in shouts. A strobe light flickered across the club and it looked like sunlight passing over shut eyelids. "Chris Selden." As she said the name, she seemed to look past her friend, past the dance floor, past the club; a glance outside of time and space . . . "I think he's a writer now."

"No, no—the other one," the girl sitting next to Alice shook her head, furrowed her brow, slapped her delicate thighs, sheathed in a floral skirt. "Billy?"

"Bailey," Alice said. "He's in . . ." her mind raced. Berlin, Buenos Aires, Rio? He said he'd only be gone a month, but that was a year ago . . . "I really don't have a clue," she said, and placed her lips on the rim of her highball, not really taking a sip, just letting the vodka graze her mouth.

"I think there's more coming," the girl shouted over the thumping bass, pointing to Alice's iPhone vibrating wildly on the table, hiccupping past glasses and bowls of ice, threatening to drop off the edge. "Should we send someone outside to get them?"

But Alice only stared deeper into the alcove of her memories. *More coming?* She was thinking about Bailey, his pale face, his small dark eyes, his sharp laugh like a snicker in a squeal—something flashing erratically like strobe lights—where was he? Where did he go?

In purgatory. Still waiting. ☹

•

. . . In another sense, this "interference" is always occurring; technology only emphasizes it, while at the same time reminding us who we are . . . what we are, which is persons deferred: a mind that is constantly somewhere else, with our bodies in quite another place.

Q: Humor—a kind of playfulness, a kind of meta-dialogue—seems to be an important component in your work.

A: I like to communicate with the reader, you know? Ask a question, place a footnote here, follow the route or take a detour. Read the stories in any order you'd like.

Q: Any order?

A: Sure. Critics want to talk about plot, about sequence, about *characters*. But the only element that interests me in my work is the reader. I suppose I've always been characterized as . . .

•

. . . the emotional type, a real romantic—él tiene la pasión, you know? Capable of loving on the intuitive level. Very sensitive. He's the kind of guy who writes poetry at the dentist office. He likes holding hands in the dark, the tingle of a black-and-white movie, and Lauren Bacall in 1946. It says it right here . . .

I threw down the magazine and slowly turned my head. Nobody was looking at me and yet I felt like I was on the inside of somebody else's joke. Was someone writing *this*? The words seemed to be communicating through the page, as if they were winking, whispering something that had never occurred to me. I glanced back at the pile of magazines, at the one spread open on the carpeted floor—

He's the kind of guy who writes poetry at the dentist office.

—and looked at the poem I had been absentmindedly scribbling as I flipped pages, tearing through people, places, images, coordinates; the interminable space between arrival and exit.

In the middle of my life, I lost myself
In the middle of my life, I found myself
In the middle of the lost & found,
I lost my way & found you

Each word seemed to be expressing more than the accumulation of its letters. It existed below the surface, deeper than sound. A wisp of hair, a whisper. Tendrils of wind. Barren branches. The glaze of frost this morning. Air. I looked for traces of you—a reader, sitting somewhere, maybe even a waiting room—but saw nothing to indicate anything out of the ordinary, least of all alarm; I saw nothing except for the young brunette that called from her desk behind the glass window, blowing bubbles:

"Doctor Johnson's
still tied up.
Sorry."
The bubble burst on her lips.

I imagined my dentist with his arms tied behind his back, face down on the tiled floor—blindfolded, maybe—and turned the page.

". . . me?"

"Yes," I said, looking at my father for the first time—I mean, really seeing him. "Oh my God, yes. What a difference it is—I mean, how different everything looks!"

He smiled as I continued looking at things, darting my head up and down and sideways, only a few feet more until we reached the car. The color of the storefront's awning, the light inside the lamppost, the sidewalk curb, the way the moon lit up the street from a new angle. Things. I could no longer speak, not with words, at least. It was as if I were seeing everything again, but for the first time. I pressed both my hands to my face, pressed both my hands to the round eyeglasses propped on my nose. My face. I couldn't wait to see my face in the mirror. Look at myself. I mean, really see myself. My face.

"Is this better—or worse?"

White-brick home with a red roof in a field of poppies.

"Better or worse?"

Ten years later . . .

I remember hope, cold flesh, The Cars' "Just What I Needed," the barren smell of my cornea burning, sound of an incision, a sliver of skin, suction pressure to my eyeball, once, twice, lying still, staring at a green light

light

light

It drifted farther away until it escaped me completely.

I stood up slow. When I walked outside, the view looked hazy; a sensation like seeing things underwater. Including me.

". . . me?"

My father's voice. His hands guiding my own. A visor propped on my nose. *Just What I Needed*. I shook my head. I turned my face down toward my lap when he closed the door.

"How do you like your new eyes?"

I turned my head. Silhouettes of shapes. A faint retracing. Echo.

"Your new eyes?"

White-brick home with a red roof in a field of poppies, I thought. White-brick home with a—

"Very sensitive," I heard myself say.

A sensation like being underwater. I turned my head. Silhouette of shapes.

A faint
retracing
echo.

"Can you see me?"

". . . me?"

•

"Me?"

When my name was called I hesitated only briefly, stumbling past the reception window and along the hall until a lithe, blue-eyed attendant sat me down on the examining chair and tottered off. A magazine was unfurled on the burnished lino counter.

Marietta listened to the long, plaintive siren and shuffled her feet toward the sliding doors. There was something about a train whistle, the shrill ringing, the faint rustle of the engine. It never ceased to intone a note of melancholy. She thought of long good-byes and

I turned my head.

"Scott, thought I'd never—"

"I'm sorry for the delay," Doctor Johnson said, slapping a bib clip across my chest and propping my mouth open with a bite block. The rest of my salutation surfaced as babble.

I began drooling, saliva sliding down my chin. Vanilla, honey, blackcurrant. The blue-eyed attendant's scent lingered in the room. Doctor Johnson inched closer. The scent grew stronger.

Babble.

"Yes, sorry about that," Scott repeated, humming an old Madonna song. He was thumbing at a smear of crimson on his neck.

"Were you waiting long?"

Everyone Born in 1985

Are you really wearing that?

—What's wrong with this?

—What's wrong? (laughs) You call that a coat?

—Whoa, listen to Beau Brummel over here.

—Who?

—Never mind.

—Are those . . . glow-in-the-dark? Hey—we are making one stop, okay?

—Where do you want to go now?

—T.J. Maxx. We can find you a better outfit there.

—. . . . .

—Okay, I'm joking. Listen, this is a big night, isn't it? Four-year retrospective. Chris Selden isn't going to want to talk to me if you—

—If nothing, Selden doesn't give a shit for clothes, and he certainly doesn't give a shit about events like these.

—But it's his movie.

—It's not *his*, it's Dave Goldstein's. From what I know, Selden's terrified of the whole thing. I don't even think he knew he was in the film, let alone starring. Not until he read about it. Not until he woke up in Cannes.

—Anyway, there'll be lots of people there. And Chris, of course. You can introduce us again, right? He wasn't much of a talker when we first met. But he'll remember me—I mean, how could he—

—Sure, but listen, he's not the same person he was when I knew him. I mean, when I saw him every night in the newsroom. Before he left. Before I left.

—How do you mean?

—When you look at him, you don't see a person, you see a ghost. That's who I see. Absent and present at the same time—is that even possible? Of course it's possible—and see, he's gone too far. He's on the other side. It's clear to me . . . when I look in his eyes, I see someone far off away from here. I see someone who likes to remember things more than he likes to live them.

—That's a good line of dialogue, right there.

—You got that right. (lengthy pause) Anyway, he got rehabilitated—but that was a long time ago. A long time ago . . .

—*Rehabilitated?* What the hell does that mean?

—Just what I said. Awhile back. Before I left for Austin. Before I came back. Before you two—when did you two meet? Anyway, hospitals are getting more and more like nightclubs. People want a good time to the end. That's all he could say about it. Apparently, he'd moved on from song lyrics to film dialogue.

—A curious specimen.

—He's the only person I ever knew who went to grad school because he was curious what'd it be like.

—Sounds a lot like me.

—Not quite. You're bored; he's fascinated—by everything. Like a five-year-old. A precocious five-year-old. He gets his Master's because he's desperate to learn, to soak it up; all of life is rapture for him, you see? Pornography. Sensual explosion. Emotional, erotic. I see it in his eyes, like it was yesterday, like it was today. It's a different game, he said, and I like this one better. He gets his Master's then he tells me, after he graduates, he tells me on the phone,

How can I understand anything about literature when all I've done is read books?

—Deep.

—Last I saw him, after he got back from Brazil, after the whole readjustment, the hospital-cum-nightclub . . . he looked like a fucking vampire.

—He was wearing a cape?

—No, like a model vampire. Like *Interview with the Vampire*. That's what we were doing actually. At some point. I don't remember when. Except I fell asleep because he just rambled for forty minutes. Maybe an hour.

—I think I read that interview.

—Is it wrong to get a boner after seeing your book in the storefront at Barnes & Noble?

—A valid question.

—Something he asked me once, a little while ago.

—What'd you say?

—Only if you're a girl.

—"Leave Me Alone"—New Order! I love this.

—We're standing still.

—*"You get these words wrong, You get these words wrong, Every time . . ."* Hey—turn this up higher!

—Goddamn rush hour traffic. You have an awful voice for singing, by the way.

—. . . . .

—Are you crying? You're crying. Why are you—

—I'm too sensitive. Like my dentist says.

—The thing is, I can never tell when you're joking, or being real. If you're ever being real.

—Why don't we take an alternate route? What about straight down Riverside? I love riding down Riverside. Hands halfway out the window. The ripping wind . . . there'll be food, right? I'm ravenous. That feeling? That's real, Charlie.

—You're always hungry.

—I have a tapeworm inside my stomach, sucking everything up. I eat for two.

—How about Monica? She's not pregnant, is she?

—No . . . unless she has been spitting out the pill every night. Anyway, we mostly do it the other way.

—The other way?

—Yeah man, I am obsessed. Those beautiful buns. I just want to bury my face in there, sometimes.

—Don't choke.

—Speaking of choking, check this out: "Jane Fonda says that she is not afraid of death anymore." Wow. Bravo. Why is that on the news ticker? Would you run that shit in the *Star-Ledger*, Charlie?

—On the front page.

—Hey, you got any floss?

—Floss?

—Things get stuck to me. Stuck in me.

—. . . . .

—I'm very tactile, is all I'm saying. Very—

—Shut up, Clarence. For just a second.

—. . . . .

—Okay, resume.

—Oh fuck.

—What?

—I forgot the tickets . . .

—Forgot the tickets!

—Do you hear an echo?

—Jesus, Clarence. What the fuck? I only gave them to you because you wanted to show them off to Monica's friends and now you've left them at your apartment.

—Hey, can we turn around? Take Broadway, please.

—No, we're never going to make it.

—But we are VIP, right? Friends of the star. Use some of that V-Man charm, Charlie.

—Fuck you. You have the worst memory, Clarence. The worst memory.

—It's because I'm only ever thinking about me. It takes practice . . .

—You got that right.

—. . . but inevitably, I find myself forgetting about everyone and everything else. Time evaporates. Like I'm lost in space.

—We are never going to make it. I'll use my press pass. You can play photographer.

—Press pass?

—I kept mine.

—Isn't that . . . illegal?

—Maybe I figured I'd be back someday. Who knows.

—Danger-danger (danger-danger) . . . like that White Williams song. Oh, this sounds like it will be a good night.

—Yeah, a night to remember. Or completely forget. In one way, out the other, right? That's how you operate.

—What day is it again?

—Case in point. Shit, we are going in the wrong direction. Hey—make the next left. I hate missing the previews.

—There'll be previews? Shit!

—. . . . .

—Relax, we'll get there fashionably late! (nudges Charlie) Some of us more than others. And then you can introduce me, right? Right?

—You know, sometimes I feel like he's off, burned-out, inconsolable—but sometimes I feel the same way, like I am suffocating, like I am drowning in it, whatever it is that makes people feel anxious, and nervous, and desperate, and alone, so alone, plodding toward an empty house, with an empty room, no bed either, nowhere to rest and nowhere to fuck, and nothing to do and never enough time to do it anyway, or else no sense of time at all, *no time*, nada, nothing and nowhere to be, like everyone born in 1985 is doomed.

—1985?

—Yeah, 1985. Something he told me once. And I believe it.

—But that can't be. I was born that year, too.

—And then I realize this isn't a story written by Bret Easton Ellis. This isn't about how fucked up the world is and has been and can be. You read one, you've read 'em all. This is a story about hope.

—Amen. Well-put, Charlie. Exactly what I was thinking.

—Thank you.

—And I hope we get there soon.

WINTER

How It Cuts

I am standing at baggage claim reaching my hands in my jeans pocket. Reaching for my iPod, staring at the concourse, the luggage, the briefcases, the boxes, the conveyor belt, slouching forward—me and the bags—watching the bags until they all begin to look like one bag, and it isn't my own.

DON'T RIDE WITH STRANGERS catches my eye and I look away at the nearly vacant concourse, running one hand through my hair—they had it cut before the flight—feeling the folds and the waves and the way it's been shaped; imagining what it must look like because I hate mirrors; I try to avoid mirrors when I can, and one night I had a dream in which I smashed all of them.

I feel the meticulous part, the tight, buzzed edges where the brown-blond strands stop, how they bleed into each sideburn and how one hair is much longer than all the rest, how one hair reaches down past my left eye, how one hair obscures my vision, how it cuts it in half—WITH STRANGERS—and then I get bored and I remember my iPod, finding it, clasping it, flipping on *play*.

The tuning is out of whack because I sweat too much; I sweat too much and I sweat all over my iPod and now the tuning is out of whack and the sound goes in and out, in and out, louder and softer and sometimes clearly audible for half-a-second (maybe more) but I think I like it that way: in between, halfway in the music and halfway outside of it, and it occurs to me: I like myself that way, too.

In and out, in and out.

And in between this thought I look up as another bag passes me. *Swoosh.* I look up and I stare at the television monitor propped on the white wall.

Because a building is blowing up in slow motion.

A Slice of Life

I remember it like it was yesterday. And maybe it was.

Or at least it feels that way, because there was a camera. A man with a big, black video camera, the red light turned on, recording everything.

So now I remember it again and again, but each time, I remember it differently.

We were all sitting around an oval table. *Ovoid*, according to the hostess who seated us. "Ovoid," she said, "like the cosmic egg of all creation." (She was wearing a refurbished checkered kimono and her breasts popped out around the same time she spoke.)

Introductions, salutations, kisses and hugs. Everyone was touching each other without touching each other, and I tried to count the space—maybe the exact amount of molecules—that separated flesh from flesh, a pair of eyes gazing and reclaiming each other pair.

I took a look around the room: recycled wood from the Andes, flora from the south of France, a rustic swing set from—Paterson? The menu didn't say—in the center, and breathed deeply. Maybe I sighed. We were at the grand opening of À Votre God. I didn't get the joke but then again, I don't speak French. We clapped our hands, we rolled our eyes, maybe we tittered. I'm watching this with the sound muted. We were Clarence Byrne, Chris Selden, Alice Waters, Joël, Dave Goldstein, Barney—no, Bailey—Lazar, and me, well you know my name.

It smelled like cotton candy. Everything smelled like cotton candy. Burning sugar. Thermal infusion. Centrifuge. Current immersion. Aromatic accompaniment. I'm making these terms up but I remember the smell. The scent of progress?

Bailey was looking at Alice who was looking at Chris who was looking at nothing. Because his eyes were closed. He wasn't sleeping, but he seemed to be dreaming, because his forehead was slightly furrowed and I could see a pale light under each eyelid, which I knew was the light of someone reimagining everything.

I wanted to prod him, poke him, maybe slap him on the cheek, but Alice had planted one gloved hand there, caressing his mouth, opening his lips with her webbed fingers and trying to stick her tongue through.

". . . featuring sustainable, local, artisan indigenous, salvaged, recycled and good-wood materials, including found, salvaged, reclaimed AND recycled building materials; handmade porcelain dinnerware by local artisans; bread baskets handcrafted by the indigenous Mapuche people of Patagonia; salvaged wood tables handcrafted by . . ."

The waitress—who looked just like the hostess except with blond (refurbished?) hair—continued her homily and I wondered where the rest of the players were. The dining room, draped by an enormous fluorescent chandelier, was almost empty.

Time stretched like a rubber band, it stopped, it started, it lengthened each time a voice track clicked in ("Still? Sparkling?"). Hours passed, a minute or two went by, unless I'd been sitting there, surrounded and alone, making time stop myself, making it assume an untangled ribbon of hair (blond? Refurbished?) and glancing at my phone, too, wondering if À Votre God was on a list, somewhere, wondering when the moment would arrive. Some big bang.

"A little pepper please?" Clarence implored, massaging his teeth with his tongue, and he looked disconcerted. That's the word. I hardly know him but he looked *disconcerted*. "A few more shakes?"

"Do they have kin-know-ah here?" Alice asked. She wore glasses; she sounded as if she were reading the words from a card. "Do they have *chickpeas?*"

"Of course they have chickpeas," Joél cut in. "Reconstituted too."

"Naturally."

"It's keen-wah," Clarence corrected, shaking his head and muttering, while the black pepper spewed forth, above him, and from the right. I wonder what Clarence looks like when he's not wearing that mask he puts on when he speaks; that mask he puts on when he does anything.

"Keen what?"

"Exactly."

"Super indigenous," Bailey cut in.

"Everything," Chris interrupted, opening his eyes for the first time that evening, "is indigenous."

I didn't think anyone was here for chickpeas; I didn't think anyone was here for quinoa. Arugula spaghetti, oven-baked beer, disappearing ravioli, and of course, Lifé, which was the hottest thing on the market. Never-before-seen, or at least not like this. And it was the special of the night. Harvested, hand-picked, and bottled, then blown up in a lab to resemble a polyhedral soufflé. *Equilateral* was the word on everyone's lips and the press was making a big deal of it.

"Thrilling"

"Addictive"

"Lecherous"

I didn't know what they meant by that last bit, but it was enough for Clarence to secure a table on opening night.

Clarence, who was looking more disconcerted with every passing plate.

It is getting hotter all the time—I think now, as I thought then.

Hotter, hotter. So damn hot.

It was heavy with heat and my clothes clung to me; the collared golf shirt, the olive slacks, the fanny pack around my waist (ol' reliable ensemble of the Tourist). It was heavy with heat and still, the air-conditioner roared, the flat-blades circled, my damp calves stiffened.

The presentation would begin any minute. I was only confused as to whether I was attending the performance, or a part of it.

Everyone was exchanging satisfied looks, feeling that lovely feeling of being surrounded by friends, swallowing their own saliva, smoothing out the folds of each reprocessed towelette on their laps. The pleasure of chewing and swallowing. Swallowing and chewing. I watched Chris run a hand through his hair—once, twice—and saw his lips tighten; a sprinter waiting for the gunshot. Waiting, waiting . . . a slight pause—not a full stop, not even a semicolon, more like an interruption or interference ("Still? Sparkling?") just an em dash—and then the sound of bells, a shrill whistle, the roar of a plane overhead, outside, on its route to JFK.

"Is it time?"

I sat back and watched the procession enter: a long succession of kimonos, all specked in different checkered patterns, and each hand holding something hidden under a shiny, silver-plated dish.

"This is better than TV," Alice mouthed, letting one glove slip to her lap, as something by Schubert[x] strummed majestically on the PA.

---

[x] I only know because I Shazam'd.

"No—" I said, shaking my head, letting Dave—the man behind the camera—letting him catch my gaze. "This *is* TV."

When we were finally presented with Lifé, half the party was drunk (edible cocktails), Clarence was talking loudly about the prospect of an *All My Children* go-see, more ravioli were disappearing into Joél's mouth, Chris was sitting with his eyes closed—maybe he was actually sleeping this time—and Dave, Dave was still filming all of it. I spit out a dehydrated olive's pit and reached for my cell phone in the bag around my waist. Business was good; business was always good if you were in the business I was in.

"A slice of Lifé," a hovering waitress announced, and almost immediately, the sound of clinking forks followed.

Lifé looked just like how I imagined it. Reverse Gelatin—they call it gelification; the molecular change of a liquid food to a solid, jelly-like substance—re-liquidated into a puddle on the plate. A pyramidal puddle with hints of pop rocks.

"You sip it," another man—the chef?—whispered in my ear. "Slowly."

"Well—is it better?" Clarence asked, looking at me for approval, looking at me for any sign of satisfaction, for any intuition that it might not be worth whatever he was investing in it—effort, energy, money. Time.

"Better than what?" I asked, removing my lips from the bowl as the whole table laughed. The ground shook. The chandelier—well, it looked like it was teetering from the ceiling, and I heard a few more whispers, a few more forks clinking, a few more exclamations. A few more snaps.

"Better than life."

A Work of Art

The act of creation comes when I arch my back and turn my head in profile, and catch Julie's furrowed brow, her scrutinizing gaze, the way her eyes look through me like I'm dust, like I'm dust on a piece of pasteboard. A mannequin with hazel eyes. Dust.

Before that look, I was minding my own business, acting polite and even a little interested—I'm a good actor and I made some money moving from one ABC soap to another a few years back—simultaneously engaged and nonchalant, and aware of my surroundings: the smell of steamed polyester and dark coffee, the way the sun cast a shadow over everyone, the clipboards, the pencils in each hand, five of them jotting down notes, everyone seated at a conference table, the chalkboard at the head of the room with the list—

SUPERHEROES
CELEBRITIES
CLASSIC UNDERWEAR ADS
WARDROBE MALFUNCTIONS
CROSS-DRESSING/OPPOSITES
HALLOWEEN IN JULY
DEVILS/ANGELS
MARDI GRAS/CARNIVAL
DECADES* HISTORY OF UNDERWEAR

—remnants from a marketing meeting fifteen minutes earlier, I thought, and started to shape my lips into a smile. I know what people want, and I was playing to the field. "Now *that* is something I'd wear to a family barbecue . . ." ". . . What's this fabric called? . . ." ". . . I think the jock would sell quite nice . . ." "Was Jack Rogers your *first* choice for a brand name? . . ." I don't even register what I'm saying; as soon as the words leave my lips they're gone, dispersed into the stale air or out the open window, flung breathless toward the wind tunnel on Broadway, but I hear my tone, how I underscore certain words, the hint of a laugh curling under my tongue after each line.

I was in the moment. Or at least pretending to be. But now I'm out of it, thinking about that gaze while Julie cocks her head and purses her lips and jots something else down, and Donna makes a noise in between a hiccup and a wheeze and I think of something clever to say, something that would betray any sense of extrasensory perception, something that would make me seem totally involved in this fitting when Michael, the president of the company, says: "Look at that torso! My goodness. A torso like a salamander . . ." and nods at his own assessment. I am at the office of Whipped Skivvies on the fifth floor of 610 Broadway, in a room with five strangers; two of them buyers, one of them a designer, trying on samples while everyone gapes and take notes. Some only gape.

"Yeah, salamander torso," I say, creasing my lips into a smile and rubbing my abdomen, which is now twisted and jutted forward, upon Julie's instructions. "That's actually why I can eat so much. Lots of room for food to go to."

Everyone laughs except me. Someone asks about my Web site and I give him the URL while my mind drifts to another scene completely and I think that nobody ever knows where anything goes, much less what they consume.

"Is that capitalized?"

You can never tell anyone anything about what you've seen, or where you've been, or the people you've met there, and what you've done. It's no use trying to paint them a pretty picture because they'll never see it the way you saw it, the way I see it . . . and the way I see it, not just the image but the sensations, the intangibles, the human sensibilities . . . the way I see it can't be encapsulated in a photograph or a video. It can't be translated. The thing is to express the very substance of your thoughts as you read this; nothing there but the flashing pictures in the movie in your mind, and that's enough, that's alright, that's everything.

Now I observe the billboard gleaming on the corner of Houston and Lafayette.

THE WHOLE WORLD IS TALKING

"Well, look at the color, honey, look at that *color*. Does 2(x)ist have this? Does anyone?"

"Is that the new iPad?"

"I don't know, how can you tell?"

"Smash it on the floor."

"Oh, okay."

"Does anyone have this *exact* color?"

I begin to hear everything as if I am half-asleep at a lecture, a lecture in which I only catch occasional words or phrases, except I am hardly half-asleep; I am alert, frantically trying to catch choice words or phrases, trying to recall the details.

"Yes, that's exactly why we're copying CK, right down to the stitching . . ." ". . . you bet it does . . ." ". . . I say let's do it before they can . . ." ". . . stealing costs a lot of money . . ." ". . . look at that LIFT! For chrissake . . ." ". . . then get Reggie in Accounts to make the call . . ." ". . . the power of suggestion works best when suggested over and over . . ." and here I pause, thinking hard, concentrating, because that is *really* good, I think; I think that is something worth jotting down, and I even think it sounds good enough to be an advertisement, scrawled in cursive below a picture of my sweat-stained body, like the one on the bus stop on Bowery and Fourth: me in khaki shorts, palm trees dancing in the background. Donna makes another high-pitch squeal, that sound between a hiccup and a wheeze; she does it every time she says the word "lift" and I don't blush but I begin to smirk; I can't help it. Is that a tick? I wonder. I wonder: Is she just embarrassed?

The mouths move, talking about pouches, fabrics, contours, two-tones, inseams, elastics, talking about the inept manufacturer in Thailand, and I think about an underwear exposé, I think about trade secrets; fashion industry backstabbing and style-scooping; maybe I think about my other career as a journalist, and I think that these people will say anything around me. Around and behind and through me.

I've been a journalist, a teacher, an actor, a model. I was only ever a writer. I've done too much, and too often, and now I think I'm destined to merely go through the motions, destined to roam the earth, hoping, restless, like the earliest Americans, except not even this land is a part of me; I am forever an exile.

Did I suck too much out of life or did I suck all the life out of me?

"Julie, how is the baby? Is it Samantha? Is she walking?" And now this in between my crotch and a tape measure that Julie has brought out to make sure she's got the *right* specifications and I wonder why in the world my crotch, my ass, I wonder why in the world a tape measure millimeters from my penis would make anyone think about this lady's newborn. It occurs to me that the mind is a funny thing. It occurs to me that there are many ways in which to enter a story. And each point of entry is open; each point connects back to every other point, so that the story can be reversed, reworked, rearranged, and read like an uninterrupted season bleeding across the year.

Google my name and the first eight modifiers that come up are:

Model
Muscle
Facebook
Bulge
Cuba
Weight
Recline
Writer

People ask me everything: What's your diet? What's your workout? What's it like to be on the cover of *DNA*? What's it like to be on TV? What's it *like* . . . but no one ever asks me what it takes to be like me.

I don't know the answer to that myself. I think it's half-comic, half-peculiar, and wholly tragic. The fact that I can't look at someone, at anyone, without sizing them up, without writing them into the story. Every encounter in life viewed from above; a tracking shot from the camera eye of a cruising hawk. It wears on me.

Most people think the real tragedy of writers is that we are destined to be appreciated for our art long after we are dead, but the real tragedy is our inability to live as anything other than unconscious observers.

It has always been this way. As if I can only view any experience as a series of scenes with an unseen stagehand directing traffic. Something in my chemicals, I don't know. The way I've been programmed. Or, I think, the program itself. I think that's why I began writing. For a kind of recognition, not of my talent, not for an audience, but to know that I was not deranged.

"Are you crazy?" a man in a prison-orange vest and khakis rolled up to his ankles mouths. "The pouch is *not* too big. The pouch is fine," he says, scratching his scalp furiously, tearing his skin. Does this guy have a tick too? I think. "The pouch is absolutely *perfecto*." Then he looks at me and I already know what he's going to say.

"Chris—you speak Spanish, right?"

I nod and he claps his hands wildly, like I've just recited the ABCs backward.

"But Selden—Selden is . . ."

"Irish," I fill in.

Don't these people know all of this already? I think. I think: Haven't they seen the movie?

"—" was a remarkable hit in 2008; so big it won the Palme d'Or at Cannes, so big it surpassed *Twilight* at the box office for a week and even if they haven't seen it, they must have heard about it, because the blurbs were everywhere.

> *"Shocking." "Post-Postmodern."*
> *"Disarming." "Revolutionary."*

The French called it avant-garde, the British dubbed it sci-fi, and the Muslim community in Singapore somehow saw it as a romantic comedy. Dave Goldstein's post-postmodern masterpiece. Everyone hailed it differently, and everyone hailed it just the same. It is peculiar how so many people can see so many different things in the same thing. But I guess it's like anything else.

"Irish . . ." Michael repeats and hangs on the word for a while, lowering his glasses on the bridge of his nose. "Jake—" he looks at the short man in the prison-orange vest—"I would have never guessed," and Jake just whistles, maybe imagining what I look like without the polka-dot briefs I'm wearing now.

My name is Chris Selden and I am Cuban and I am Irish, and for this fitting I am *Caucasian* and for a Macy's catalog later today I'll be *Hispanic*. My name comes from the Old English *scylf* meaning *shelf* and the family crest translates into: *To suffer is best*, but I decide not to fill him in on this little detail. Instead, Jake recites the particulars from my comp card. I have hazel eyes and dirty blond hair and I'm five-eleven and three-quarters but the card, as I can see now, flopping wildly in Jake's upturned hand, the card says I'm six-foot and one inch, so I guess you can't believe everything you read. And certainly not anything you see.

CHRIS SELDEN UNCUT!

When my eyes catch the *Soap Digest* the young brunette is reading, she slides it on her lap and her apple cheeks grow rosy. Pigtails and thick, oval eyeglasses. An intern? I wonder. I wonder if the magazine is referring to my interview, or my dick.

My mind drifts to the interviews.

"My parents got used to it by the time I was nine, and every day, I walked around the house completely nude."

"I like holding hands in the dark, the tingle of a black-and-white movie, and Lauren Bacall in 1946."

"Worse than that. Like a thing to buy and sell. Like a commodity. Except I wasn't only selling myself, I was selling them. I was selling them back to themselves. Follow?"

"Acting is very different to modeling in that I don't think you can just pick it up one day out of the blue and run with it, unless perhaps you're Britney Spears. I heard she was really outstanding in *Crossroads*."

"It's not my doing. I'm available to be consumed electronically, and *you*, you get the aura while everyone else gets the traces, and yet they love it and keep eating, not knowing that there is a real meal they will never taste."

"You *cannot* ignite a stick of dynamite and wonder why it is about to explode when it is inches from your lips."

"I wrote a trilogy out of order and then rearranged it, because the whole of life is like that—a cut-up—and when you cut into the present, the future leaks out."

"Boredom is a bomb in your brain. And it hurts."

No one could tell if I was putting them on or if I was being serious, but I said things that in the years between then were debated and critiqued and valued in ways that only a four-page spread in a glossy magazine can provide. But it was all nothing and that was the artistic expression: Nothing. And nothing can be art. And more than that, nothing is the best art.

"I was touched by the hand of God, never knew it, but I guess I was . . ." and the result was that *Nylon* ran a story gushing about the importance of religion in my life. Looking back now, the people, their faces . . . Josefina and Bailey and Alice and Francis and Dave, even Dave, looking back now they seem like ghosts, like characters that evaporate the moment you change the channel.

When I began to speak only in song lyrics, even I couldn't predict what the result would be, and the result was that no one actually noticed. The spectacle didn't fall back on itself. The upshot was only a sudden acknowledgement, a fear worse than I could have ever imagined: people really are walking around with their receptors excised, receivers cut; the line goes dead, and everyone *is* talking, talking, yes (I glance out the window again, my eyes lock on the letters sprawled across the billboard); everyone is talking over everyone else.

But no one ever looks at me; they prefer to look at me without my looking back. And eye contact is extremely important. Eye contact is the best kind of contact. But no one ever looks me in the eye, no one ever returns my gaze. So when Julie did, when she looked into me with a look that seemed to say that there was nothing there, nothing there at all, a look that told me I was nothing, *I am nothing, nothing, could I be nothing?* I almost flinched.

Instead, I thought of lines for a short story.

Or a novel. Another novel? I wrote a novel and used myself as the main character, thinking that people could identify my experiences with their own, thinking that I, the writer, the protagonist, had something to offer. Something to return other than my unrequited gaze. What big balls I have.

"What big balls!"

I hear it loud and vibrant, like it arrived through a megaphone. Have I been speaking out loud this whole time?

"Seriously, Chris," Jake mouths, pointing to my package, to my testicles hanging out the pouch of the polka-dot briefs. "You should tuck that in, no?"

I adjust the underwear and wait for further instruction, all the while thinking about the novel. But no one understood anything. A coming-of-age story. A story about fashion and media. A story about first-generation Latino identity. A story about livelihood. A Pop story. A story that begins where it ends. A New York City story. A story about *communication.*

Except when I wrote it down, when I wrote it *in*, everyone took it as satire, or worse, erotica. All anybody wants to write about is how well I wear a hat. It is as if once reality becomes written, it becomes more perverse and more exaggerated and more unreal and yet more commonplace every day.

Which is why I think you can't tell a thing to anybody. You can only make them see, and they'll only catch a glimpse. You can only make them *feel*, and hope that your feelings become their own. Because even if we switched places, if say, you were me, you'd see the same things differently.

"Turn around again, please . . ." someone mumbles, and I don't even nod, I just turn my hips like they're on a swivel.

And what was better? To be the art, or the artist? I asked myself that a long time ago, oh so long ago, back when I was writing the first novel. That coming-of-age story. And now I knew the real answer:

Who said you had to choose?

"If you had to pick, do you think this fits *better* or *worse* than the charcoal bikini . . ."

Life is short, and art is long.

And years from now, when I am dust, when I am soil vegetating someone's garden, maybe Julie's daughter's, people will see my photo in *Cosmopolitan* or *Men's Health* or very likely, *DNA*, and remember me as what? Some guy with a salamander torso. Some guy with the horrible luck of having to wear the polka-dot Jack Rogers briefs.

Five minutes later, I am back in my jeans and collared shirt, with my backpack slung across my shoulder, walking toward the elevator doors. I press *L* and hold the door for a few employees. The doors stutter and groan and open wide for five others, familiar faces, smiling and laughing, and circling their fingers around their cell phones. Everyone crams in, limbs on top of limbs, and I think that these people will finally be forced to look at one another, I mean really *look*, or else they'd get a chance to touch one another without *having* to look. All of us hurtling toward an eventual stop. I look at the big white button on the top-left, above all the numbers.

HELP IS ON THE WAY

And then, finally, the elevator doors close.

Going Further Down

"Are you lost?"

Alice was lost, but she was also looking. Looking for something, or rather, for someone.

"Are you lost?" the girl with the dirty blond hair and copper skin repeated her question. And Alice thought, yes, I'm lost. Yes, I'm looking. To be lost and looking, what a novel idea. But then it occurred to her (and this was only brief) that that went for everyone. Lost and looking. Still looking. Lost. But the thought passed before it had time to register, before the world collapsed before her eyes.

She nodded her head, ran her hand through her pale hair, nodded again. "Yes, I'm totally lost. I'm looking for Rua . . ." she paused at the pronunciation of the street name. "Naskimien. . ."

"Nascimento Silva," the girl nodded. "I'm Josefina," she smiled, taking her hand, bringing her closer. "Josefina Tristessa Consuela. Welcome to Rio."

Alice thanked her and looked around the avenue; every corner had a digital clock radiating from a billboard. Everyone always kept the time in Rio, and it was fitting, because it seemed like the whole morning had moved in slow motion, ever since she arrived.

"Are you here on holiday?" Josefina asked, pointing to a shop-front's sign which said BEACH SUCOS. People were huddled close, sitting at the counter or standing, in board shorts and bikinis. "You ever had açaí?"

Alice shook her head. "I'm actually looking for my

boyfriend. He was doing modeling work here. He was here last winter, for the season, I mean . . ."

"A model?" Josefina smiled; her brown eyes turned green. "I know a few." And then she paused, looking at Alice without really looking at her. "His name doesn't happen to be Chris, does it?"

Alice laughed. "Selden?"

Josefina nodded.

"Oh wow—you have *got* to be kidding me." Alice's voice wavered between excitement and irritation; and about Chris Selden, too, she could no longer fix the anomaly in place or straighten it; make him straight-forward or at least comprehensible. She had never seen a man cry; she had never seen a man piss sitting down. "No, he is *not* my boyfriend. But Bailey—do you know Bailey Lazar? Light blond hair, almost gray, and pale, very pale, six-foot. . ." she paused, thinking hard; thinking hard about Bailey Lazar's comp card, his picture, all those measurements . . . "two? Six-foot two," she repeated, the comp card replacing the person in her mind. She liked the firm texture of the cardboard, the way the black border framed and bisected each photograph; she even liked the sprawling typeface. *MEGA, BAILEY* . . . "That's who I'm looking for."

Josefina's hazel eyes went blank and she slowly shook her head. "He was working here, in Ipanema?"

Alice nodded. "Last I heard . . ." and she trailed off, thinking about Bailey, about his pale hair like her own, about his thin lips and his small eyes, and the evening where everything had come into view—more coming; there had to be more coming; there had to be something else because people just don't disappear off the face of the earth like that, do they?—while Josefina thought about Chris, and amid the turbulence of the world, amid all the people who had come and gone, all the people whom she had abandoned and who had abandoned her, Josefina had felt some texture in the little wedge of his life that interacted with the little wedge of her own; she had felt some contact, and that was enough, wasn't it? Even if it hadn't lasted long.

Underneath it all, Josefina thought, we are just children. Just children. Inventing games, tracing imaginary steps in the sand or the street . . . playing Hide-and-Seek or Ring Around the Rosie until we all fall down.

•

"What's that—over there?"

"Ahh . . ." Josefina smiled, and it was as if she were walking alongside Chris again, it was as if she were looking into *his* eyes. "That's Cristo Redentor." She gazed at the figure of Christ, at his outstretched arms . . . they were visible from almost every corner in the city. Touching everyone. No wonder he was haunted by it, she thought. "Our mutual friend loved that."

"Who? Chris?" Alice asked, rubbing her slender arms, scratching away at mosquito bites. "They work quick here."

"Yes. And if you drink enough cachaça, they won't come near you." Josefina nodded and smiled. "Or you'll be too wasted to notice."

Alice gripped her cell phone in one hand and snapped a photo of Christ the Redeemer. Now it's living in me, she thought, and wondered if she captured the best angle.

She tugged at her scarf—she had suffered one of those unbearable outbreaks during the twelve-hour journey (the air is so *toxic* on planes): a trio of pimples on her neck, and bought the first one she saw at Galeão International. It was green and yellow and blue. She kept tugging and talking, tugging and talking, as Josefina stared. Do people—do people here wear . . . Alice wondered (tugging again), taking note of Josefina's gaze; the way her lips were curved in a half-smile . . . scarves?

They sat under the shade of a green awning at a bar near Posto Nove, and were clinking glasses within minutes. Alice wasn't shy; she was telling Josefina her life story. She was explaining about her lifestyle; she was talking about her time working as a promoter; she was discussing particulars. Models that were more like call-girls. Crowds of swarming wannabes. Hiked-up club tickets, bottle fees, table charges, costs and outlays. The price of pretending you were a somebody. A safe place for cocaine, ecstasy, marijuana (of course), China white heroin, more money exchanged in a night than at her father's famed auctions; inherited capital meets acquired capital. Party planning. Facts, figures, various faces; an image of Manhattan slid across the wooden table, and Josefina took it in, but she didn't exactly like it.

"Money makes people do stupid things, dumb and terrible things," Alice said, noticing Josefina's scowl. "Awful things."

Josefina thought about her cousin. *Awful things*. And all of it recorded on film. Arroyo, she murmured. Chris. Bailey—was that Bailey? Was Bailey . . . but she didn't complete the thought, as if by talking about it, as if by speaking the words, it would transpose them into reality. The reality, Josefina knew, was that Bailey was gone. The same as Chris.

"And what about love?" Josefina asked.

"Love will make you do *any*thing," Alice ran a hand through her hair again and sighed. "That's why I'm here."

Josefina nodded. Isso é verdade, she thought. Maybe this preened and pampered princess knows more about life than I'd figured fifteen minutes ago. And who am I to judge? Who am I to make up my mind about her just from the way she looks, the way she talks, the way her teeth chatters when she stops speaking. If she stops speaking.

"And desire?" Alice went on, between quick sips of her caipirinha. "Reality can be pure desire."

Josefina bit her lips. Maybe she'd find Chris again. Maybe even next week. New York City-bound. Everyone passes through Rio, but the whole world stops in New York City. That's what Chris had told her, and now a year later, she knew it was true. "Want another round?" she asked, and Alice responded by sucking down the rest of her drink.

"Is that free?" she asked, spying a coconut rolling on the sidewalk at her feet. Again, Alice thought about the dark clubs, the snaking lines at the front door, the party favors. And no one paid, no one paid for anything—at least no one Alice knew by anything other than a name.

Josefina hailed the bartender and smiled.

"Nothing is free."

•

She walked and walked, moving from Ipanema to Copacabana to Leblon . . . looking wildly, darting her eyes from every corner in her field of vision. She passed the Jardim Botânico, she passed the Real Gabinete Português da Leitura, and by the time she walked alongside Cristo Redentor, she was exhausted. (Still tugging.) Where had Josefina gone? Where the hell was her hotel? Royal Caesar? . . . and where the hell was she now, anyway?

She reached for her phone and cursed when she realized she had left it at the bar. She spotted the Cristo's outstretched arms, palms reaching forever outward, and it gave her strength. She kept walking, moving, moving, plodding further, not realizing that she was going down, spiraling downhill on the cobblestone streets of Corcovado, and the image of Christ the Redeemer was sinking from her view; the image and everything else was sinking.

ATERRO METROPOLITANO
DE GRAMACHO
FECHADO
PROIBIDO JOGAR LIXO NESTE LOCAL

What the hell does that mean? she wondered. The post was blue, and it looked like it was new, supported by thick, green steel beams. Maybe it's a welcome sign? Alice smiled. She was drunk. She continued walking further down, deeper into the lot of land, which was actually a landfill. Jardim Gramacho, Rio's wasteland, the largest wasteland in the world.

She spotted T-shirts and telephones. She spotted soda bottles and beer cans, and sneakers and flip-flops, and high heels and slip-ons—is that a vintage Manolo?—and broken rocking chairs, and tattered billboards and microwaves, and a familiar smile, and cereal boxes, and flimsy photographs, and broken cameras and VCRs. The scarf. Green and yellow and blue. The scarf, too. (She tugged, but this time, only felt her own flesh.) She spotted men and women with towels wrapped around their foreheads and large green and black plastic bags in their hands, picking up as many useful items as they could, the things that could be recycled, lixo extraordinário; scavenging.

Catadors, she heard someone yell in the distance. Catadors. And big black birds with white-tipped wings flew overhead, circling, circling, and descended on her, and around her, and flew past her, and she kept sinking, sinking. More catadors. Old and withered, and bruised and aged. Aged. They looked like flowers. If that flower were human, she thought, it would look like some older people do, a person whose head drops down from their vertebrate as if the neck is too tired and weak to support it. Flowers. And she kept walking deeper, not quite moving so much as slipping, tripping further, falling in a heap of trash. It was the largest landfill in the world. It is where all the garbage goes, she realized. All of it, and everything . . .

And then Alice heard a tractor, or what sounded like a tractor, gears moving, gyrating, turning, spinning on its wheels and the sound of dirt being lifted and tossed, lifted and tossed, and it was a lullaby. Lifted and tossed. Where is Bailey? she murmured. Did he abandon me, or did he simply vanish? Was he somewhere in this wasteland? Was he nearby? Can he hear me? Lifted and tossed. Deeper, deeper. Further down. And then she fell asleep.

Buried in garbage.

Talking Heads

March 6, 2012 7:41pm

Chris! Great to "see you" again. Just checking in.
Greetings, Roy . . .

March 15, 2012 3:15am

hi, how are u?
i hope u have a lovely day today . . .
can we be friends??
hmmm juz let me know
bye for now
see ya

March 20, 2012 5:30pm

I sit and wait for you in Skype, I watch video in YouTube,
your video, incidentally, there is your name not "Selden"? will
explain?

March 28, 2012 10:29am

Chris! Hey man! Long time. Are you still acting? When did
you drop "Cuba"? Hope all is well.

March 31, 2012 4:17am

Hi. Omg. The strangest thing has happened, but I don't
know if you know this, but there is some man in South Africa
who has sorta stolen your identity and your pictures. He has
photos of you and he has put them up as his own. His name
is Chris Sinclair. Or so he says. It's so weird. Ok thanks. Bye

April 4, 2012 7:38pm

Salut! Je trouve tes photos vraiment magnifique, ta carrière fait envie.

April 10, 2012 3:46am

Hello I'm interested in knowing more about you and let's see what we lead us for the future and discover the qualities and adventurous in both of us because I'm seeking a serious long term relationship and more. Someone special to capture my heart and knows how to handle it with care, one who will cherish me and be willing to share life's greatest joys and sorrows. Someone who's willing to spoil, pamper and love me unconditionally, who is kind, sincere, honest, passionate, loyal, sense of humor, loving and wants a lifetime of passion. I'm ready to relocate anywhere in the world to spend the rest of my life with the right person . . . Would you IM me at my yahoo id kateespender67. I can't wait to have a word with you and let's see what develops from there

April 17, 2012 8:44pm

you look familiar why?

April 17, 2012 9:35pm

Hello, can you please give me your address? I am not stalking you . . . I just want to send you your birthday cake, but I need to know where I should send it. Please message me back ASAP, preferably with your cell number

April 25, 2012 1:09am

Hey My name is Manny, I am a Club Promoter, I just wanted to invite you check out some of my parties in NYC, here is a link to my group if you would like to join some of my events:

[REDACTED] and here is my page if you would like to check out some pictures, video, sign my guestbook, all of those good things: [REDACTED]

258

Don't think, don't hesitate, just embrace . . .
GET YOURSELF CONNECTED

May 2, 2012 7:45am

Good morning.

I just discovered you today as:

1) a writer and poet influenced by the XX century avant garde and the Situationist International;

2) the legendary headless model for Undergear (well, I think it's you. Are you. . .?)

I'm a writer too (middle aged and overweight, sadly) and I've already ordered GOING DOWN (not translated in Italian at the moment). Can you accept my, well, 'friendship'?

May 6, 2012 2:24pm

cool! u r a model, in ftv i saw you in dkny show. nice!!

May 10, 2012 3:01am

chris every time i type a name of a photographer i find a picture of you

May 12, 2012 6:00pm

Another thing we've in common. You're a writer/poet/actor/model (and what model!) and your work, for what I can see, is mostly about the blurred borders between public and private personas and public and private image.

May 15, 2012 1:06am

Hola chico, te escribo a decirte que te queiro tanto, que me muero si no me aceptas la Amistad. Pues, no me muero pero me pongo muy triste, jaja. Este, cuando tienes tiempo por que no escribes unas palabras, algunas palabras que vienen de tu boca, de la boca donde queda un mundo. Nuevo y maravilloso. Hasta luego, guapo, hasta luego.

May 17, 2012 3:11am

I'm a somewhat literary writer who could publish (with a rather big publisher) only through taking part as a contestant in a TV talent show called Masterpiece, a kind of 'American Idol' or 'X-Factor' for writers. It flopped, both on TV and in bookshops, but here I am, a little but definite TV personality.

May 20, 2012 3:07am

Chris, will you be in town at all before the festival ends? Dave Goldstein is here making a mess of everything, shoving his camera in everyone's face, et cetera. It is all very four-years-ago and you want to know what else? He is still holding the Palme d'Or over his head, and over all of ours too. Everyone is looking for you along the Croisette. Shall we meet at the Marriott lobby around half-nine? Where did you say you are?

May 22, 2012 4:35am

And of course, having obtained a contract through a TV show, I was largely ostracized by the Italian critical community. Anyway, a martial arts literary fiction was a tough sell from the start. . .

May 27, 2012 4:14pm

hay dear friend . . . chris . . . how are you . . . i am zlatko by croatia . . . your big fan . . . i want be your friend . . . in internet . . . you look very, very beautiful . . . please you . . . ADD me as friend in internet . . . ok!!!!

i am zlatko by croatia . . . i have 26 year old . . . 189-74 . . . brown hair ok boy . . . i live alone with my mother . . . my father is dead . . . i have not job . . .i love in my life . . . movies, dance, fashion, music, art, style, etc . . . and . . . eurovision song contest . . .

how goes your life, job, love etc !!! do you ever be in croatia !!!! . . . I am so happy to see you in internet you look very beautiful and sexy and you are great artist . . . i give you the best my compliments . . .

. . . please you sweet . . . chris . . . send me . . . your some photos+autograph . . . on my home adr . . . on memory of you . . . ok . . .!!!!!!!!!!!!!!!!!!!!! i will be very, very happy on your nice kindnesses and your gifts . . .

My home adr . . . [REDACTED]

my cell . . . [REDACTED]

send your family and you lot lot hot nice greetings from beautiful country . . . please you . . . your new friend . . . zlatko by croatia . . .

June 1, 2012 3:00pm

At dusk, hovering above the city: a sensual, seductive rooftop society comes out to play. Bathed in neon, high on glamour, the look of polished penthouse perfection shimmers against a glowing skyline. Guests may join in, watch in awe and learn, or simply take photos.

June 3, 2012 1:06am

Chris, do you remember Bailey Lazar? I heard you two knew each other pretty well. Do you know where he went? Do you know how I can reach him? Did he tell you anything at all?

June 8, 2012 6:26pm

I'm from Austria (Europe) and I would love to get in touch with some people from foreign countries. I'm 21 and study Law. Are you interested in talking a little?

Kind regards, Sarah.

June 15, 2012 7:19am

Bro. Jus' droppin' by to see how ya 'R' these days, man! Thinkin' about cha. Ya kno'? And you're RIGHT . . . "nothing lasts"! That IS something to THINK about, isn't it? Really! Hit me back man. A.J.

June 17, 2012 8:11pm

Hi there. I've been following you for a while now. I guess you can call me a fan. I really respect you and what you are doing. Your interviews are funny because I have no idea what you are actually talking about but it sounds like some serious shit.

June 20, 2012 4:30am

Whom do I contact to set up your Author Q&A at BookCourt? I assume you don't check your e-mail, which means . . .

June 27, 2012 1:18am

hello i wanna be ur friend but i dont know why! and i cant add u ☹ i hope u wanna add me . . . pleaseeeeeeee . . .

July 1, 2012 3:00pm

Just saw your Harper's Bazaar feature! Fucking FANTASTIC. That thing you do—with your mouth, half-open, the curve of the upper lip, asymmetrical?—where in the world did you LEARN THAT? A "Night on the Town" is RIGHT, although I looked at those shots all weekend.

But wasn't there supposed to be a girl in that story too? The captions say there's also a girl.

July 4, 2012 1:00pm

HI I LOVE YOU

July 8, 2012 8:14pm

hi how are? im erick from ecuador y me gustaría ser tu amigo espero me aceptes gracias

July 15, 2012 2:10am

hi dear friend—can you tell me what foods you eat SPECIFICALLY? when and how do you prepare your foods? recipes? please!

July 23, 2012 3:51am

i am just a fake page but i would like to know where i could find pictures of you

August 9, 2012 6:21pm

Such a huge fan of yours! ☺ You're my phone and computer wallpaper lol

August 15, 2012 4:14pm

Tell me how you can sing so well without ever opening your mouth?

August 23, 2012 10:05am

Hey Chris I'm Simon, I just want to let you know you are a huge inspiration to me, I always wanted to be a model and when I saw your pictures I knew I wanted to be just like you, I guess what I'm trying to say is thanks for being a role model to someone like me.

September 1, 2012 7:57pm

Buenas tardes, Cris, Habla tu amigo, René. Yo soy de Uruguay y te encontre aqui en el internet. Tengo unas preguntas para ti. Que es tu color favorito? Que te gusta comer en la manana? En donde encuentras toda la ropa que llevas? Cuantas novias tienes? Come se llaman? Gracias para tu tiempo y ojalal no ponemos hacer amistades mejores. Gracias otra vez. Gracias.

September 10, 2012 3:45pm

Chris, just finished GOING DOWN. The first chapter I mean. You are crackers. What's up with all these footnotes?

September 15, 2012 8:10pm

Hi, I know this is gonna sound weird and you'll probably laugh at me but to me this is no laughing matter. This past couple of months I have been falling for a guy on the internet who has been using your photos as his own. No need to tell you that I got a slap in the mouth. Anyway I have put myself in a position where I still have to keep him sweet so that my husband (with whom I have been going thru hard times lately) does not find out. I am not expecting anything from you. I don't even know why I am sending you this massage. Despair I guess. This person has been feeding me your photos for weeks (by the way, you are amazingly handsome). Anyway this person's ex told me that he was fake and that he got your photos of internet. It took me all day but I finally found you. I don't know whether to be relived or sad to find out that the person I have been falling deeply in live with knows nothing about me and that it was all a lie. You must think I am crazy. I am not. Just stupid. Stupid to have let myself be misled. It would make my day to add you as a friend. Please believe me when I say that this is not a prank from me. If you go on my profile and scroll thru my friends you will soon find the person I am talking about. Thank you for reading me. I have fantasize on some of your photos. Nothing inappropriate. All sweet and romantic. Finding you is the wake up call I needed. Not that you would need it but I wish you all the very best and hope that we can be at the very least internet friends

    Ree

September 15, 2012 8:15pm
    ps excuse my spelling lol I'm a bit emotional. Bye

September 23, 2012 7:30am
    Hi Chris My name is Davi and I live in Brazil . . . so I'm your fan and I think I saw you in person one day when you were here walking somewhere, so add me here please, I wanna keep touch!

October 1, 2012 1:23pm

I mean it, you are C-R-A-Z-Y. What's with all these song lyrics? Madonna? Really?

October 5, 2012 11:58am

Hi Mr Chris, just one question can u speak spanish?

October 10, 2012 9:11am

I love your poetry. I can't believe you actually wrote a NOVEL. I didn't even think you could read . . . LOL . . . seriously, I would have never known, just by looking at you . . .

October 15, 2012 7:40am

Chris,

I am really interested in health and fitness and I'm trying to mimic what has worked for other people. You have an amazing body and I would really appreciate if you could tell me a little about what your diet consists of or what you eat typically in a day. Also what are your exercise routines. How often do you train? Where do you train? I look forward to hearing from you.

Thank You

October 18, 2012 3:35pm

Chris!

Long time, my friend! And I am ecstatic to find you here again and connect! Have definitely been thinking about you bro. If I never told you, I've ALWAYS held you in the HIGHEST esteem in spite of whatever, and even tho' I've never hung out with you! You have ALWAYS been one of my ALL TIME FAVORITE people, and I've always wanted you to 'know' it bro. And the Love is outstanding to say the least! And I wanted to uplift your heart with that, bro, because I know the power of it! I hope that you are doing well . . . and from the looks of it, it seems to be so. I remember the afternoon at Cosmo like it was yesterday! Maybe it was and we just have been time-travelin' you feel me? Hanging out the window, about to jump! Damn, man. I owe the world to you and I praise the Lord every moment of my waking life. IF you WOULD, please keep in touch man. Really!

1 love, and God Bless . . .

Your bro.

A.J.

October 22, 2012 6:27pm

Hey Chris. I hope all is going well. What are you teaching in your class now? I love teaching the basics. How is it going for you? I know lots of students are not excited by the topics. I am sure your students love you, and I bet the girls (and even the closeted guys) are pleased to have you as their teacher.

November 1, 2012 3:15pm

We all miss you in Quilmes. Besos de Argentina!

November 7, 2012 3:33pm

I thank Steve Jobs every day for letting me have your literature and your pictures on my phone at all times

November 10, 2012 5:30am

¿Habla usted español o no?

November 15, 2012 7:17am

Hey Chris. I am just back from two great weeks in east Maine. I hope all is going well for you. Maine was lovely and I know you would like it even though I have never met you. I can just tell these things. I was with friends at a lakeside cottage (where one can swim as it is too cold to swim in the ocean). We had some nice visits with high school and college friends as well as local friends. One professional photographer let each of us choose one of her works—and I have a beautiful photograph of blueberry fields turning in their fall colors. Your photograph was given to one of my good friends Alec Jolson, as a present for his 54th birthday party last night. It is the one you did for Izod . . . very handsome as always.

November 17, 2012 10:10pm

Dear Chris, may I send you a friendship request. So I can learn a lot from your stories, your words, vision and way of life. I am a writer as well or I try to be one ☺

November 20, 2012 4:18pm

Okay, I get it. Reevaluating narrative, producing agency for readers, engaging in a conversation with your own work. But why footnotes? Why not, for instance, asterisks? An asterisk, from the Latin asteriscus, from the Greek asteriskos—"little star," as you may already know—has various functions, all of which directly relate to your work. Let's look, for example, at the use of bounding asterisks to signify stage directions. How about mathematics? I understand you're not good with numbers but think about multiplication, think about the little star we use to signify multiples and multiplicity and . . . well, do I need to even verbalize it? Repetition. I would rather not linger on computer science (wildcard characters; limitless substitutions), so let's move to linguistics, specifically historical linguistics, in which an asterisk immediately before a word indicates that the word is not directly attested, but has been reconstructed on the basis of other linguistic material. Need I say more? Without saying too much, I associate the asterisks which indicate the blotting out—the blotting OUT—of certain words, of certain epithets, with the (self)censorship, really the self-dissolution, which is essential to understanding your oeuvre of ghost stories, your seesaw between physicality and fantasy, the overarching idea that you can be both present and absent at the same time . . . that you can exist in this negative space . . . that this non-existence is actually normal . . .

Because, you know, the asterisk—not to be confused with the six-pointed Arabic star (each point like a teardrop emoting from an ovate face)—is a lot like you, or how I've always thought of you (yes, I sometimes think of you): always finding yourself in one place, with your mind in quite another . . . and the function of the asterisk—at least how Hera used it on Zeus (inscribed on his brow, no less)—was to remind him that he should always be somewhere else.[xi]

November 21, 2012 8:43am
Gorgeous model Chris!!! Hope to work with you one day. I'm Guy from Greece. You can see my work at [REDACTED]

November 24, 2012 6:30pm
Chris, once again I listened with respect and delight to your amazing words. Thank you for making the movie "Memories" and others on YouTube and the story you are telling. Unfortunately I cannot buy your book in the Netherlands. But when I'm in the States I will buy it at Barnes & Noble. Please keep writing.
Greetings and respect from the Netherlands,
Aart den Dekker

December 5, 2012 6:38pm
Hey man, I wanted to ask you, how did you get your body so toned and muscular, but not huge . . . what different things did you do? THANKS, from Belgium!

December 5, 2012 3:30pm
Contact Sergio Cemitas when you get in to Galeão International. He has all the details. Everyone at 40 Graus is excited to see you again. I mean, in person.

[xi] This particular asterisk was written by the author himself.

December 7, 2012 1:11am

Let me straddle your mind. Can I do that? Can I wrap myself around that head? Can I get inside?

December 8, 2012 7:34am

I spotted you at a Devils game once, and didn't know where I knew you from. It drove me crazy for weeks. Lol. Do you think we can be friends?

December 10, 2012 5:47pm

Chris, IF I haven't said it, I say "THANKS bro." For "connecting" with me! I'm in a daze travelin' thru ya pix man. So MANY! And they're AWESOME bro. Check out MY profile too, and even sign my guestbook if ya feelin' me! I'd be MOST honored. It's right on the wall. Click the link next to it and it'll open! Don't forget a PIC, man. And KEEP in touch for sure! Aight? 1 love bro, A.J.

December 15, 2012 4:03am

Hi Chris. Your work sounds very interesting whenever I get a chance to Google it. I shall hope to finish your second novel before you come to Annapolis for a reading. What's the name of that one? . . . Let me know, please. Will you continue to teach once you have your PhD? Be nice to have you at Washington College, here in Chestertown! My Thanksgiving was excellent—sang in the choir for Wednesday evening service and on Thanksgiving Day joined friends for a great meal and lots of good conversation. I guess by now you know I am one of your great fans. I admire your intellect as well as your good humor and, of course, your incredible modeling career. I hope you will not be upset to know you are my screen background. ☺

Today 10:57am

Is that what you were really thinking, all this time?

Is It Here Yet?

"Is it here yet?"

Johnny Baker was not exactly asking.

He'd been pouting on the couch, reclined and frowning, holding his cell phone as if it were a microphone. Now he shouted. "Is it here yet?"

He was referring to the General Tso's chicken he had ordered over an hour ago, the wonton soup and moo shu pork, and fuck if he was going to miss out on his favorite Chinese takeout, on his last supper altogether, on the final day of his life. His and everybody else's.

"This is a matter of life and death," he was saying into his speaker, as bodies and faces roved around him and he lifted up his free hand to catch the passing handshake or slap of the wrist from his guests. Of course it's a matter of life and death, Johnny was thinking. And for once, he wasn't exaggerating. "Burning Down the House" by Talking Heads erupted on the sound system Johnny Baker had installed hours earlier, wiring the stereo to all available electronic outlets. Who the hell made this mix? he thought, I've never heard this before . . . but he bobbed his own head to the beat anyway, maybe pretending, or maybe just letting go, letting the music slide past his skin and through him.

Clarence Byrne looked around the apartment, strangers and acquaintances but no one he *really* knew (as if anyone really knew anyone, let alone themselves . . . although there was somebody whom he had known, and who had known him, really known him, he thought faintly, didn't she?) and thought about why he had come.

Just ten minutes ago, he remembered, he was standing on the corner of Rivington and Clinton, outside Johnny Baker's apartment, pretending to wait for the telephone. It had to be the last telephone booth in the city, Clarence thought, maybe in the world. And it was being occupied by a five-foot six (five-foot seven?) chica with curly dark blond almost brown hair and eyes that were green or brown or both, maybe both, and secrets under her charcoal blouse and faded jeans and black scarf.

Ten minutes ago, he was waiting, hands jammed in his pockets, glancing furtively out of the corners of each eye at her face, at her mouth, her lips, and every other moment, she seemed to be looking back at him. By the time she finished speaking to whomever it was on the other line, she said, "All yours" with an accent that Clarence couldn't place and he was dumbfounded and intrigued as she walked away; he had no idea what she was referring to, because he had all but forgotten the excuse for being there in the first place, which was an excuse to make contact. He shrugged and saw her silhouette slide away, into the evening and the taxis and the clamor of the city until she disappeared completely. He walked three steps and rang the bell and when he arrived, he fished out a CD from his jeans pocket.

Why did I come? "There will be hummus . . ." one of his roommate's cousins had mentioned and, until now, hummus had been the party's main selling point. But now he saw the five-foot seven (she was definitely at least five-foot seven, he considered, sizing her up) chica standing in the corner, nursing a Bud Lite con Limón and talking to a group of men and women but really just nodding her head, and it was clear she was bored, completely bored, utterly and absolutely *bored*, and *that's* why he had come, wasn't it? To make some contact, Clarence thought. To fill the boredom.

"This is good," Clarence said, darting his eyes from each face, each body, trying to will the girl in the corner to look back at him. "I will let her court me. Wait for her," he said, nodding his head. She was looking out the window. "I will be her coy mistress."

With one deft movement, Clarence flicked his wrist and re-emerged in the scene with a raw carrot glistening with a glob of beige hummus. Cilantro, he mumbled, as he chewed, beaming, as if after eating anything, he could appreciate the good, the hopeful, the fabricated details of his situation.

"So what do you do?" the chica, whose name was Josefina—or is it Tristessa? or is it Consuela?—asked him, between sips of beer.

He thought about all the possible answers. Poet, personal trainer, print model, tennis instructor, keyboardist in a pop band, waiter, graduate student, bartender/cabana boy on CBS's *The Young and the Restless*, before deciding on: "I would prefer not to say because anything I will say will diminish me."

But he was cut off at "prefer."

". . . *Hold tight. Wait till the party's over. Hold tight. We're in for nasty weather . . .*"

"Oh my God! His voice . . . he modulates *so* well."

"He could read the telephone book to me."

"Just *look* at him."

And half the party was looking, crowding around Johnny Baker's 27-inch Apple iMac, watching clips of an ABC soap opera—ABC, what the fuck, Clarence grumbled—where the same actor was shown in a variety of scenes and outfits, sometimes wearing a cut-off shirt, sometimes shirtless. "Who's that?" He pointed to the blinking monitor and Johnny Baker answered for him.

"Chris Selden," Johnny said, shaking his head, bristling. "I went to school with that fucking kid—you believe that? True story. He wrote poetry and shit in between classes, even at parties. Do you believe that?"

Johnny ran one hand roughly through his thinning scalp, his eyes glazed over and far away, as if he were remembering a scene from long ago: a long line of zombies pouring into the old apartment on a decrepit street, and Beirut and flip-cup, and making out on the couch, and Dave Goldstein, and the undercover cop; do you believe that?

Francis Carter pointed to the YouTube clip and said he also knew Chris Selden. "He used to cater here and there," Francis said. "Way before he was on ABC. (Clarence shuddered.) And you know, I've done some print work too," he pointed out, puffing out his chest, smiling at the crowd. "I've done some TV. I was dedicated, you know? Used to fly down from Buffalo for extra work. Extra work! That's dedication . . ." and Clarence shook his head (What a loser, Clarence thought—but damn! ABC. . .) and Josefina—that is her name, isn't it?—also nodded her head and said *she* knew him too. And another girl, a short brunette with bows in her hair and freckles, she boasted, "That's nothing. The last party I worked, the birthday boy was presented with a blown-up print of one of Chris Selden's cover shots—the one in *DNA*, you know? 'Sexiest Man Alive '09' . . ."

"Well, I'm friends with him on Facebook," another girl said, and the man standing next to her, wearing a fedora and suspenders, nodded in agreement.

"I'm not even on Facebook," a tall, lanky, red-haired man said. "But I know Chris Selden. Very well, actually." And eyebrows raised on cue as he scratched the stubble on his chin and raised a hand. "I'm Charlie, by the way."

"If you're not on Facebook, you don't *exist*," Johnny Baker said, and a host of murmurs and mumbles and chatters and jabbers followed, and people briefly stole glances at Charlie, as if he suddenly disappeared, but he was still standing, holding a high ball, patting his knees to the beat of the music, still scratching his chin. Charlie was thinking about his recurring dreams, which were actually nightmares. In one of them, he was having sex with his wife (he didn't even have a girlfriend), him on top, rising over her while she was videotaping and when they played it back an hour later, or fifteen minutes, or fifty seconds—dream-time existed in no-time—they both saw the outline of a woman's torso, a woman's bony hands and fingers, in the background, as if she were behind them the whole time. In another dream, sirens blared across the neighborhood where he was living and one by one, people he once knew—neighbors and friends, familiar faces—all walked into his home, trudging like zombies, eyes glazed over, eyebrows hardly raised an inch, and all of them took turns fucking different dogs; purebreds, mutts, Shiba Inus (means "small dog" in Nagano, Charlie remembered), and Dachshunds, and big, red and brown Doberman pinschers, and Golden Retrievers, all of them fucking away, and when he started to feel his eyelids pull back, when he started to feel his eyes glaze over and his body go slack, as if he were the next one to go into a trance, he woke up. If he could have dreams as fucked up as that, Charlie thought, then he was either going crazy, or the world really was about to end.

Who the hell didn't know Chris Selden? Clarence thought, besides me. When the pregnant girl drinking a Snapple mint iced tea volunteered that she didn't know who Chris Selden was, Clarence felt relieved, if only momentarily. "I hardly watch television," Miranda said, rubbing her stomach, maybe feeling her baby kick, Clarence thought, and who the hell would want to bring a child into this place—not this party; the world. Didn't you hear? He remembered the headline like it was this morning instead of one week ago:

27 PEOPLE DEAD, MOSTLY CHILDREN, IN CONNECTICUT SCHOOL SHOOTING

Didn't you hear? But nobody heard that. Nobody knew what he was talking about. Nobody seemed to notice.

"*. . . into the blue again, into the silent water, under the rocks and stone . . .*"

Josefina Tristessa Consuela scrolled down on the viewer comments while Chris Selden continued to utter a few lines above her field of vision. The filet mignon of men was kissed off with three emoticons ☺ ☺ ☺ and Clarence instinctively rubbed his stomach. He was ravenous. As he retreated to the mortar of hummus, he thought about the reading he had just given the night before at KGB Bar. He had only recently become a poet, and he reimagined the scene: the dark room sectioned off with a red curtain, the faint echo reverberating from each brick in the walls, everybody's astonished face when he had finished reading; a hush in the room like he had just told them that their sons or daughters had died, or that they had never existed, or that they themselves had died, or that they themselves had never existed . . . But I wish I could have seen the look on *my* face, Clarence was actually thinking. I wish someone was recording *that*—had they?—so that I could see exactly what I looked like, what it was that emoted in my eyes at that particular moment, what it was that radiated from me and could send me spiraling back to the moment, like actual time-travel, *flash*, just like that. The moment that could interrupt all other moments. The whisper that held the secret to life, but that also made life dissolve. "If you write the perfect poem, the world will end" is how his creative writing professor had put it. Had he been referring to tonight?

"*. . . there was a shopping mall, now it's all covered with flowers . . . if this is paradise, I wish I had a lawnmower . . .*"

The TVs that had been blaring an uninterrupted stream of FOX sitcoms now radiated the news. Footage showed a crowd of several hundred people, kneeling in water, on the banks of what looked like a jungle or a forest, and the caption underneath read:

Ceremony in Bacuranao, Cuba, marks end of Mayan calendar cycle
'New dawn' near, not apocalypse, sage explains

and another report about a riot in Moscow, and a looting in Beijing, and a calculated mail-order bombing in Berlin, and Clarence took another bite and shuddered, the crack of carrot seeming to echo in the crowded apartment, which had never before felt so quiet.

I got it, Clarence thought. I know Chris Selden, too. Food—food had brought us together, hadn't it? The memory finally returning to him as he put another carrot to his mouth, as he chewed, loudly, as he swallowed. Opening night. À Votre . . . À Votre . . . À Votre . . . his words searched for the name (another carrot, another wedge between his teeth).

God?

Playa del Carmen, Mexico

"¿Qué tipo desea? ¿Mexicano o Americano?"

"Excuse me?" Jack Anders stared blank-faced at the waiter hovering above him. He had whiskers and beady eyes and his hair was gelled and slicked in a wave to the side of his face, as if the shiny black oil was about to spill over, onto shore.

"Los tacos, señor," the waiter repeated, this time, in English. "The Mexican, or the American kind?"

Jack put down the menu he had been scanning for the past fifteen minutes and his expressionless face became one of exasperation. Sandra, his wife, inched closer and extended her hand toward him, as if she could pull him back from the abyss, the brink of doom.

"Why would I want the American kind?" he retorted, staring at the waiter's small eyes, at his whiskers and thin lips. "I'm in Mexico, dammit."

They were in Playa del Carmen, actually, on the Mexican Riviera, staying at the Rosewood Mayakoba.

How did I get here? Sandra wondered. Before the forty-two mile stretch of chauffeured resort service and the two hour and fifty-minute flight from JFK to Cancun International, and the car service—a maroon Lincoln with a Russian driver—that had brought them from their home in North Jersey to JFK (an hour and a half?), it began two weeks ago, two weeks and three days, at the Byrne's home, Nancy and Walter, and her and Jack huddled around their coffee table, sipping something affable from a ceramic mug, and talking vibrantly about their child—Clarence— gushing and regaling them with stories which only made her feel nauseated, since she and Jack had none of their own, and they kept talking about life, about jobs, about vacations—Bermuda and Mykonos and the lovely trip that they had just taken to Mexico, actually, to this very spot— and then there was silence while Jack looked at her and she nodded, and the two agreed telepathically that they would have to go too, while Nancy secretly wished she hadn't told them a thing about it, because she wanted Playa del Carmen to remain her little secret, her own private oasis. But she kept talking anyway . . .

"And when we got back, we were changed," she said, looking seriously at both Jack and Sandra, while her husband, Walter, nodded his head beside her as if to affirm everything. "You know, you have no idea what's going there, no idea whatsoever . . ." and Jack kept smiling, delirious with the idea of taking his own trip there, and Sandra too, was infected, giddy with the prospect of adventure. Real adventure. But all they had experienced so far was a buffet brunch, and a massage and spa service, and cable television, and high-speed Internet, and the opportunity to not only ride dolphins, but to do yoga with them—downward facing dolphin? she wondered—and it was not the life-altering experience she had hoped for, the one she had wished for, and now where were they? Getting into a heated argument over American tacos versus Mexican tacos, as the sun beat down on their backs, and the sweat dripped from her chin into a bowl of granola imported from Maine—why did I come all the way to Mexico for that?—and she envisioned just what the ruins of Chichen Itza would look like this afternoon, when all of *this*, whatever it was, the arguing, the picnicking, the nitpicking, the talking just to hear a voice, was over.

The waiter hurried away and Jack sighed. "Fucking Mexico," he said, looking at Sandra and managing a smile, taking his earbuds out and letting the wind and the smells and sounds of Mexico envelop him. He had been listening to a playlist Walter had given him prior to their trip, one that Walter had been given by Clarence, that blue-eyed son of theirs. "I thought I was going to be enveloped with an authentic experience," Jack continued, shaking his head and squinting. "What the hell happened to our checklist? Things-to-do in Mexico. I knew we should have just gone to Paris."

But of course we couldn't have gone to Paris, he considered. Because this was Mexico. This was the heart of Mayan country. "Imbued with the spirit of Mexico's Yucatán Peninsula," as the Rosewood Web site put it. *A journey to this serene world captivates the soul* . . . This was where the end of the world begins, and they would be the privileged witnesses. Hah. Walter and Nancy hadn't thought about that, had they? They would never get *my* experience, they would never have the photo at Chichen Itza, or the magnet we'd receive at Xcaret Eco Park, etched with *December 21, 2012—Welcome to the End of the World* . . . "You have no idea . . ." Jack replayed Nancy's grating words, her grating voice, in his head and smiled. You got that right, he muttered.

Huevos con nopales
Huevos con tocino
Cemitas de carnitas
Torta de lengua
Mole poblano
Quesadillas Suaves
Tacos Americanos (orden de dos)
Granola de Maine
Tostadas Oaxaca
Horchata
Jamaica
Café (orden de dos)
Jugo de Naranja

An hour later, Jack and Sandra received the bill (the idiots charged me for the *American* tacos . . .) and well-fed and restored, they retired to their hotel rooms to pack a small duffel bag for their sojourn through the playa. Water, bring plenty of water, Jack reminded Sandra, and she nodded, throwing a handful of Poland Springs in the bag. "Can't trust the water here."

He added: "What can you trust anymore?" He inserted his earbuds again and let the Talking Heads flow through his receptors, let the song flow through his whole body.

". . . warning sign of things to come (take it over, take it over) . . . it happened before, it will happen again . . ."

Main Street, Hackensack, New Jersey

Chris Selden was leaning over the bar counter at The Pourhouse when Jillian Aguilera walked in. A gust of December wind blew through as she tottered closer, the door seesawing to a stop behind her, hinges clicking in the distance. He pretended not to notice and instead fixed his gaze on the bartender working the tap. Weary and suntanned and wearing too much perfume and not enough makeup. Let the barmaid squeeze an orange in so I can feel classy, Chris was thinking, when Jillian put her slender arms around his neck and pulled him into her. They kissed. The bartender slid the pint glass over to Chris with a broad smile. No orange, Chris thought, and frowned.

"I can't believe you're back in town," Jillian said, taking Chris's hands into her own and walking to a booth in the center of the bar. The Pourhouse was secluded, except for a few stragglers. It's early, Chris thought, glancing at the time stamp on his last text message from Jillian Aguilera: 8:55 p.m.

let's grab drinks and chill, catch up, you know ;p

And then

it's been a minute!

That was half an hour ago.

"Only for two days," Chris said, in between sips of Blue Moon. Why didn't I demand the orange? he thought, considering whether or not to walk back toward the bar until Jillian started to rub his crotch with one exposed knee, hiking up her black skirt with either the force of gravity or the slight wind blowing in from the entrance (it takes practice), and he decided he'd sit down a little while longer. "I'm heading back to Rio for some work."

"Oh my God—Rio?" Her knee left Chris's crotch and he frowned. "You are so effing lucky." She slurped down a little more from her vodka cranberry and shook her head. "Are they doing Fashion Week over there now?"

Chris glanced at the mistletoe hanging at the doorway and nodded. "'Tis the season . . ."

Jillian motioned to a waitress for another drink and Chris's eyes roved the rest of the room. He saw René de la Rosa throwing darts in the corner, next to two old men in guinea tees and jeans (Wrangler? Chris thought) shooting pool. Chris indicated a *Hey what's up?* with a nod of his head and pointed to his wrist as if to ask: How long have you been out?

René smiled, his eyes lit up, but he continued throwing darts.

"I saw René when he picked me up from Grand Central," Chris said, nodding his head toward the dartboard. Three torpedoes in the double-top. "Next time I saw him, he was in a jail cell."

"I want you to give *me* photos," Jillian said, unmoved, or nonplussed, or just not listening. "I don't want to Google you and get what's on the public domain." She blushed and wet her lips. "Because I'd feel like I'd be looking at someone I don't know."

"That's how *I* feel," Chris said. But when he looked back at Jillian, she was only smiling wider.

In the time it takes to take hold and let go again, Chris had written a novel about the world of the newsroom and the runway . . . and what else? He still didn't know, or rather, he was still writing it.

"So tell me more about *fashion*," she gushed, inching closer, and she was thinking that he was, at this particular moment, never more beautiful and they were never more beautiful, and everything was never more beautiful than now, and Chris was thinking: She's trying too hard.

The last time he had seen her was before he moved out of his parents' home in Oradell. New York City boy, she had said then, rubbing her hands playfully through his hair, touching his smooth scalp, before she bent down and slid his cock down her throat. The faraway wet warmth.

That was five years ago.

Girl must be desperate, he thought. But what does that say about me?

He took another pronounced gulp from his pint glass, the frothy pale liquid leaving a trace of foam on his thick lips, and René was sending darting glances over at his high school buddy, wondering why Chris seemed to always be smirking; a half-smile gleaming across his lips and his hazel eyes, as if he had some secret knowledge of something, as if he were telling himself a joke while the whole world was just talking.

Why did she want to know so much about modeling? he was thinking, and why would anyone give so much shit about a thing they know nothing about? What did she think fashion was, some sort of trip? But everything I've done has left me more disappointed, and more depressed. It is like kissing a beautiful woman with bad breath (he looked over at Jillian, Jillian flashing her pearly whites, her ruby lips, her chalky throat jutting with every breath and every heave . . . yes, a beautiful girl with bad breath). The shock of it. Or like getting hit by lightning while picking up the paper. The paper. That, too. Journalism had been shit, was still shit. No one read anymore anyway, and I don't blame them, he was thinking, because there was nothing worth reading. Everything, in fact, was still being reproduced, copied, passed around and published under different headlines below different dates. And everything came through the same channels, from the same source; and everything that was written was written for a de-classified audience: the revelation only of a generic consumer identity. It was *no news*.

He thought about the *San Francisco Chronicle*, the *Star-Ledger*, the motherfucking Dow Jones Newspaper Fund, my alumnus ID; what a waste of credentials. What credentials? Everything was shit. Life was shit.[xii] The only recourse was to write about it. So he wrote about the horrors and absurdities and upshots of boredom, about people who got bored and did wild things, crazy things (he looked at René), people who broke into people's houses and rearranged all the furniture, people who performed experiments on their patients while lip-singing karaoke, people who posed as tourists to become terrorists . . .

But even the worst bits, even the drudgery, the monotony, the shit, the anesthesia, even the sound of everybody typing separately at the same time could be beautiful, because there was music in everything. But it took him a while to hear that.

Because Chris wasn't responding, Jillian just kept talking, asking him questions that she answered with more questions, wondering all about casting calls and editorial shoots, and what was the difference between being on hold and being booked? And was Rio nice this time of year? And do you watch all the TV shows you are on the moment they air or do you tape them beforehand, or both? And so on, and so on, and Chris's eyes lingered to the sign above the bar.

[xii] Whenever I did anything I always wanted to be doing something else but when I started doing something else I knew I didn't want to do that either. I was at a loss, I was a loss addict.

UNA MUJER EMBARAZADA
NUNCA TOMA SOLA

Jillian saw that his gaze was focused elsewhere, so she pointed to the sign and asked Chris what it meant, all the while bending over farther, farther and further, an indeterminate distance even as both nipples almost rose into view, if Chris had been looking.

"A pregnant woman never drinks alone," he said.

"Got that right," Jillian whistled and shook her head. "Oh, I almost forgot . . ." she dug into her purse, pulling out her birth control. "I can take Yaz with vodka, right?"

But Chris was still staring at the sign, shaking his head, staring.

A pregnant woman never drinks alone

But even she was alone. And so was Jillian, and so was he, and so was everyone, all of them. Alone.

Playa del Carmen, Mexico

Before they left the lobby, the concierge informed Jack that there were reports of a serial killer in the area. In the area? What the fuck does that mean? Jack asked him, livid again. "In the general proximity, señor," the concierge said, sweat beginning to form on his forehead, on his thin lips and whiskers (does everyone grow whiskers in this hotel?). "How typical," Jack said, turning to his wife. "I mean, really. Serial killers? This is straight out of *2666*."

"What's *2666*?" Sandra asked. Jack's face grew hotter.

"Are you kidding me? You're kidding me. Sandy, really? It's a massive novel. Five books," he said, remembering that he'd only read three. "Five. And it's incomplete, for starters. It's laden with tragedy—Bolaño, the author—

"I know Bolaño—"

"He wrote it *knowing* he was dying. Europeans, Americans, Mexicans, everyone lost in Mexico. (He looked around.) A surfeit of unsolved murders. A boxing match. Provincial pre-war Prussian life. Mental illness and the world of academia. Time itself as one long nightmare. Something secret, and horrible, and cosmic. You have to suggest *that* to your book club."

"Don't talk to me like that," Sandra said, her eyes sharp and her brow furrowed. "You always talk to me like that."

"Like what?" Jack wanted to know.

Sandra shook her head. "What makes it so good?"

"Because . . ." Jack paused. The waterfall lapping behind him made him suddenly calm and reflective. "It scared the shit out of me. It terrified me. It made me ask questions I had never asked before." He paused. A fly flew by his face, landed on his cheek. He let it rest there. "Questions I'd never thought to ask."

"And what were those questions?"

But Jack just shrugged, because he had not anticipated another response from his wife, and also, he had already forgotten. The questions. The book itself. He looked back at the concierge. "So are you suggesting we close our doors and double-lock?" he laughed. "Yeah right, compadre," he added. The concierge looked at him with a blank expression. "Sí," Jack continued, swatting the fly with a slap to his face. "I know some español. Enough to survive."

He grabbed Sandra and the two headed toward the revolving doors, out into the sunlight of the approaching afternoon, the last day of the world. An air-conditioned van with tinted windows and a friendly driver who wouldn't stop smiling picked them up fifteen minutes later.

"¿A dónde va, señor?"

"We're going to Chichen Itza, amigo," Jack replied, rubbing at the dark smear on his cheek while Sandra settled in beside him. She pulled down the headrest and grabbed for her travel guide as the driver flipped through the radio and the static shrieked. "Chichen Itza."

Main Street, Hackensack, New Jersey

Chris had to escape. He motioned to the restroom and excused himself while Jillian continued to talk, talk, talk . . . the whole while Chris listened in rapt attention, playing the child, knees up around the campfire, nodding seriously, as if the story were so terrifying, so horrific, that it was all he could do—and it was terrifying, it *was* horrific—but he was only pretending to listen. He didn't hear a thing.

Inside the relative privacy of the stall, Chris unrolled toilet paper and unzipped his jeans, sliding his ass onto the cool toilet seat. He enjoyed these rare moments of introspection; it afforded him with something that amounted to pleasure, and he drifted back to life, back to the past, the moments that zigzagged between now and then and the voices that collided in thoughts . . . The End of the World Party, Johnny Baker's apartment, Lehigh, everybody slouching toward Bethlehem in some shape or form, Johnny Baker . . . What the hell was that idiot up to these days? . . . A stream of images transmitted in Chris's mind, coming quick and sporadic like a montage reel, a montage in which he saw all of the girls he had ever loved, all of the women he had fallen in love with, those lives . . . Is it possible that any of them have ever thought about me again; is it possible that any of them are thinking about me right now? The girl with the small button nose, the blue eyes, the brown bangs . . . May? All of these lives entangled in my own. Again, he asked himself: Do people stop existing the minute I stop contact? Do they stop existing the moment I stop thinking about them? . . . But of course they do . . . and doesn't that go for everyone? And he thought about more people, more voices, as if they were ghosts, as if they lived inside of him . . . "The idea isn't to find things, kid, it's *not* to find them." The best proofs were the ones in which mistakes had gone unnoticed. The best proofs were the ones that preserved the errors, the inaccuracies, and cut and printed and packaged them for the public the next morning. Proof of lies. Every editor-in-chief who hired me to hear a diverse viewpoint in the newsroom and promptly shut their ears, he murmured. It is no wonder that print journalism had gone extinct. And what is worse—that no one seemed to realize on the outside? Or that I thought I could make a difference from the inside?

A vibration near Chris's ankles cut him off. He felt for his phone.

OMG! Out with CHRIS SELDEN ☺ Pourhouse all night. Popping bottles with celebs. Don't hate—appreciate!

Jillian had tagged him on Facebook in a recent wall post. How recent? The time stamp said 9:57. Thirty-three seconds ago. Shit, Chris thought, the girl is quick. He briefly scrolled through his news feed and then exited the Facebook application, clicking on Instagram until he found a picture of a man lying with his body twisted but his eyes staring straight ahead, in profile, looking at the train that would arrive at 49th Street and crush him. The caption read: "This man will die in 2 minutes." Christ, Chris shuddered. Why the fuck did no one pull him up, give him a hand? The obvious answer was because everyone's hands were already full. Their fingers on their cell phones. A word formed on his lips and he opened Google. He began typing until "subway deaths" popped up and he found deaths per year, and deaths per city, and deaths per line in each city, and deaths per line and year in each city, and also: subway directions, and also: subway construction, and also: subway diet, and also: subway restrictions, and also: subway menu, and also: subway surfers, and also: surf lessons, and also: surf and turf, and also: surface, and also: surf taco, and also: Subaru, and also: substitute, and also: sub-human . . .

And he kept clicking on more search results as Google supplied him with them until, exasperated and bored, he clicked out and placed his cell phone back in his pocket, and flushed the toilet (had he even urinated?), and zipped up his jeans, and forgot what it was he'd been searching for in the first place, which was *survival*.

A rolled up, folded newspaper caught his eye as he exited the bathroom. A headline read

MILLIONAIRE ART COLLECTOR'S HEIRESS
DISAPPEARS IN SOUTH AMERICA

And Chris wondered if that was possible, for people—for anything—to just disappear, no trace left to salvage, nothing to hold onto, and if he had clicked back into Facebook, and refreshed his news feed, he would have seen exactly what Johnny Baker was up to now.

Rivington and Clinton, New York, New York
"You guys had to be there. You would have *died*."

Johnny Baker had placed the phone down momentarily, or just muted it, to regale his guests with tales from college. The last time he threw a party for The End of the World, he had to run away from his own apartment. Now he'd have to—what? Run away from the motherfucking end of the world. Shit. Imagine that, he was thinking. And then he did. Houston blocked off completely. Williamsburg Bridge collapsed. Lots of red cones, yellow tape. No way in or out of the city, let alone the Lower East Side. Lines around the block at Meng's Dynasty. A shortage of wontons. Helicopters spiraling overhead as fireballs erupted in the sky—fireballs?—is it going to be like that? he wondered. Or would everyone just vanish at the stroke of midnight? *Poof.* Like they had never existed at all. Everyone except him, of course. He knew the score. He was ahead of the game. He could see the future.

"The future, I can see yours," Francis was saying to him, poking him in the ribs playfully, directing his gaze toward Josefina. "And it's wearing a charcoal blouse and faded jeans." Johnny smiled confidently, running one hand through his hair once more. Shit, he was thinking. I'm getting old, I'm getting tired (he thought about his job at Bank of America: quarters, nickels, dimes, most of all, dollars . . . analytically dying . . .) and upon the invitation, he was looking at Josefina, he was gazing into her in-between eyes, green one moment and brown the next, or concurrently green and brown, but she was looking elsewhere, her eyes fixed on Clarence, concentrating on his form-fitting button-down and his strong jawbone, Clarence who was stuffing more carrots in his mouth, Clarence who wouldn't die starving, who would settle for nothing less than gluttony.

Playa del Carmen, Mexico

The ancient Mayans possessed one of the most precise and hermetically controlled calendars ever used on this planet, a calendar that, in effect, controlled what the populace did, thought, and felt on any given day. Knowledge of the calendar was the monopoly of a priestly caste which maintained its position with minimal police and military force. The priests had to start with a very accurate calendar for the tropical year consisting of 365 days divided into 18 months of 20 days and a final period of 5 days, the "Ouab days," which were considered especially unlucky and, in consequence, turned out to be so. An accurate calendar was essential to the foundation and maintenance of the priests' power. In addition to the yearly calendar, which regulated agricultural operations, there was a sacred almanac of 260 days. This ceremonial calendar governed 13 festivals of 20 days each. The ceremonial calendar rolled through the year like a wheel and, consequently, the festivals occurred at different dates each year but always in the same sequence. The festivals consisted of religious ceremonies, music, feasts, sometimes human sacrifice. Accordingly, the priests could calculate into the future or the past exactly what the populace would be doing, hearing, or seeing on a given date. This alone would have enabled them to predict the future or reconstruct the past with considerable accuracy since they could determine what conditioning would be or had been applied on any given date to a population which for many years remained in hermetic seclusion, protected by impassable mountains and jungles (Sandra averted her gaze from the pamphlet she was reading to glance out the window. She saw: a P.F. Chang's, a Cheesecake Factory, a Hard Rock Café, a Ruth's Chris, and half a dozen designer boutiques dotting the Avenida Quinta.) *from the waves of invaders who swept down the central plateau of Mexico. The goal to submit was implanted by a threat so horrible that the people could not confront it, and the Mayan secret books consisted of such horrific pictures. The few volumes that have survived bear witness to this. Men are depicted turning into centipedes, crabs, plants. All of them, human sacrifices . . .*

"Se presume que los asesinos están armados y son peligrosos."

The radio kept blaring, tuning in and out, but now the driver turned the volume up. "Los asesinos fueron vistos en Tulum."

He turned his head to meet Jack's gaze.

"Vicious," he said in English. Jack nodded and the driver spoke again. "Very dangerous people." He turned the air up and Sandra shivered. Jack realized the driver was still smiling.

Main Street, Hackensack, New Jersey

"Everything alright?"

Chris looked at Jillian, at her vivid eyes, at her too-much mascara, at her too-caked cheeks; he looked at her like she was stupid. Stupid? That's an understatement. The world is about to end, bitch, he was thinking, of course I'm not alright. But instead, he nodded his head and kissed her warmly on the cheek, the too-caked cheek.

"The Great Curve" came on the bar's speakers as people began to mill around The Pourhouse, some of them even dancing, some of them even touching each other, but mostly burping and shouting and probably farting, Chris thought, letting it all go. And he was thinking of the Penthouse at 81 Irving Place, of Alice and Joél and Francis and all of them, all the waifs and ogres at every casting, the guys that looked more like girls, the guys that looked like they were about to explode right out of their skin, veins bulging, eyes about to pop right out of their sockets, and still popping, popping . . . the raisin diet, the Master Cleanse, all of that bullshit, and all for what? So they could all look the same when they were perfumed and tucked in and kissed off to sleep in their caskets, and Chris was thinking, we can only cleanse our bodies so much before we realize it's not our bodies that need cleansing.

"Crazy."

"I heard Rio is crazy," Jillian was saying, drinking another vodka cranberry, the yellow umbrella floating toward the rim. ". . . *Night must fall now-darker, darker . . .*" "Crazy

292

dangerous. Isn't it? I mean, I hear people get attacked on the street, on the beach, I hear people get attacked seven different times in the same day. Did you hear that?"

Chris laughed. "I hear a lot of things," he said. Jillian inched closer like she was expecting him to say more, but he was only listening—but really listening this time. And if René was looking up from his dartboard, he would have seen that look again, like a world was being created before his eyes, like he was the privileged witness to the genesis, like—

"Like, how do you even do what you do?" Jillian continued, and she resumed rubbing Chris's crotch with her knee. "You've got boundless energy. And you say you don't even sleep a wink?"

Chris nodded.

"Not even a wink?"

"*. . . Night must fall now-darker, darker . . .*"

"I like life too much," he said, and he was thinking about Rio, about his first trip there, about how dangerous it really was. But the most dangerous thing he found in Rio was himself; the most dangerous thing he found in Rio was self-knowledge. And hope. And everything that happens is again and again a beginning and it was this hope—not youth, not beauty, not love—but *hope* that kept him moving. "I like what life has to offer me—not only me, not me alone . . . and I soak it up, all of it," he continued. "Everything rubs off on me, rubs into me. Rubs me. (He put his hand on Jillian's exposed knee and he could feel her whole body, damp and hot.) They used to call me the sponge. I wanted to be everyone and do everything." He did not mention that they also called him Jack. *Do you want to be a jack-of-all-trades, or do you want to be a king?* And he knew that he was good enough to be good at a few things; and he knew that he was good at modeling because of his innate and inherited custom of assimilating. Ana and Robert and the ever-enduring process of *becoming American.* Assimilation was, after all, the practice of mimicry. And assimilation was . . . he was thinking now, even as he leaned in closer, even as he re-assembled his face into a somber smile. Assimilation was his greatest pose. And he knew—even now, even on the last night on earth—he was passing. And he knew that to pass meant that he was also being passed around; he was being passed on.

He glanced at the clock. Quarter after ten. He didn't have long. No one did.

"*. . . Night must fall now-darker, darker . . .*"

After Chris paid the bill he took the plastic click pen and pressed hard into the wooden table, deeper and with conviction, engraving his name in ink, preserving the reality that he had come, at some point, which meant he existed. Except it wasn't his name.

PETER DENTON WAS HERE

Chris stood up and walked outside, and telephoned the only person he felt he could still talk to.

Rivington and Clinton, New York, New York
"I was dying of boredom," the short brunette with the bow in her hair drawled when Francis appeared before her. "Where the hell did you run off to?"

"Me? Oh, I just . . ." he paused. He had retreated to his bedroom in the hopes that he could actually follow through with it. *It* was suicide. *It* was teetering perilously from his desk chair while tightening the noose around his neck. Hangings are the work of the melancholic, he thought, even while he was slipping his head into the knot. (His legs were teetering now, but both toes were still scraping the stool.) Hanging is long, drawn-out, dramatic. Is this the effect I want to produce? Francis thought. Is this the effect I *want*? He felt his throat tighten and burn, until he felt a release. (He yawned.) Francis had failed, Francis had failed in everything, he was thinking. Shit model, shit actor, shit caterer. That's all Francis has done—all Francis'll ever do. Catering the same parties my girlfriends attend with their parents, he thought. It's my custom. My costume. Always living above my own means. And why was I even here? Why did I even come? I am from Buffalo, he was thinking, not Manhattan. I was supposed to be an architect . . . I was supposed to design office buildings, apartment complexes, people's homes. People's *homes*. Francis had made a habit of spending whole afternoons standing, silent, eyes shut, on the corner of Trinity and Courtland. In front of the empty lot that was the Twin Towers. It was the first thing he saw when he came to the city. "Had to call my parents," he finished, finally, forcing a smile. "You know, final good-byes and all."

Dying of boredom, Clarence thought, overhearing the conversation from a few feet away, standing above the mortar of hummus, that was, with every passing moment, diminishing. Dying of boredom! He laughed. Aren't we all.

Francis's parents were already dead and he thought about them both, thinking about them the way you would think about ghosts, ghosts that haunt you, ghosts that overtake you, ghosts that talk to you but ghosts that you could never answer (because that was what parents were like, Francis understood, two strangers that give you life, two strangers whom you try as hard as you can to forget about, two strangers who are actually your mother and father and who know less about you than your most distant acquaintance). The girl with the bow in her hair brushed up against him, inched closer, wrapped her short arms around his neck, moved in to touch his lips with hers.

"What's your type?" she purred, and he answered: "Straight, long hair."

"Straight, long hair?" she muttered. "That's all?"

He nodded, looking back at Miranda, lavishing a half-smile a la *Chris Selden*, circa 2009. The world is about to end, Francis thought, but no one ever stops fucking. Everybody needs that last hit of body-to-body contact. And whom he really wanted—if he had the choice—was Miranda. She is blossoming, he thought. She would have made a good mother. He glanced back at her, her hands still rubbing her stomach, her green eyes gripping and soothing and beautiful all in one . . .

". . . *no time for dancing, or lovey-dovey, I got no time for that now . . .*"

"Who made this mix?" Johnny Baker was asking, in between shouts into his cell phone's receiver. "What the hell are 'Talking Heads'?"

Clarence was about to answer when he spotted a break in the conversation and made his move. "So buddy," he sidled up, hummus in hand, and with the other, patted Francis's shoulder, "you stay in touch with anyone over at ABC?"

"Guys," Francis announced, not looking at Clarence but addressing the whole room with his eyes fixed down, as if he were reading his own palm. "There's a series of murders in Mexico. Playa del—"

"Maybe someone's doing everybody else a favor," Clarence cut in, but he wasn't smiling. "Would you really rather be alive for the end of the world?"

"Speak for yourself," Charlie replied, shaking his head, stepping into the narrow hallway to answer his phone.

Chris Star-Ledger

It would always be Chris Star-Ledger to him, even

though he had finally stopped waiting for Chris to return to the newsroom. *But I know Chris Selden. Very well, actually.* Yes, he thought, I know Chris Selden, even if Chris Selden doesn't really know himself.

"It's the end of the world," Charlie was saying, agitated, almost shouting into the receiver. "At least try to have some fun."

"What's that mean?" Chris's voice came scratchy through the cell phone.

"You became an object," Charlie said. "And now you can only see people through the same objectifying gaze; the same way you think people see you."

There was a pause, harsh static, and finally Chris laughed. "The process of reification is complete."

"What's that?" Charlie asked. Johnny Baker was talking loudly in his ear, drunk and drooling, slipping on his words.

"You always save me from myself—" Chris began.

"Are you there?" Charlie asked. "Hello?"

But the line was dead.

Main Street, Hackensack, New Jersey

We all have to die someday, Chris was thinking, and when it came, would it be better for it to be long, drawn-out, a diagnosis like an impending deadline, inevitable expiry, the date scrawled in black across a hollow tin . . . or would it be better to come quick, and without warning, like Thomas Merton, the writer, the Trappist monk, who died flipping the switch on an electric fan (Chris flipped the light switch on), death by misplaced wires, and what did all of it amount to anyway? The search and struggle, the striving for what? Some higher idea, some excuse to stave off boredom, and it was the motion that mattered more than anything, the movement, as if everything depended on action, kinesis, the ability to move past everything and everyone, and Chris was thinking that maybe the whole world was waiting for tonight—the whole world, not just Jillian Aguilera, not just him, but the whole world—waiting for the moment the world would end, hoping, secretly, that it would, since then—and only for a brief moment—everyone would have something to feel, and everyone would be feeling the same thing differently. He was thinking all of these things when Jillian pinned him down on the bed, her hands to his chest, and *I love you I love you I love you I love you* started gyrating, turning and turning as the clock seemed to tick to its inevitable midnight.

Playa del Carmen, Mexico

Chichen Itza was not as close as the Rosewood Mayakoba tour guide promised. They drove along the 180 Federal Highway for what seemed like days, if not weeks, an actual distance of 188 kilometers, or roughly 116 miles. The sun was beginning to recede into the clouds when they pulled up to a crumbling stone arcade marked "Chichen Itza: Pre-Hispanic City" and a crowd of people snapping photos, standing like a big bag of bricks in the sweltering heat.

"I thought it'd be bigger," Jack mumbled and Sandra nodded, directing his gaze past the sign.

"I think it's actually the pyramid behind it. 'El Castillo,'" she recited from her guidebook.

"Well, that's not marked," Jack said in defense, and reached for his digital camera. Wait till Walter and Nancy see this, he was thinking. *Chichen Itza at sunset*—done. "Hey Sandy," he waved to his wife while the bus driver stood off to the side, still smiling. "Mind if you shoot me?"

She flashed a few shots, horizontal and vertical, Jack in profile and then in three-quarters, and then straight on, and two more without his sunglasses on, and then it was her turn. But the sun had gone down already. "Shit," Jack whispered. "The damn 'night capture' isn't working. You want me to just take a photo of the pyramid instead?"

Sandra raised both hands, as if to say, Are you kidding me? "We came all the way here for *your* picture, Jack," she screamed back, through the wind picking up, through the air growing colder, growing heavy. "Let me get *mine*."

He fiddled around with the settings, snapping a few more, shaking his head after every other while Sandra scowled and by the time she re-joined him on the edge of Chichen Itza, it was dark, utterly and absolutely dark, a foreboding dark, a dark that was final. Everyone had left except the driver, who was still smiling. Jack gave him a look, a look Sandra had never seen before and if she had, it was a look that communicated nothing to her or anyone, a look that might just as well have meant, "Take me to the nearest El Rey del Taco; I'm fucking starving."

Jack rubbed his stomach and Sandra wondered if she actually translated the look. But the driver hadn't because he refused to get in the van. Instead, he pushed Jack down on his knees. Jack spit out blood and sand. The moon reflected off the crumbled stones, the columned arcades, the ruined temples, and Sandra saw a look of exhaustion in Jack's eyes, but when she looked again, she saw a look of horror.

The driver was still smiling but now he was also carrying a gun. If Jack had listened to the reports on the news, he would have known it was a Webley .455 automatic revolver. But it could have been a Cougar Magnum for all he knew; it could have been a Snickers bar. He felt nauseated. He began spitting, burying his face in the sand and sobbing. The driver asked Sandra to step closer and she did. She was acting like she was in a daze, Jack thought, briefly glancing up, too afraid to look for too long, but it was long enough.

She was acting as if she were a zombie. He wondered what time it was. Should I bother glancing at my watch? His wrist was bruised, bloody, and the driver kept poking him with the steel, kept kicking him with his boots. Jack coughed. Jack thought his lungs were going to explode.

"You want to see the real Mexico, eh?" he said calmly, kicking more sand into Jack's mouth, circling him like a piñata. "You want to see the spirit of Mexico's Yucatán Peninsula, wasn't it?"

Sandra gurgled. The bitch, Jack thought. Is she laughing at me?

"Well, now you've seen it my friend." He smiled again, his teeth gleaming like fangs. "Mi amigo, right?" *Hahahahaha* . . . and the laughter echoed in the evening, the only noise besides the wind: Jack sobbing, Jack cursing, Jack praying under his breath, Jack still.

Sometimes, human sacrifice . . .

The driver wiped the sweat from his brow with his left forearm and handed the gun to Sandra. Sandra's eyes lit up. Is she thinking about *2666*? Jack wondered, moments from death. Is this what makes *2666* so great? Sandra was thinking, holding the gun in her small hands, feeling the cool smoothness of the steel, the weight of it, the kinetic energy and the power, the curve of the trigger. Now I have an adventure to call my own, Sandra was thinking. Now you get to sit in the corner for a very long timeout. Now you get to shut your mouth.

Mind if you shoot me?

And Jack's mind raced. What were those questions he was forced to ask himself; why wouldn't they come to him now? And instead: other questions, more pressing questions. What time is it? Is it midnight? Is it past midnight? Have I survived after all?

Bang!

Have I survived the end of the world?

Rivington and Clinton, New York, New York
Everything was so cozy, Francis was thinking, laying in his bed, the sheets up to his knees, so why did the world have to end *now*? And everything was perfect, and the TV was blaring, all three of them, and the music was blasting, and the people were laughing and talking—all of them talking—and shouting, too, shouting over everyone else, but cozy, cozy . . . and

Bang! Bang!

Champagne was popping, and Veuve was flowing, and everyone and everything was so cozy, so why did the . . .

Bang!

And more champagne? And Johnny was still on the phone with the bus boy, or the waiter, or the manager, or the motherfucking chef at Meng's Dynasty, yelling, screaming, demanding his dinner, and Francis could imagine his face, his gestures, the particular expression, and why did the world have to end *now*? *". . . it's always showtime, here at the edge of the stage . . ."* And Francis looked out the window, everything was dark and silent but still, tranquil, as if someone had just hit *pause* and there was silence, finally silence, which had its own sound, and it was beautiful, it was heaven, or something like heaven *". . . home is where I want to be, pick me up and turn me round . . ."* and it was as if the whole world were listening to the same song, or at least the same mixtape *". . . cover up and say goodnight . . . say goodnight . . ."* but then Johnny kept talking, shouting into the receiver, and then Francis heard a few thuds, past his bedroom door, past the apartment, outside, far away and yet so close, sounds like bodies hitting the dirt.

Bang!

"Is it here yet?

OUTOFSEASON

"Live without dead time"
(anonymous graffiti, May 1968, Paris)

Halfway through the matinee, I
wake up watching a film to find myself
in the lead role.

The smell of Miami always brings me back.

The smell of damp earth, tropic glades, palm trees trembling. The smell of café cubano and croquetas in La Carreta's window. And each smell brings on other smells, smells from every time of my life and always in Miami. The smell of the old house on Southwest 44th Street, the musty garage, the rusted smell of old tools and old cars and gasoline; the pine-soled floor in the parlor, the smell of Cuban bread pressed on a pan, butter and oil and fat and pillowy galleticas stacked high in plastic packages in the wooden cupboard, black beans cooking on the stove and the sweet barley smell of Malta. The smell of the mango trees, the cotton hammock and the stiff blades of grass that crunch under my feet with every step. The smell of the salt in the wind from the sea; the chemical smell of the pool cleaner and the smell of charcoal burning on the grill. The musty plastic lounge chairs inside the Florida Room, and all the caguayos slipping past my feet, staring at me with their big caguayo eyes.

"Caguayo! Caguayo!"

The smell of my own saliva, my own blood and breath and sweat, and probably baby powder too. The smell of my abuela's perfume, Agua de Colonia, orange and lemon and lavender. Clinging to my abuela's breast, rocking on her lap. Clinging to her breast, her lap, her neck, clasping her tight. Because she was the biggest woman I'd ever seen. And the most beautiful.

And this is why I love Miami. And this is why no matter what time it is, no matter what year, I step out of the airport and I am a child.

A child, a child.

The Fleeting Moments
Between Here and There

TITLE AND REGISTRATION

"Despiértate."

Sense the shifting of weight, the heavy eyes still laden with dreams, the halitosis breathing fire at our face.

"Abre tus ojos ahora."

We do and catch a top down view of Miami in August: palm trees, crooked sidewalks that are rain-soaked on one block and sun-burnt on the next, cicadas buzzing, mosquitoes sucking, the stench of sweat and bodies, splashes in a nearby pool. Spiral smoke from barbecue, smell of mojo marinating on pork, ropa vieja boiling on a stove drifting through an open window, close by abuela cradles niño on rocking chair, whispering, whimpering, "Tranquilito bebito, tranquilito. Abre tus ojos ahora," hand on forehand comes away damp and clammy; the baby is sick. Backyard full of guava and mamey and grass that's grown too high; a little boy singing under a mango tree. Laughter and congas in the background. Somewhere, someone is dancing the merengue. Blond hair reflects gold in the sun. Humming sound of frames changing.

Cut to a young boy mimicking his father as he dresses for work, crossing a tie twice in a knot and pulling it over the top gently then nudging it tightly under his chin.

Cut to a young man rolling over wispy sheets. He leaves a note with his number and address on her nightstand. It flutters away in the wind. Or, it dissolves like dust clinging to old furniture. Or, it falls in a trash bin. She never finds it.

Cut to university. Green everywhere, snaking hills that twist and turn around a mountain-top campus. When it snows you're in the North Pole, the treetops glisten crystalline with a glow that reminds you of heaven if you knew what heaven looked like. Food that makes you sick before you eat it.

Cut to a dark room with a dark man, his face obscured or bandaged.

Cut to silence.

Cut to white walls overlapping blank stares.

Cut to nothing.

LEFT TO MY OWN DEVICES (ACT I)

Awake. Finger the crusty remains of a dream out of lashes and sit up, already flexing, eyes waver from side to side, trying to lose themselves in familiar surroundings but it's not working, so instead, I stare.

A knock at the door can mean any one of various things; trouble in a hard-boiled detective flick, the closing shot in a dramatic comedy about wine and friendship, rising action in a spy thriller set in the dark alleyways and derelict motels of Eastern Europe: Who is at the door? you wonder but you open it anyway, half expecting trouble, half wanting to find it.

Shake my legs awake and I'm on my feet, sockless, scanning my surroundings: white walls flanking white ceilings, white pillow, white mattress. White tile decorates the floor where a single white couch rests, unperturbed.

Mentos commercials, Western musicals, a couple of artsy indies, trashy sci-fi Bs, straight-to-TV romances, true crime docudramas, a diverse résumé that's landed me a one-room studio apartment for the past three days while on set with my latest project.

By Balloon to the Sahara
(re-issued in Mexico as *Danger in the Desert*)

I forget why I was awakened in the first place and instead find myself browsing through a heap of magazines scattered across the floor. I can see the headlines, the cam-

313

eras, the big, burly security guards ushering me into movie premieres and award shows, nouveau restaurants, clubs, discos. I can see everything but me.

"Personal assistants tend to his every wish. He's fed at the proper times, exercises on a strict schedule, and is watched over by security personnel vigilantly."

I'm reading some monthly with my face emblazoned on the cover, smiling like someone at the dentist after they got their caps removed. A shard of sunlight peeks through early afternoon clouds and infiltrates a small window at the rear of the room, characterless except for the locks adorning the panes.

Pause for a moment, allowing myself to breathe this all in before I continue reading aloud; the thought of what I've done or haven't yet is dizzying and I envision the sensory overload an admirer, female or otherwise, must feel upon catching sight of my visage in the newest issue of *GQ* or *Vogue*, *Cosmopolitan*, *Teen*, or my personal favorite, *Youthanasia*, where I was recently outlined in a four-page spread complete with an inspiring montage: Peter after shower, Peter getting dressed, Peter at the beach, Peter eating breakfast—a tasteful series re-appearing on coffee tables next month—Peter flicking off the camera in a sensational display of naughtiness that had adolescents and adults alike screaming for more. Insubordination is the new fad.

You get the picture.

I continue reading like the subject is something new and fascinating.

"His face is emblazoned on everything from cereal boxes to toothpaste ads; he endorses everything from automobiles to deodorant. And now he is appearing in Green Light's latest production in a role so challenging and powerful that it's sure to earn him a heap of nominations and awards . . ."

"So, you're as interested in yourself as the rest of the world is?"

314

Look up and I'm met with the breezy gaze of Freddy Douglass with the press pass to prove it, I think feature writer for *Glam Star*, 37ish, bisexual and loving it but who isn't these days, sporting a goatee that's very last month, if not last year, clad in beige Dockers, a shit-colored tweed polo shirt, gray Sperry slip-ons, and in his hand: a white office pad that matches the room. An equally boring cameraman is situated, crouching, behind him. Or he could just be a complete stranger. But there's always a cameraman behind someone.

"Can you blame me?"

I shrug casually, my eyes scanning the room for the magazine I was just reading, the one I must have misplaced, the muscles in my shoulders bulging unintentionally from a white undershirt suffocated by an indigo jumpsuit. I'm going for that new age space explorer meets Fred Flintstone look and I can tell by Douglass' speechless smile I've nailed it perfectly.

"How'd you get in? I wasn't notified . . ."

Freddy cuts me off, easing my alarm somewhat by asking for an autograph, laughing violently, and telling me that his thirteen-year-old daughter is a big fan, and I'm about to ask for her name when he tells me the reason for his business, which, of course, is another interview.

"Did I okay this deal?" I glance at a white-gold Breguet that isn't there. "I've got to be on set in half an hour," I lie.

"Actually," he smiles, "your publicist did."

I'm startled when he finishes this with an obnoxious giggle, as if he's testing me and I can't even see the questions, let alone the exam, but my thoughts are comforted when I realize he must be attracted to my publicist, Jean Petaire, who is charming and semi-hip in his own way despite the French Decadence act he's been performing, though I still haven't met him in person.

"And this won't take long," Freddy adds for good measure. He pauses, inhaling the texture and shape of the sterile room. "Pretty modest place, I expected better from the son of . . ."

"Don't mention my father," I cut in. "I don't have any problems here; it's quiet and . . ." my eyes circle the room, "I never have to worry about remodeling."

Nervous laughter.

"So you got here, what, three days ago?"

"Three days, three months, it's all the same to me." I shrug. A practiced gesture, except I don't know what I'm practicing. "Any place feels like home eventually."

I force a chuckle and playing the role of real estate agent, stretch one arm out to the side, an open invitation to further inspect the colorless ceilings and walls, the bleached tile and furniture. I direct my hand to the dusty window behind me, the only source of natural light in a room full of synthetic glow. "Anyway, I'm not one for glamour."

"You could have fooled me," he shoots back.

Freddy glances over to the balding man behind him and the cameraman nods, signaling the cue to begin filming. I catch the action and put a face on.

"Everybody likes to hear about this kind of story," he intones. "*Your* story. It's attractive, it's shocking, it's lucrative. Did you ever imagine in your wildest dreams you'd end up here?"

Freddy asks this like he expects a logical answer. He's speaking in his game-show voice and I do my best to please.

"I'd like to think the opportunity was . . ." I halt dramatically, ". . . serendipitous, for the both of us."

I have no idea what I mean, or even what I just said, the words floating past me the moment they leave my lips.

He doesn't seem to be smiling and I'm unnerved but his next question allows me to open up; asking how it all started; he obviously means my life. I anticipate more banter on "the early years of Peter Denton" and I'm too eager to oblige, I've run through it a thousand times, plunging into a vast ocean of thoughts and recollections.

Next I hear only my own voice resonating, a lively chatter; I'm in high spirits now, no drone, the faint chirping of birds, an airplane flying overhead, the tapping of my knees, or his, or someone else's, the rolling of film.

WILD WILD LIFE (OBLIGATORY EXPOSITION)

I know what you're thinking. Rich kid gets everything handed to him, grows up, becomes a rich man that has his hands in everything. It wasn't like that, not always.

Before the thirsty fans and publicity agents, there was just me. Me and my mother, my father, two dogs, and a goldfish. And of course, the cameras. Always the cameras. But mostly my father. You know him; everyone else in the world does.

Except my father was barely ever home, and when he was, he'd disappear for long hours at a time.

Sometimes I did my best to disappear too.

I remember men in suits with briefcases and ten-dollar smiles walking in and out of our house like they owned the place; they shook my hand and asked me how school was going just shooting the shit as if they were part of the family, but I didn't even know their names and I doubt they knew mine. They were just shooting.

Home was a ranch on Flagler in Miami far enough from high school that I'd had to take the bus. The rides were something I looked forward to; some scattered moments where I could prepare my face and learn to think; to practice conveying as the sun shot through me. Palm trees surrounded the ranch's perimeter like our very own jungle except it was anything but natural, guards stationed outside the gates because the security system I never learned to work wasn't enough. Nothing is ever enough. Attendants, waiters, maids, butlers zigzagging through the house inside and out of my life as if it were a circus; sometimes I felt like I was the punch line in a long-running joke. Born under punches. Waiting, waiting. Maybe I'm still waiting for it. I can't remember a time in which my parents were ever alone for more than ten minutes. She played it off well enough but sometimes the whimpers and crying were just too audible not to ignore while I feigned sleep in the next room.

My mother would arise every morning at five and go to bed sometime after dinner but she never really slept until she knew I was safe. Imagine that, but I didn't have to imagine because that was her life, the way she lived, and I often tried my best to put myself in her place, in her mind. All of that worrying, all of that anxiety. Of course, this presented obvious problems when I got shipped off to boarding school in New York halfway through my junior year, and four months later, when she died on my seventeenth birthday, but that's my mother for you. She was beautiful when she was breathing.

Afterward, my father took a more "active" role in our relationship, his first duty deciding on the best university his reputation could buy, and his next, shelling out as much cash as would be necessary to prevent communication with me for the next four years. Suddenly, I drop out and get semi-famous and he walks back into my life like this all happened yesterday.

But I still don't see his face, only hear his voice in the voices of all the assistants that follow me wherever I go.

Our Dobermans—Amy and Lexie—were my best friends until I found people like Henry VIII and Juanita to hang out with one afternoon, walking home from the bus stop near Hialeah, on holiday. It was like all the drapes had been removed from the window of my life, all the dirt and wax and mold, and I could finally look through and see the world as it really was. It reminded me of the first time I got glasses; I used to think the blur and obscurity was just God's way of reminding us we were only human. Now it's death. After an experience like that, who needed anything else?

I spent my adolescence carefree on the sand and shores of Miami Beach when I should have been in Manhattan, at school, cutting everything except History, sleepwalking through class and exams, racing through hallways in various states; worn, sullen, suddenly ablaze (how a mood can change), bodysurfing each morning, groaning with a new lover every Monday without the comfort of love. Taking everything in: sweat, salt, seashells speaking through the drift of generations, baitfish barely touching my feet in the shallow end, the morning joggers with their backs against the sun, forever pushing forward like a Hallmark postcard . . . Making passes at my poetry teacher as I sat in class, rolling my tongue around my lips as she read something I would never read by Kerouac, on the road speeding headfirst, full-force ahead, stopping only to belt out a chorus, or a refrain, taking myself too seriously, or not seriously enough, slipping through the halls of my parents' home as a ghost, cruising along Calle Ocho or Ocean Drive in my father's silver '63 split-window Corvette, top down and shifting, blasting the Talking Heads, inwardly wondering what he would do if I took his car for little more than a joyride until I met him at a rest stop in Tennessee . . . Falling in love with every girl that laid her eyes on me, writing poetry at lunch, between classes, during lectures on scraps of tissue paper and napkins, reading every moment I wasn't, imagining things that weren't really there . . . Stealing my best friend's candy on multiple occasions—Gushers? AirHeads? Jolly Ranchers? All the flavors, particularly watermelon—Going to church every Saturday night instead of Sunday morning with my mother, never too early for salvation . . . Writing the same love poem to four different girlfriends on four different Valentine's Days, coughing too loudly whenever I passed anyone I used to love, or who used to love me, no such medicine for lovesickness; recording all the memories I had solely from the ways in which I wished the events occurred . . . Throwing Ping-Pong balls into plastic cups balancing on railings, or cushions, or curbs, or my own two feet, kicking back, replacing sentiments with bland phrases, expressions I mistook for meanings . . . Unofficially aging every April, hanging out at Coco Walk and Dolphin Mall, in smoke-filled bowling alleys and billiard halls, in swimming pools, in saunas, in Jacuzzis too hot to sweat, in decrepit arcades I thought I outgrew in elementary school or junior high, in back alleys and dirt tracks, at weekend matinees, every movie conflated into only one long preview with no context or storyline, repeated without pauses one two three times as a frame imperceptibly clicked . . . Head slung low in the back of Range Rovers and station wagons, in empty discos and dance halls, in dusty weight rooms that outlive their patrons, amid advertisements such as *Thirst Is Everything*, images of a Sprite can, gleam of sweat, an orangutan, basketball shorts worn inside out or simply reversible . . . Never early or late, or rather only ever out of time, refusing to look at clocks, watches, calendars, and the front page of the *Times*, or even mirrors (I only saw myself in passing), retrospective glances here and there about what I could have done or could be doing or would never do, or what would never be done by me or hardly anyone, parallel realities traced on parchment, each revision moving gradually through time and space, a lifetime of conjectures rooted in hypotheses . . . In a void, imagining things that weren't really there, and would never be.

WORLD OF TWO

Sometimes you think you're the weirdest person in the whole world. You've got these insane, forlorn, lovely thoughts running through your mind that you think nobody else could ever conceive. These thoughts that jump out at you at the most arbitrary times and from the loneliest recesses of your heart, stir you and scare you until you imagine that you are the only person in the whole world that could ever feel this way.

Until you meet these other people and realize you're perfectly normal.

These people that go door-to-door imploring you to switch religions or selling dental insurance, or the ones wearing green checkered flannel underwear and crusty white Reebok high-tops, asking the girl next to them if she farted because they heard something and it wasn't them while they're wondering out loud which Ed Wood film they'd watch tonight, maybe *Plan 9 from Outer Space*, maybe *Revenge of the Virgins*, while you're waiting impatiently at the bus stop near a couple conversing only in song lyrics. Or maybe it's the guy in the lobby of the therapist you overhear talking about the affair he had with his neighbor's black Lab named Bogey and how he's dreading breaking the news to his wife but is worried about approaching DNA tests and the like. Who even admits to a thing like that?

You meet these people and maybe you think *you're* the only normal person in this world. Maybe.

This is what happened when I met Wes outside the only phone booth left on campus my sophomore year at college. Wes was a businessman, except his company boardroom meetings took place in the shade of an abandoned steel mill. He had a curly black mop that was rarely combed and a beard that may have actually been a smattering of dirt stains accumulated over the years. His off-campus apartment also doubled as a porn set affectionately nicknamed "The Boneyard" by its loyal clientele. Wes was a heroin dealer. He wasn't the kind of guy you'd bring home to your parents on the Fourth of July, but then again, I don't know many people I'd want to introduce to my father.

Wes changed majors three times before settling on sculpture. He made a double-sided dildo—one side was for transmitting, like a walkie-talkie—for his senior independent research project and got kicked out of school two weeks before commencement, complaining ardently about "the fallacies of a liberal education" and citing the Kinsey Reports as proof of his project's social value. He had never heard of Kinsey until he saw the film.

My last image of Wes was actually of his pale, lumpy ass. He mooned the Dean of Student Affairs in her pristine, porcelain-lined office, handing his letter of expulsion back to her, after he removed it from his boxer shorts. When he started a footrace with two security officers, he should have known he was toast. With Dead or Alive's "You Spin Me Round" blasting, they chased him up and down campus, past the old stone mill on hillside, across the quad where sorority girls and their boyfriends were facedown, tanning, up through the brick watchtower, pausing at the very top to watch the bell shake before scampering back to the Office of Admissions, as a tour began to settle in. When it was all over, Wes had steel cuffs slapped around his wrists, defeated but smirking, since a squad car had to finish the job.

That was the last I saw of Wes, and probably the last he saw of a college campus.

TRANSMISSION

Could I tell you that it hurt me to smile? To sit there and pretend. That the actual movement of my lips, the crease I had to create in each cheek, the look in my eyes . . . that it hurt. That it felt like dying, and that sometimes, I felt as if I would die. That sometimes, I wondered what else there was, what else there could be, and if there was anything else, if life was waiting, somewhere, how I could ever escape. How I could ever begin again. To sit there and pretend.

I felt defective. Like there was something wrong, something off. Like I was missing something but that that thing was *me*. Like I was a monster. Like I was incapable of being like the others, fitting in, having friendship, or at least friends, people I could call by name and even confide in. Like I was destined to die alone.

Could I tell you any of this? And would you believe me?

ATROCITY EXHIBITION

Sometimes waking is the slow fading panorama of some indistinct shoreline of wherever from inside an airplane window seat, shades pulled up, every person, automobile, factory, stadium disappearing between each cloud. Waking can be the screaming of a stereo from the adjoining room—thin walls, obnoxious roommate—or the frantic beep of an alarm clock that, left unattended, can be mistaken for a high school fire alarm or an emergency meltdown procedure in some neo-fascist clandestine nuclear testing facility if your imagination is wild enough. You wake up outside, on the grass, sprawled out, all wet from the rain but at least you don't have to take a shower.

Sometimes you wake up and you don't know where you are or what you've done.

"Come in, come in—Bravo five-niner where in God's name are you?"—and then muttering in disgust—"for Pete's sa—"

"Hold it, I'm here. No time to buckle your dust, it's too dangerous; we'll cut our losses, save the lambs. Rendezvous at six clicks north by northeast of the eagle's nest—*move out!*"

A voice, vaguely familiar, maybe mine. Can't be more hackneyed except if I tried—unless that's what I'm doing. Going for *stale*. The sound of static on both ends, an explosion, and then a bigger one. I'm running around like I know what I'm doing, bypassing reports of detonations and sonic booms and picking off snipers from the hillside, faint little flashes in the hills, scooping up survivors from the rubble, carrying bodies or maybe just body parts on my shoulder, smiling wistfully. *Wistfully.* Cameras pan to every other building in view, cement blocks shot out like sandwich-bites, gaping holes and withered flags, blue, white, red, and yellow like a parade except it's war. Portrait of holes in nondescript warehouses and homes, mortar shells exploding every time I turn my head someone else is on fire, bullets, metal casings, primers, propellants rattle down in a symphony of chaos. Magazines unloaded into skin like machine breathing *put-put-put.* Wind blows dust and cacti across the camera's gaze. *Urban Desert.* Minimal props, low-budget, but we get the point.

Sometimes you wake up and find yourself the self-appointed captain of a freedom force in the post-nuclear era, 3 AE (After Eradication), on a pretty standard mission to destroy basic artillery, missile supplies, underground lab-testing, the whole nine yards, save as many innocents as possible. As if there were even still innocents to be saved.

This all started three years ago when someone's asshole father decided to blow up the world.

Fade out.

We see a room full of television screens, big 72-inchers, plasma TVs, flat-screen monitors, small gray cubes wedged into the corners of the room. Each screen projects a different video.

Exhibit A: Hundreds of red-beret soldiers wearing green camo marching along the shores of maybe St. George's Channel, lots of green and you think of Leprechauns, no end in sight. One man at the head stops, salutes his company, speaks loud and vulgar in a guttural tongue, "März zur Hölle!" Smiles turned on for tourists. We see torches lighting, fires spreading, children screaming, skin painted red stuck to alleyways and walls of factories, whir-

whir-whir of helicopter propellers flattened down to earth
. . . more soldiers pour out, AK-47s with silencers, 105 mm
Howitzers, flamethrowers too big to carry in two hands,
automatic shotguns, standard-issue combat knives, killing,
shooting, cutting, burning things we can't speak of or die if
we say, get shot in a crowd or hang like a puppet in a town
square full of mannequins too afraid to do anything else
but stare. For once, people are *speechless*. Sound vacuums
that suck the words right out of your throats. Right out
from your lips . . .

The camera moves in a clockwise motion and then back
again.

Exhibit B: Children: black, white, brown, yellow, purple
playing in the street. *Purple?* Hopscotch turns into jump
rope, turns into stickball, turns into target practice. Parents
on sidewalks with roses and daffodils laughing to friends,
speaking affectionately of their sons and daughters playing
on the street turn vicious and pale in the August sun.
Twenty-two-cal rifles replace roses and they cut them down
laughing, cackling like they just won the lottery. Faces and
costumes torn off, we see the same men and women no
jeans and T-shirts and K-Swiss walking shoes but weathered
battle gear, belts and pockets to fit more weapons than
would ever be able to use, thick heavy leather boots,
weather-proof Kevlar jackets. A pack of Menthol Lights.
Raise their guns up to the sky and triumph.

Exhibit C: Middle-aged man, accountant maybe, typing
at computer. We see a view of New York City from his
thirty-story office building lit up like a birthday cake. It's
nearing midnight, deadline's tomorrow, no one else but
a cleaning crew around at this hour and they are secretly
smoking joints in the sixth-floor bathroom with the fire
alarm cupped. Man works fervently, pausing once or twice

to pick snot from nose then cracking his neck, stretching to the side, peers out window. Ash replaces buildings and nightlife in a split second of atomic warfare glory. BOOM. Man worries if he will still make deadline.

Exhibit D: Renowned red button in a dark, dank cellar of a room. Mr. President, celebrated public figure and before that, big-shot businessman, looks around furtively. Excited, eyes open wide in anticipation, bulging sockets, fingers tense and shaking, rushing blood flow to phallus, smell of moisture, saliva forming at mouth foaming can't wait a second longer, sweating, burning, screaming, he orgasms nuclear fury as twitching finger points *down*, explosions and airplanes heard overhead.

Sigh.

Exhibit E: Time of terror, whispers in phone calls and static announcements through megaphones all over towns and rural villages and big, sprawling cities spared in onslaught intermixed with scenes from *The Exorcist*. Everywhere else is dark, decrepit, shells of civilization. People knife each other in their sleep for crusts of bread and lollipops while dogs bark viciously in the background. A slow pan of wild, starving faces . . . hungry for something they can't get on the market. Fruit is worth much more than dollar bills, filet mignons and T-bones and thick slabs of skirt steak. Shit-stained buildings ablaze make these places look like candles from a birthday cake. Ready to blow? People punch through department store glass windows and drive over children for fun. Black jets flying overhead bring gusts of wind: smother candles, smother light. Hanging loose like a disused lantern. Everywhere except here is dark. Shadows emerge on projection reels, sprawled out, legs spread, some crouched over still dying, breathing last breaths no last rites looks like they're dancing. Soul Train. The world is either asleep or in hibernation.

Sometimes you wake up and you wish you hadn't.

REMAIN IN LIGHT

Remember the drive to Miami? Remember the motel we used to stay at, the one with the neon eagle, the wings blinking sporadically, the beak not quite lit? Remember the name? The Firebird, and it was either North Carolina or South Carolina, unless it was actually Virginia. Remember the traffic around D.C.? I remember sleeping through it, I remember asking a million different questions, like: what state are we in now? And: what do they eat here? And: are they nice people, are they good people? And: what are their names? And: what do they look like? As if I could imagine them in my dreams, when I closed my eyes, in the backseat, or gazing out the window at a million different things, everything floating by, everything passing me, a life like riding in trains, landscapes rising from nowhere, but I never rode in a train, at least not back then. Remember the all-you-can-eat breakfast at The Firebird? Remember the looks of the waiters—were they called "waiters"?—the look of someone ashamed, or maybe perturbed, or maybe shocked, or maybe all three, the moment they caught my gaze, and I was looking at them with my hands full and my mouth open; half a dozen cereal boxes, crusty waffles, pillow pancakes, everything dripping with powdered sugar and artificial syrup, margarine, strawberry jam, too much, never enough variety . . . do you remember how it coated your lips and your tongue and eventually your stomach and made you drowsy—you called it *dopey*? . . . Do you remember Pedro? Do you remember those billboards?

South of the Border . . . do you remember driving farther down, going further down, accelerating through Georgia and Jacksonville . . . do you remember the firecrackers, or the time we couldn't find a hotel so we slept in the car—at least I slept—do you remember that? Do you remember when we finally got to abuela's home? Do you remember her home, the cul-de-sac driveway—it was the first one I'd ever seen—the palm trees, the mangos and papayas in the back, the screen doors, the rocking chair, the smell of abuela—a smell I've been searching for my whole life—the way her lips moved when she talked, when she kissed, what her kisses tasted like on my cheeks? Do you remember the twin beds we'd sleep on, all of us huddled close in the same room, and how comfortable it was to be together? Do you remember the time we stayed up late and you parked the car at abuela's, right on that cul-de-sac driveway, but we didn't get out, and we didn't turn off the radio either. Do you remember how you turned the dial on the tuner, in that rental sedan—a Volvo, wasn't it?—and how the song came in clearer, how the static melted in the night? Do you remember the song? I do. *"Bye bye, Miss American Pie, drove my Chevy to the levee but the levee was dry . . . "* Do you remember singing the lyrics to me? Do you remember the look on my face, wonder and delight, and still, trying to remember everything . . . Do you remember the funeral? Or a week earlier, when we got the phone call? *"This'll be the day that I die . . . "* Do you remember the poem I wrote? Do you remember my oath? To never let anyone die again. And to never die myself. Do you remember how I smiled, finally, when I read you my poem? The look on my face when I said: Death is nothing. Do you? *Death is nothing.*

Or am I remembering things differently?

SCHOOL DAZE

Clanking seats far back and to the left of some nondescript lecture hall just like any other lecture hall: EES 11— Environmental Geology; or: *Rocks for Jocks*.

Take your pick I'm bored regardless same old shit and I wonder why I'm even here if I'm an English major, or supposed to be.

"Much of the delay in selection of a site for disposal of high-level radioactive waste has resulted from the need for thorough investigation of the geology of any proposed site. However, in the United States at least . . ."

All I need right now is one pill.

". . . there is also a . . ."

Just

". . . political component . . ."

one

". . . to the delay."

pill

Sigh.

"Howdy, partner!"

The projection screen Dr. Ydobon uses for his slideshows becomes the picturesque cacti rubble of an Old West saloon stroll inside barnyard doors swing back at your ass and you're met with obscene laughter and bottles smashing across the room or maybe on someone's face; old Western saloon duels before noon are not unheard of. Sound of rattlesnakes outside and revolvers tucked neatly in buckskin brown holsters where card players lose more than their teeth for cheating, the fleeting chorus of the Old West plays, bar maids boogie like a more erotic version of the Rockettes in their blue and white checkered blouses red locks sinking downward to a mound of cleavage.

"Get your back straight, you look like something in a zoo acting funny you wouldn't want your mama to see, up down up down, c'mon now your babysitters worked you harder than this!"

Mud in your face dropping hard on the ground you think in between snot rockets of dirt that you were better off staying in school but those flashy commercials were just too tantalizing and anyway, who reads books these days?

"What the FUCK are you doing boy? You got a problem doing push-ups? I said DROP, not stop!"

The drill sergeant, gray-haired, forty-five if a day, buck-toothed and wild-eyed, spits a lump of tobacco in your face and before you can wipe it off your forehead, he rubs it in for you.

"Putain mec! Où est le pain grillé?"

Sun-streaked brick streets lead us onto a path of chardons and acacias and big, rosy amaryllis clumps fuchsia-streaked where an old farmer is teaching his youngest son how to churn the butter, resembling something perverted to the trained eye. Accordions bounce off Parisian sidewalks and find their way into the palace of King Louis III. Attendants scurry back and forth, frantic, knowing all too well the price they'll pay for being late with monsieur Louie's liverwurst sandwich.

Images, same as the first, replay and overlap, unceasing, irregular click of frames changing and I get the sense I'm reading the same sentence over and over and over; a lack of focus.

Over and out.

My eyes divert to the head of the room and nothing much has changed except the hands of the clock hanging from the upper right corner of the auditorium.

"And I'm afraid that's all we have for today. Remember—review session in Baldwin at 7:30 tomorrow."

Over and out.

LIFE DURING WARTIME

Dusty pamphlet banded with rubber bands, torn pages, a tattered cover, notes and recollections scrawled in black ink, no author named or a name rubbed out, excavated somewhere years later more intact than the tomb of Ozymandias. Which is to say *unread*.

Day 7, Year 2

At dawn, we journeyed to Coconut Incorporated on disposable rafts so as to not give away our presence to helicopter patrols and flashing strobe lights. About noon we reached shores, cut open rafts, quietly throwing shrunken rubber in foliage set about path to the Holy City. Skulls littered our path like yellow bricks if we knew which way to go, shrieks in distance rapidly approaching, hawks with steel eyes and camera lenses for talons hover by, circling us, watching while recording. We stay close to one another and shoulder on. Heavy equipment combined with lack of water gasping for air freezing wind rips apart flesh gasping for breath and nutrients, substance, warmth, anything with a hole to be inside. We come to a fork in the road about two clicks later, dense berry bushes separate the path, pick a few, split up; I go left with two others. Four go right. Hear screams and splatter of blood on bodies no more than a hundred yards away, shake head, whistling silently, wild mongrels pick your breed mutated by scientists I've never met or Coconut's vigilant patrols, or else sick stagehand joke, continue on. These patrols have ways of dealing with you explosive diarrhea for one you could cough until your lungs collapse they have instruments of torture you might think they are perfect gentleman or ladies when they smile bow courteously but you can always tell a spook by the color of their eyes—silver—and when they catch you it's usually over before it begins.

Day 21, Year 2

We reach the Holy City inappropriately named except for the blood baptized foreheads of bodies littered like patron saints as far as eyes can see Ash Wednesday came early. Only one left besides me. Johnny barely walks, I drag him along invisible leash in one hand and .357-caliber magnum in the other. The city is deserted but for mutilated bodies and the glare of Satan, stinks of death and vomit and cum between the crumbled half-eaten basilicas of the Byzantine Empire blasted through by big German B-52 bombers, a set of aviators left behind from ages ago or another set. No sign of rendezvous point or reinforcements; the setting is desolate, typical of old apocalyptic dreamscapes and tumbleweed Westerns, evidently someone got here before me, before me and after a whole crew evacuated, I begin to think I've made a mistake in my own arrival, smile wistfully and shoulder on. Wistfully. Straddle the scene stragglers roam sidewalks see more clearly between dust balls and sweat piercing eyes city streets reduced to nothing knives in hand they've got towels over faces to protect from sandstorms. Looks dangerous, chances—who's taking any? Shoot one, then two pop-pop-popping of bullets into flesh like suction-cup screams barely audible (I've got a silencer). Third vagrant turns my way I wonder if this was my rendezvous out of ammo only clicks of air in exhaust don't waste time looking back drop Johnny and run.

(day and year omitted)

Alone in the jungle just like any other jungle serpent vines that sway like swings in all directions, foliage, thick, dense, menacing eyes glaring, smell of fruits and wild passion, something dirty and beautiful both feet in quick sand, maybe, I don't like to find out, screeches and howls, comforting knowing I'm not alone I've never been in a jungle before. So many smells you can't quite classify because you never quite smelled them before the only thing left to do is guess, veered off course, Holy City got me nothing, no new information, no visual transmission, no reed to keep writing (almost), supposed to rendezvous with the others, take out remainder of Coconut's men, seize fortress, move onto next objective, et cetera, this one in our own backyard but lost whole company eight days ago no fortress even standing to seize big joke blew up in my face no punch line thoughts of "who set me up?" and "where the hell am I?" particularly the last one. Born under punches. Radio broken reduced to nothing makes survival impossible syntax breaks, separates, dissolves, starving lungs gasping for breath and nutrients, substance, warmth, anything with a hole to be inside. Street signs characteristically pointing me in different directions follow one, folded knees on mound of dirt beneath a palm tree temple in the background tropical forest sounds smooth jazz drums and silent whistles as I fall asleep. Fade out.

MORE THAN A FEELING

It was the hallucinogens that did me in. Queens of Diamonds, or Daisy. In college, I got serious about my drug habit. It provided a good backstory. Everyone loves a comeback; everyone loves to see an egg crack. For a long time, me and Wes had this mutual relationship; I'd hook him up with as many girls as he could stick in a film at The Boneyard and he'd supply me with the mind-fuck of my choice. But it was hallucinogens that really got my blood pumping. Or made it stop altogether.

After I did Special K, everything else was just supplementary. Fentanyl, morphine, marijuana, heroin?—that was child's play instead of the play, the film, the movie that was always on if you had the cruising eye of a camera to see it.

I had dreams. I also had nightmares. Fires burning everywhere, whole cities evacuated or else vanished to ashes, no graves, no sign, no traces to say London, Paris, Tokyo ever existed.

I tried calling newspapers, public service stations, local politicians, even my father; warning, protesting, anything, but all I got was a one-way ticket to a psychiatrist who gave me red and blue stress balls and told me I looked like a young Harrison Ford. Stresses of academia . . . It's practically an Ivy! . . . Just a stage . . . Just a stage . . . Doctor Ralph Cohen wore whatever hair he had left parted to the side in an attempt to hide his receding hairline and asked me if I was ever sexually attracted to my mother or else afraid of my father's power to castrate me—Freud, I suppose, and I think I replied *yes* to at least the last question.

"Ever seen *Blade Runner*? Ever seen *The Frisco Kid*?"

"*The Frisco Kid*?"

"It's just . . ." Dr. Cohen reaches for my stress ball. "Remarkable. The chin, definitely the chin." Thumb and index finger pressing deeper. "The similarities!"

"Excuse me?"

"I'm sorry," he says, squeezing and squirming, alternating between a smile and a lopsided frown.

"Can I have my—"

"I'm sorry but I *need* to write this down."

"Stress ball—"

"I think *I'm* having a breakthrough."

"A breakthrough?" I ask.

"A veritable eruption," he says, still fingering the red ball. "The pimple has popped."

"The pimple?"

"Metaphorically speaking," he says, letting the ball drop, rubbing his cheek. "Shall we attend to the evidence?"

He flips a switch and now the lights are off. The curtains close. Light pours in from a projector. "How about *Hanover Street*?"

Both chairs begin to vibrate, tremble, recline.

"But I thought you wanted to talk about my past?"

UNKNOWN PLEASURES

Peter was the kind of boy who liked games. Hide-and-Seek, hopscotch, Hot Cross Buns, who'll blink first? (he always lost) . . . in an old video he stands for hours, silent, eyes closed, listening for any sign the earth is actually moving. Clickety-clickety-clack . . . the wheels go round and round . . .

He viewed his life as a moving picture; he saw himself as a superhero, an alien, sometimes invisible, sometimes barely-there.

At twelve, he picked up a new act: Shy boy with wide-brimmed glasses. Soft, worn eyes like flannel. He felt it could be his thing, since all the world knew: you had to have a thing. If you didn't have a thing, what were you?

Shy boy with wide-brimmed glasses

He still remembers the first time he shot himself to pieces. It tickled tremendously . . . (he was disposed to tickle-fits), it burned and it screamed, and he could see his hips heaving but oh, how it felt so good . . .

Removing his hand from his pants with webbed fingers, rubbing out the sap or sometimes letting it dry there, right on his jeans, maybe saving it for a reminder of being outside himself, a possibility of escape.

He'd rush to hump another bedspread, close his eyes and sigh in the back of the bus, or play pocket pool while roaming the halls, one hand holding his books (an old stage trick). Long, striped diner straws, Bunsen burners, the butterfly stretch in gym class . . . sometimes all it took was a depraved smile.

He liked danger, forbidden things; any kind of kick that felt a little wrong was at least a little right. And everything right was worth doing.

But everything he arrived at sank away from him. Scholarships, girlfriends, Varsity letters, even the love of his mother.

Boredom is a killer.

He could speak, at least when he wasn't on his act. When he wasn't doing anything but inventing whatever it was he was saying. I mean the words . . .

Probably he was disgusted with language, probably he was bored, again, and he liked the surprise that exists in any moment of creation, but he would invent every single word. And each word he invented could mean any number of things but it was all understood, and it was all picked up and tried on and passed along . . . and he shared this language with his mother, and she returned his words with her own, and it was like they were inventing a new language out of the old one. Like they were saying something and nothing at all, except what they were really saying was this: Anything could be turned into anything else.

It was a sort of salvation.

MEMORIES CAN WAIT (LAST NIGHT'S DREAM)

In my dream I came back to Miami. I came back to 8530 Southwest 44th Street. Except this time I was with my girlfriend and her parents, neither of whom speak Spanish. I had a sense of foreboding which haunted me all day.

We walked around an outdoor market that I had never been to before, with shops I had never seen, with clothes and jewelry and items—so many items, contraptions, utensils, sockets and plugs, video cameras and projectors and lights—that I had never seen before. There was a sense of foreboding, and it followed me. Followed me.

The phone rang. "Your mother's died." Wailing, down on my knees, wailing, crying, sobbing, slapping the floor. Thwack. Thwack. My flesh hitting wood, wood hitting flesh. Some kind of contact. An echo. Thwack. I continued to wail, putting my palms across my face, as if I could gouge out my eyeballs, and if I could, as if that would solve everything. As if that would give me peace. It is a frightening thing to have so many memories center around one person. You risk, one day, being left only with the memories.

I ran. I ran screaming through Miami, which looked more like New Orleans than Miami. Rivers and ridges and hollows, and big hanging evergreen oaks; the Miami of my dreams, through the market, and the gardens, and the park, and the streets. Eventually I found my way back to my girlfriend's house. Or my house, in which my girlfriend was staying. I couldn't remember which it was now—mine, hers, neither of ours—but I slipped through the front door, the knob turning slowly, haltingly, as if the foreboding had followed me here, all the way back.

My mother and father looked at me like I had never left. We die with the same unconcern that we live.

What's for dinner? What's for lunch? Have you eaten? You look tired. You look ravenous, my mother purred, pinching my cheek. The phone rang. "It wasn't your mother," the voice said. I looked at my mother. She was still smiling, still looking at me like she wanted to feed me. Maybe to hold me too, to hug and kiss me. "It was your grandmother. Tu abuela."

The air went out. Gasping for breath. Men know that the mist is not their friend. Regret. Crying. And wailing, wailing . . . I never got a chance to see her . . . I never got a chance to say good-bye, I moaned, banging my fist on the carpet, my fist burning and bruised and bleeding. It is a frightening thing to have so many memories center around one person. You risk, one day, being left only with the memories.

My grandmother. Mi abuela. I thought of her wide eyes, her thick lips, her sing-song Spanish, her flowing gray hair, streaks of charcoal through the center, and her heavy laugh, and her galletas, her Galleticas María, and the way the crackers sounded in her mouth, and every chew, and her broom, her big wooden soup spoon by which she stirred her frijoles, her black beans. Black, black . . . back back . . .

And then it occurs to me that my grandmother, mi abuela, has been dead for eighteen years.

BIZARRE LOVE TRIANGLE

And here he was, so different from you but just enough of the same, so that you could identify his habits, attitudes, actions . . . his manias, even his perversions as your own. Just enough that, like any character, he'd cease to be a person on a page in favor of becoming you; your own image. Like any character, it is you, in the end, who does the creating . . .

And it's still the same, whether or not your eyes are closed. Whether or not you are looking right at me.

BREAK FOR STATION IDENTIFICATION (ACT II)

Awake. Groggy, either from the abrupt arousal or the codeine shots (I guess) they gave me. Rubbing arm gingerly, grimacing, "Where the hell am I?" and other similar thoughts.

ABDUCTED?

The words splash across the screen like a puddle of blood in a smoky San Francisco film noir and I shiver on cue.

Recollection is hazy. In fact, I can barely remember the plot. Inner conflict, I think. Are we already at the *Inner Conflict?* Somewhere, a violin is playing. Deep thoughts, anguish, isolation, loneliness. Melancholy and the infinite sadness. Is this what I'm supposed to be feeling? Montage of my besieged face drooping solemnly, unshaven, unkempt, in an indigo jumpsuit looking out my nine by five space, furnished with a lovely cot I bet's not Sealy Posturepedic, a toilet, a sink. One mirror.

Crack my neck a little, senses return, scents of anise, tarragon, confectioner's glaze. Just open space. Open space and a bevy of beeps and whirs. I'm not in any prison and if this is a sanitarium, it's doubling as a spaceship.

A voice startles me.

"Peter Peter *pumpkin* eater!"

The childlike voice of the sister I never had.

"How are *you* this afternoon!"

The tone is more excited than inquiring and I'm about

to say something frank and rude and you can use your imagination when I look up and catch her gaze and take her in: blond hair and soft blue eyes almost gray in the dim light you think of meadows and ponds and backyard swing sets, and I'm smiling and privately embarrassed about my appearance; how I appear.

She turns her head to the side and repeats the question, this time with a question mark, running a gloved hand through hair spun by Rumpelstiltskin.

Somewhere, a violin is playing.

Or maybe a whole Philharmonic Orchestra.

"Peter? Pe—"

"Waitaminute, first let's ask *where* am I?" I'm blurting this out and it can be construed as bad manners, which I regret now, looking back on it.

"Where do you want to be?"

Looking back on it . . .

Devil in a blue dress and I almost smirk, is that an invitation?

"I can think of a few nice places, what do you think?" I ask, staring at her lips and thinking the dirtiest thoughts permitted in a hospital, if this is a hospital. If she is my sister. She's wearing a blue satin dress and those white latex gloves that make me wonder if Vaseline was sold separately.

"Depends."

"On what?"

I don't hear her answer because she disappears. *Poof.* Maybe she was never there. I close my eyes and open them again and again.

And again.

No girl, only a stream of light. I float higher and higher lying face up in the air I think of Jesus Christ pass receptions desks with no lines and offices dimly lit through pellucid glass rusted panes above each doctor's name and several terracotta flower pots and vases synthetic hyacinths that add a sense of comfort to this house of the dead and dying, and some other things I can't identify or begin to describe; I've never been in this kind of hospital before.

And believe me, if you're lost I'm some oil tycoon's wife alone in the Andes wearing high heels and sporting an umbrella for the shade.

I turn my head and see the white bedspread, the crumpled pillow my head rests on, the shrieking wheels; I'm on the bed and the bed is moving; I'm being carted off, calm, smiling faces all around me, no sign of the blond I was just talking to, lots of clipboards and clinical talk— nystagmus? Dancing Eyes?—and sporadic interjections of laughter, sarcastic or otherwise and it's all very *Jacob's Ladder* it takes me a while to realize I was never floating in the first place when the tram ride comes to a halt.

I'm let off rather roughly, thrown face-first in another room with an array of colorful monitors as the beeps and whirs return, a compact disc of mating calls and salutations, heavy doors that close behind me. Another stream of light and this time I'm seated, strapped down to a wooden chair while nurses take turns looking at me and taking notes as an eighth-grade science project. Frog legs kicking in the distance. Madonna's "Like a Prayer" blares from nondescript speakers I can't see and her voice gets louder and louder until I'm sure it's not just in my head but I close my eyes anyway.

"The subject's name is Peter Denton."

"I hear you call my name" and the voice goes on talking as if I'm not here, as if I never was, whispers in the background, nodding of the head, brief pause to consider my next possible move.

"The subject went comatose and just awoke this afternoon. He is unaware of his surroundings."

"You can say that again."

"He is unaware—"

I curl into a ball; I close my eyes; I tap my bare feet against each other until they're a bruised sierra red; I pretend to be dead or else asleep, anything to be invisible and *"I'm down on my knees"* another voice breaks the meditation before it even can begin.

"The subject is not responsive to any method of provocation."

"Have we tried them all?"

"One wonders, dear fellows . . ." allowing his glasses to drop onto the bridge of his nose, "how he can perform—"

"With such élan—"

"Such style and vigor—

"Given the circumstances—"

"Effortless."

"Vitals are normal though he is incapable of remembering anything directly before the incident."

"No surprise there."

"Well, good ol' Ydobon could swap brains on the interstate doing sixty."

It's either raining outside or there is a leak in a nearby room, series of audible splashes and this can get annoying after a while, I think this can get downright painful, horrible, the monotony of it, the absence of silence, the drip-drip-dripping and *"You are a mystery"* smile inwardly and maybe I laugh at the irony; at least they've retained a trace of humor.

And a trace is better than nothing at all.

"At least he's still alive."

"Alive and kicking."

"He sure can kick."

"Take him to the lab for more testing. The subject must be operated on further before he is permitted to exit."

"Before he is permitted to enter."

"Before he is permitted to—"

It becomes easy to float after enough morphine. After enough Demerol, methadone, opium. After enough.

"What we are doing here is simply an exercise."

Open my eyes and I'm in another room. I have the sense that what I see is becoming closer to real as I continue to look. They call it "Dancing Eyes." They say I sure can kick. Twirling, twisting, dancing eyes, and I continue to look. Grimy white walls turning putrid gray and yellow and filthy brown discolored, crooked signs pointing THIS WAY to the Operating Room screams and howls in the background, mainly for effect, I think, but shiver anyway. I imagine nuns with shotguns and clowns that don't smile. These things scare me and I am petrified. Rodents dressed in lab coats and white gloves and funny-looking glasses you know are not prescription playing with my insides with a pair of plastic toys. I can't move so instead I stare. A frame skips (the unending replay of a scene), a sound like a dashboard directional clicking as if a blur. I am stuck here forever *"Heaven help me"* and I never thought I'd be living vicariously through a Madonna song as much as I am now.

VANISHING POINT (RISING ACTION)

Some of what happens next I forget, or perhaps better I never remember.

"I trust you had a nice brunch earlier, how is your appetite progressing?"

And sometimes: "Would you rather have sponges for feet, or not be able to distinguish babies from English muffins?"

Like that's an easy question.

"Mr. Denton, Peter—can I call you Peter—when did you first realize you were *cracked*?" when I am particularly well-behaved. The voice, sniffling monotone harmless nasal pitch, is always the same.

If I'm not being carted off to provide the spare parts for some LEGO project I am usually left to my own devices. I explore the inner workings of the facility and discover that it is much bigger than I ever imagined. Imperial Chinese temple? Ruined towers of Russia? French landscape garden? Hermit's retreat? Turkish tent? *Eccentric*? The architect had tried hard. Plastic flora flourishes around the artificial waterfall flowing from the second-floor lobby to the scientists' quarters below where they take the most esteemed guests on adventures—they call them visual journeys— to Renaissance Italy, Hellenistic Greece, Teutonic Order Prussia, Apocalyptic Earth in the distant future jungle terrain and mushroom clouds of dust, Ancient Samaria, 1890s London smack dab in the middle of the Industrial

Revolution, soot-covered slave boys climb out of chimneys to say hello. *Hello.*

Subjects who misbehave get any number of worldly tortures, maybe it's the Judas Chair or Strappado (also known as "reverse hanging" or "Palestinian hanging") practiced during the Spanish Inquisition, maybe it's the Iron Maiden of Nuremberg or the Chinese Water torture popular in Italy during the sixteenth century. Lunch with the Duchess and a bath with the neighborhood dandy.

They force you to work long hours at low wages, stick you in fine homes with people you don't really know called *families*, make you wish you were more successful and prosperous all the while tying you down to plush couches, green leather recliners and La-Z-Boys watching television, break for vowel movements and commercials, or just shit yourself lest you miss the Final Spin.

"Shall we run the film backward?"

We watch live footage of the ordinary world gone crazy where mobs converge with dynamite and bowler hats and plenty of KY, assembling inside the Liberty Bell and other national monuments, looting the residential sections of every great sprawling city and flicking matches over shoulders toward gasoline-spritzed skyscrapers, stopping only to pose for the fearless news reporter trailing each one, and if you think Black Monday at the Palisades Mall during the great rush of '76 was ugly, honey, you have no idea.

They send special technicians down there on clandestine operations in the name of advancing science with gloved hands if you're lucky open up your assholes and glide cameras inside shivering from the wind machine you shudder wondering what the bipolar cutting forceps are for or where your tonsils went while the same scientists replace your skin with another animal's and you watch it happen with the mirror they place in front of your eyes, kept intact to remind you who you used to be—the insides don't match the outside—and when you're trying to speak, when your lips start to quiver, when you're fumbling for just the right word, *le mot juste*, you really know the meaning of spilling your guts.

If you're lucky.

A quick shift in the hips and you are looking out through someone else's eyes.

So I devise plans. Calculate formulas. Draw elaborate maps. Forge documents. Anything that needs to be done and most things that don't. I play the mission's actions out in my head. I contemplate what I will say in the event of capture (likely) and what I will tell my friends and distant acquaintances supposing I escape. I make weapons out of crude material, bludgeons out of the most unexpected things. Toothbrushes and tweezers become twin daggers, lethal weapons in the hands of a trained assassin. I do push-ups (five sets of fifty) when nobody is looking and especially when they are. I look the part. And I like the part. I spend hours at the hospital's library; I read Dostoyevsky, I read Trotsky. I part my hair to the side. I write letters to my district's congressmen complaining of the harsh realities of the public healthcare system.

For a week (I guess), I become James Bond, Jason Bourne, Angus-fucking-MacGyver. Every character plays the role of a character who plays a role. In the absence of kings, the tradition of succession and the succession of tradition is played by celebrity archetypes. And the curtains rise.

"Peter Pan—room service has arrived . . ." mouthing faux chimes of a bell, Dr. Ydobon with an oversized mole on his cheek and a shiatsu for a hairpiece arouses me for breakfast. "And this belongs to me."

He forces a gloved hand toward my bedside and grabs a black composition notebook labeled *Reflections from Damaged Life*.

I'm quick on the uptake, spring from the mattress wide-eyed startling him with a preemptive strike, knocking him out with two quick jabs and a pillow-throw for good measure. Quickly undressing the old geezer, I strip too and we switch clothes. I tuck him back in bed and whisper closed captioning in his ear then glance in the mirror and fix my collar. The rest is up to fate, I think, but I know better. Reality favors coincidences and slight anachronisms.

I race out the room until I remember my disguise, walking slower, taking in the sights, breathing in the stale air and pretending to be late for an appointment. Create a distraction just so long and long enough.

The frantic drumbeat in the background picks up tempo, "Take On Me" by A-Ha (excellent choice, I think) matching my footsteps, adrenaline's pumping but I'm not nervous so I shake it off and crumple my brow into a sad contortion, my best wrinkled face, hiding my broad lips and vibrant eyes while dozens of hospital employees and nurses wave and smile, nodding with probing stares like a mother who doesn't know her teenage son is having sexual intercourse, something's different, she thinks, but she can't quite make it out. I reach the waterfall, climbing one foot past the other, almost tripping up the stairs, water splashing beside me, drops pelting my white jacket and maybe I can see the light at the end of the tunnel but all I see is Alberta, the overweight, pasty receptionist freckles and curly black hair, foaming at the mouth with the bulge of a retainer and I think God, what a stereotype, shoot the writer, the director, and especially, the cinema MC, and send the projectionist home. She knows my face and this vital fact eludes me, her half-smile is telling, but she whistles a 1920s fox-trot tune and brushes past and I'm up the steps in an instant, hearing the rush of the waterfall behind me, waving good-bye to the camera at the double door entrance as the music comes to a halt—"I'LL BE GONE . . . IN A DAY . . ."

This is how it could have happened.

Instead, I'm roused earlier than usual for breakfast and this time it's not Dr. Ydobon with the oversized mole on his cheek and a shiatsu for a hairpiece but my mysterious friend, the blond I met when I arrived three days or three hours ago.

"Peter! I can't believe it—it's been so long."

"Too long," I mouth.

It's like having a conversation with my girlfriend from junior high. We speak in that roundabout way, talking in silences and the spare moments of quiet between thoughts, like we're telling spy secrets, giving signals for something much greater but not actually saying what it is. Speaking in silence.

"Maybe not long enough?" I try.

I'm playing it cool—telephone two days past the first Sunday after you get her number, right? The number-one dating rule I remember from the earliest days of adolescence, when the parameters were drawn—pretending like I expected her here, at this exact place, at this exact moment, as I'm strapped to a bed.

"Well, I'm glad we got the chance to talk before you headed out."

"Headed out?" I return, "When am I leaving?"

"Well," she smiles, pointing to a clock in the rear of the room, "your time is almost up! And anyway . . ." she nods enthusiastically, "you can leave whenever you want."

NEXT EXIT

I take one step outside and look back for the last time. On the surface, the hospital looks more like a hastily-assembled trailer park than a high-tech medical facility. Stone-faced men and women on go-karts packing up the set.

The insides don't match the outside.

I rub my feet roughly on the dirt road and wonder what's underneath. I imagine elaborate tunnels created by another race, another species maybe, those small men with green hats and pointy ears in the Keebler Elves cookie packages. Tunneling deeper and deeper, occasionally one or two extraordinary elves would volunteer to escape to the world above the earth to gather intelligence, trade secrets, pass themselves off as worried parents, suit-clad businessmen and underappreciated teachers, workaholics doing overtime, gung-ho unabashed feminists, liberal lobbyists, right-wing extremists on radio talk shows, the prototypical American.

Who am I kidding? I am having a tumultuous day, a terrifying, turbulent day, a day that has the quality of a dream. Dreaming.

Maybe what I need is some rest. That's the problem with the paranoid mind: inquisitive, lingering, aware of something and nothing at all.

The paranoid mind is never at rest. The paranoid mind is always drawing conclusions, inventing elaborate plots and impenetrable mysteries, alert, uneasy, disquieted, alarmed, chasing shadow men in and out of shadow buildings, shadow rooms, dark, decrepit alcoves of the shadow brain. A headache becomes migraines becomes brain cancer. A sore throat is obviously the first signs of hepatitis and should be checked out immediately. One minute you're working an office job at some multifaceted conglomerate of wherever, the next you're a computer hacker joining forces with rebel warriors to battle a malevolent cyber intelligence system.

There are no longer any coincidences. No room for chance, luck, or any other word we assign to amputate the nebulous from the inexplicable. Constellations become horoscopes to arrange your life by; shapes of the clouds become decrees. Ancient Romans went to war over bird sightings—augurs called them divinations. Maybe the whole world is paranoid. Maybe that's the only way it's ever been.

I walk past cardboard cutouts of defunct factories, seedy motels with letters missing from their neon signs, seldom-used saloons and cattle ranches of the Old West, overdone restaurants promising steak and pasta and fat, deep-fried crab cakes on their flashy posters. I feel like an anonymous gunslinger ready to swing my Webley .455 from its holster and give somebody a lesson in humility.

"Do you feel lucky?"

But all I really feel now is tired and lost. And about to find a nice cozy corner on the side of the road to retire for the night until I hear a honk and I turn, eye-catching a cab strolling slowly from behind.

I reach for my pockets, finding a Jackson I don't remember putting there—I don't think I've ever called one that before—and without hesitation, hop in. The driver is dressed unusual for the occasion, a droll gray suit and greasy hair parted to the side; I think of Mr. Rogers.

He's got silver eyes but I don't register this fact because he's wearing shades.

What happened to me?

366

The question lurks behind every dead-end alleyway that we pass driving back to university. I see it in the way the moon reflects a glare on the glass windows of the nondescript shops and anonymous street signs where I can make out letters but not any legible words and I'm wondering where exactly I am and who's writing my lines. The parts don't add up and I've missed out somewhere, the way it feels when you exit a cinema and see the puddles of water collecting near the sidewalk, slapped on every scrap of parked metal that you walk by walking to your own, indicators of a passing storm that's already passed without you.

I don't want to think about it anymore so I just stare out the window and pretend to watch the scenery, a seated somnambulist waiting for someone to hit me over the head.

Twenty minutes later, the car stops at the entrance to campus and I place the folded up twenty in his hand, telling him to keep the change, calling it a *Jackson* again, getting out and slamming the door behind me so quick I never realize until I'm in my dorm again: I never gave him a destination.

GRIEF POINT

Her disease had no true beginning—does anything, ever, start as a stopwatch does, clicking on and off, on and off? Off . . .—only gradients of degradation, misery, only her: gradually peeling away like an unripe orange; stiff, rigid, cool to the touch, embittered, even a bit acerbic . . . peeling until she was fleshless, a skeleton—no, not even a skeleton, not even a . . .—until she had disappeared completely. Memory is a sieve, a slit between fingers, images and sensations dispersed right down to the digits . . . the cold fingers clasping a bedpost. Memory. A muslin that unfurls to let the cold breath through. I can still feel hers. Just as I can hear her voice—her real voice, her lively, sing-song Spanish voice . . . playing as the music I grew up with, the music I heard when I was a child and still hear today.

No true beginning, no true beginning, no true beginning . . . does anything, ever?

•

When was the last time she called? The last time she telephoned you, I mean.

—The last time? The most recent time?

—Yes, the last time.

—Before, or after she died?

LOVE FOR SALE

"And for you, monsieur?"

The subject's name is Peter Denton.

"West End Girls" by the Pet Shop Boys opens gently, cascading on the lobes of each ear as the camera glides through Café Arcadia on the corner of 40th and Maine of some bustling metropolitan city, lights dimmed though it's the middle of the day, bus boys hastily walking from one table to the next, waiters with fake mustaches and even less authentic French accents, violins playing somewhere, golden chandeliers and china silverware, coffee-burnt menus for effect and prices amounting to a minimum wage month's pay, which make me wonder why I keep going back to these places.

Most likely because of her.

"Oh Peter . . . are you feeling alright? You look a little pale. A little dead in the eyes."

A sinking feeling like you've been here before no longer is it a case of déjà vu, a question of whether you've dreamed this or done this but rather whether you've done this or only *seen* it happen; whether you've watched it on screen.

She talks about her internship at 40 West clothing, the new Cher CD, the Beyoncé, the parents' summer home in Seaside, the brother's bar mitzvah. She talks about getting a new washing machine, a leopard skin recliner, a sliding door navy minivan, the bare standards of American living that would make even the loneliest person happy. She talks about marriage and three kids and a townhouse in Boca that would be perfect to start off with and she saw the ad in the paper the other day. She talks and talks and I can't hear any of it.

To start off with—

Nod, nod, smile. Rinse, wash, repeat. I am a washing machine that never stops spinning. This is going surprisingly well. Nod, nod, smile and I think maybe if I keep smiling she won't know the difference.

"And we have to start picking out window drapes. I read in the latest *Kitchen Living* that the house is *negligible* compared to its furnishings and I quote, 'a good set of drapes makes a secondary home first rate.' Notice the rhyme?"

How clever, I would think if I actually were listening, but I'm not. And as I read back the transcription, I'm stone-faced. This is about four months after I dropped out of school and moved to the city and got a call that sounded like: "Peter Denton I would have never guessed look who's dropped into town and I thought we'd never meet again my friend Sandy *swore* she saw you walking alone downtown last week but she couldn't say for sure since she said you were in a big rush or something and, well, anyway, I *had* to call!"

Someone always sees me; someone who looks exactly like me.

To the uninformed, Cindy was my first girlfriend. Junior high. They say old flames die hard and I can't blame her. But God, she can get a little overzealous. She can get a little *too much*.

"Excuse me—Peter, answer me!"

She inches closer, revealing perky tits, a number flashes in my head I think C cups or at least they used to be, wearing Prada, Marc Jacobs, Hermès, the works but I'm not looking. I'm staring in her general direction but I can't see a thing.

The last time we had been together was the summer I was sixteen, sidewalks paved with sweat, no rain in three weeks, local pools more popular than ever. I was taking summer classes with an instructor who rattled on about the American fascination with being watched, as if we were the object of some intense scrutiny, and how this also creates a perpetual state of fear borne out by boredom; MTV execs stole his idea for the *Real World* but he wasn't saying how.

After classes I'd walk four blocks to Cindy's house on Manchester and we'd fuck in the shower because it was too hot to do it anywhere else and her parents wondered where all the hot water was going during the drought.

"There you go again."

Every day I keep reading about perfectly good husbands, hard-working businessmen, bright high school students beaming with aspiration, successful musicians, middle-class blue-collar nuclear suburbanites, nurturing mothers turned serial killers and "who would have thought, Mr. and Mrs. so and so were model neighbors."

Acedia, recession . . . everything is fading *out*.

You could be sitting at a park bench loitering, relaxing, whatever, and a certain person passes by; you met them at a party last month and talked about how bad the beer was and since then, exchanged enthusiastic smiles but now, maybe, there's no greeting at all; perhaps a shy "hey" or grunt or nod and you just sit or stand with uncertainty, inaction, gazing down at the sidewalk wondering what it all means. It's like shoes worn less and less each year. I think of sex and I'm reminded of vampires. They don't simply fuck you, they suck your insides.

"Check, please," I blurt out, raising my arm waving my hand at the waiter while Cindy stares at me wild-eyed, probably expecting an explanation or at least an apology.

"Hey I was thinking why not let's just go back to my place instead," I say without pause or comma or even a breath, "this whole Four Seasons vibe is not for me."

A smile breaks across her frown and those electric green eyes soften up almost immediately.

"I don't like seafood anyway!" she lies.

Twenty minutes later we're in my Holiday Inn suite funded on a new gig as a projectionist at the Regal on Airport Road and our conversation moves from the den to the bedroom and I'm thinking I know where this is going but I can't be too sure so I ask if she's dating anyone and she thinks I'm joking and shoves me down to the bed.

Sex sells, I think and kiss her hard on the lips, hands fumbling downward lifting her dress and squeezing her ass until she coos like a newborn duckling waking to a sun shower for the first time. *Sex cells*, feeling like a great wave of rushing water; feeling like I've got the whole Atlantic Ocean inside me.

I imagine someone yelling "cut!" and I drop my pants.

BORN UNDER PUNCHES

The things I recall, I recall in zip pan, POV, a pullback shot without mise-en-scène. Or in darting moments, a brief flash, a passing scent, transposing and unblinking, and utterly distinct. Yet the whole of history favors similarities and slight anachronisms. The schism of time is in a class all its own, and even now I am racing through hallways of my subconscious without taking notice of the hall itself. The lino. A railing. Reverse angles by which you see your own self speaking. Everyday details. Everything passes. As a rule, I strive for lucidity in loneliness, long takes in cover shots, covering myself with the candy of imagination, the sweet gaze of the mind's eye that seeks amusement and finds instead the truth. It strikes without warning. I am either writing it down, or scurrying for a pen. And of course, my palm as paper never does the trick. Too many callouses, rough spots or swollen joints makes for disjointed prose, words rising and falling on the flesh, out of frame, a chronic fear like a cough, or coughing fits in an elevator filled with mysophobics without relief of medicine. Time is relentless. All the memories I have of a certain age arrive with an eye for dissolves and split screens, ellipsis narration, the Kodak Junior camcorder above me, rising higher, slung across somebody's shoulder. The older I got, the more conflated I became: rapid cuts into a montage set to something serious by Radiohead or Kurt Cobain's hoarse voice asking to be raped. Again and again. Only every five seconds, three more images arrive in the form of bridging shots: a birthday party, Carvel cake, wrapping paper unfolding a gown and tassel. In the interest of time and patience, the camera skips the in-between phases, puberty, the Middle Ages, and suddenly time's up, or forever passing, the screen goes dim. Remove the reel and I don't exist, unfilled as an indecision, a figure shot from extreme distance, an unrequited gaze . . . The memories I have as a child, eyes agape in solicitous childhood, of five years and five months, or at nine, balloon mind, afraid of almost everything—¡Tribilin!—every converging train and each whistle and telephone ring and my mother's laugh and my dad's demands, and under tables all the faces I never knew from just their feet rising higher in the address of my dreams, conflated voices all talking separately at the same time around a dinner table, or at a cocktail party, or in my own mind, into and out of intuition . . . Readjust the lens to find emptiness, which is only thirty-three frames per second, a vast expanse of images, the darkness of the cinema, the places my mind goes when I stop to think, an isthmus for hermetic memories lost in the time it takes for perceiving anything. And time's passing.

ATROCITY EXHIBITION II.

Exhibit A: Somewhere deep in the hills of North Dakota or South Dakota or Washington State is a made-to-order Victorian mansion estate, hundred-year-old oaks and fern trees surrounding the perimeter, its own runway stretching for four miles and, of course, a private jet that the Director uses to fly to and from Miami every Wednesday and Sunday. Across vast gardens and marble statues, some spouting water from imaginary orifices into an artificial stream running the length of the gated entrance to the doorway, we peer inside past framed Vermeer paintings as Chopin plays casually in an office, letters on the door etched in gold plating of a name we might find familiar. The base of operations for Greener Pastures, a Health & Wellness company in name that controls everything this world has to offer. Radio, Internet, TV, newspapers with circulations in the stratosphere, all forms of media, big government, rogue government, bureaucrats on the street corner and in Congress, CIA, FBI, DEA, IRS, PACs, AC/DC, more acronyms than you can find groups for, terrorist organizations, religious fundamentalists, gentlemen clubs for the social elite obsessed with the color green (money, money—you get what you pay for, and if you pay enough . . .) in bustling cities that fund all the projects, right wingers disguised as leftist liberals and vice versa (in here nobody is themselves), Black Ops, trendy clothing stores with two names asking questions like, "If you could be any animal, which one would you be and *why?*" during job interviews, blacklisted scientists that perform experiments on selected patients, Don King's barber. Responsible for every major political or social event in the past twenty years. Tango in the Sahara sand? Blitzkrieg in Belgium? Johnny Leprechaun's Last Stand? You name it, they've done it. A vast network of operators, connections they've got 'em, intricate layers of communication ensure everything remains clandestine. In the real world. Behind covers though, they know who's running the show and maybe YOU know it too. There are no questions, and hardly any answers. The only question is, what *don't* they control?

Exhibit B:

December 4, 2003

  To Our Esteemed Stockholders:

  I hope this letter finds you well during this frantic holiday season. As you know, the company continues to develop and our increased sales reflect this exponential growth. Enclosed are the most recent figures as well as our initial predictions for the 2004 fiscal year. But the real news comes from inside our own corporation. It is with great pleasure that I announce the Presidential candidacy of Greener Pasture's very own Jack Denton running under the Independent affiliation. The long road ahead will surely be a challenge but Mr. Denton is confident of his preparation for the approaching months. We know all of you will support him in this election year and our only regret is that he will be temporarily stepping down from Director of the company due to his new responsibilities. Enjoy the rest of this newsletter and have a safe and happy holiday! Go Jack Denton, go Greener Pastures!

  Signed,
  Alvin Morris
  Communication Chair, Greener Pastures

Exhibit C: He bit his fingers until they bled; he scratched himself to sleep, waking up with scabs all over his face from day to day. He routinely cried. Wishing he could be somehow *removed*, wishing he could be *out* of himself for more than a moment at a time, wishing he were normal, not realizing that being *normal* meant dying in slow motion.

It was clear to anyone who would notice (who would notice?): Peter wanted to destroy himself.

Exhibit D: Quick cut to a shoddy Venezuelan farm that's seen better days overlooking scorching mountains and sun-tipped peaks. It is the middle of summer and ranchers work hastily, picking crops, filling woven baskets, planting seeds, cultivating growth with splashes of water from a grimy bucket. One young boy, round, cabbage face, eyes like evening, sits knees bent leaning on a wooden fence. "Mira, aquí." Camera pans across until a llama comes into view. Yelping in llama tones, the llama has a look of fierce tenacity in his eyes like the natural world has gone crazy. "Se siente tan bueno, ¿eh? Se siente tan bueno." Tito Puente's "Ran Kan Kan" starts playing and the cabbage-faced boy laughs, his hand shooting up and down rough like rushing water in a ravine jerking off the llama oops, wrong movie. Somewhere, a man utters in disgust, the natural world gone crazy audiences everywhere reel in terror and bewilderment wondering, waiting, eyes still glued to the screen maybe just for explanation's-sake, or simply because they were expecting a love story.

Exhibit E: Through the glass, the sky had no color.

Exhibit F: Newly-elected Mr. President takes office but the fanfare rubs off after about two weeks. His penis didn't grow any bigger; his hair is still falling out. His greed grows exponentially, he muses in the gray area between night and dawn, the discontinuous hours of daze like dreams and lost hours of sleep where burning passions fizzle flickering only in ambition and wild, carnal thoughts the prototypical hopeless romantic, or rather hungry romantic, "What can I do *now*?" You want to be the happiest man in the world? Power can only give you so much, but he hasn't learned that yet.

Exhibit G: The upshot of capitalist distribution is always with a view of its own reproduction: natives reprocessed into a sellable labor force—mimicking itself through its own conquest; an iteration or imitation toward a desired result, which ends in refuse and refusal; material waste and wasted humans. Organization, not barbarism, is the first step in a systematic process of dehumanization.

Exhibit H: When we are hungry we eat our ghosts.

IN BETWEEN DAYS

Walking across a busy intersection one week later at noon crisp July day clouds cars zigzagging past moisture forming at my back I get the gradual sense I'm being followed. I can't be sure at first but it's a creeping feeling you know is there without seeing like an itch on the roof of your mouth you tongue at, desperately, without much success. You might wake up in the confusion and chaos of a chase scene and you're clueless as to what to do next. People are always looking behind them, afraid, anxious, catching furtive glances in innocent gazes, pretending they know something no one else does.

I don't remember a destination at any rate glance casually to my right, slap shades over hazel eyes and turn around like I forgot my wallet at the diner and I hope the waiter retrieved it.

Hopscotch past traffic lights no rhythm and I think that's my problem right there so easy to pick out from the crowd, *look!* a man being followed and how exciting this must be for the both of them, the hunter and the one being tracked, and if only they knew what the other was thinking. Besides how good it'll taste.

Scamper past liberals in scarves and wool jackets and berets playing chess on makeshift tables near Ashgrove Park swing sets mirroring sway of ivory pieces as each player makes his move, careful and deliberate. Onlookers crowd around, some playing hacky sack, some just playing with their sacks, cupping their fingers under the saggy skin.

I reverse on Orchard Avenue past the Turkish café smiling hello to the owner loitering outside, "Ağzını hayra aç!" puffing rolled up cigarettes and blowing smoke in the languid breeze although I never spoke Turkish until today.

I imagine my actions on camera, the jerky movements of my limbs like a robot out of synch and probably even malfunctioning, my hair blowing wildly tousled in the rush, ducking into a nearby 7-Eleven, pretend to look for an item, something common and everyday, eyes squinting, staring at labels after about five minutes of this people squinting at *me* casually walk out the door, eyes taking one glance behind me and above; standard security camera, my aloof face peering up watching me watch *it*, my life on film.

You can always feel the cool whisper of surveillance when the film hits your flesh, the eye of the camera or simply the camera eye . . . faces of passersby, clientele, unpaid extras change completely as soon as they're no longer observed . . . double-slit experiment, quantum theory . . . a memory from Physics lab . . .

I walk steadily now picking up pace hit with a revelation: there are no coincidences no chances or accidents, a situation is always deliberately produced . . . stop suddenly, eyes peer up slow and dramatic . . . a towering banner: *Prayer of the Rollerboys* at 1:30 also at 4 and 6:45 undoubtedly a sign, duck in double glass doors make small talk with the cashier, short, brunette, soft blue eyes the way I like it or how I've been taught to, and she even knows my name. I walk coolly into the black of the cinema.

In the darkness and the spurts of silence between clicking of frames I start to think maybe it's not a fear of someone watching me.

Maybe it's a desire.

SHADOW STABBING

Sometimes you feel like a zero, a nobody. Invisible. No one. Anyone.

The winter of my sophomore year at college brought snowstorm after snowstorm. The first barrage would barely be sticking when a second and third came pouring down. Stuck inside, nothing to do besides get iced, Wes and I took to the streets. We didn't sell drugs or pornography; we only wanted to get out of our Converse low-tops for a while. Every Wednesday and Sunday night we played a role. The play within a play. We dressed the part, adopted accents, facial expressions, distinct scents, particular textures of our palms when we shook hands. And then we made reservations.

On a Wednesday night at Biaggio's we were Jed and Tom Brown sightseeing from Kentucky where we owned the last real cattle ranch in the country and dozens of authentic homestead clothes from Kohl's and Macy's including the beaver fur hats we were wearing now next week same place I checked our reservations as Tony Rigatony with a *y* and this is my friend Paulie from the Bronx Zoo his last name ain't important and we're lookin' for una cena deliziosa and how you doin' how you doin' ham sand-weech lots of hairspray and kisses on the cheek Sunday was the Sea Shack hello darling Brian and Tyler for two yes I called about half an hour ago and I'll take a booth, gasping at the slightest delay looking petulant and peevish oh we're from Greenwich go to Columbia yes, scholars, I'm Pre-med, he's Philosophy yes, such a long drive we know wearing too much mascara one of us with a cheap-looking black sari snagged from Salvation and you can guess the rest. *Yes.*

"You got coffee with that, mistah?" or "Excuse me, dear, was that the pan seared *south* Asian herring or the orange basted *codfish* with fresh *string* beans?"

It was amazing the way people looked at you each night. You get served, you get noticed, you start italicizing your words at random. You are the object of intense scrutiny and suddenly—you're not very invisible at all. You want to be an actor, dentist, rock star, President's son, displaced farmer?

The subject's name is Peter Denton.

It's such a bore to be one person all the time.

YOU CAN CALL ME AL

About a week after me and Cindy reunite I'm in my hotel room 4 a.m. can't sleep flipping through channels reading passages at random the latest *New Yorker* playing with my hair's part wasting time doing things I feel bad and good about I hear the phone ring expect Cindy since she's the only one who knows my number but I can't be more off.

"So it's late at night all alone and you're wondering what do I have to do to get in bed with Peter Denton, am I right?"

"Mr. Denton? Peter Denton?"

The subject's name is Peter Denton.

"Oh, um sorry, I thought you were . . . someone else, yes this is he, to whom am I speaking?"

"My name is Alvin Morris. I apologize for the late call but I've been trying to track you down for a while now and . . .

"Is this about those pornographic movies I made in college? Because that was for an art project and—"

"Heheh . . . ahem, no. But I *am* involved with films, specifically *major* motion pictures and—"

"Whoa slow down mister; what is it that you want? I can't afford any made-to-order laxatives or those ThighMasters they keep pushing on TV . . ."

"Nothing like that," Alvin says, and then his tone turns heavy, becomes deliberate. "I just want to use your pretty face in front of the cameras. And besides," he adds, clicking his tongue twice, "you're practically a star already."

"No shit."

"I saw you on TV last weekend."

"But I don't think . . . it's Alvin, right? . . . Alvin, let me put it country simple: I've never done anything."

"You mean besides the premiere of *Who's-Who in South Beach*? Listen, to make a short story shorter, the first thing I thought was: Who is this guy?—I mean, outside of South Beach. I wanted to know what's in your head; what's behind the eyes, you dig? The producers, Joel and Jerry Shapiro—I know them pretty well—I called immediately I said, 'frankly, I need to know who this young buck is.' There was no bullshit, Pete. Can I call you Pete? No beating around the bush. Last in a long line of dirty blonds with hazel eyes. I needed to find you and maybe you needed to find me. So here we are."

I try telling him I've never been on TV or in films, that I'm a movie projectionist at the local Regal, a tennis instructor in the summer, I like the outdoors and yeah, maybe I've got a face for smiling and a body that's nice to look at but that's about it, so here we are.

I don't mention my father but I guess I don't have to.

"Well, what do you say?"

(A long pause in which you swallow.)

"Where can we talk in person?" I say. I say, "I like the idea of being in front of a camera."

I leave out the part about never taking acting classes and dropping out of college one year early and my old drug habits—I think bad publicity but somehow—

"We'll worry about that later. I see a natural talent. Guys like you, they don't come along every day. I know. I've been in this business for longer than I'd like to admit. Peter Denton is built to *last*."

"But what is it that you want me to do, Alvin?"

"All you have to do is act."

Silence.

"The difference between an actor and a star is simple, Petey. Actors play a role. Stars are only always playing themselves."

"But I—"

"Can you do that? Can you play *yourself*?"

"Well," I say, thinking hard, "I can certainly try."

"So meet me for brunch at 11:30 tomorrow at—what do you think, you know Green Palms? Corner of Kamera and—"

"I'm a regular," I lie.

"I bet you are," he laughs. It sounds like a gurgle. It sounds like he's being choked. "See you then."

"Hold on, how do I know what you look like?"

"You'll know."

"I'll know?"

"There'll be an audience. Live bodies."

"Spectators?"

"We don't deal in laugh tracks."

"Okay," I sigh. "I'll see you tomorrow then, Mr. Morris."

"Just call me Al."

Click.

The camera pans out revealing my face, the nondescript talking of characters on screen from an old detective movie, Humphrey Bogart and Mary Astor, black spots on the film, crackling voices of old sound recording lost in the translation of time, dull gray and brown curtains hiding the dawn breaking in a few short minutes, crumpled pillows and ruffled sheets—I haven't gone out all day—coffee stains on various magazines; *U.S. News, Life, Time, The New Yorker* sprawled across a bed stand where a black hotel telephone lies unplugged.

I WISH YOU WOULDN'T SAY THAT

"We require certain skills," the man sitting next to me in the café on the corner of Bird Road was saying. Was he talking to me? Was he talking to his phone? Was he talking to himself? I glanced at him. He had a pen in his hand, one of those cheap plastic click pens, and he was scrawling fast and wild in his notebook. Click-click. He was smiling and his eyes were spread wide, and his body shook in odd spasms, like he was thinking wild things, wonderful things, like he was reimagining everything. When he noticed me staring at him, he stopped.

"Ever heard of the Situationists?"

I shook my head.

"The Situationist International?"

My head was still shaking when he said: "I've been writing a book about 'em." He neglected to say that he had been writing the book for the past eight years, that every book he had ever written had been about the Situationist International, that every line he ever put on paper—whether it was ink, whether it was pixel—was about the Situationist International, and everything he thought, and the motives and the reasons and the occasion to have thoughts, to be thinking at all, to be thinking anything, anything there was to know, or anything he had known, everything he *knew*, was in service of the Situationist International.

I shook my head.

"What's your name?"

"Peter Denton," I said, and extended my hand. He had

hair that was somewhere in between blond and brown—dirty blond?—and hazel eyes, and a tan not unlike mine.

He wrote something in his notebook and gazed at me thoughtfully, and wrote something else.

I flashed a friendly smile but before I could ask him who the Situationist International was, before I could even ask him who *he* was, he was gone.

He left his notebook on the counter.

ATROCITY EXHIBITION III.

Exhibit A: A young boy mimics his father as he dresses for work, crossing a tie twice in a knot and pulling it over the top gently then nudging it tightly under his chin. The boy loses patience with *his* tie and shrugs complaining; father laughs and corrects his son, arm around shoulders now, gaze in the mirror, "You'll get it sooner or later, someday you'll be even sharper than your old man," but somehow we get the feeling father is afraid of this notion.

Exhibit B: Three eggs on kitchen table. Butter melting on a pan, stove heating blue flames the kind they use in science fiction soaps to evaporate corpses. One egg cracks, falls to the wooden floor, yolk running between tiles to form letters: two M's and an O.

Exhibit C: Huddled around dining room, an older boy and aging father, "What's for dinner?" "Takeout." For two weeks since, always takeout. Silence speaks more than words, grunts substituted for sentences when there's a death in the family.

Exhibit D: A fancy ballroom, silver chandeliers, gold candles, only the best china on satin table cloths that get thrown away the minute they're used, long lines of old men and women—we'll call them senior citizens—ushered into the party wearing the finest tailored suits, gowns more stunning than the bodies inside of them, waves of makeup, various exotic perfumes and colognes, a pocket watch in each palm, the whole nine yards. A voice emanating from speakers says things like, "You are the young and famous, the rich and wealthy. The social elite. Rock idols, movie stars, successful bankers, lawyers, politicians, and here are your endearing wives, mothers of three, four, five children, caring, fostering, the prototypical nurturers." The men and women, some with canes, others on rollers, nod like a bunch of concrete bags, unaware, obtuse, smiles plastered on, eyes gleaming a silver shine, they think of their lives full of promise and youth and immortality in history.

Exhibit E: It was dark and rainy, and looking at the world was like looking through tinted glass.

Exhibit F:

>*Dear diary,*
>
>*He's got so much money I'm surprised he hasn't bought himself a new wife . . . I guess he really loved her. But who wouldn't? She was the one person holding our family together. Now he's seldom at the house, even less often than before. He's got clients, business, secrets.*
>
>*Who will save us now?*

Exhibit G: Fireworks ignite a Manhattan sky, some loom larger than others, hovering in the night for what seems like seconds, actual minutes, but they all fall down, eventually evaporating into thin whispers in the New Year's air full of drunk laughter and nervous chatter. Among youngsters without dates, murmurs of "Who will kiss me at midnight?" permeate the sky-rise apartments overlooking Times Square. "Let's get married"—a man, tanned and confident, holding hands with a beautiful blond woman, sierra brown skin, green eyes reflect the rainbow sparks outside the window where couples hold hands and embrace on balconies.

"Let's have a baby" is her reply; a sing-song accent to tell the audience she wasn't born around the corner. The man becomes nervous, thoughts race through his head: flashes of responsibility, selflessness, sacrifice, all things he could do without but he says *yes* anyway because it's midnight now and besides, who can say no to a woman like that?

Exhibit H: Snapshots of the boy's life: family is wealthy, father is well-known, mother delicate at times and stern when she needs to be. He is a familiar face, a natural socialite, popular in school, surrounded by friends. Adored. Not loved. A father's forgotten son. A close-up of a sand castle dissipating in the tide; somewhere, an egg is cracking, blistering on a street corner in heavy July sun you're reminded of anti-drug commercials in the Nineties, "This is your brain" becomes "This is your life." The yolk spells *mom*.

Exhibit I: When I talked to him again, he told me he believed every person born between 1983 and 1988 was destined to be doomed, and that the end of the world was only a byproduct of this unconscious upshot. He told me the end of the world was only window dressing.

Exhibit J: Hard to control and it begins.

Exhibit K: Didn't anyone ever tell you how to gracefully disappear in a room?

Exhibit L: "People don't want freedom, kid. They want the freedom to buy whatever's on the market. They want the shelves to be stocked. They want to consume. Sometimes the only thing stopping 'em is a date of expiration. Classic case, boyfriend gets so sick and tired waiting around for his sweetheart to try on *another* pair of heels, he jumps from a seventh-floor railing in a shopping mall in China. Dead upon impact. It's like a Nick at Nite rerun of *Shop 'til You Drop* set in Xuzhou. It's the smiling on the package. You dig?"

Exhibit M: She bent down and pressed both cheeks closer to her mouth. I closed and then I opened. Sounds of a beach breeze recorded years ago spliced with rushing water and an inimitable voice-over: "Go slow but not too slow. Stop when I say when."

Exhibit N: "What we want—what we intend to do—is turn you into your greatest self. What we are *doing* here is shaping a commodity that can be manufactured through publicity," he said, pausing to flick the lighter in his hand, "not by building an audience but by building the perception that one already exists." The flame went out before I had a chance to blow.

Exhibit O: The last line in the notebook read:

Halfway through the matinee, I wake up watching a film to find myself in the lead role.

NO ONE RECEIVING

I never knew exactly where I was.

Even with the signs, directions, markers affixed to almost every hall. I never knew exactly where I was.

There was really no end to its windings—to its incomprehensible subdivisions . . .

When I think about the apartment, I can only think about it in terms of something by Edgar Allan Poe.

When I think about the apartment, I can only think about that uncertainty; the fleeting feeling of always being under surveillance, of always being taped, of always being arrested by the gaze of the gargoyle that sat, unseen, on the roof. Twenty-three levels up . . . and twenty-three people (more?) passing through, neither ascending nor descending but only passing, doors sliding behind them as they grunted, heaved, maybe breathed, got on with the whole business . . . and my own view: each room turning sideways eventually, turning in upon itself; the kitchen leading to the parlor leading to the study leading to the dark room—

I was never able to ascertain with precision . . .

Here, he paused. Paused, eyes vacillating, nostrils breathing in his own secretion. He paused and I saw him look above me.

"I was never able to ascertain with precision anything at all."

"*William Wilson?*" I tried.

He smiled, sniffing out more snot. "You have a wonderful memory."

"Photographic."

"What'd you say?"

"Photographic," I repeated.

He laughed.

"I said," I repeated, "photographic."

THIS MUST BE THE PLACE

So where am I?

I am in a restaurant, I am telling a story.

"Where are they?"

I'm asking Cindy, I think.

That's the thing with memories; they are just distorted images, unreliable, altering and shifting in each passing moment, but then again, memories are all we have.

Memory can change the shape of a room; it can change the color of eyes, hair, a name or a face. It is not a record, it is an interpretation. A representation of the actual experience.

A fake.

There is nothing short of terrible when you realize you are forgetting. The sliding feeling of memories eclipsing until people whom you love are just glimpses or specs of a feeling, just traces, fading traces—even the ones you thought you would never in a million years forget, a woman, a mother, and suddenly, you can't see their face in your memories; suddenly, you can only visualize a round blur with hair on top. Unless, of course, they're bald.

Today is our one-month anniversary if you celebrate that type of thing (we do) and tonight it's reservations at an ultra-snob SoBe supper club with two of Cindy's friends from college that just happened to get married. I am less than enthused about the whole thing but I haven't met many of Cindy's friends and I can't turn down a good eggplant a la vodka. Dinner is a table for four in a tight corner of The Green Grove at eight o'clock and to think I used to fake reservations to these places, now I am walking in as myself.

When the frantic hostess shows us to our table, Cindy's friends are already seated, menus in hand, placing forward welcoming fingers for me to touch. I smile like a skeleton and slide right in.

Vanessa introduces herself as a psychiatrist in Coral Gables who specializes in Rorschach tests, or maybe she just likes to say the word.

"Yes, it's very fascinating actually; the *Rorschach* blot is all about you, not the blot. It's such a huge misconception, these *Rorschach* blots. There is no authorized meaning, no definitive answer. An *O* becomes a *Q* a *C* blurs into a *G* when the handwriting is vague enough, an *l* can be mistaken as an uppercase *I* and suddenly, everything alters. It's the same way with the *Rorschach*."

"I can only imagine."

"Oh—but that's just it!" Vanessa screams. "Everything can be interpreted in so many ways. Are you finding it or making it? That's what *Rorschach* was trying to figure out."

Maybe you ask yourself: Do I really want to find the truth?

Her husband, Phil, is twenty-six and already growing gray with the few hairs left flanking his ears: a pair of wings, the kind that make you wonder if he will fly away in the middle of a conversation when it gets too personal.

I suppose these—the gray, the wings—are just repercussions of his hectic lifestyle, working bonus hours compressed in the same nine-by-five cubicle as his subordinates (new company policy did away with offices to boost morale amid equality issues until it became clear: It is more cost-effective to stick three or four workers in *one* cubicle) would do that to most everyone, he admits between crunches of calamari. Each crunch is like an hour, maybe an hour and a half of salary, I'm thinking. Each crunch sounds like the clamp of a dollar bill.

Phil is scratching his pointed ears and talking about his favorite sitcoms. I'm only listening because I know Cindy will quiz me the minute we get in the car.

Furtive glances will be directed. Passion will ignite. Lust will be felt.

"Tonight is a big night," he's saying. "We have *Candid Controversy* at eight and *The Marketplace* half an hour later followed by *Living Large*, that new one about fat people and their true stories, obesity discrimination, the dangers of flying in coach, et cetera, for an hour. I taped *Cabbies* before we got here just in case we miss it; I really don't know what's going on with Tabitha and her ex-junkie boyfriend . . ." he frowns, looking over at Vanessa, "or was that ex-boyfriend junkie, Ness?"

Thankfully, Vanessa doesn't answer and I'm about to announce that, by the numbers, every family in China owns a television set when he asks me:

"Do you follow ABC's Thursday night lineup at all?"

That's more than 1.3 billion televisions in one country to go around, and I think: People have been living their lives through a TV set for years. Raised on cable cord and commercials.

Probably our memories aren't even our own. Probably they belong to someone else; someone else's TV family.

"Peter?"

And then the shaking starts.

Phil has this peculiar tic, like he is about to begin convulsing in the middle of conversation. He says he's had it since he was a child but I can tell; I would know. Too many uppers and you're the lady from an old Dirt Devil commercial. Eyes blinking faster than you can count teeth chattering legs swerving back and forth hopping up and down; it takes your whole effort just to sit in one place. Consequences of work, eh? I wouldn't know.

I turn my gaze slowly to the bar, zoning out of Phil's sitcom dissertation and it's her. Still wearing a blue dress, minus one latex glove.

Shall we run the film backward?

"Excuse me, I have to go to the boy's room."

I motion to her at the bar the moment I spring to my feet and next I know we're locking lips in the second stall from the left (the first one is taken). Her kiss is hard and I can feel the passion between her teeth; her tongue dances with mine and I get that aching sensation between my legs. It starts to hurt; it starts to burn real bad.

"Sorry," she murmurs, pushing me away, "there's no time for this now."

I'm about to say I've got all night because Phil is one hell of a talker but she stops my thoughts with some frantic talking of her own, staring me straight in the eye and I get the impression that what she's got to say is a little more important than playing patty cakes in the water closet.

"You've got to get away, Mr. Denton. Hide. Run."

"Hey, hey, slow down, and it's Peter, but . . . "

"But nothing! They know that you *know* . . ."

"What are you *talking* about lady?"

"Peter, shut up and listen," she says, grabbing my shoulder, flushing the toilet with her glove hand. "Just listen to me for a second . . . you have to *get away*. You're in danger. They're on to you—on to *us*."

"Need a hand?"

A vested gentleman hovers over us, moist towelette at his fingertips.

We simultaneously shake our heads.

"Just leave town," she resumes, "we'll play nurse and patient another time, soon, trust me . . . please." She pushes me, her fingers cold and firm and bare. The latex glove on the tip of my shoe. Doors swinging on their hinges. A tissue still hangs on the edge of a ledge. "Hold your nose and run."

IS THERE SOMETHING I SHOULD KNOW?

Am I original?
 —Yeah . . .
 —Am I the only one?
 —Yeah . . .
 —Am I *sexual?*
 —Yeah . . .
 —Am I everything you need?
 —Let me get back to you on that one.

GIRLS ON FILM

Slapstick whirlwind of synth drums and quick cuts of the Miami skyline hovering down past corner cafeterias selling café cubano and cortado, past old men with corduroys and cigars looking at their lives through weary eyes, past kids on skateboards and red bikes and spraying fire hydrants creating crescendo of thoughts like a waterfall in the street toward South Beach, Stevie B's "Party Your Body" blaring from speakers in the clouds, fast cars (are there any other kind?) race up and down I-97 screaming around corners top down, hair beating back and forth with the beat of the music, the camera scans the shore closing in on palms blowing languidly as if betraying the excitement in the air, young men walking from water, bathing suits clinging to thighs, the texture of salt and wind and sun, young girls wearing skimpy thongs you think you can substitute for floss maybe tops maybe not, cat-calls from college students lots of Spanish and English intermixed with laughter and the ebb and flow of waves as the sun burns down on the sand and the stench of sweat and bodies, smooth, wet, perspiring mouths parched from the heat of the day or the moment. In the background, expensive condos and sky-rise apartments overlook the beach. Old pale businessmen and their pale trophy wives sip sparkling water, nibble caviar on balconies, umbrellas over heads; these people can't take the sun. Montage of young beautiful people tanning, walking hand in hand on the sand, one is picking sea shells one is taking pictures, Newport tank top "Alive With Pleasure" muscles a bronze sculpture in the sun, pink and green volleyballs rolling in the sand, waiters in white polos with flamingoes emblazoned on their upper right breast serve the most esteemed guests chilled ice tea and maybe Cuban rum if they tip well while the most beautiful women in the world shake their ass to the rhythm, shirts damp with sweat or maybe from a nearby hose (sex sells), hair curly or straight however you like it brown, black, china ivory, you're either in South Beach or you're watching a music video.

It's night now, camera shifts focus to Azúcar about a block from shore, same song still playing. I appear on the corner walking coolly with Cindy wearing a sultry red skirt—her, not me—she's got pearls around her neck and high heels not meant for dancing, flashing white teeth and winking at funny-looking bouncers, chests too big for each body, straws for legs, brushing past curious onlookers and anxious young faces in the crowd, desperate, fed-up, annoyed, feeling left out, abused, forgotten, and maybe I know the feeling too.

Walk in the club dark except for flashing lights that might induce euphoria, or else a seizure. *"Party your body"* keeps repeating, sweat drips off the bodies on the dance floor united as a whole save for the few inches of space between them that we call breathing room or simply breath, legs swaying back and forth frantic and *"Don't you believe it? Well I can party your body and I can do it right"* limbs moving in the same direction at the same time grinding up and down against each other in a sex simulation, I laugh at the implications and order Cindy a drink.

"So what do you think?"

"What do I *think*? Peter, I love this place! Why didn't you take me here sooner?"

"I was waiting to surprise you."

The truth is, I've never been here before either.

My eyes wander from Cindy to the herd of cameramen hustling in through the doors and out near the dance floor. I'm taken by surprise; how did they find me HERE, I wonder, but Cindy tells me they are filming for a new episode of some music television party guide who's-who of South Beach and that's probably why we got in so easily— because of who we are or rather what we are: young, attractive, wearing the right clothes; it's all an image, a fabricated world to show viewers in their homes what the scene is really like more or less if less is more; disfigured and decaying things, accidental remains, and apart from them and everyone, and all of us, simply accidents, but they manufacture it, no room for error or deviation.

"Simulacra." She finishes this with a swirl of Long Island ice tea and grabs my hand. "That's what they call it."

"Who's *they*?"

"C'mon party boy, let's dance." And when she takes my hand:

"Maybe we'll get on TV."

INSIDE-OUTSIDE (ACT III)

Curtains open to an old, 1930s hotel. Black and white, static, smudges of black between the rolling of film the sign pointing THIS WAY to Holiday Inn missing letters on the ends of both words, crooked, lopsided, cheaply done with paint rusting off the edges. Inside the revolving doors is a reception area, thrashing music more ominous than charming, violent surges of instruments clanging against one another creates a jarring sound, screeching, howling, then submitting to eerie silence before it begins again.

Camera pans around the corner and we realize an orchestra of five teenagers is practicing for a gig; punk rock meets The Doobie Brothers and it doesn't sound good.

We don't hear much more because a piano overture begins. Sweet elegant inviting to the mind our eyes wander from hallway to hallway, same pasty beige wallpaper cracking from the top, stained white in places or else those are the only places *not* stained, stairs that creak when you step on them up up up to the third floor we hear a TV blaring through a closed room, peer through the keyhole: I'm sitting on a loveseat with Cindy watching a recent spy thriller set in an old black and white discolored hotel. The piano keys go mute.

WOMAN (in exaggerated tones): Well, what would you think if you were me? It's just . . . I get so worried about you.

MAN: It's difficult to explain. But I think it's best if we stay here tonight; tomorrow is a very important day. My phone's been off the hook. It's finally happening. Aren't you excited?

(One hand doesn't know what the other is doing and by the time I know it my hands are down my pants.)

WOMAN: Oh, darling. Peter, Peter—I'm sorry I ever argued with you in the first place. (camera fixated on eyes: a close-up as she turns her gaze intensely toward his) The truth is, I'm concerned . . . but only about losing you again.

PETER (rough): Shut up and make love to me.

The two embrace as the title forms at the center of the screen, LOST IN LENINGRAD *starring Peter Denton as himself, Rocko DiPisa as the hotel manager, Pip Roberts as Monkey Man Abrams, Francis Carter as Randy Rizzo, Johnny Baker as General Garbof, Betty LaRoche as Cindy Schultz, Bailey Lazar as . . .*

I am lying down with Cindy inside my Holiday Inn suite.

I am watching myself lying down with Cindy inside my Holiday Inn suite.

The effect is too startling to think about so I quickly flip the channel.

Sometimes I feel as if I'm getting other people's memories. Images I only recognize in dreams or TV, old films, faces I've never seen before and places I've never been . . . somebody's switched the reel.

"What's the matter, baby?"

"What, you thought I was kidding?"

"Huh?"

I rip off my tank top and force one hand down her sweatpants cold fingers meeting warm hips her thighs are sweaty and taste of salt when I lick them, gently first then firmer until she coos like a newborn duckling waking to a sun shower for the first time.

LOVE FOR SALE (TAKE TWO)

EXT. — ELEGANT RESTAURANT — AFTERNOON

WOMAN: Oh, Peter . . . are you feeling alright? You look a little pale. A little dead in the eyes.

PETER: (uncertain, reticent) I'm . . . I'm fine. Sorry, Cindy. Please continue. I apologize. My mind . . . I was just staring off into space, thinking about something else. You know how I get.

(It looks familiar but he can't remember when or where he may have seen such a room, the exact layout of the tables, hammocks for chairs, the bartender's curled mustache, ornamental music boxes in bread baskets and unlit chandeliers . . . a kind of spotlight, and once again he feels the hushed chill of surveillance . . .)

CINDY: (frantic, excited) It's way too early to start thinking about marriage but I think it's kind of cool, you know? The word that comes to mind is *fate*. I mean, I didn't think I was ever going to see you again after high school. Look how the world works . . . I want two kids— no! Three: two boys, one girl. Don't quote me though. My mind is always changing about this, but we need at least three, got it?—*3* is my favorite number. Haha, ahem, and coming from the two of us? We'll have the most beautiful kids in the world, don't you think? I think we should look at this great place, in Boca, I saw the ad in the paper today. Very affordable and it's even got a swimming pool— very affordable though—right next to the docks. Fifteen minutes from the beach, we'd love it. Where are you living now, anyway? I just got a new job actually—fashion, you know how THAT is. Comes and goes. Trends. Are you still playing tennis? I really think we could use a new washing machine if we're going to be thinking about a house, what do you think Peter? What do you *think?*

PETER: (looking straight at the camera) That sounds *fabulouso.*

(Cue "West End Girls" and a whip pan: the bartender juggling bottles of wine like they're tennis balls)

CINDY: And we have to start picking out window drapes. I read in the latest *Kitchen Living* that the house is *negligible* compared to its furnishings and I quote, "a good set of drapes makes a secondary home first rate."

PETER: (tipping back his head in laughter) Is that Blake? Is that Marvell?

CINDY: You are adorable.

PETER: Please, Cin—(smiling) can I call you Cin?—you don't have to tell *me.* (pause, to collect breath) Hey I was thinking why not let's just go back to my place instead this whole Four Seasons vibe is not for me.

CINDY: (expression becomes joyous, confident, smiling as she stops popping jumbo raw shrimp in her mouth) I don't like seafood anyway!

LOVE WILL TEAR US APART

It was the spring of my twenty-third birthday and things were going well. I ditched the Holiday Inn for a condo in Kendall and Cindy couldn't be happier. We even had a washing machine. It wasn't Boca Raton but really, what *is*? We went for long walks around town, talking about our future together, our pasts apart, our lives, our careers. According to various magazines, advertisements, billboards, pamphlets you see at the Publix checkout, mine was on the rise. I had just finished filming a new movie, *Cowboys Don't Say Please*, about a gruff California kid who rides to the Big Apple on his trusty Spanish colt sidekick in the late nineteenth century "Finding love and a whole lot of trouble," according to the tagline.

We went to night clubs, nouveau riche restaurants, lounges, lofts, hangouts, bars. We went to Denny's diners disguised as normal hard-working Americans searching for our slice of the pie. But they knew better. Cameras followed us everywhere and just like Garbo, I could tell when the image was crisp just by feeling the light. I was on the upswing, I thought, and it was a natural price for fame. We were photographed for magazines whose sole purpose is to show pictures of the rich and famous, the wealthy, the socialites, the *in* crowd. We were the subject of various talk shows, radio, Internet blurbs, commercial advertisements I didn't remember doing.

(Montage of sex scenes set to Pakito's "Living On Video" . . . slow-motion close-ups of suffocating erections

413

in blue jeans, swaying asses, Johnson & Johnson's baby lotion squeezed slowly, trembling fingers, karate chops and jumping-jacks in a playground, blistering swing sets, round, open lips, lipstick traces, the purple sky . . .)

"Peter . . ."

"Cindy, what's up?" I say, cradling the phone on my shoulder, recognizing her voice immediately. "I was meaning to call you. I've been looking over my itinerary. My flight is in two hours. I'll be sky-high."

"Well, see that's the problem," she says. "There's something I need to tell you . . ."

OMD's "If You Leave" starts playing on a stereo I don't own.

"Things just aren't the same . . ." she blabbers. "I just don't know what to say."

So she says nothing for a few moments of impenetrable silence while I mouth the lyrics. *We've always had time on our sides, now it's fading fast . . ."* "They just aren't." *". . . Every second, every moment, we've got to, we've got to make it last . . ."* "I can't love you anymore. I just can't do it." *". . . I won't let go at any price . . ."* I can't pretend. I'm sorry, Peter, I'm so sorry . . . but things are simply *out of hand.*"

"Hey," I return, still bobbing my head to the beat, "whose hands are we talking about here?"

"Peter, you are fucking *loony!*" she shouts. "Sky-high."

"Okay, well yeah, in two hours, babe. I'll ah . . . I'll talk to you later, right?"

No words, just sobs, now a wailing and I think she's being overly dramatic given the arc of the scene *". . . I need you now like I needed you then . . ."* and I at least seem to be capturing the essence of missed connections and insouciant romance.

"Okay then," I continue, unfazed, even, somehow, rising higher, "well, feel better, honey. I'll catch you later, okay? Bye-bye, babe."

". . . You always said we'd meet again someday."
Click.

Suddenly I feel very much alone. I am at the center of the world with nobody else in it. How many licks does it take?

I cannot dwell on this for very long. I am an actor, I feign emotions, create new ones, that's what I do. Slipping into people's clothes, people's skin, people's minds. And tomorrow is a very big day.

I've never killed anyone on camera before.

STORMY WEATHER (CLIMAX)

Drop down to a crowded Main Street of wherever, lunch break businessmen hustling back and forth bustling in suits and ties with briefcases and an umbrella for the rain the five-course meal. The city could be Los Angeles, San Francisco, Miami, Moscow, London; today, it's Manhattan. Rain-slicked sidewalks make splashes with every step as the camera pulls up to a looming view of the Empire State Building while lightning rips across the sky you get the feeling it's not going to be a good day. Someone yells "action!" and film rolls, Peter Denton comes into view playing himself today dressed in a tweed suit and fedora the people in wardrobe hope will give him that effortless tough sophisticated look but he's trying too hard and the naïve face untouched eyes give it away in a waning moment.

(He knew what he had to do without quite knowing what it was . . .)

The Chemical Brother's "Believe" starts blaring from a cloud in the sky real frenetic and head-throbbing the way you like it and I throw down the fedora, overdone splashing sound effect behind me to start sprinting toward The Green Tea Society, a gentleman's club for the social elite on the corner of 49th and Broadway. Cold-hearted revenge story the kind audiences love best; the owner[xiii] killed the love

---

[xiii] Coco Jones, also known as Rough and Tumble Billy, also known as Kaka Monsoon, also known as Clarinet Larry (strictly on stage), also known as Huckleberry Jones, also known as Coconut Soufflé.

of my life and set me up for murder now I'll finally get the chance to commit the crime.

"Hey, where you goin' Jack?"

I push the servant boy out of the way and throw him hard on the floor without looking back. The music gets louder, more intense *"I needed to believe in something"* the jarring synth noises match my racing thoughts rescinding to a standstill at any given moment where I might go off the edge or just come down and catch a taxi back to the Verde Saloon where I checked in three days ago, according to the narrative voice-over.

"You one of those Shake Men?"

"What the—? What the . . . hell are you doing!"

More of an exclamation than a question the little twit springs back and is on his feet chasing me through the building, across the lobby through the dining room down the stairwell (while I take the elevator) and then back up the stairs (while he wonders which way I went) it is all very comical, a turn-of-the-century talkie until he telephones the cops. Then the music breaks to a standstill as I stop mid-stride and stare at the office door in front of me—*Coco Jones, OWNER & OPERATOR*—camera slowly gazes up building anticipation budding excitement on my trigger finger *"I needed to believe."* I jam one hand into my gray tweed coat pocket and pull out a standard-issue Webley .455 automatic revolver, no silencer, just steel, the kind manufactured for precisely these scenes.

"Knock, knock."

"Ahem, Marcy, will you see who it is please?"

The pale platinum blond secretary, fortyish, with wrinkles beginning to form in places she wishes she could hide—maybe two kids and a cheating husband, maybe not—opens the door and I blow her head off and adlib a line for good measure:

"You were supposed to say, *Who's there.*"

"What the fuck!" someone screams. Someone screams: "Holy shit, Jesus Christ! Who are you?"

"You an impersonator or the real thing?"

Those were his lines I think but Jones is just sitting at his swivel chair, shivering from fear and an overactive air-conditioner eyes wavering from left to right holding tight on the busted brains on the carpet already stinking hairs on edge snot flowing down his lips teary-eyed screams of nonsense.

"Don't play dumb, mister."

He starts to speak over the hum-hum-hum but I don't let him utter anything worth mentioning because I don't think I'm supposed to, blowing him away with two more slugs, servant of a body collapsing like an old bladder before walking calmly to a navy blue suede three-seater with red pillows meant for visitors and sit down, sighing while ambulances and police cars dance in the distance, their sirens ringing in my ears like bad static or maybe a bad dream, drifting into a doze, nodding and twitching.

There you go again.

I wake up before they hit the entrance, face covered in a black ski mask that might look intimidating on the wrong person being rocked back and forth like the time I had chicken pox as a baby, forehead damp and clammy, whispering, whimpering, "Tranquilito bebito, tranquilito . . . abre tus ojos ahora," open your eyes *now*, my hands tied behind my back in the matinee darkness of an old cellar somewhere in the deep hills of North Dakota.

Or Washington State.

A MEANS TO AN END

An old dusty book dug up in the sands somewhere between Africa and Argentina or maybe found in an old attic of some nondescript picket-fence home in suburban New Jersey; two young boys go searching in the darkness flashlights in hand rain making music outside while curiosity hangs in the air like a kite on a breezy day.

Morning Bell

After the destruction comes the realization. Murders, executions, cover-ups. Fires (real and figurative) blaze unceasingly for forty days fertile forests rural landscapes the kind you only read about in poems you think Wordsworth whole cities and sprinkler-soaked lawns of suburbia evaporate in ash. The world falls back on its heels, buckled knees, international banking system topples, stock market crumples, poetry is a word that falls out of our vocabulary and mechanically purged from memory, communication via computers which create their own responses to messages based on people's probable replies, GPS locations, Internet tracking, and previous posts. Speaking in stream-lines.*

The privileged set get so many transplants they forget what's original and what's replacement. They forget even who they are but at least they remember they're immortal.

Basically—

Projected via hologram or prolonged via patchwork, some careful assembly is always required, squeezing out an unmistakable stench of rusted steel and oil in place of excrement at the most unexpected moments.

Crude means of journalism tell of pop stars and socialites from every major country murdered in their sleep by angry mobs, confused citizenry, devious imperial guards, faceless patsies, cheeky tourists, the prototypical assassin. Extras run rampant, screaming and crying, running down the streets bare in the strictest sense of the word, voices without bodies . . . it's an every-man-for-himself scenario . . . mobs flee to lands still rich in wealth or at least vegetation and capable of relative autonomy amid the Summer of Ardor as it comes to be called years later while pretentious experimental music with hushed voices and sibilant whispers plays over the montage. The whole of history is laid out on a roll of film, crisscrossed and double-sided it's so long, re-played every three days as an encore . . .

Summer of Ardor? Texas City Disaster? Great Fire of Warwick? Sack of Constantinople? Montana's Big Burn? San Francisco Shakedown? Flame of the Barbary Coast? The Torches of Nero? . . . Everyone on the street is saying the same thing differently . . .

Scenes selected at random and presented intermittently, like memories in passing or evening dreams . . . awake only to find the semblance of storyline: a tight-lipped script. The man responsible is murdered two days after he lets the first fleet of bombs drop only to have a stronger, more nefarious group of men take over in his place, controlling the five sectors of the globe (Canada cut in half as a broad-tipped marker runs dry . . .); collectively they call themselves "Coconut Incorporated" and collaborate to form some sort of security over the broken territories and various freedom forces scouring the world, underground agencies and patchwork networks that assemble their own means of influence, double agents and deceptive reporters working under deep cover while self-help books line the bestseller's list at every major book store magazines which tell you how to dress, how to act, how to look and often you wonder if people still wiped their own asses anymore without wondering about the most appealing form. There is an intense fascination with the color green. Noise pollution—a wordless vacuum of din and hysteria, traffic sounds, tire screeches, honks and mobile rings, routine interferences—and a knock at the door. People can't hear themselves think, so they stop thinking altogether. After the destruction comes the realization and the question lingers amid the chaos:

Who will save us now?

ATROCITY EXHIBITION IV.
(REFLECTIONS FROM DAMAGED LIFE)

Exhibit A: The key to a frittata is a very hot pan.

Exhibit B: Sometimes I feel giddy when I think about what life affords me, what life breathes into me. And sometimes I am weak in the knees and feel faint, and terrified, and paralyzed. And other times all I want to do is sit down and think about things, and think about everything, and write it down, or write it in to a story, which is really *the* story, the only story, any story. Every story.

Exhibit C: This is best read with the music turned up.

Exhibit D: "Death came of age on the assembly line, mind you. Tuberculosis, diabetes, cancer moving steadily along through the years, stamped out and sorted for shelves. Wall Street stands to profit from AIDS, obesity, explosive flatulence, and heart conditions of every kind, including heart*break*. Money can fix just about anything. You dig?"

Exhibit E: The first club I ever went to was called The Graveyard and it was dark, and it was strobe-lit, and it was vast, and everybody looked at each other. Nobody danced.

Exhibit F: We went to Balthazar to celebrate your birthday and the two of us ordered the duck confit, the caramelized onion tart, the pumpkin agnolotti, the roast lamb sandwich, the pan-seared salmon. The caramelized banana ricotta tart with a flambé garnish. Ashes.

The world will end in four days. And everybody on Spring Street, and everybody on Broadway, and everybody everywhere talked faster than ever, and louder than ever, and no one heard a thing.

Exhibit G: "What we are doing here is simply an exercise."

"Come again?"

"Precisely. Keep returning. Upside down, inside out, round and round . . . round and round . . ."

Exhibit H: The sky opened—for a moment, I saw white. Then the clouds came in: big, bulbous, like pillows which separated the pale sun. Pale, pink, gray, gold. The gradient spread across my eyes and I heard a whistle.

"If the clouds look too good to be true, it's cuz they ain't."

I tried to block out his voice; I tried to block out the noise. I felt a click and registered the scene in my mind before he broke in again.

"You dig?"

Exhibit I: The nineteenth-century Italian aristocrat, better known as La Castiglione, was an iconic model, muse, mistress, narcissist, and queen of drama.

Exhibit J: "What do you want? Cocaine, heroin, crack, LSD, E, ice, a toilet that doubles as a TV, inflatable erections (a stiff bargain if I ever saw one), girls with mustaches, girls who look like boys, boys with two dicks or none at all, talking dolphins, jellyfish kisses, a slave for shitting, Haitian love doll, marijuana by the pound, PCP, Puerto Rican police chief assassination?

Cigarette junkies, liquor lips, sex-crazed-nannies, *image addicts*. We satisfy 'em all. But those image addicts are a tough lot to satiate, Johnny.

Can I call you Johnny?

See, sometimes we gotta bring in the Repro Vampires. These creatures come storming in while "Satisfaction" by the Stones hits. Tall and spindly, with faces like a lunchbox, vacuum hoses for hands, they suck it all outta ya. Only leave pure image. Unadulterated imago, baby. Back to the basics."

Swoosh

"But it ain't a pretty picture."

Exhibit K: A black-and-white postcard with gilt edges and scattered coffee stains: three nuns wielding shotguns and the words, "See you in *Sindicado*!" etched in bubble letters sprawled across the center; silhouette of the Sistine Chapel exploding in the distance.

Exhibit L: When I close my eyes I can still see the fires.

Exhibit M: Shall we run the film backward?

Exhibit N: Unlike most models, though, the Countess dictated all aspects of her photos, creating the scenarios and characters herself.

Exhibit O: Unlike most dramas, there is no pretense that the audience is not there.

Exhibit P: "When I was young, I wanted to be a movie."

Exhibit Q: Walking is an art, an art that can be learned and eventually mastered. It's all in the heels. Heels, knees, arms swinging in the opposite direction of the trembling toes. You'll find yourself gliding in no time.

Exhibit R: Going and coming returning and departing—it's all the same, it's all the same—everything present in the same moment when no one is watching the moment pass. When no one is counting and there is nothing to count.

Exhibit S: Instead, we are given an apparently less constructed scene; the camera takes us, for example, into the living room of a house after showing its exterior.

Exhibit T: I made it a point not to shower after seeing her, after being inside of her. I could smell her on me the whole day, as if she lived on me, as if she lived in me. But of course she already did.

Exhibit U: I can't hear you. Can you whisper?

AUTOMATIC STOP

Awake. What is it about an echo that is so lonely?

I'm talking to no one, I'm talking to myself. White walls flanking white ceilings, white pillows. White mattress. White lies. I guess I fell asleep somewhere in between then and now.

Time collapses like a Mexican fiesta, Día de los Muertos, it pulses and it trembles and it shatters into fragments, picked up and rearranged until the clock runs backward—*tock-tick*, *tock-tick*—an itch in the groin like chance, risk, the fleeting feeling of being alive, and really feeling it this time.

My words trail off trapped between the locks adorning the windows; Freddy Douglass isn't beside me anymore. Disappeared. Maybe never there. You have to take these realizations in stride, compensate for visual inaccuracies, the way the light hits the shade, memory lapses, the representation of the image in front of you has changed, a gag reel placed over the film, out of order, sped up or held shut on changeover, your whole ground of belief blows up in your face like a cheap microwave dinner and maybe you start to feel like a East Berliner in '89.

Now there's no cameraman tailing me everything is quiet and you think things are going well but I get the sinking feeling I'm still being watched, the phantom touch of the lens on flesh, gentle as swallowing or the air before a breeze. You can always feel the film.

"Are you ready?"

The words emerge from an invisible Walkman attached to my ears pre-recorded questions and I already know the answer because I've been ready my whole life. The final scene and I think this is how stars are born so I slowly get up and open the door. Locked.

Two knocks at the door and I'm nonplussed.

"Take him to the Green Room."

The Director's wishes.

I look down, already wearing my gown cut low at the back so you might catch a glimpse of my ass. If you're lucky.

Two rough-looking men grab me when I open the door and I think they're characterless or simply caricatures, short, brown hair, high and tight, muscles like balloons, one has a mustache and they both have silver eyes. I wonder if we started filming yet because these guys don't look like nurses. They aren't carrying alcohol swabs, a gait belt, or stethoscopes, but they do have silver eyes.

On set now they drag me to the Green Room, which is actually a deep royal blue filled with men in masks and supervisors with clipboards and funny-looking glasses I think I'd never wear out of the house. The Director motions for the men to let me loose and he nods his head, whistling, smiling, offering his hand to shake after he sets his clipboard down.

"You are some kind of marvel."

I am flattered but I can only muster an embarrassed smile as he removes his surgeon's mask.

Father.

"Place him down gently, please."

His voice betrays any semblance of familiarity but I catch a knowing glance, maybe heartbreak, maybe sorrow, as he puts his mask back on and over his mouth.

Blank, serious faces from everyone and I do my best to look panicked while the rolling of film prowls somewhere in the back.

"Good. Now get to work."

They lower the bed on a decline and I close my eyes just to see if the world stops moving. I close my eyes and I picture my first kiss my first love that moment when hearts collided with the tension and anxiety of growing up rich wealthy popular beyond anyone's wishes and ever-lonely I think about seeing Cindy's face, cutting class just to meet her outside on the quad and talk, her wide, open lips, the faraway wet warm maybe this is just a love story masquerading as something greater but the fleeting moments between here and there seem endless, frozen in a crux of time to be relived infinitely and the Director, dressed now in full surgeon garb complete with latex gloves and a breathable mask starts yelling "OK, cut" followed by more precise terms I've never heard before but no one stops filming and I'm still strapped here on the bed, my head the only part of my body not held down, enclosed with a metal apparatus, actual bars, and I'm jerking up to get a better glimpse thinking, the portrait of the American hero, is this it? when I hear the buzzing behind me, a very big drill not to be used for recreational purposes, the scalpel flashes in the Director's hands and I finally realize what kind of *cut* he was referring to, stare in horror while the drill inches closer to my flesh, to my head, I can only blurt out one last lucid thought hastily assembled before they cut my tongue out to prevent the screams:

"Does my contract cover this?"

The Evergreen Express
"All the news your nickel can buy"

July 7, 2005

PRESIDENTIAL TRAGEDY
Staff Writer
Freddy Douglass

MIAMI—President Jack Denton's son is believed to be dead after his boat was found capsized on the coast of Key Biscayne three days after leaving on a fishing expedition, according to friends. No bodies have been found in the area around the wreckage.

Peter Denton, 23, was enrolled at prestigious Highlands University from 2000 through 2003 before inexplicably dropping out halfway through his senior year. Although the President was not available for comment, Cabinet Member Alvin Morris gave a brief statement on his behalf. "As you can imagine, the President is experiencing a time of deep anguish and kindly requests the media to respect his wishes."

The tragedy comes at a turbulent moment for President Denton, who was sworn in on January 20, as he juggles multiple wars in the Middle East, and contends with a divided Congress and plummeting approval ratings. Only one of the initiatives from the ambitious reform package he campaigned on has made it into law: a sizeable increase in the budget of the Department of Defense, affecting military spending and tripling funding for the Defense Advanced Research Projects Agency. Despite vehement protests and last week's "Natural Woman" marches across the nation, the President has maintained pronounced support for several biotech companies devoted to "life extension"—or as one Silicon Valley billionaire put it, to "solving the problem of death." Google's billion-dollar Calico longevity lab, along with The National Academy of Medicine, formerly known as Greener Pastures, an independent group, and hefty investments by Amazon's . . .

Continued on Page A6

434

COMPANY CALLS EPILOGUE

This is how it could have happened.

Rewind to the point where I'm lying in the hospital bed, nondescript faces hovering and my father's too, hovering and blinking, looking at me like he's never looked at me before.

"Hey, Peter, did you miss me?"

A different voice, warm, familiar. A woman's voice.

He throws down his scalpel and removes a thin layer of flesh across his face, his features slowly dissolving until they become molded feminine, blond hair and blue eyes so soft they're almost gray. One hand holding a synthetic human face, a replica. A mask.

It's her.

"Are we gonna play . . ." I sputter. "Nurse and patient?"

"Let's go we don't have much time," she returns while the other doctors and nurses in the room rip off their white caps and smocks, revealing stonewashed Levi's and brightly colored T-shirts, unassuming tennis shoes and rusted belt buckles and fanny packs across their hips, the prototypical everyman, spectator tourist: the perfect disguise.

We scramble through the tight corridors of the hospital, actual employees looking at us through eyes bowled over and glances so funny you wish you had a camera, but of course everyone does, bursting through the revolving doors like a pack of wolves and she pushes me into the open arms of a waiting limousine, shadowy black with tinted windows

435

and a driver with a face I know pretty well and the press pass to prove it.

Freddy Douglass.

She sits down beside me and yells at Freddy to get a move on, looking into my eyes like it's the first genuine thing she's seen in years. The first thing that didn't have to be practiced and cropped. I'm privately embarrassed about my hospital gown but our lips lock anyway, climaxing in a knockout Hollywood kiss and for the first time in my life, I am perfectly sure I'm awake.

ATROCITY EXHIBITION V.
(ONCE IN A LIFETIME)

Exhibit A: "You left me a voicemail? When did you call? I didn't hear the phone."

I pointed to my lips.

"I whispered in your ear," I said. "And you felt the air of my lips."

I was blowing my breath on the window, writing out my name.

I said: "But you only registered the touch a moment after it occurred."

And here I paused.

I said: "Like everything in life that comes into us from the outside."

Exhibit B: I grew my mustache and my beard so I could taste her kisses and her hips, and her lips, her lips . . . and her nectar, and all of her, and everything, as if I were tasting her for the first time, as if I were tasting her all the time and every time, and again, and again.

Exhibit C: Every image, sound, smell, taste, and object is associated with a keyword. All one has to do is to allow a space to be touched. (I want the reader to get the feeling that the text is trying to rearrange itself, upon every reading. I don't want the presentation of narrative; I want a life told out of order.)

Exhibit D: What about your face? Is it sweet, piercing, clever, desolate, childlike, guarded? Have you ever considered? Probably you haven't, and yet your face is your *centerpiece*.

Exhibit E: These three-minute screen tests purported to show everyday people as a continuous stream of faces, each framed in close-up. The faces, almost like a re-presentation of the reel of film which carries its image, became a series of twitches; facial spasms or fleshy blips against a barren background.

Exhibit F: The world ended on December 22, 2012.

Exhibit G: Viewers wait for something to happen—lips to move or a pair of eyes to blink, or even the uttering of words. In this way, the stars and the viewers switch places; really, they occupy the same space, straddling the ever-moving boundary of *becoming something else*. The faces on screen stare, star-stuck in moments of their own recurrence, looking at people who have not yet arrived (other stars on set) or who will never arrive (the audience). The audience stares in expectation of something other than the repetition of a face. No one actually exchanges glances, yet everyone continues to wait.

Exhibit H: "A movie? Don't you mean a movie star?"
   "No," I shook my head. "I mean a movie."

Exhibit I: People had to re-think concepts of motion.

LEAVE IN SILENCE

In sanctity and solitude we find who we are in the dark as in the light, terrified and softened to know that when we are stripped away, we can be nothing too. (Another shard of sun; the day cutting in through a lens.) And over the curb, a mosaic of trash littered on the lawn: rolled-up newspapers, a corroded copper lighter, a tattered notepad. A black rectangular box, facedown on the dew. In a cutaway close-up, you reach your hand to bring the black box closer; to turn it over and hold it up: a tape recorder, the red key jammed as to prohibit pausing and anyway (you think) it's only one key which does both—record, stop recording—it's only ever the same.

A fog so thick it sinks you. The dirt and the wind and the current from the river just in the distance, lapping like an echo in your ears, damp and red from the sweat and the cold. A sloping curve, a sky still dark; the self-immolation of a run in winter. The sound of your own footsteps, each breath and each step so in sync as to forget which is which, the body and what's leaving it. A fog too thick for treetops and streetlamps and your outstretched arms, lunging the way you learned when you were counting time. The face of someone who's just realized that their world is over. All tenderness, revulsion, reverie, regret, violence and recreation, erotic eye-contact, all pleasure of not seeing, of not being seen, vertiginous distraction, boredom and oppression, oblivion and hunger and guilt (is it better if I close your eyes; is it better if I tell you you deserve this?), all painful awareness, all beauty, all horror: another savage night at the opera. (The sound of a car passing, to your left.) The look of your face and its expectation. Fear and yearning and the will to live, something stronger than faith. (Another car, another stoplight; the sun beginning to puncture the clouds.) History, the accumulated suffering of a thousand-billion-and-still-counting strangers, the ones who aren't counted, the invisible ones, all of them, all of *us*—a mountain of bones and unborn ghosts. (The silhouette of a city.) Your joints cracking with every twist of your limbs, the fog falling into and out of your breath, the hoarse heat rising, the absence of birds. Breathe, *breathe*. Your heartbeat or the beating in your brain, the pulsing, the twitching, neurons and electrons and divisions of your organism, gyrating, colliding, held together by what— whatever holds anything together long enough to persist? (Another pant, the sound of your own footsteps breaking in again, clearer: the river bank's edge.)

Leakage, circulation, outpour; the direction or the directing of the displaced. The inscription of borders along the earth and on the body, sealed and at the same time amputated by walls, trenches, electrical fences, barbed wire: a space that is at the same time inside and outside. The ritual processing of flesh, the screening and examination, the waiting, the interminable and unrelenting waiting, the cracked-open waiting (the small of the back, the thighs, the throat beginning to burn), the management of human flow. To be written off or out. And yet—to return . . .

Imagine the space beneath your eyelids the moment before you wake. The running tap, the cool collapse, the silence that is not silence, the mirror, the polished glass, the weighty frame—a mirror or two mirrors, each reflecting the other but neither reflecting you. So you wake each morning and drift toward the Hudson on Atlantic, or at least you used to, when you lived here. When you lived there. The

Hudson flickers, the park lights flicker, the speeding yellow taxis and black sedans and the other runners flicker and dance around you (but not now; now there's nothing, but nothing) and you care about this intensely, with no recognition except of being inside your flesh for a moment more, unable let go. Everything that happens happens again and again, and repetition, too, becomes its own movement. (Another lunge, your legs kicking out to a stop.) Imagine a house you've seen before, mistaken or misremembered: palm prints on a window, the laughter of children (but not now; now there's nothing)

—Brooklyn, May 22, 2013

ACKNOWLEDGEMENTS

These stories were written during a period of eight years, beginning in 2005. Until that time, I had never thought to write anything other than poetry. I read WSB's *The Wild Boys* (which inspired Duran Duran's hit single of the same name) and discovered my own wild, fervent desires. Several of these were written under the influence and instruction of David Hawkes, Edward Cahill, Scott Paul Gordon, Stephanie Powell Watts, Daniel Contreras, Meera Nair, and John Reed; instructors at Lehigh University and Fordham University. Much of this work is indebted to the city of Bethlehem, through which I first learned to explore my own inner life. I could not have written this novel without the continual mentorship of Sophie and John Campanioni. And finally, to the readers who pored over this in its early and various iterations: Jonathan Marcantoni, Madeleine Díaz Quilichini, Giancarlo Lombardi, Michael Kazepis, and Chris Lambert. Thank you for catching the drift, and carrying it to today.

2.24.18

Available from King Shot Press

Leverage by Eric Nelson
Strategies Against Nature by Cody Goodfellow
Killer &Victim by Chris Lambert
Noctuidae by Scott Nicolay
Marigold by Troy James Weaver
I Miss The World by Violet LeVoit
All-Monster Action! by Cody Goodfellow
Nasty! (ed. Tiffany Scandal)
The Deadheart Shelters by Forrest Armstrong
Drift by Chris Campanioni

CPSIA information can be obtained
at www.ICGtesting.com
Printed in the USA
FFOW03n0924160318
45625583-46444FF